SPLIT ENDS

Also by Sarah Harvey

Misbehaving
Fly-Fishing

SPLIT ENDS

Sarah Harvey

HEADLINE

First published in 2001
by HEADLINE BOOK PUBLISHING

10 9 8 7 6 5 4 3

British Library Cataloguing in Publication Data

Harvey, Sarah
Split ends
1.Love stories
I.Title
823.9'14[F]

ISBN 07472 6911 4

Typeset by
Letterpart Limited, Reigate, Surrey

Printed and bound in Great Britain by
Clays Ltd St Ives plc

HEADLINE BOOK PUBLISHING
A division of Hodder Headline
338 Euston Road
London NW1 3BH

www.headline.co.uk
www.hodderheadline.com

For Terry,
forever.

I got the idea for this book from the fact that there are an awful lot of people in my life in relationships that could be considered slightly unconventional, or who have had to fight certain prejudice and untoward circumstance to stay together. Although the characters in this novel are purely fictitious, the following people may find this book strikes a cord, and my love and thanks are always with them: The gorgeous, irreplaceable Imogen Taylor and her hubby, Richard; the beautiful Barbie – cleavage of doom – Alvis, and Darren. Dad Brucey and Sil, Louise and Des, my mum Diane and her old Bill, Phil and Sarah, Ayshea and Dave, and Gorgeous Gazza. I should also mention my brother James, who will be amazed to find that he's not in this one at all, Linda, Nuala, Brenda, Belinda, Doddy, Andrew Gunns, and a tentative thank you to Graham, Alex and Phil for scaring me with their theories on men and the meaning of love. A huge thank you must also go to Luigi Bonomi, John Rush, Amelia Cummins, and Amanda Preston of Sheil Land, and Clare Foss, Frances Coward and the rest of the team at Headline, who have all worked so hard on my behalf.

And finally, but most importantly, my constant love and heartfelt thanks to Terry, who always encourages, drives and inspires me.

Chapter One

I lean on my horn for the third time, this time letting it sound for a good five seconds. Apart from a furious face at the window of the flat below Tanya's, I'm rewarded with absolutely no response whatsoever. Grumbling like a granny with no teeth, I root around in my bag for my mobile phone and hastily punch in her number. She finally answers on the twelfth ring, purring hello in the familiar sexy, throaty voice which always becomes slightly more breathy than usual on the telephone, as though she's auditioning for a job on an 0898.

'Tanya!' I bark, frustration making me ratty. 'What the hell are you up to? I've been sitting outside for twenty minutes.'

'Ollie darling!' Despite my frosty tone, Tanya's greeting is as enthusiastically friendly as usual. 'I was drying my hair, Babe . . . What's the time?'

'Twenty to nine . . .'

There's a small shriek and the line goes dead. Two minutes later the main door to the baroque Mayfair building, where Tanya rents a flat from her rich father at a pauper's rent, is flung open, and she hurtles through like a greyhound out of a trap.

As soon as she's in my car I realise that the reason for her haste isn't the fact that we're running later than a Virgin train, it's the fact that she's practically naked. She's wearing a set of purple silk La Perla's, a pair of high-heeled fluffy pink slippers and a rather smug smile.

'Sorry, darling!' she beams. 'I've had the plumber round. Rather lost track of time.'

'Again!' I sigh, rolling my eyes at her in the rear-view mirror.

'You know how I like to keep my pipe work in order.'

1

Tanya's plumber is her on-call shag. Every time her bits are feeling a little rusty due to lack of use, she's straight onto her hot line number for a guaranteed 'within the hour' call-out. Unfortunately within the hour only refers to the time it takes him to get there and not the time it takes him to do the job, and she is therefore running horrendously late.

I pull away at great speed as Tanya rummages around in the sack of a bag she's dragged with her. She pulls out a make-up bag that contains more MAC than the sales counter at Selfridge's, and proceeds to paint her face with practised dexterity, despite the fact that because we're late, I'm now throwing my car around corners like Schumacher at Monaco.

The face finished, a little black number from the last Moschino sale is pulled out of the bag, and whilst the guy in the next car at the set of traffic lights I've just screeched to a halt at ogles through our windows in grinning disbelief, Tanya wriggles her terrific body into its tight-fitting confines.

'How long have we got?' she asks, head emerging through the neckline.

'Minus thirty minutes and counting. We were supposed to be there at eight-thirty. I thought *I* was late until I hit your place.'

'Shit! Sorry, darling.' A pair of gorgeous kitten-heel mules are next from the magic bag to replace the pink Barbie-girl slippers.

'I don't know what's more scary, meeting our best mate's new man for the first time, or travelling in the back of your car with no seat belt on.' Tanya laughs as, her feet pointing to the roof as she pulls on her shoes, I charge off the lights like Starsky and Hutch on a mission to rescue Huggy Bear, skid around a left-hand bend and slide her head first into the door console.

'Yeah, especially with your legs in the air.'

'Oh that's not scary,' she quips. 'I'm used to that position. So what's he like then?'

'Grace's new man?'

'Yeah, she must have given you the goss. What does he do?'

'Gray said he was into leather or something.'

'Sounds like my kind of guy!'

Finally fully clothed, Tanya squeezes between the front seats and slides down next to me, her Lycra-clad arse squeaking

2

onto the car's leather seat, skirt rising to reveal endless legs, toned through innumerable sessions at the gym ogling her personal trainer.

'Not wearing leather, you old tart; manufacturing, textiles or something.'

'What a shame . . . what else did she tell you?'

'Well, his name's Stuart, he's thirty-three, completely single, got his own business, all of his own hair and teeth, lives in the country, up North somewhere . . .'

Tanya yawns, her attention wandering out of the window to the rather hunky figure of a traffic cop who's just pulled alongside us on a motorbike, making me hit the brakes in a feeble attempt to get within the thirty-mile-an-hour speed limit. Fortunately he's too busy gazing through my window into Tanya's amazing cleavage, whilst she bats her long eyelashes at him, to notice my lack of respect for the local traffic laws.

'And Gray said he's hung like a donkey,' I finish.

'Really?' She immediately snaps back round to face me.

'Haven't got a clue, but I needed to get your attention somehow. We're nearly there. If I drop you outside, then you can go in and grovel for our shocking tardiness, whilst I try and find somewhere to park.'

It's another fifteen minutes before I've managed to somehow shoehorn my car into a parking space that's really only just big enough for a small hatchback, and trot back to the Soho wine bar that we were supposed to be meeting Gray in nearly an hour ago. I look at my watch. Nine-twenty. I have a reputation for being late for everything, but this was one occasion when my promise to be on time was one I would have liked to have kept.

Grace is my best friend. Grace is also a serial monogamist. A true romantic in a quest for, yes, you guessed it, true romance. As I'm sure you can imagine, her search for Mr Right has meant a long haul through a catalogue of Mr Wrongs.

One such Mr Wrong was her last man, Arty. The Artful Dodger, we used to call him. He had a certain indefinable easy-going charm that made everyone who met him fall madly in love with him, not in a lustful, sexual kind of way – although Gray would disagree with that, having spent the majority of the relationship in bed with him – but he was the kind of guy that everyone wanted for their best friend. Always sociable, funny, easy to talk to, and got on with absolutely everybody.

He was also however the total personification of unreliable, and therefore ended up becoming a brief chapter in Gray's life, rather than the permanent fixture we all thought or hoped he might become.

This hasn't put Gray off in her hunt for true love, but although she's launched headlong into a few relationships since she split up with him five months ago, she hasn't actually maintained any of them for long enough to warrant an introduction to us.

Until this one. That's why this is an occasion I didn't want to be late for. This one apparently merits an introduction, and as she's only been seeing him for a few short weeks, he must be pretty special to earn this accolade.

I push through the heavy glass door of the busy Neal Street wine bar, a favourite meeting place for pre-club clubbers, and our usual haunt when we're in this area. It's surprisingly packed for a Tuesday night, but it doesn't take long to find Tanya. To my surprise, instead of hugging the bar, loudly demanding alcohol whilst eyeing up the talent, she's waiting for me just inside the door, her normally pouting lips pulled into a tight, thin line that I immediately recognise from almost six years of Tanya-watching as concern.

'What's up, chuck? Are they here? Or have they given us up as no-show and gone home?'

'Well, I've found Gray, at least I think I have.'

Grabbing my wrist, she pulls me further into the crowded room, and nods over to the bar where Grace, my oldest, and – apart from Tan – my dearest friend and partner in crime since the first year of secondary school, is currently being served.

I start to wave, but Tanya catches my wrist.

'Hang on a mo. Tell me what's wrong with this scenario?'

Laughing nervously at Tanya's perturbed expression, I peer a little closer. Well, Grace looks okay. She's standing at a bar, which is a pretty normal place to find her. Then I notice the bottle of Pellagrino the barman's handing over.

'She's ordering mineral water instead of Smirnoff.'

'And?'

'It's not unheard of, although it's unusual I must admit, but maybe she's still got a mega hangover from partying till dawn last night or something. Maybe the new man took her clubbing.'

'Maybe.' Tanya replies as if she doesn't believe this theory. 'But what else is weird?'

The heaving crowd of boozing honking people shifts a little, and I get a full-length view.

'Gray's wearing her mother's clothes?' I reply incredulously. 'No, strike that, I think they must be her grandmother's.'

'Great-great-grandmother,' agrees Tanya. 'That dress is straight out of Victorian Britain: thou shall not shit, swear, shag or work for a living . . .'

Tanya gropes in her Baguette for a Marlboro and, lighting up, inhales deeply as though the smoke will give her strength to cope with the sight of our normally extrovert Gray dressed up like a nun on her day off and sipping water instead of slugging Smirnoff.

'If the neckline was any higher she'd suffocate.' I nod my agreement.

Grace's copper hair, which normally tumbles past her slender shoulders in a shock of rather unruly curls, is also pulled uncharacteristically away from her face in a severe chignon, and instead of the usual pillar-box-red lips, she's taken the definition of nude make-up to new heights, with just a smudge of grey eyeshadow to match her grey eyes, and the lightest smear of sheer gloss.

The lips bearing this new minimal-look break into a huge smile when Gray spots me staring over at her like a Cardinal who's just spotted the Pope sporting a Marks and Sparks' twinset instead of his usual white robes.

'Ollie!' Despite the subdued clothing, the Gray greeting is still as effervescent as ever. She shrieks my name at the top of her voice then, a mineral water in each hand, elbows her way through the crowd, and envelops me in a breath-threatening embrace as though she hasn't seen me for a month, instead of just three days.

'Did you forget to shave your legs?' I ask when she finally releases me from a Hugo-for-Women-enhanced hug, and turns her over-zealous greetings to a still open-mouthed Tanny.

'What?' Gray drops Tanya and smiles distractedly at me.

5

I stand back and look her up and down pointedly. 'The up-to-your chin, down-to-your-toenails number. Not exactly you, is it?'

Gray's distracted smile turns into a huge beaming grin, her grey eyes twinkling with laughter. 'This is the new Me,' she giggles. 'Respectable with a capital R.'

She stands back and pretends to twirl like a cat-walk model, violently elbowing the man behind her so that he hurls the large scotch-on-the-rocks he was clutching all over the friend he was chatting with. He turns round angrily to complain to a completely oblivious Grace, only to come face to face with Tanya instead.

'I like the old you. You know, R for Raunchy, R for Revealing,' I reply, watching with amusement as the business-man's face melts instantly from furious to fawning at the sight of the delectable Tanya.

'Well, tonight,' Gray grins, leaning in and whispering con-spiratorially, 'I'm even wearing knickers! Although that's more in the hope that tonight might possibly be the night he slowly peels them off me with his teeth!'

'You mean he hasn't already? You've been seeing the guy for nearly three weeks now, what's wrong with you, darling, you've normally got them tried and tested by now.'

'This one's different.'

'I thought our philosophy was that all men are the same.'

'He's shy.'

'Shy! You don't do shy.'

'And he's very nice . . .' she continues.

'And you definitely don't do nice!' I shriek in concern.

Grinning, she balances both glasses in one hand and, taking my hand with her recently freed one, starts to lead me through the bar toward the restaurant. 'Come and meet the man, and be nice. Like I said, he's a bit shy.'

'I'm always nice.'

'I know that, babe, but he doesn't. I think he's finding it a bit nerve-racking being introduced to the gang.'

'Who's here then?'

'Well, I left him talking to Louis, who unlike you managed to arrive on time.'

'And has the Dancing Queen toned it down a bit too? Or is he wearing his usual gold lamé hot pants.'

6

'Silver.'

'What?'

'Louis's hot pants are silver lamé. Gold doesn't go with his skin tone.'

'Whatever, just tell me he hasn't squeezed his hot little bot into anything too outrageous, otherwise all of your efforts at looking respectable are going to be completely ruined by your friends. As usual Miss Mathers here is wearing a little off-the-crotch number, with enough cleavage to park your bike in.'

I indicate toward Tanya, who has somehow managed to persuade the guy who lost his drink to not only pay for his own replacement, but buy us a couple of large G and Ts as well in return for her phone number, and is now tottering along behind us on her delicate little heels, gazing open mouthed at the sight of Gray in so much cloth.

'Jeans and a T-shirt,' Grace announces, referring to Louis's attire. 'Although the T-shirt *is* Morgan!'

I look over to the noisy group of people in the corner. Louis is instantly recognisable, despite the fact that he appears to have dyed his spiky black hair an unusual shade of cobalt blue to match his eyes.

Except for the hair, Louis's usual flamboyancy has indeed been toned down a little in honour of the occasion. In fact he looks positively tame in a pair of jeans that are more rip than material, and a black-and-gold Morgan top with a flower motif on the front; the only key to the normal Louis mode of dress being the electric blue mascara framing his bright-blue eyes.

Apart from Louis there are three or four people in the little group that I think I recognise from Grace's work place. There's also another guy standing next to Louis. I don't recognise this one, and therefore it's pretty safe to assume that he must be Gray's new man.

At least I think it must be. It certainly doesn't look like it *should* be. Gray has a very eclectic taste in men. Each one has been different – and trust me, there have been quite a few – but they've all shared one characteristic: confidence, sometimes a touch too much of it I must admit, but a touch too much is far better than a bucketload of too little.

This guy looks about as confident as a eunuch in a wet

Y-front competition! He's looking strangely out of place and embarrassingly uncomfortable, finger tugging almost constantly at the collar of his polo neck as though there's a pair of polyester hands tightening around his epiglottis. Although Louis, who could talk the hind legs off a donkey, is babbling away to him, he's obviously not really listening, his eyes scouting the room in search of Gray, like a stranded mountaineer seeking the rescue helicopters.

He has floppy brown hair that looks as if it's been cut with a pudding bowl and polished with high-gloss wax it's so squeaky clean and shiny, and a sizeable slightly red nose. Two large brown eyes are made bigger by the lenses in a pair of tortoiseshell glasses, which keep slipping down his nose, only to be pushed back up again with the long index finger of his large right hand. He has the earnest, studious, dependable, healthy air of a headboy from a rural public school. And he's *very* quiet. It's pretty obvious that busy bars are not his scene. He's standing slightly behind a pillar, as if for protection, looking about him at the noisy scenes of drunken debauchery with the air of a vicar who's taken the wrong turn and ended up at an organised rave instead of the WI fund-raising tea party he was heading for. If he had an anorak he'd have slipped it on, and be sitting quietly in the corner waiting to go home.

I turn to Tanya and raise my eyebrows. She's already spotted him and is staring open mouthed, like someone who's just caught sight of the bouncing bosom of an enthusiastic streaker at Twickenham. She puts a hand on my wrist and pulls me back a little from Gray, level with her, hissing in my ear, 'That can't be him.'

'Maybe it's a friend of Louis?' I venture uncertainly.

'Is he wearing Lycra, sequins and make-up?'

'Hardly, lip gloss doesn't go with a three-year-old Armani jacket, faded cords, and a polo neck jumper.'

'Well, that rules out that possibility then, doesn't it?'

'Maybe Louis's changed his type.'

'Somehow I don't think so; that's got to be him.'

'Well, in that case Gray has *definitely* changed her type,' I reply incredulously.

The fact that this is indeed Gray's new fella is verified when, on reaching the small group, she grabs his hand, eyes shining with pleasure, and pulls him away from a still-gabbling Louis to meet us.

'This is Ollie and Tan,' she tells him. 'My two best friends in the whole world. Ollie, Tan.' She takes a deep breath, and smiles, as though she's just about to announce a winner at the Brits, pushing the hesitant headboy gently toward us. 'This is Stuart.'

He holds out his hand. 'With a u and an a, not an e, w, a.'

'I beg your pardon?'

'Stuart with a U,' he repeats, smiling slightly, and thrusting his hand further toward me.

'Oh right, great,' I reply, only one side of my mouth managing to follow through with the smile I was attempting.

'Ollie's the one I was telling you about who runs the restaurant in Battersea,' Grace announces proudly.

Stuart has rather sweaty hands. After a handshake that is a touch too close for comfort, I slip – literally – out of his grip, just resisting the urge to wipe my hand down the side of my Oasis boot-cuts.

'And this is Tanya.'

The fact that Stuart's the first man ever to be introduced to Tanya whose eyes aren't immediately diverted from her face to her cleavage, earns him some brownie points here, which redeems him a little from the fact that shaking hands with him is a bit like shaking hands with a large damp fish.

'Tanya's an estate agent,' Gray tells him breezily. 'But we still love her.'

'I'm a property consultant . . .' Tanya corrects her.

'There's a difference?'

'Only in fee,' I tease.

'Ooh look, there's Cornelia.' Grace spots her boss from the PR firm heading hesitantly through the front door of the wine bar, and drops Stuart's spare hand, which she had been clutching a little too tightly for somebody who's not normally a clingy kind of girl. 'Must go and let her know where we are. She hates coming into these places on her own. Promised I'd buy her a large G and T for letting me leave an hour early tonight,' she says in an aside as she brushes past me. 'I needed the extra time to get my glad rags on.'

'I suppose it would have taken at least an hour to lace up your corset,' I rib her.

Grace sticks her long tongue out at me. 'Me, need a corset?' She indicates her incredibly slender waist. 'But think of the fun it would be to slowly remove one though . . .' she winks, 'hook by hook . . .'

'A three-hour wait whilst you unlace your stays is a bit of an overkill on the anticipation stakes, babe,' I murmur dryly. 'Especially on the first night.'

'Good job I'm only wearing edible knickers then, isn't it?' she giggles in my ear. She turns back to Stuart and smiles broadly. 'I'll leave you three to get acquainted. Back in a mo.'

'Glad rags?' Tanya mouths to me incredulously as Gray sashays across the room, skirt swishing round her ankles in a most disconcerting fashion. 'Queen Victoria wore happier clothes than that when she was in mourning for Bertie.'

I turn to Stuart, hoping he didn't catch this comment.

He smiles at me, so I don't think he did.

I smile back.

He smiles.

Tanya smiles.

He smiles.

I smile again.

Tanya grimaces at me, then quickly turns the grimace into a rather strained smile as Stuart turns to look at her and smiles awkwardly again, but still says nothing.

For some reason I, too, seem to have suddenly lost all power of communication, it must be contagious. I rack my brain for an opener. 'So, Stuart, do you live nearby?' is all I finally manage. I know full well that he doesn't, but as we all seem to be completely stumped for conversation . . .

'No, fortunately. Family's got a small flat in Kensington, but I'm actually based in Leicestershire.'

'You say fortunately? Not keen on London then?' Tanya asks somewhat archly. A city girl born and bred, Tanya thinks anything beyond the M25 is tantamount to the Deep South.

'It's not my favourite place. I must admit I only come up to town when I absolutely have to.'

Tanya crosses her eyes at me, as Stuart smiles nervously again, then buries his face in his glass of water, managing to remain in there for a breath-holding-record length of time, until Gray returns with Cornelia, a rather po-faced redhead, of the Alice-band-and-sensible-shoe variety, just in time to stop

10

him from drowning in mineral water.

I've met Cornelia a couple of times before. She's one of those people who is a veritable dynamo in the office, but a complete damp squib in social situations. Our Grace, however, is the human equivalent of the Battersea Dogs Home. She has this tendency to pick up waifs and strays and try to find them, not a new home, but a social life at least.

Not everyone is as kind hearted or magnanimous as Grace though. Now that Cornelia has arrived, the other girls who work with Gray decide it's time for them to leave.

Tanya watches them head off to a club with a wistful expression on her face. Having tried and failed to engage Stuart in conversation about her three favourite subjects, shopping, clubbing and sex, she has now given up and headed for the safety of the bar to buy more drinks.

After introducing Cornelia to Stuart, Grace and she are now talking work, so I decide it's my turn to try to bring Stuart, if not out of his shell, at least out of his mineral water. After what seems like an eternity of polite if somewhat stilted chitchat, though, he once again lapses into nearly total silence, submerging into his drink like a submarine in enemy waters diving for cover at every sign of potential danger.

Leaving him, once he finally emerges, in the safety of a conversation with Louis, the gorgeous gas bag, where all you really have to do if you don't feel like chatting is look as if you're listening, and murmur 'uhuh' every few minutes to encourage the flow, Tanya and I head for a confab in the ladies loo.

'So what do you think?' I perch my bum on the edge of the basin units, and search in my handbag for the make-up I didn't have time to apply before picking up Tanya, due to a last-minute minor kitchen crisis at the restaurant.

'He's wearing cords!' Tanya shakes her head in disbelief.

'I must admit he's very country casual,' I reply, digging out my favourite Ruby & Millie lippy. 'But I meant, what do you think of his personality?'

'You mean you found one?'

'Oh dear, you too . . . maybe he's just shy. Gray did say he was shy.'

'Maybe he just hasn't got one.'

'Got one what, girlies? Are you dishing the dirt on Gray's

11

new bit of stuff . . . and that's stuff with a "y" on the end. You know I've never seen Grace go to such an effort to impress a man before though. The formal intro thing's pretty novel too. We normally get to meet the latest beau by bumping into her snogging him in the corner of a nightclub or something.' We're disturbed by Louis, who waltzes through the door, parks his bum next to Tanya on the edge of the washbasins, and offers her a cigarette.

'You're not supposed to be in here,' I tell him, narrowing my eyes as cigarette smoke curls about our heads.

'But your loos are so much nicer.' Louis blinks his striking blue eyes at me disarmingly. 'You know I think loos are so un-PC.' Shifting sideways, he peers into the mirror behind us, and wipes away a stray blob of mascara from his lower lid with his little finger. 'It shouldn't just be girls and guys, it should be girls, guys and gays.'

'What? With little pink loo mats?' I taunt him.

'We should just cut the crap and go unisex,' growls Tanya, her lungs full of Rothmans.

'Horrible thought.' I wrinkle my nose at her. 'You just want to stand in line at the urinals willy-watching don't you?'

'Well, I suppose there is that advantage . . .' Louis agrees, trawling through my bag and helping himself to a shell-pink lipstick.

'So what *do* you think about lover boy?' he murmurs, rejecting it, and rummaging for another.

'That's what we were just discussing.'

'He's not her usual type.'

'Gray doesn't have a usual type, her tastes are extremely varied, that's why she's best buds with all of us.'

'The Saint, the Slapper and the Sex God,' laughs Louis. 'Me being the Sex God, of course.'

'Oh yeah, and which one am I?' Tanya asks him, throwing back her head challengingly.

'You need to ask?' I reply, taking back a bright-red lippy from Louis, and passing him a not-quite-so-violent blush one instead. 'I'm the one that hasn't had sex since RaRa skirts were in fashion.'

'Yeah, Miss Fussy Knickers.'

'To have sex, you actually have to have a man.'

'Well, that depends on what turns you on, baby!' drawls

12

Louis in a fake Southern accent.

'And I don't think I want one of those at the moment,' I finish, ignoring him and attempting to push some life back into my long, dark-brown, and infuriatingly poker-straight hair with my fingers.

'You don't?' Tanya asks incredulously. 'Not even for leisure pursuits? You don't have to have a relationship to have good sex, you know.'

'I know, but if I'm just aiming for an orgasm I think I'd rather buy a vibrator. Anyway, how did the subject get from Stuart to sex?'

'Yeah, not the most obvious link,' snipes Louis.

'You haven't just abandoned him, have you?' I ask in concern. 'I think he felt a bit awkward out there.'

'Nah. I left him talking to Cornelia. I think they're having a competition to see who can outbore the other one first.'

'He's not exactly scintillating company, is he?'

'Definitely not what I expected,' I agree, shaking my head.

'Maybe Gray's getting a bit desperate.'

'Desperate for a bit.' Louis turns it around. 'Perhaps he's a good shag.'

'To be honest, I don't think she's slept with him yet.'

'No?' they both ask in surprise.

'Well, I haven't had the usual full match replay, no. And she was hinting earlier that tonight could be the night she finally gets him out of his Calvin's.'

'A man like that wouldn't wear Calvin's,' Louis, the total fashion victim, scoffs.

'No?'

'Boxer shorts,' Tanya states emphatically. 'And tartan ones at that.'

'How on earth did they meet?'

'Ah, now this one I do know. Do you remember when she ditched her car on the way back from visiting Granny Ellerington in Uppingham?'

Louis lights another cigarette, shuddering at the thought as he does so. 'Do I ever,' he murmurs protectively.

'Well *he's* the one that found her, pulled her out, and towed her to civilisation – well, the nearest garage anyway. Her knight in shining Land Rover.'

'At least we know he's a good guy then.'

13

'A very very very nice man.'

'So now he's been brought forth for our approval – or disapproval.'

We all fall silent for a moment.

Louis is the first to speak. 'I don't want to be horrible, but did Gray get a bloody hard bump on the head when she crashed her car?'

'Stuart pulled her out of a ditch and then pulled her,' Tanya tells him. 'It could be the nurse–patient syndrome.'

'What's that then?'

'You know, when somebody takes care of you, wipes your fevered brow, brings you Lucozade, tucks you in. It makes you feel loved and protected. Most people are far more needy than they let on.'

'So he was her Florence Knight-ingale in shining Land Rover then?'

'Something like that, yeah.'

'I still go with the bump-on-the-head theory,' Louis pouts.

'Perhaps we should give the guy a chance,' I interject a little guiltily. 'We've only known him for an hour.'

Tan shrugs. 'I suppose so. He's just really not Gray's type at all.'

'Correction,' I tell her. 'He's not *our* type. There's a difference. We should be kind for Gray's sake. Besides we all know she's good at spotting the potential in something.'

'Yeah, look at her house when she first bought it, now that was a right dump.' There's just a hint of sarcasm in Louis's voice at my bargain-renovation theory.

It's fortunate that we all fall silent at this moment, as Grace, up to her ears in mineral water, decides to come in for a quick pee.

'I might have guessed you'd be hiding out in here,' she calls from her cubicle. 'And I know exactly what you've been discussing, so don't pretend otherwise.'

The loo flushes and Grace comes back out. Gently pushing Tanya out of the way of one of the sinks, she begins to wash her hands. 'So, what do you think then?' She grins broadly, looking at us all in the mirror. She's bubbling over with excitement, awaiting our verdict on Stuart with an expectant smile on her face. 'Come on,' she demands, as nobody speaks. 'What's your verdict?'

14

'Well, he's certainly not what we expected,' I say carefully, throwing a warning glance at the not-quite-so-diplomatic Tanya.

'We wouldn't have put the two of you together as a couple,' Tanya adds, choosing her words very carefully.

'Me neither,' Grace grins. 'When I first met him I thought he was awful! I mean, I was really grateful that he helped me out the way he did, but if you'd told me then that I'd end up seeing him, I'd have laughed in your face.'

'So what happened to change your mind?'

'He grows on you.' She smiles slowly.

'What, like fungus?' Louis mutters. 'Or mould,' he adds, rolling the 'o' as well as his eyes.

Grace grabs Louis and ruffles his hair affectionately. He shies away, grinning coyly. 'Watch the do!' he moans, running his fingers through the blue in an attempt to spike it back up again.

'Well, be nice, you,' Grace admonishes him. 'I told you, he's shy, but he's actually a lovely guy.'

'If you say so.' Louis runs his hands under the cold tap, and uses wet fingers on his flattened hair.

'I do say so. You'll get used to him.' She looks round at us all appealingly. 'Trust me. You'll soon get to like him as much as I do. In fact . . .' The appealing smile turns to the cheeky wicked grin I've known and loved for over seventeen years. 'My only concern is whether or not he'll get used to you horrible lot. I mean it's taken me *years* . . .'

Stuart with a U and Gray get into a taxi at ten-thirty holding hands.

'She left before last orders,' Tanya mouths incredulously, shaking her head and knocking back her seventh gin, the tonic getting less obvious with each drink.

'And she left without me!' Louis howls. 'I thought we were sharing a taxi back!'

Louis and Grace both live in Islington. Grace in a beautiful terrace she's spent a lot of time and money renovating over the past three years, and Louis in a huge old rented house which is home to him and about eight of his mad friends, and has therefore been dubbed the Pink Party Palace.

15

'Don't worry, sweetie.' I tuck my arm under his. 'I'll take you.'

'But it's miles out of your way.'

'I know, it just shows what a kind, sweet-natured, loving friend I really am.'

'You feel guilty about slagging him off, don't you?'

'What, Stuart with a U,' Tanya mocks.

'Yep,' I reply to Louis, ignoring the fish face that Tanya is pulling. 'So I'm compensating by being overly nice to you. Take advantage while you can.'

We walk the mile or so back to my car, arm in arm, like the Monkees without the silly walk. Well, actually I'm lying, we do break into the silly walk, at frequent intervals, but seeing as I'm twenty-eight, Louis is twenty-seven and Tanya's just hit thirty-three, it's a kind-of-embarrassing thing to admit.

Louis, who by this point is just the right side of drunk not to fall over, piles into the back of the car, still clutching a bottle of Bud. 'Stuart with a U!' he cries mournfully, plugging the bottle into his mouth and taking a slug, head shaking from side to side incredulously. 'He was drinking mineral water all night.'

'So was I. Well, most of it anyway.'

'Yeah, but you're driving.'

'You don't have to drink to be interesting.'

'I know, but in his case I think it might help!'

'I think this could just be a reaction to her last relationship.' Tanya slides into the front seat, pulls down the sunshield and, flicking open the mirror, begins to reapply her lipstick. 'Arty was so totally unreliable she's gone for Mr Security.'

'Mr Boring,' growls Louis from the depths of the back seat.

'Come on,' I cajole. 'We promised Gray we'd get to know him a bit better before we passed final judgement.'

'I know we did,' Louis replies a touch guiltily. 'I did try in there, Ollie, honestly, but it was like trying to thaw an iceberg with a hairdryer.'

'We all tried,' I sigh. 'I must admit he didn't even laugh at my nun joke.'

'Great!' mocks Tanya. 'At least that shows he has some taste then.'

'Everybody laughs at my nun joke.'

'Only because you normally tell it when we're so pissed

16

we'd laugh at a party political broadcast.'

'We normally laugh at those anyway.'

'I liked Arty,' Louis states mournfully.

'Arty was a drunk.' Lipstick finished, Tan finds a mascara wand in my centre console, and attacks her lashes.

'Exactly, I liked Arty. He knew how to party. Party-hearty Arty.'

'Maybe he *was* just shy like Gray said,' I muse. 'We can be a bit hard to take on the first dose.'

'Like foul-tasting medicine? Cheers, babe . . .' Tanya tuts at me. 'I always thought I was more like a glass of champagne – for the obvious reasons, you know, sparkling personality, expensive taste . . .'

'Totally flat in the morning after getting popped at wild parties,' I add.

Louis shakes his head despondently. 'It's just like Marilyn and Arthur Miller.'

'The whore and the bore,' Tanya teases cruelly, knowing full well that the gorgeous Marilyn is Louis's idol.

'Don't worry, lovey,' I murmur soothingly. 'I know Grace. I have a feeling that Stuart with a U is just a phase. She wants to try something different to the party animals she usually hooks up with. She'll have moved on to a new one in a few weeks' time.'

'Well, let's hope it's one with a bit more life than a piece of old carpet everyone's wiped their boots on.'

We drop Louis off at his house share four streets away from Grace, and are just heading toward Mayfair for the second leg of the journey, when Tanya spots a late-night takeaway. Tanya's one of these enviable people who could eat for Great Britain at the junk-food Olympics and still come out weighing less than when she first started munching.

'Pull over, I'm starving!'

'You're a human dustbin.'

'I'm a human dynamo.'

'Thought that was your plumber.'

'No, he's a human Dynorod; reaches the parts other plumbers cannot reach. Pull over, I need a burger.'

'How can you eat that junk?' I shudder.

'Well, normally I just open my mouth.'

'Ha, bloody ha! Why don't you come back to Tates with me and have some proper food?'

'And run the risk of getting goosed by Claude the shameless chef? No thanks, his food may be divine but he's hellish, especially when he's pissed, which,' she looks at her Gucci, 'he most certainly will be by now.'

'He's like all geniuses,' I reply, 'a little unhinged.'

'That's a polite way of describing him.'

'He's nice when he's sober.'

'Which is as frequent as an appearance by Haley's comet. There's a rat in the kitchen . . .' Tanya starts to sing.

'Yeah and it's called Claude the Chef,' I reply dryly.

'Is he still attempting to shag all the waitresses?'

'Is Posh Spice skinny? He even goosed Louis the other day as he was backing through the door with an armful of dirty dishes. Although I must admit Louis was wearing a pair of boot-cuts from Miss Selfridge. I think he thought that it was the arse of my gorgeous head waitress heading temptingly into his domain.'

Tanya shudders. 'He's dreadful. I don't know why you keep him on.'

'Simple, he's a complete nightmare, but he cooks like a dream . . . He doesn't cost me a fortune either because he's been sacked by nearly every other restaurant in London for his totally appalling behaviour.'

'I thought all chefs were *supposed* to behave appallingly.'

'A lot of them are renowned for their temper, yes,' I reply guardedly.

'So what makes Claude worse?'

'Well, have you seen that part in *The War of the Roses* . . . where Michael Douglas you know . . . er . . . relieves himself in Kathleen Turner's fishkettle? Well, there was kind of a similar incident at the last restaurant he worked in. Something to do with a very expensive bottle of Chablis.'

'Euk!' Tanya shrieks. 'And you want me to come and eat at your place!'

'Don't worry, honey, his last boss upset in him a way I never could.'

'How's that then?'

'He slept with his wife.'

'I still think I'd rather risk a bout of mild salmonella.'

I give in, pull into the kerb, and Tanya gets out of the car and sashays into the late-night burger bar. A few minutes later she gets back in the car clutching a huge paper bag full of chips, a large bacon burger with sweetcorn relish, and the phone number of the greasy Greek Adonis behind the counter.

'Brings an entirely new meaning to *fast* food,' she grins, winking flirtatiously at the still-watching guy, and then offering me a chip as we pull away.

'You'd pull in a monastery.'

'He's got a brother, perhaps we could double date.'

'No, thanks.'

'Why not?'

'Not my type.'

'How do you know, you haven't even met him,' Tan replies in exasperation. 'Honestly, Ollie, sometimes I think you haven't got a type at all! Either that or you're a closet lesbian, and you just haven't told me yet.'

'I'm a closet lesbian,' I reply dryly. 'I just haven't told you yet.'

After dropping Tanya off, I head back down over Chelsea Bridge and finally arrive in Battersea sometime after midnight. I'm just in time to help Melanie my head waitress – strike that, she's practically my only waitress – finish loading the industrial dishwasher, after what was apparently a fairly quiet evening in the restaurant. Despite Tanya's misgivings, and despite the fact that I like to feel I'm completely indispensable when it comes to the running of Tates, Claude my chef spent the entire evening sober, and seems to have pretty much held the place together without me.

After Melanie's gone, I head back into the restaurant from the kitchen and wander round, supposedly checking the doors and windows are locked, all candles are snuffed, and that there are no sneaked cigarettes left smouldering in hidden corners. I carry out this ritual every night after closing, but not just out of a concern for health and safety. It's a time to potter around my beloved restaurant, wallowing in the hard-earned pleasure of the fact that I've actually made a major ambition into solid reality.

Just over two years ago, I gave up a well-paid job in marketing to indulge in this wild dream of running my own restaurant. So far the wild dream has turned into a pretty

19

decent reality. It's been a hard slog, but I think I'm finally getting there. We're not quite River Café league yet, and we don't have a waiting list backed up for two months, but to my extreme satisfaction you do have to pre-book these days to guarantee getting a table. Tates used to be an old-fashioned bakery, and the theme has been kept pretty rustic, with soft-washed ochre walls, stone floors, solid wood tables and an eclectic mix of chairs ranging from old church pews to black wrought iron, with even a fake wood-and-gilt throne, which Grace nicked for me from her mother's last operatic-society production, taking pride of place at the head of my biggest table.

The restaurant itself is really one large room, which is a thoroughly odd shape. A bit like a large backwards L with extensions at either end, providing quaint little alcoves, perfect for couples in search of privacy. There are two fireplaces, one in the centre of the room, which used to house a huge oven, but is now a stone arch containing a black grate open to both sides. This divides the foot of the backwards L. The other fireplace, huge enough to roast a small pig in – if one ever felt like roasting a small pig – is set in the wall. This blasts heat throughout the entire building, making the bathroom of my flat, which is directly above, feel like a sauna no matter what time of year.

Old black-and-white family prints adorn the walls. I thought it was appropriate as the place is called by my family name. It was nearly called 'The Bakery', a more obvious and less egotistical choice, but it was such bloody hard slog getting the place open, I wanted the world – in particular my bank manager and rogue building contractors – to know that I'd finally done it. Hence the unusually large plate above the front door, stating 'Olivia Tate – Proprietor'.

The photographs are fun to look at – well for me, anyway – and a not-to-be-missed chance to embarrass certain members of my family. Particular causes of family distress are a picture of my brother Jack, when he was about two, dressed as Noddy for a fancy-dress party, stroppy face on, hat-with-bell thrown onto the floor in a fit of childish pique – highly embarrassing for someone who's now a high-ranking barrister – and the corresponding picture of my big sister Ella dressed as Big Ears – she was quite a podgy child and doesn't want this fact displayed to half of little Chelsea – and a wonderful picture of my mother in winklepickers, with a beehive bigger than the Millennium Dome, and more black eyeliner than Morticia Adams – enough to make her adamant that this particular snapshot certainly shouldn't be on display to the general public. There are also more up-to-date photos; a lot of them pictures of me and the gang, mostly ones where one or all of us are pissed and doing something hideously embarrassing.

Grace, Tanya, Louis and I are the four musketeers.

Grace and I have known each other since we were kids, and Tanya, Louis and I met up when we all started in the marketing department of a large commercial company at roughly the same time. We're all completely different, but we all share the same zest for life, and a totally mad sense of humour. We also share an unbreakable bond of friendship that, apart from Tates, is one of the things I value most in the whole world.

I know that any one of them would be there for me in a crisis. I'm very lucky in that I have a lot of good friends. I'm doubly lucky in that I have three particular friends who'd walk on water for me if they had to.

Louis is what he calls an 'Artiste'. Tanya, somewhat predictably I think, says that if he adds 'Piss' to the front of this self-awarded title, then he can just about get away with it. I think the problem with Louis is he hasn't quite decided what sort of artiste he wants to be, so he's tried his hand at practically everything. Singing was his first love, and he still belts out surprisingly good rock numbers in pubs around the East End. He's also been writing a book for the last four years, although I think he's still only on Chapter Three, and the plot's changed more times than Madonna's image. Acting is his rising passion though. He's actually done quite well so far – he's been seen lurking in the background of most of the well-known soaps, and even got to throw up over PC Garfield's boots as a drunk clubber in an episode of *The Bill*.

In order to have time to pursue his dreams, Louis has also given up a blossoming marketing career – the last of us to escape from the aforementioned large commercial company – and now spends what time he has left between casting calls, gigs, and his trusty laptop, working for me in the restaurant,

21

as head barman, and the official most-talented waiter in London.

Tanya: well, we call Tanya the Tart with the Heart, but despite the ribbing and in-jokes, she's really a paragon of virtue – NOT! Tanya is a bloke in a girl's body. I'm not saying that she fancies women, simply that she has a male mentality toward sex. Instead of emotional, it's mainly recreational. She also swears that she's never once fallen in love, and doesn't quite believe that such an emotion exists. Her theory is that love is lust gone haywire. This, however, doesn't detract from the fact that she's thoughtfulness personified when it comes to her friends. Despite the designer lifestyle, she was one of the first to don a pair of overalls and muck in when I needed help setting up and sorting out Tates, and if I ever need a sympathetic ear at an ungodly hour of the morning, hers is the first number I call.

And then there's Grace: bright, beautiful, funny, kind and, judging by her latest conquest, a bit of a soft touch! Mothers us all and yet is as mad as a hatter.

All so different and yet so together.

I pity Stuart with a U a little in that we are so close. Let's face it, even Mel Gibson would be given a pretty thorough appraisal if Gray brought him round for our approval – once we'd stopped drooling and begging for autographs, that is.

There's something else that worries me as well.

Strange though it may sound, Grace and I have such different tastes that I've never actually really fancied any of her men. However, this is the first one that I've actively *not* fancied. You know, the sort of guy you'd run away from during Kiss Chase in the playground because the thought of actually having to snog him was so unappealing.

Never mind. Each to their own. If we all fancied the same type of person, then there'd be a lot of lonely people around. And a few very big-headed ones as well, but I digress.

Reassuring myself that all is well, that Tates *is* reality and I'm not dreaming, and am still actually tied to a nine-to-five I hate, I lock up, and then stagger upstairs to the flat above the restaurant that I've called home for the past two years.

My flat is decorated in what I call a minimalist style. In other words it's much too small for me *and* furniture. In fact there are only four rooms, all of which were painted ochre by

Tanya, a total whiz with a roller, with paint left over from the restaurant. The most important is my bedroom, my haven from the outside world, in the form of a huge bed, with a pepper-red king-size duvet as a major splash of colour, which I can hide under when the going gets just a touch too tough sometimes. If you can't find me slumped at the huge scrubbed-wood table in the kitchen of Tates, which is my favourite place to be in the whole world – especially when I'm feeling flush enough to raid the better part of the wine cellar – then you'll probably find me in bed, buried under my duvet with the portable TV on.

The bathroom is my next-favourite room. Although it's not big enough to swing a runt kitten let alone a cat, I like nothing better – apart from slumping at the kitchen table, or falling into bed obviously – than to fall into a tub of bubbles with a good book and a bottle, until my skin is the texture of a sun-dried raisin.

Bliss.

Then there's the living room – the cat would get a touch more headroom in here, fewer bruises on the bonce maybe, but not many. There's enough room for a sofa, a load more family photographs – I'm a bit of an amateur camera buff – and a TV which only gets watched at about two in the morning when there's nothing on but what I call trash TV. Because of the strange hours that I work, I've developed this really bad habit of staying up late to watch crap American made-for-TV films, and then falling asleep just before you get to the usual dramatic climax, i.e. The End. I normally then wake up in the morning, totally knackered, and bloody frustrated that I didn't get to see whether Sharon, late thirties, successful, but single, managed to personally trap Robert, potential man of her dreams, who turned out to be an axe-wielding obsessive, without the aid of the sexy policeman, tall, dark, handsome and maverick, with more than a truncheon down the front of his trousers that in my opinion are far too tight to be able to chase criminals in.

The last room is the kitchen. This only gets used for the odd cup of coffee, because I usually eat downstairs in the restaurant.

There are advantages and disadvantages to living 'above the shop'. Midnight munchies have never before been so easily

23

assuaged and therefore so dangerous. At times I have thought of resorting to padlocking the fridge and sending the key home with one of the staff: chocolate cake was never meant to be *that* readily available.

All in all, despite my lack of willpower, life finally seems to be coming together. I've got my mates, and Tates, both of which can be bloody hard work, but make me incredibly happy. No man, of course, but unlike Tanya and Grace, I think one of those is a luxury rather than a necessity.

I wonder which category Stuart falls into – luxury or necessity?

I feel a bit cruel when the word 'Oddity' immediately springs to mind, but the fact is, it really is strange that someone like Grace is dating a man like him.

Oh well! I don't suppose I should get too concerned. She's tried sporty, haughty, naughty, dynamic, demanding and devious. I suppose now is as good a time as any for her to get 'Desperately Dull' out of her system.

Chapter Two

As predicted, Grace's hemlines start to rise again after a few days, an inch at a time maybe, but slowly and surely going back in the right direction, but after a further two weeks she still hasn't come to her senses and ditched Captain Sensible. In fact, despite our initial prognosis that he was a fairly weak flash in the pan, things seem to be getting pretty serious between them pretty fast.

Since she's been with him, we've only seen her about twice. It's not that she's with him all the time. Fortunately he lives too far away for them to have been able to progress to the 'can't bear to be apart' stage of a new relationship. It's just that you can *never* get hold of her. Her mobile's constantly switched off, and her landline's permanently engaged, either because they're having three-hour telephone conversations, or chatting constantly via the Internet.

Tanya, Louis and I are seated in the kitchen of Tates. Louis and I have just finished the Sunday lunchtime shift, and have collapsed at the huge scrubbed kitchen table, helping ourselves to the last pieces of a wickedly dark chocolate torte that was on the lunch menu. Tanya is bemoaning yet another Saturday night without Grace as her ever-present ready-to-dance-till-she-dropped and flirt-for-England club buddy.

'You still had a good time, didn't you?' I ask her.

Louis and I were both working the previous night and are slightly jealous, in a very good-natured way, of the fact that Tanya got to go out at all.

'Of course I had a good time, I always have a good time, but it's just not the same without Gray. Do you know they've subscribed to the same internet chat room, so that they can talk to each other all night? I never thought I'd see the day where Gray would choose to be stuck indoors on her computer on a

25

Saturday night, instead of coming out to play. I just knew Stuart would be a computer nerd,' Tan moans.

'He doesn't need a computer to be a nerd,' Louis remarks bitchily.

'Maybe we should give him another chance,' I interject, feeling vaguely magnanimous. 'I mean we've only met the guy once. Perhaps he *is* shy. She did say he was shy.' I repeat for about the eighth time. 'Perhaps we should organise another night out. Get to know him a bit better, bring him out a bit.'

The other two look at each other and shrug.

'I suppose it's only fair,' says Louis.

'For Grace's sake.' Tanya nods.

'How about JoJo's?' Louis suggests.

'When we said we wanted to bring him out, we didn't have quite that type of outing in mind!'

'Oh please, I haven't been there for ages and it's such fun, we could have dinner at the Groucho first or Max – they're both just round the corner.'

'I was thinking more along the lines of a few drinks, then perhaps going on to Abigail's Party?'

Louis's face falls.

'There are lots of gorgeous blokes there.'

'All *straight*,' he replies in disappointment.

'I doubt that very much.'

'Well, if it is full of straight men, maybe we could find one for Gray,' Tanya suggests hopefully.

'The point of the evening is to get to know Stuart, not get rid of him . . .' I reply, as Louis looks at me hopefully. 'Besides, she seems to be pretty happy with him.'

'God knows why!'

'If Gray likes him then he must have some redeeming qualities.' I'm trying to be the voice of reason here, but it's difficult when my feelings are actually the same as my friends.

'Yeah,' Tanya waves her fork, 'but you know what she's like about sad cases.'

'True, but she's never actually dated one of her lost causes before,' replies Louis, pouring some fresh cream straight onto a spoon and licking it off slowly.

'That's why I think we should make the effort to get to

26

know him a bit better. For Gray's sake, if nothing else. Maybe she sees something we don't.'

'Maybe. Either that or the Gray we know and love isn't the Gray we know and love,' Louis says mysteriously.

'What on earth do you mean?' Tanya good-naturedly slaps his outstretched hand as he reaches for her plate and attempts to steal her untouched piece of torte.

'You don't want it,' he coaxes her, batting his long eyelashes disarmingly.

'I might, just because I didn't wolf mine down like I haven't been fed for three days . . . What do you mean anyway?'

'Well, the way Grace has been acting recently I think she's been taken by the body snatchers. You know, looks like Grace from the outside, but underneath she's actually a pod person from the planet Zarg.' Louis sneaks his fork onto my plate instead, and gets away with the theft of my torte without reprimand.

I shake my head. Not at the theft of my dessert, but at Louis's last comment. He's right in a way, it is as if Grace has suddenly become a whole new person, changing her likes and dislikes to fit in with Stuart. I suppose we all do this to a degree when in a new relationship, it's just that Stuart's likes and dislikes are so vastly different from Grace's as to make this change in her personality extremely and radically noticeable.

The next Friday evening, we sit and wait nervously in our chosen restaurant for Grace and Stuart to arrive. We've made a pact to be as nice as pie, and really make an effort with Stuart. Nothing too OTT, just try to make him feel comfortable and perhaps bring him out of his shell a little.

Grace arrives sporting a skirt that comes to mid-calf. It's a huge improvement on the Victoriana, but still vastly different from her usual style. She's also proudly wearing a floral silk scarf knotted over her hair. This turns out to be a gift from Stuart. I might have guessed he'd have a hand in it some-where. If Grace had bought something like that for herself she'd no doubt have ended up looking sassy Bohemian; as it is, the style is definitely more sad Sloane housewife.

Stuart on the other hand, is actually looking rather better. He's had his hair cut a little shorter all over, which suits him much better than the previous pudding-basin cut. He's still wearing the same three-year-old Armani jacket, but this time has new black cords and a fresh black polo neck, which Louis is delighted to find on slightly closer inspection has a Paul Smith label.

I still find him about as attractive as the prospect of snogging a garden slug for kicks though.

Grace obviously doesn't have this problem, as throughout dinner they ignore their food and simply eat one another. They're all over each other, necking like teenagers when they think that no-one's looking, much to Louis and Tanya's disgust.

'Honestly, Ollie,' Tanya hisses to me, toying with a piece of radicchio. 'I wish she'd put him down, it's putting me off my salad.

I look over at Louis who is morosely cutting up his calves liver, whilst watching them sharing tongues, and smile at him encouragingly.

'I'm surprised we managed to drag you up to London again so soon, seeing as you dislike the place so much.' This is Tanya's opener to Stuart, when he finally releases Gray for long enough to remember they have company. So much for second chances. I throw her a 'please behave' look, and she sticks her tongue out at me.

'Well, it does have an added attraction now,' Stuart replies, smiling at Grace and taking her hand, which is resting on the table, and squeezing it.

Ah. Now that's sweet.

Stuart gets a big tick on my list for this one. Even Louis manages a slight smile, and trying hard, bless him, starts to ask Stuart about his new clothes. Unfortunately Stuart promptly loses the tick minutes later by telling a complimentary Louis that he didn't buy the Paul Smith, it was a present from Grace, and then announcing in front of Tanya that he hardly ever buys new clothes, because he absolutely HATES and DETESTS shopping.

This is like announcing to the Misses Pankhurst that you don't believe in equality for women. Tanya waves away the waiter who was offering her the dessert menu, and looks down her nose at Stuart as though he's a bad smell. 'So, Stuart,' she says slowly, resting her chin in her hand, and gazing levelly at him. 'You don't like London, and you don't like shopping. Is there anything that you do like?' The barb in Tanya's voice is a bit too obvious to go unnoticed.

Stuart looks vaguely embarrassed. 'Well, I do love gardening.'

'He grows all of his own veggies,' Grace interrupts proudly. 'Totally organic. I said *organic*, Tanya. You should have some for the restaurant, Ollie, they taste so much better than supermarket stuff.'

'That would be great,' I reply enthusiastically, determined to try my hardest for the sake of my best friend. 'More drinks anyone?'

'I'll have another gin,' growls Tanya. 'A large one.'

'Louis?'

'Arsenic, a double,' he replies.

Fortunately Grace doesn't hear this one. 'Nothing for us, hon,' she tells me. 'We're going to make a move soon.'

'You're going?' I cry disappointedly. 'But we're supposed to be going on!'

'Yeah, I know, but nightclubs aren't really Stuart's scene. Are they, darling?'

Stuart shakes his head.

Well, that doesn't surprise me.

'Maybe not,' I coax her as Stuart, possibly sensing further disapproval, heads off to the loos. 'But they're yours. Come on, Gray, we haven't been clubbing together for ages.'

'If Stuart doesn't want to come, can't you just send him home in a cab?' Louis adds.

'All the way to Leicester?' Grace shakes her head. 'He's staying at mine tonight, I can't really send him home on his own. Besides, I'm not really in the mood, I'm a bit tired myself to be honest.' This is the woman who could boogie until four in the morning, and still get up at six the next day as bright and breezy as a Spring morning.

'He doesn't grow organic vegetables at the bottom of his garden. He grows strange substances instead and brews them into love potions with which to trap poor unsuspecting members of the opposite sex!' I mutter grumpily, as Grace and Stuart head for the door hand in hand.

'Do you think he'd sell the recipe?' Tanya grins lasciviously.

'You don't need it. You already produce it instead of sweat.'

'He's Prince Charles without the kudos or connections,' murmurs Louis, watching them get into a cab still holding hands.

29

Well, this evening didn't exactly achieve what I'd hoped. I love my friend so much; I really want to get on with the person she loves. Unfortunately we just seem to have confirmed that Stuart is about as easy to bond with as wet Sellotape.

At least I think I've worked out one of the reasons why we find him so difficult to get on with. He'll sit and chat with Grace, but he doesn't actually attempt conversation with anyone else, simply sits and looks at us, whilst Grace talks to us, with an expression on his face that I can't quite work out.

Tanya insists it's contempt, but I don't think so. I think it could be that he quite simply doesn't know how to take us: the cleavage-toting sexpot, the flamboyantly pretty big-hearted gay, and me, the only vaguely normal one of the lot of us. I feel quite boring in comparison with the other two. Not the sort of people that I think Stuart with a U is used to socialising with. I suddenly feel a little flat.

'You know, I don't know if I fancy going on to a club after all. You two go on if you want to. I think I'm just going to finish my drink and get a cab home.'

'I don't know about organic love potions, I think he must brew a party-pooper aftershave,' Tanya huffs. 'I don't much feel like clubbing either. Can I come back with you?'

Tanya and I share a cab back to my place, leaving Louis the Dancing Queen to head off with a group of friends he bumped into outside the bar to rave the night away in a local club.

After a minor detour via the fridge, to assuage Tanya's desperate desire for the dessert that she didn't get in Soho, we head upstairs to the flat and bed. I just fall into bed as I am, minus clothes of course.

Tan, however, sits down at my dressing-table mirror and begins the long laborious process of removing every single trace of make-up from her face. This is probably how she manages to stay looking so good all the time. Maybe I should adopt the cleanse, tone and moisturise regime, before my minor wrinkles turn into major crevices.

'What's happened to the mad scatty fun monster we know and love?' I sigh sadly, as Tanya slips out of her dress, and gets into the other side of my bed.

'Maybe the party animal's been tamed.' She leans over and hugs me reassuringly. 'Don't worry, darling, you know what it's like: new man equals huge effort. She'll get over it. She'll soon be back in her crotch-brushing bumhuggers and flirting with barmen.'

'And what if she doesn't?'

Tanya shakes her head. 'I wouldn't worry too much, babe. Can you honestly see it lasting?'

Tanya may have a point here. Grace is bright, bubbly, gregarious, a real party animal with a taste for high living, high fashion, high jinks, high hemlines and low necklines. She's like Tanya, but with a social conscience, and a slightly lower sex drive.

Stuart is quiet and shy, hates clubbing, hates shopping, and hates London: three of Grace's all-time favourite things. Admittedly he wears Armani jackets, but at least three years old, and with a clashing roll-neck jumper!

'I know they say that opposites attract but this one really is ridiculous!' Tanya adds.

'I don't know, we may think they have about as much in common as a feather duster and a g-string, but she seems really keen.'

'I can think of a few things that involve a feather duster and a g-string at the same time.' Tan grins.

I sigh heavily. 'Maybe Gray will just grow out of him,' I say hopefully.

'It's just the novelty factor,' agrees Tan.

'Yeah, she's never dated an anorak before.'

'Never gone off-roading in a Land Rover.'

'Never shagged in a caravan.'

'Never worn his and hers pullovers.'

'So he's providing a whole new spectrum of life experiences,' I say sarcastically.

We wake up late the next day, having slept through my alarm, with just enough time for me to give Tanya a lift home on my way to the wholesaler's before I start preparing for the Saturday-lunchtime rush.

I finally arrive back at the restaurant two hours later, the boot and back seat of my car loaded with supplies; fresh vegetables, cuts of meat, flowers for the tables. I work off some of my bad humour lugging boxes in and out of the restaurant, and am just starting to feel a little more chirpy,

31

when the second post arrives. I might have known with the way things seem to be going at the moment that my happy mood would be seriously short-lived.

'They cannot be serious!' I shriek John-McEnroe style, making the postman, who was loitering by the range necking a cup of coffee, jump three feet in the air, grab his bag and head out to finish his round, away from the mad woman with a meat cleaver in her right hand, and one of his freshly delivered letters in the other.

'What's the matter, babe?' Louis comes rushing in from the restaurant where he's been laying tables for the lunchtime session.

'I don't believe it.' I slump down at the table, shaking my head. 'Just when everything was coming together.'

'What is it, Ollie, what's wrong?'

I wave the letter at him. 'This! This is what's wrong.'

'What's it say?'

I take a deep breath, to try and calm myself down.

'What is it?' Louis repeats in fearful exasperation. 'Ollie, you've gone completely white, tell me what's wrong.'

'Well, you know old Mr Forsythe, the guy who owns this building, and the ones either side.'

Louis nods impatiently, and sits down opposite me.

'He's retired.'

'Is that it? Honestly, I thought you were going to tell me someone had died or something!' Louis tuts, letting out the breath he'd been holding. 'Well, it's a shame, babe, he's a nice guy and all that, but I'd hardly call it the end of the world!'

'It is when he's sold the buildings to a property developer, Louis!'

'You're joking?' It's Louis's turn to go white.

I shake my head. 'It's here in black and white,' I exclaim, jabbing a finger rather viciously at the letter I'm holding. 'Slater Enterprises. They're the ones who bought up those old factory buildings near the Heliport eighteen months ago, turfed everyone out, and converted them into ridiculously expensive apartments. And as if that isn't bad enough, do you know what else they want to do? No? Well, I'll tell you. They want to put the rent up by over thirty percent!'

'You're joking,' Louis repeats flatly, his face now the same fetching puce colour that my face is currently sporting.

32

'I wish I was. I know I was lucky in that the rent was pretty low before, but this is ridiculous! Besides, a property developer usually buys property in order to develop it. Putting up my rent by thirty percent is obviously an effective but sneaky way to try and push me out.'

'Can they actually do that? Don't you have any rent clauses in your lease or something that says that they can't just bump up the rent when they feel like it?'

'My lease is due for renewal in just under three months, Louis. After that they can negotiate whatever terms they want.'

'Shit.'

'Exactly. Shit. And we're now right in it.'

Louis gets up and pulls his chair round next to mine. 'Don't worry, babe.' He hugs me reassuringly. 'There'll be something we can do. You'll work it out . . . *we'll* work it out.'

'There's a number to phone here. They want me to call in if I have any queries.'

'Are you going to ring them?'

'You bet I'm going to bloody ring them! In fact I'm going to do it right now!'

'Are you sure that's a good idea? Maybe you should take a few deep breaths, or perhaps a few large gins, and calm down a bit?'

'Strike while the iron's hot.' I smile at him but there's no humour in the smile. 'Or perhaps that should be strike whilst my temper's hot.'

Seven minutes later I head back into the kitchen. Louis, bless him, has made a pot of coffee and is waiting with open arms and an open biscuit tin.

'Well?' he demands, pushing a cup into my trembling hands, and offering me a double chocolate cookie.

'I was right!' I pull out a chair and sit down heavily. 'They *are* trying to push us out.'

'Why? How do you know? What did they say?'

'They said that if I can't cope with the increase, then they'd be more than happy to offer me a deal to buy out the rest of my lease.'

'Really? What did you say?'

'Told them to get stuffed.'

33

'You didn't?'

I nod. 'Yep, then I told them to put me through to the person in charge. Well, actually I asked to speak to the organ grinder instead of the monkey.'

'Literally?'

'Literally.' I nod, a touch ashamed. 'I was just so angry, and the bloody woman I got through to first-off was so officious, I can't believe how rude I can be when someone puts my back up . . .'

'And then what happened?' Louis asks, wide eyed. 'Did they put you through to the organ grinder?'

'Of course they didn't. She just put me on hold for a few minutes, and then came back and said that Mr Slater was unavailable at the moment, but "understood my position" and reiterated the offer to purchase the remainder of my lease for a "very good rate".'

'And what did you say?'

'I told her to tell that bastard to stick his offers up his backside.'

'Ooh, Ollie, you didn't!' Louis drops his third biscuit into his coffee, where it promptly melts into a soggy mess at the bottom.

Biting my bottom lip to suppress a badly timed smile, I nod at Louis. 'I know, I can't believe I said it either.'

'Good for you!'

'Well, if they think they're going to get me out of here that easily then they've got another think coming.'

'Yeah! You tell 'em, babe!' Louis thrusts a fist in the air in front of his face in a sympathetic power salute.

'They've got a fight on their hands,' I state determinedly. 'I've worked too hard for this business to let some jumped-up little shit of a property developer get his hands on it.'

I phone Tanya at work.

'Daniel Slater,' she murmurs. 'Name rings a bell.'

'Well, it would, you being an estate agent.'

'Property consultant . . .' she corrects me.

'And him being a property developer. Do you think you've ever met him?'

'Don't think so,' Tanya muses. 'Heard of him, but never actually seen him in the flesh. I wonder what he's like?'

34

'I know what he's like,' I growl.

'You've met him?'

'I don't need to meet him to know what he's like. He's a bastard! He'll probably be just like someone out of a Chaucer story. You know, lots of physical defects manifesting from all the times he's put some poor sod out of business.'

'What, short, bald and ugly with lots of moles and prominent birthmarks denoting his mean streak; oh and don't forget the hump.'

'Well, he's certainly giving me the bloody hump, so he deserves one.'

'Hump,' says Tanya thoughtfully. 'A word with many varied connotations.'

'What am I going to do, Tan?' I can hear Tanya tapping the end of her pen on her desk as she thinks.

'You know, I really don't think there's an awful lot you can do at the moment, babe, apart from sit tight and wait for his next move.'

'Do you think he wants to turn Tates into a des res?'

'I really don't know, darling, but you are in an area that's classed as up and coming, they don't call your part of Battersea little Chelsea for nothing. But that said, all you can do for the time being is sit tight and wait and see what happens. It's my guess you'll be hearing from them again pretty soon anyway.'

I've begun to dread the arrival of the post. I always used to be quite excited by this part of the day; despite the fact that I normally only receive bills and slightly scary bank statements, there's always the chance that you'll get something nice or even exciting, like a letter from a friend, or a party invite or, my favourite at the moment, a nice big cheque.

When the next white envelope arrives bearing the now familiar frank of 'Slater Enterprises' in big red letters, I'm tempted just to leave it on the table and spend all day eyeing it suspiciously every time I walk past. Louis, however, hasn't the patience to wait and after much nagging, watches as I finally rip it open, straining over my shoulder in an attempt to read it as quickly as possible. I put him out of his misery and read it aloud.

'*Dear Sir.* Dear Sir! They can't even get my gender right, let alone put my name!' I exclaim in disgust. I bet they really had to restrain themselves on that one. I can just envisage them itching to put *Dear Right Madam*.

'Following our recent telephone conversation, please accept this letter as confirmation of our offer to purchase . . .'

That's as far as I get. 'What part of "stick your offers up your backside" don't they get?' I yell angrily, slamming the letter down on the table. 'I'm not selling out!'

Talk about adding insult to injury!

I'm straight on the phone again, and through to the old battleaxe I argued with the last time. 'I'm afraid Mr Slater isn't in the office at the moment,' she tells me imperiously.

Not in the office my arse. He just doesn't want to talk to me. Slamming down the phone, without the usual pleasantries – ie thanks for nothing, and goodbye arsewipe – I reach for my coat, which is hanging on the back of the door, and grab my car keys from the window ledge above the sink.

'What are you doing, Ol?' Louis's face is a picture of concern.

'I'm going round there.'

'Are you sure that's a good idea?'

'No, but I'm going anyway.'

'And what exactly are you going to do when you get there?' Louis asks rationally.

'Murder someone . . .' I reply savagely.

Slater Enterprises takes up the whole of the penultimate and penthouse floors of an imposing glass-and-steel building in the Euston Road. Scurrying past the reception desk, hidden in a crowd of office workers returning from lunch, I hop in the lift and head past the Slater Enterprise reception area on the penultimate floor, straight to the top floor, which is where I assume a man such as Daniel Slater will have sited his office.

I am right. The lift doors open onto a very plush lobby with the softest of pale blue carpets, which must have been ridiculously expensive and probably hell to keep clean, and heavy, also no doubt ridiculously expensive, oak furniture. I suppose he can afford it, going round fleecing innocent businesses like a one-man swarm of locusts.

An immaculately presented woman in her forties is seated like a sentry at a desk placed at right angles to the lift door. I'd try to slide past her, but she's trained to spot interlopers and moves in for a swift kill.

'Can I help you?' The voice is polite but frosty, and instantly recognisable as the 'monkey' I spoke to two days ago, and very briefly this morning.

Her face as she takes in my somewhat dishevelled appearance is distinctly unwelcoming. For the first time I realise that I just pulled on my jacket over my grubby kitchen whites before heading over here. I must look a total state. I quickly grapple a hand over my head and whip off my hair net. She's probably pressing a panic button under her desk right now to call in security. Running a rather pointless hand through my hair, which only succeeds in making it stick out more, I take a deep breath and try to sound authoritative. 'I'm here on behalf of Tates in Battersea. I want to see Daniel Slater.'

She hesitates.

'I have an appointment,' I state grandly, pleased at how smoothly I manage this lie.

A slow smile spreads over her perfectly made-up face. It's not a friendly smile. 'I'm afraid you can't possibly have an appointment, as Mr Slater is out of the country at the moment,' she announces in her clipped voice.

She has every right to look smug here, after catching me out telling a bare-faced lie, but the fact that she does, and with such relish, takes my blood pressure up another point. I look past her to the imposing double doors, where a big brass plate states 'Daniel Slater – Chairman'.

The very fact that she looks so bloody smug at catching me out should tell me that she's being truthful and Dan Slater is actually reeking havoc on small businesses elsewhere in the world today, but I haven't come this far just to leave with my tail between my legs. Besides, there's still a slim possibility she's just covering for him, after all that's what she's paid to do – be a human Rottweiler. Despite what she said, he could actually be sat in his office at this very moment. Ignoring Miss Smugpants, I start to walk toward the doors.

She's out of her seat in seconds. 'Excuse me . . . *Excuse* me! You can't just go in there.' The controlled tone gets a little shrill.

Ignoring her, I barge straight past her desk and burst through the door to find . . .

A very empty room.

Oh shit. It looks as if she was telling the truth. Now what do

I do? I've already made myself look a total prat, so there's only one way I can think of to salvage some joy from the situation. It may be childish, but I cannot describe how much better it makes me feel to take that bloody letter from my handbag and tear it into shreds, then sprinkle it confetti style over Dan Slater's far too tidy desk.

I turn around, pause to look down my nose at Miss Smug, who's mouthing wordlessly like a shocked beached fish, then march back to the lift with my head held high. The regal effect is only ruined by the fact that the dirty tea towel I still have trailing from the back pocket of my Rupert Bear trousers gets caught in the closing doors of the lift as I march inside, affording the other elderly be-suited occupant of the lift a brief view of my pink G-string.

By the time I get back to Tates, Louis has closed up and gone, leaving me a note to say that he's supposed to be meeting friends, but I can get him on his mobile if I need a sympathetic ear, or bailing out of jail. Although he continues that as he's only currently got twelve pounds fifty, a half eaten mini Mars Bar, and a packet of three with one missing in his pocket, I'd probably be better off ringing Tanya on that score.

Bless him.

This puts a smile on my face for the first time since the rather manic one I was sporting in Dan Slater's office. All the way home I've been frowning like a shortsighted patient trying to read an optician's test chart. I've probably got more lines than a Klingon on my forehead now.

Why on earth did I just do that?

Yes, I was angry, but I'm not normally the impetuous type. Especially when the impetuous is coupled with the words 'stupid pointless gesture'. I do need a sympathetic ear, but I also need a sensible one. Someone who'll not just applaud what I did because they love me, and who'd be eternally on my side even if I'd just declared war on the Vatican. Someone who's not afraid to tell me when they think I've done wrong, and who's prepared to help me work out a sane solution to my problems.

I phone Grace, only to be told that she's not in work today.

I try her home number and get her answer machine.

I try her mobile. It's switched off.

It doesn't take a genius to work out where she is, or who she's with for that matter. Grace has been sucked even further into the confines of Stuart with a U world. Every sentence she utters nowadays starts with 'Stuart says'. That's when we actually get to talk to her. I'm not saying that she's not entitled to her own life. Of course she is. Maybe we lived in each other's pockets a little too much when we were both single, but since she met Stuart we seem to have gone to the other extreme with frightening rapidity.

I miss her. I'm used to Grace always being there for me when I need her. It works both ways of course. Well, it would if she was ever around.

I phone Tanya instead. She's at work, but she still finds time to listen for half an hour whilst I moan about 'Satan' Slater and missing best friends, without pause for breath.

'We need a night out,' she announces when I finally grumble myself to a halt. 'And we need to persuade Grace to come with us. It'll do you both good. Take your mind off your business problems, and give us a chance to catch up.'

To my surprise, we actually manage to tempt Gray away from Stuart for one evening by arranging a girlies' gossip night at Tates with just the three of us. It's a bit like being summoned to a meeting of the Masons or something. Attendance mandatory. It helps that treacle pudding and custard, Gray's favourite, just *happen* to be on my menu tonight.

The evening doesn't get off to a particularly good start however. Grace arrives glued to her mobile, and spends the first twenty minutes curled up on a seat by the fire drooling down the phone to Stuart, who from the sounds of things has been re-christened some sickeningly gooey pet name, that sounds a little like Stuey Pooey. Tanya, who's sitting as close as she can to eavesdrop without being too noticeable, pretends to barf in her wine glass.

Grace finally gets off the phone after another sickening five minutes of blowing kisses, and 'you go first's, and 'I MISS you's. 'You know I really think that he could be the one,' she announces, after finally joining us at the table. She sighs happily, and stares dreamily into the depths of her glass of Chardonnay.

I just manage to clamp a hand over Tanya's mouth before

she screams. 'But you've only known him for just under two months,' I mutter, quickly letting go of Tanya as Grace stops mooning into her wine and looks up at us.

'How long does love take?' she replies philosophically.

'You're in love with him!' Tanya exclaims, glaring at me as my hand hovers toward her mouth again.

'Well to be honest, I'm not sure, but I think I could be.'

'Loo!' Tanya grabs my hand, and drags me up from the table. 'Now!'

'What's up?' Gray stops grinning into her glass and stares up at Tanya in surprise. 'Where are you going?'

'Er . . . I just need to borrow Ollie, I mean, er . . . I need . . . er, I need to borrow . . . in the loos, I need to borrow, you know, girlie things . . . Tampax,' Tan exclaims a little too loudly, when her brain finally thinks of a plausible excuse to drag me away from the table for a private confab. 'Back in a mo!'

Gray watches us in some confusion as Tanya drags me across the restaurant and into the kitchen rather than the loo.

'It's worse than I thought,' she gasps as the door swings to behind us, and Mel, who's on a speedy coffee break turns round and blinks at us in surprise.

'What do you mean?'

'I've seen this before, never in Gray, but I've definitely seen it before.'

'What do you mean?' I repeat in exasperation.

'She's in love.'

'She's not in love. She just thinks she is. She's been brainwashed.'

'More like lobotomised. What does she see in him? The next thing we know they'll be getting married and having . . .' Tanya swallows before she can force the word out of her mouth, '. . . babies! Can you imagine a horde of little Stuart clones running round in mini cords and mini polo-necks? Ugh!'

'I think you're getting a bit carried away, babe. She's only known him for a few weeks, I hardly think marriage could be on the agenda.'

'Of course he'll ask her to marry him,' Tanya insists, 'before she comes to her senses and dumps him! Probably can't believe his luck. Stops to tow a car out of a ditch, and ends up

40

pulling a babe who's well out of his league. Besides, he's Mr Traditional if ever I met him, that's what they do . . .'

'You think?'

Tanya nods vigorously. 'I'd bet my monthly clothing allowance,' she replies gravely.

When we get back to the table Grace is fortunately too keen to get back onto the subject of Stuart with a U to quiz us on our sudden departure into the depths of the kitchen. 'I'm having him round for a romantic meal for two on Saturday,' is the first thing she tells us, 'just him, me, good food, soft music.'

'You don't want to do that!' I exclaim, Tanya's dire forewarnings of imminent proposals springing instantly to mind.

'Why on earth not?'

'Because . . . er . . . because . . .' I stutter stupidly.

'Because,' cuts in Tanya, coming to my rescue, 'you'll spend half the evening running in and out of the kitchen making sure you don't burn anything. Then there's all that washing-up you have to do before you go to bed in case he thinks you're a total slut for leaving it till the morning. Hardly conducive to a romantic evening.'

'I've got a dishwasher, Tan.'

'Yeah, sure, but you've still got to stack it, and he might be one of these guys who thinks it's tantamount to sluttishness not to wash your saucepans by hand or some-thing.'

'Why don't you bring him here instead?' I offer, a germ of an idea tickling my brain. Tanya, catching on quickly, does a thumbs up under our side of the table so only I can see. 'That way we can keep an eye on you . . . er, I mean things, keep an eye on things, you know, make sure everything goes smoothly. You can have Snoggers Corner.' I indicate the table in an alcove in a corner where we always stick love birds due to the fact that it's the most secluded in the place. It overlooks the little courtyard garden to the back, which is just big enough to house a few climbing plants, and a fountain that Louis insisted we install, sporting a small Cupid perched on top on tiptoe, arrow pointing directly in at anyone seated at the table.

'Yeah,' Tanya encourages her, 'then all you've got to do at

41

home is put the champagne in to chill and turn down the covers.'

'You'd do that for me?' A huge smile floods Gray's face, and lifting a little from her chair, she reaches over and hugs me. 'That's wonderful.'

'No problem, babe, you're my best friend. I'd do anything to make you happy.'

I quash the flood of guilt that rushes through me with the thought that all we are actually trying to do is make her happy. We're trying to save her from herself. Grace would do the same for us if the tables were turned. I mean she once stopped me from buying a Gucci dress in the sale that I really thought I had to have. I fell heavily in love with that dress, and was adamant I'd be instantly transformed into Liz Hurley the moment I put it on, but Gray knew that no matter how much I steamed up the shop window with my drool, it didn't actually suit me, and I couldn't really afford it. I may have hated her when she dragged me away from the Gucci sale kicking and screaming, but my bank balance and my dress sense thanked her for it afterwards.

Tanya obviously has the same feelings of guilt. She stays after Grace has shot off home to curl up under her duvet and make her long uninterrupted good-night phone call to Stuffy, and helps me finish the second bottle of wine we opened.

'I'm sure he's a decent guy, but I'm also sure that he's not the right guy for Gray.' She shakes her head despondently. 'Maybe we shouldn't interfere, but I don't want to see her get caught in a long-term relationship for all of the wrong reasons.'

'I agree. If she wants to date the guy, then fine, that's her prerogative, we really have no right to interfere, and as long as she's happy, we wouldn't, but it's like pairing up Madonna with Steve Davies. You just know when Mads gets over the novelty of being Mrs Boring, it's going to end up messy.'

'Do you think we should have stayed out of this "evening of lurve" thing?'

Tanya takes a gulp of wine and shakes her head vehemently. 'Definitely not. We're just keeping a friendly eye on things, that's all. Because it really wouldn't be right for them to get too heavy too soon, would it?'

'Perhaps we shouldn't interfere.'

'We're not really interfering, simply making sure that they

don't get out of hand. You know, looking after Gray's best interests.'

'We can just hover in the background, and make sure it all goes okay.'

'Like a maitre d' at a major banquet,' Tanya adds. 'Making sure everything goes off smoothly, whilst safeguarding etiquette.'

'At an unobtrusive distance,' I add.

'We don't have to interfere *at all*!' Tanya agrees.

'They're here!' Mel pushes through the door, balancing plates, calling out to us in her best Jack-Nicholson impression. Tanya, Louis and I stampede for the kitchen door, heads popping through, one above the other, like Indians on a totem pole.

Stuart is holding the door open for Grace. He's abandoned the favourite cords, but is still wearing the three-year-old Armani jacket, although he appears to have hunted through his wardrobe for the rather creased pair of trousers which I think used to match, but through lack of wear are now a shade darker than the jacket. The polo-neck jumper has also been abandoned in favour of a shirt, and, unless my eyes deceive me, a tie!

Louis, Tanya, and I all look at each other with raised eyebrows, the same fear echoing on each of our faces. Stuffy in a shirt and tie equals HUGE effort.

'Are you sure you want to put them in Snoggers Corner?' Tanya asks in concern.

'We already told Gray that we would.'

'But it's *far* too romantic.'

'Well, we'd better un-romanticise it then, hadn't we?' states Louis, heading hurriedly out of the kitchen door.

Mel goes back out again to take Grace and Stuart to their table, delaying them at the bar long enough for Louis to sprint round snuffing out the candles, switching on the overhead lights, and whisking away the vase of red and yellow roses that was sitting on the table. He then replaces Annie Lennox's 'Diva', which is currently playing, with something delightfully head banging from Motorhead, making my other customers look up from their meals in surprise.

I think this is a slight overkill. Before everybody can walk out, I slip 'The Ace of Spades' out of the CD player and pop in something a little less frenetic, but not quite so soul clenching as Diva. I can see Mel giggling as she heads back toward the kitchen having seated Grace and Stuart at their table.

'You won't believe what Louis has done.' She catches my arm and we push through the swing door into the kitchen together.

'Want to bet?' I reply. 'Try me.'

'Well, when he hung up Stuart's jacket for him, he put it by the radiator and slipped some unwrapped after-dinner mints in his pocket,' she sniggers. 'So when he puts his hand in . . .' She mimes putting her hand in a pocket, spreading her fingers and shaking them, her face cringing at the thought of the melted mess Stuart's going to find when he puts his jacket back on.

'Oh no, that's *so* mean!' I reply, feeling a little bad, but not quite bad enough to go and retrieve them.

'And that's not all,' Mel continues, sliding her eyes toward the door. 'He put Stuart on one of the old school chairs – you know, the ones we can only use at the table in the far corner because they're too low for anywhere else – so he looks like a kid seated at the table. The table top's practically in line with his nipples! And you know the seats in those chairs have got a kind of arse-shaped dip, well he put two little pools of bleach, one on each side, so that when he gets up again the seat of his trousers is going to be all stained . . .'

'Oh no!' I groan. 'That's awful . . .'

'Don't you dare!' Tanya warns me.

'What?' I protest innocently.

'I know you, you're coming over all nice. Don't you dare go out there and rescue him. This is a really good chance for Grace to see what a prat Stuart is, and if we have to help this enlightening process, so be it. I'm not having you taking pity on Stuffy and ruining our plans.'

Louis walks in waving his note pad. 'Order for Snoggers Corner! Stuffy wants the soup to start,' Louis beams demonically, practically rubbing his hands together with glee. 'Couldn't have asked for a better choice. Ooh, the possibilities with that one!'

Whilst I make up Grace's hot mackerel with fresh ginger, Louis ladles Stuart a bowl of steaming homemade soup from one of the bains-maries, and sets to work. A far-too-liberal sprinkling with the pepper grinder, and a not-so-little dash of

44

Tabasco are added to what should be simply a fresh-tomato-and-basil soup. He adds a sprig of fresh parsley and a swirl of cream to make it look tempting and innocuous, and then as an afterthought, returns to the cupboard for a jar of garlic pepper and adds an entire teaspoonful.

Louis dashes back into the kitchen two minutes after serving them. 'He's just coughed his guts up all over the table,' he crows in delight. 'It was disgusting! He took this huge spoonful, whilst he was still talking and he just covered Grace in soup spit!'

Louis dances around the kitchen table like a native American Indian doing a celebratory war dance. 'And that was just for starters!' he laughs wickedly. 'Pardon the pun.'

Over the next hour, Louis subjects Stuart to every subtle assault that a waiter can possibly carry out on a customer, short of spitting in his food. By the time we reach the dessert course, Stuffy appears to have more food on his clothes than in his stomach.

'Need a cloth!' Louis yells, barging through the swing door backwards and heading for the sink at great speed.

'What have you done now?'

Louis emerges from the cupboard under the sink where I keep the cleaning materials, grinning like a Cheshire cat who's just drunk a pint of Guinness. 'Well, let's just say if he wants his wine he'll have to suck it from the crotch of his trousers!'

'Louis!' I exclaim, my voice a mixture of admiration and horror. 'You didn't!'

'Well, he was reaching into his pocket, so I thought he might be going for a Boodle & Dunthorne box or something.'

'He was only taking out his handkerchief to wipe away the gravy you'd already spilt on his tie during the main course,' announces Melanie, backing through the swing door with a pile of dirty plates.

'Well, that's didn't work,' Louis tries to justify himself, 'they're bloody snogging now!'

'I knew you shouldn't have put them in Snoggers Corner,' Tanya wails accusingly at me, before rushing to the door to peer into the restaurant. 'Ooh yuk!' she cries in horror, 'they're doing it again, and with tongues! It must be like a chewing on an escargot the chef forgot to cook!'

'There's a bulge in his pocket,' Louis announces dramatically.

'You shouldn't be looking, Louis!'

'Not *that* sort of bulge, unless he's got square balls.'

'You're imagining it. We're all totally paranoid he's going to fall to his knees any minute, and produce the Hope diamond from his right pocket.'

'As long as it's the No-Hope Diamond!' Tanya grimaces.

'Paranoid or not, there's definitely a bulge,' Louis insists.

'I suppose it's up to me to redeem the situation,' I announce. Heading for one of the kitchen drawers, I reach inside, and groping around, close my fingers around my contingency back-up plan.

'How about a little laxative chocolate on his dessert, instead of the real thing?' I wave the small bar of Ex-lax that I'm holding at them.

'Ollie, you can't!' Tanya shrieks, covering her mouth with her hands in gleeful horror.

'I suppose it is a bit much,' I reply, putting the bar back down on the table.

'It's not as if it'll kill him!' Louis breezes up to the table, and taking the bar, starts to grate it over Stuart's hot chocolate-fudge cake with a little nutmeg grater.' 'It'll just put him out of action for the rest of the evening.'

We watch Louis take out Stuart's dessert with a mixture of delight and distaste, but no one tries to stop him. In fact we all stick our heads round the door and stare as he finishes every last mouthful, without uttering a word to stop him sticking the chocolate-laden fork into his mouth. Stuart hurriedly finishes every last crumb on his plate, probably scared that Louis'll breeze over any minute and up end this into his lap as well. At least he looks as if he enjoys it!

They linger over coffee, not really talking, but simply sitting together, smiling inanely in that sick-making gooey kind of way that makes you want to slap some sense into them. When the 'Ace of Spades' is on repeat play for the eighth time and has long since got rid of the last of my other customers, Grace finally sticks her head round the kitchen to tell us that they're leaving, happily smiling her thanks at everyone gathered in the kitchen, and narrowly avoiding spotting Tanya, who slides quickly under the table out of view.

'We're heading off now,' she grins. 'Thanks for everything, everybody; we've had a wonderful evening – apart from

46

Stuart's trousers which haven't seemed to fare particularly well tonight! Oh well, at least I've got a really good excuse now to speedily remove them!' She pauses and the smile turns lascivious. 'And now we're going back to my place to have a wonderful night.'

She turns to me again. 'I'll call you in the morning. Fill you in on all of the gory details!'

'Please no! Not all of the gory details.' Tanya emerges from under the table, peeling a stray piece of cold cooked tortellini from the knee of her Calvin Klein jeans, and pulling a face, as Grace trots happily back into the restaurant and takes the arm of Stuart, who is waiting by the door.

'Can you imagine what he looks like naked?'

'I could, but I don't think I want to,' I reply with a shudder.

'How did he look?' Tanya demands of Louis, who helped Stuart on with his coat before they left.

'I don't know, I haven't seen him naked either.'

'I meant as they were leaving.' Tanya rolls her eyes at him. 'Honestly!'

'Well, actually he did look a little green . . .'

'I think that's probably just wishful thinking; it takes some time to start working.'

'Their cab's just turned the corner at the end of the road,' reports Mel, who's on watch duty.

This is our cue. 'Quick! To the Batmobile!' shrieks Louis excitedly.

'You really do bring new meaning to the phrase Drama Queen,' Tanya sighs, following him out of the back door.

Leaving Mel to lock up, we stampede out to Louis's battered Union-Jack Mini, cram ourselves into the confines of its takeaway-box-littered interior and speed off to Islington as fast as the asthmatic old motor can take us. Steering with one hand, Louis reaches down into my side of the car with the other, swerving dangerously as he gropes around for a plastic bag that's in the footwell.

'Be an angel, Ollie, and grab that for me.'

I grope around for a blue-striped market bag, and on Louis's instruction, remove the contents. I hand a soft blue object to Tanya, who's crammed into the back, keep one for myself, and pass the other to Louis, who proceeds to don the article with one hand whilst changing gear with the other, and steering with his knees.

'Balaclavas!' I exclaim, as Louis pulls the wool over his spiky blue hair.

'Do you want Gray to spot us?'

'I'd rather that than get hauled off by the police on suspicion of burglary!'

'Navy?' Tanya calls disappointedly from the back. 'It's not really my colour, darling. Don't you have any in black?'

'Well, I'm not putting this on.'

'But I bought them specially,' Louis mutters through a mouthful of blue wool.

Sighing, I pull on the offending article so as not offend Louis, whose bottom lip can be seen trembling through the mouth slit of his own itchy, horrible head gear.

There's only one good thing about my new balaclava. As we park and walk down the streets towards Grace's house like rejects from the SAS, it's the only thing hiding the embarrassed red blush that I'm now sporting as well.

'We're Charlie's Angels,' giggles Louis, sliding in and out of the shadows holding his hands together like a pretend gun.

'More like proper Charlies!' I grumble. 'Did you have to park so far away?'

'Well, I figured if I parked outside my house, then Grace wouldn't wonder what my car was doing there, whereas if I parked near her house . . .'

'Er . . . Louis, I don't think Grace is going to be wandering the streets at this time of night looking for your car.'

'Exactly,' moans Tanya, tottering along behind us in Miu Miu's, Gucci, and a Camden-Market army-surplus special. 'Look, I know you bought these things specially, Louis, but I've got to take mine off.' She shoves a manicured fingernail up the woollen neck of her balaclava and scratches distractedly. 'They're so itchy, it's driving me mad!'

I cough dejectedly. 'It's all right for you, you're just itchy. I think I've got a fur ball stuck in my throat.'

'Okay, okay, you can take them off,' Louis gives in ungraciously. 'Just don't blame me when you're the ones that everyone recognises on *Crimewatch*.'

We let ourselves into Grace's small padlocked back garden

using the keys she gave me when she first moved in. Grace's house is one of those three-storey Victorian affairs, with the kitchen in the basement, and a ground floor that is slightly above eye level.

After a silent game of charades, it's finally agreed that Louis will climb aboard the metal compost bin to peer into the sitting room and report on what he can see. Unfortunately his green mock snakeskin boot-cuts are a bit tight on his hot little bot, and he can't quite get the leg-up he needs to take a permanent perch, and ends up with one toe balanced on one of the bin handles.

'Can you see anything?' Tanya demands impatiently as he wobbles precariously, back leg trying to balance his body like a ballerina attempting an arabesque.

'Shhh. Not yet.'

There's a small muffled shriek and a huge rather un-muffled crash as Louis falls off the lid of his dustbin. Seconds later Grace's face appears at the window.

I hear Tanya mutter, 'Oh shit!' beside me, as we all attempt to fall back quietly into the shadow cast by a large lilac bush, and then stuff my hand into my mouth to stop a fit of giggles as Louis begins to mew like a cat.

'Miaow, Miaow,' he wails unconvincingly.

Tanya too starts to giggle, smothering her face with the mandarin collar of her suede Harvey Nic's jacket, so as not to be heard.

After a few minutes, Louis picks a cabbage leaf out of his top pocket, and clambers back up off the floor rubbing his left knee, and pulling a face. 'Think I've done my ankle in.'

'You do look a bit white.'

'How can you tell, I'm wearing a balaclava?'

'Your face is glowing through it like a fluorescent light-bulb.'

With Louis looking as limp as the abandoned cabbage leaf we decide that it's my turn to clamber onto the bins, and peer into Grace's sitting room. Fortunately Grace must have been convinced by Louis's crap courting-cat impression; then again – she has had quite a lot to drink this evening. She's returned to the sofa, where Stuart can clearly be seen perched on the edge, looking vaguely nervous, cords ruched up at the knees to reveal diamond patterns on the ankles of his socks.

49

'What's happening?' Tanya calls up at me.

'She's pouring wine,' I hiss.

'Not champagne?'

'No, looks like a bottle of red.'

There's a collective sigh of relief.

'Where's he?'

'On the sofa . . . she's on the sofa too.'

'And!'

'They're toasting . . . they're both taking a drink . . .'

'And!'

'He's put his glass down on the table . . . he's reaching towards her . . . he's taken her glass too and put that down on the table.'

'Ollie!'

'He's leaning in to kiss her!'

'Ooh, please don't,' Louis shudders, hiding his face in his hands in horror.

'It's okay . . . he's stopped.'

Louis takes his face out of his hands and looks up hopefully.

'Shit no, it's not okay, he's reaching into his pocket!'

'Oh please God, no!' Louis cries dramatically. 'I told you there was something in there!'

'Hang on . . . he's stopped . . . he's put his hand over his mouth . . . he's pulled away . . .'

We all take a sharp intake of breath.

'And he's off!' I shriek a touch too loudly.

Even the other two can hear the thud thud thud of Stuart's footsteps as he races up the stairs two at a time to Grace's bathroom, then the slam of the bathroom door. I can see Grace's head swinging from door to window like a Wimbledon spectator, as she contemplates following Stuart or investigating the strange noises outside her window. As she heads for the door and the following-Stuart option, we decide that it's probably a good time for us to make a swift and silent exit.

Chapter Three

I'm in the kitchen the following morning, grating cheese for a seafood gratin when the telephone rings.

'Ollie, it's me.' It's Grace. She sounds friendly enough.

'Everything okay, babe?' I ask tentatively, putting down my cheese grater before my fingers get shredded through lack of concentration, and wrapping my somewhat cheesy fingers round the handset.

'Yeah, fine thanks, darling.'

We obviously didn't kill Stuart off, but is the relationship still alive and kicking?

'What are you doing tonight?' she asks casually.

'Night off,' I reply nervously. 'Why?'

'Because we're going out. You, me, and Tan.'

'Out?' I reply, shocked that Grace can actually remember how to do this. Does this mean our fiendish plan worked? It's the first time Grace has suggested a night out together since she arranged for us to meet Stuart for the first time.

'Yep. Meet me in Blakes at eight. And, Ollie, please don't be late.'

As soon as Grace puts the phone down, it rings again. It's Tanya. She's had the same summons.

'Do you think this means it worked?' she asks hopefully. 'I mean, a night out without Stuart is definitely a step in the right direction.'

'I don't know, babe. But it looks hopeful. Is Louis coming?'

'Grace said she asked him, but he's working.'

'I thought I'd given him tonight off already? I know I've got my two students coming in together tonight, heaven help Mel.'

'You have, babe, he's not working for you tonight. They're filming a fight scene on *EastEnders*, where he gets to be

51

whacked over the head with a sugar-glass bottle in the Queen Vic. It's one of Louis's lifelong ambitions to be physically assaulted by Pat Butcher.'

We meet up with Grace in the Soho wine bar where we were first introduced to Stuffy Stu. She's grabbed us a corner table and is sitting waiting for us, nursing a large glass of white. She's back on the alcohol.

This must be a good sign. I hope.

Grace greets us with a hug, then pours us each a glass from the bottle of cold Chardonnay sitting in the centre of the table. She's strangely quiet as Tanya and I sit down.

'Hi, babe!'

We take it in turns to hug a greeting.

'Did you have a good time last night then?'

Grace doesn't answer, simply looks up at us both from under her eyelashes, switching her gaze from my face to Tanya's, then back again. She's got a really strange expression on her face. Like she's just about to burst into tears or something.

We look at each other hopefully, and are just arranging our faces into suitably sympathetic expressions, when Grace pulls her left hand from under the tabletop, and waves it under our noses, her face practically bursting with excitement. The reason she's doing this is instantly noticeable due to the fact that there's a rock the size of Jupiter strapped firmly by a white-gold band to the third finger.

'Oh my goodness!' shrieks Tanya, covering her mouth with her hands.

'Isn't it fabulous!' Grace beams.

That wasn't exactly what Tanya's reaction indicated. We both stare at her in open-mouthed silence.

Gray's face falls sharply. 'What's the matter? You don't seem very happy.'

'Stunned,' Tanya mutters, grabbing her glass and holding the chilled bowl against her hot forehead.

'Stunned,' I repeat, nodding dumbly.

'Champagne,' Tanya bleats dryly.

'Champagne,' I repeat parrot fashion.

Appeased that we apparently want to drink her health, despite the fact that the champagne is actually for shock,

Grace beams at us both, and starts gabbling on about always wanting to be a Spring bride ever since she first saw *Seven Brides for Seven Brothers*, whilst Tanya goes whiter than the tablecloth she's leaning heavily on.

'So you had a good night last night then?' I finally manage, after the waiter has poured us all a fortifying glass of Moët.

'Oh goodness yes. It was wonderful, thank you so much, Ollie.'

Stuart must have the constitution of an ox. Louis grated at least half a bar of Ex-lax onto his fudge cake, and we all saw him sprinting for the bathroom like Kate and Leo heading for the last lifeboat. He must have made an amazingly swift recovery.

Tanya can't hold back any longer, she's bursting to ask. Fortunately she manages to be fairly subtle. 'So how's Stuart? Louis said he looked a bit fragile when you left, you know a little green. He thought he might not be used to so much wine.'

'Wine? No! He hardly drank anything, thanks to Louis. Heavens, a waiter that clumsy is a serious liability, Ollie, I think you should make him stay behind the bar!'

'Oh I just thought he looked a little peaky, that's all. Probably nerves, you know, building up to getting down on one knee.'

'No, you were right, he wasn't well at all, but it certainly wasn't alcohol. He spent the entire night locked in the bathroom with a dodgy tummy, and was disgustingly embarrassed in the morning.'

'Oh no, how awful.' I kick Tanya under the table, and the grin that was sliding onto her face slips off rather quickly to be replaced with a more appropriate, if fake, look of concern.

'Any idea what caused it?'

'He thinks he must have had a dodgy sandwich at lunch, you know, prawns not quite right or something.'

'Nothing I fed you then . . .'

'Oh lord no! We both had much the same, didn't we, so it couldn't have been your cooking, Ollie. Which was absolutely wonderful, by the way.'

'And he still managed to get down on one knee to propose.'

'Well, since he was doubled up on the floor anyway,' she giggles.

'And it didn't put you off, the fact that he'd spent all night . . .'

'Not at all!' Grace laughs. 'In fact, more the opposite. It actually made me realise how much I loved him.'

'How on earth . . .' Tanya and I exchange a horrified look that fortunately Grace is too ecstatic to notice.

'Well, if I still fancied him after he'd spent all night glued to my loo . . . You know, I had a feeling he might be heading for a proposal, and to be honest I was a bit worried about it.'

'Worried?'

'Yeah. We haven't been seeing each other that long after all, and I thought it was a bit too soon for something so . . . so . . . well, permanent. But I do really really care about him, and it was going to be so hard to find a way to let him down gently without damaging the relationship.' She pauses and sighs happily. 'But last night made me realise that perhaps I did love him enough to make such a big commitment at this point in our relationship.'

The awful realisation hits us both at the same time.

'So it was our . . .' Tanya starts, before closing her mouth and her eyes simultaneously.

'More champagne!' I bleat, waving for the waiter, who heads back over at a trot in anticipation of a large tip from the big spenders, or at the very least a chance to coax Tanya's phone number out of her when she's just a touch more pissed.

Grace catches hold of my wrist as I numbly thrust some notes at the hovering waiter. 'Put your money away.' She reaches down by the side of her chair for her handbag. 'This is my treat. To say thank you for last night. After all, you played a vital part in one of the most important nights of my life.'

'If only you knew,' I mutter under my breath, taking my newly refilled champagne glass and tossing it back as if it's lemonade. 'If only you knew.'

The next morning, Tanya and I hold a crisis meeting over the mega breakfast at Lorna's, our usual hangover haunt where the fried eggs will either kill or cure. We both need a cure this morning. We drank enough champagne the night before to drown a whole catholic nunnery of sorrows.

54

I'm currently attempting to eat my way through three rashers of bacon, two fried eggs, a pile of incredibly greasy mushrooms, baked beans, and two small sausages, without throwing up on top of the whole plateful.

Tanya, who's greener than the pre-game pitch at Highbury, is listlessly pushing a pile of scrambled egg round her plate with a fork, and muttering about hair of the dog perhaps having more of an effect.

Personally if I had so much as a sniff of alcohol at the moment, it would be enough to make me heave so badly I could turn my entire body inside out. We got through three bottles of Premier Cru within the space of the same number of hours, and Grace only managed a glass and a half before heading back to engaged bliss with Stuffy, so that means that Tanya and I demolished over two bottles between us.

'She's rebounding harder than a bungee jumper on the end of too much elastic,' Tanya announces, piling her egg into a yellow mountain, before miserably bashing it to the consistency of a pancake.

'If you mean Gray, I don't think that's true. She split up with Arty ages ago.'

'I know, but I don't think she's completely over him yet.'

'Well, I'd say the fact that she's just agreed to marry another man would indicate otherwise.'

'That!' Tanya puffs dismissively. 'That's a classic symptom. Rushing into a commitment with someone else, someone who's *totally* unsuitable! She *can't* do this!'

'She already has.'

'But why? I'm thirty-three, darling, and I've never felt the urge to pledge my troth.'

'It's conditioning. You know what her parents are like, if she's not married by thirty then she's failed as a human being.'

'But why Stuart?'

'Because he asked her.'

'But he's not right for her. Can't she see that?'

'Obviously not. I think she's blinded by the whole idea. A man has offered her the one thing she's wanted since she was a kid, and she's not stopping to look at the actual body that's doing the offering, she's just thinking about the fairytale, the dress, the church, the cake, the presents, the whole romantic package.'

'That's a bit harsh, babe. I thought the whole romantic package was centred round the actual man. Sure the rest of it may be nice, but would you really marry a gargoyle just to get thirty-three toasters and a honeymoon in Corfu?'

'Maybe I am being a bit melodramatic, but I'm just so worried about her. Don't you think it would be best if Gray got to know Stuart a bit better first? It's taken me *months* sometimes to realise that the person I'm dating is a total moron, and she's been seeing him for such a short time. That's why I think she shouldn't rush into things, just because Stuart's paid the ultimate compliment and done the whole proper proposal thing.'

'You're right. We may not like Stuart very much, but we wouldn't even dream of inferring if we thought she was doing the right thing.' Tanya's face sets determinedly. 'You know, it's up to us as her best friends to save her from making such a huge mistake.'

'And how do you propose we do that?'

Tanya shudders. 'Please don't use that word! It's far too scary.'

'What word?'

'Propose . . .' she mouths, as if it's an obscenity, shuddering again as she does so.

'Sorry, babe. Okay, I'll rephrase, how are we going to stop Gray from messing up the rest of her life?'

'Well, I was hoping you'd have some ideas on that one.'

'Kill Stuart?' I suggest with an evil smile.

'Nice idea, but not particularly feasible.'

'A thousand people a year are struck by lightning,' I reply hopefully, chewing morosely on a piece of char-grilled bacon.

'We could get Gray institutionalised. I think we have grounds.'

'I still think we should kill Stuart.'

Tanya shakes her head. 'I really don't understand why she's doing this.'

'Told you. A man asking you to marry him is the ultimate compliment. Think about it: he's basically telling you that you're so wonderful and gorgeous he can't contemplate the idea of spending the rest of his life without you.'

'Sucker!' Tanya drawls. 'Okay, so it's a big ego boost but it didn't mean she had to accept him. I've been proposed to a few times,' she announces smugly. 'And I never said yes.'

'I've never been proposed to.' I'm suddenly a little peeved that I'm the only one of my friends that hasn't had a man on his knees begging for a chance to be a part of the rest of my life. 'I've just been propositioned.'

'Lucky you.'

'Perhaps her life is unfulfilled.'

'And if we fill it she might move on,' Tanya suggests hopefully.

'Maybe. So what do we do? She's got a good job and a lovely house.'

'And dreadful taste in men.'

'Well, he's not what we'd expect her to go for . . .'

'That's being kind, Ollie, he's a dork.'

'Do you think our judgement could be clouded by jealousy?'

'What, that Gray's had the old down-on-one-knee, rock-in-my-pocket experience? That's not every girl's ultimate fantasy, you know.'

'That's not what I meant,' I rush, a trifle too hastily, shaking my head to dispel a sudden image of Richard Gere on a white horse, with a sparkler the size of the Millennium Dome on the end of his lance, parked under my bedroom window. Where on earth did that one come from?

'What then? Jealous of what?'

'Well we've been together for ages; you, me, Gray, Louis. The four musketeers. And now here comes Stuart and everything's changed.'

Tanya purses her lips. 'Nah, don't think so. She's had serious boyfriends before, and we haven't felt the urge to crowbar her away from any of them.'

'But none of them asked her to marry them.'

'I think Arty did a few times.'

'Yeah, but only when he was so pissed he couldn't remember in the morning. She never took him seriously.'

Tanya shakes her head. 'We all feel the same. I think we've just got to trust our judgement on this one. Stuart isn't the right guy for Gray. You, me and Louis all think so, doesn't that tell you something?'

'Yeah, we're ALL jealous,' I joke half-heartedly.

'Hardly. Getting married isn't a major ambition for any of us at the moment. You're too scared of getting hurt and getting old. I know how you think: getting married and having kids is just a stepping stone to middle age, and you don't want to be an adult just yet, do you? Louis's lifestyle means he pretty much forfeits the conventional, and I'm too scared of missing out to stick with one man, so I really don't think we're jealous of the fact that she's getting married.'

'Well, we have already agreed on that one,' I sigh testily.

'And . . .' Tanya says forcefully, 'we love her far too much to begrudge her a big dollop of happiness, so I don't believe that it's your other "just us four" jealousy theory either. If we thought Stuart would make Gray happy, then we'd be all for this wedding, but we're not, and therefore we don't, or vice versa, whichever way you care to look at it.'

'So what are we going to do about it?'

'You know, I think I might have an idea.'

'Go on then, hit me with it, although I still think we should . . .'

'I know, I know,' Tanya cuts in, exasperated. 'Kill Stuart.'

'So you've come up with a better idea?'

Tanya nods. 'I think we should find her someone else.'

'As simple as that.'

'Well, I'm not saying it's going to be simple, babe, but it's certainly worth a try. If we could find her somebody wonderful then maybe she'd realise that Stuart isn't so hot after all.'

'Well they do say that the grass is always greener . . .'

'We just need to get her to look over the fence.'

'I know,' I rush, getting into the idea. 'We could fix her up with Simon.'

'My brother?' Tanya replies incredulously.

'Well she always did have an unrequited crush on him.'

'But that was about six years ago, and as you said it was unrequited, which means Simon didn't reciprocate.'

'I know, but they're both older now.'

'Yeah, and they've had plenty of opportunity to get it together if either of them had ever felt that way inclined.'

'Haven't you got any exes she'd like . . .'

'Hundreds; but hey, if they've slept with me, would Gray want them?' Tanya jokes.

'True,' I reply airily.

Tanya kicks me under the table.

'You said it first,' I moan, rubbing my sore shin.

58

'I know.' Tanya, who's obviously feeling better, spears one of my stray mushrooms and chews thoughtfully. 'We'll take her to the gym.'

'The gym?'

'It's a good place to start. Yeah,' Tanya drools. 'Tight Lycra, sweating bodies, flexing muscles.'

'And that's just the women,' I quip, handing Tanya a paper napkin. 'Wipe your mouth, dear, you're starting to drool.'

'No, I'm serious. I'll take her along for a session with my personal trainer, he's gorgeous, a mass of marvellous muscle.'

'And you think that will help.'

'It will if she does a quick comparison with Stuart's rather, shall we say *lardy* arse.'

'It's not that bad.'

'You mean you looked?'

'Of course. Don't judge a book by its cover . . .'

'But do judge a man by his backside.'

'Exactly, I figured the rest of him was so unappealing he must have something fabulous going for him elsewhere.'

'Well, it certainly wasn't his butt, 'cause I looked too. Maybe he *is* hung like a donkey.'

'I wouldn't be surprised . . .'

'No?'

'There's nothing else left, is there?'

'Sparkling personality.'

'Did you see any evidence of one?'

I shake my head despondently. 'He must be amazing in bed.'

'Oh well, that's good.'

'Yeah, but it's not a basis for a long and happy marriage, is it?'

'Well, I don't know . . .'

'Can you get your mind out of the gusset just for a moment please, Tanny, this is important?'

'But if she's happy, maybe we shouldn't mess with it.'

'Don't change your tune just because he might be a ten in bed. She may think she's happy at the moment, but how long will that last for? She's only known him for a couple of months, for heaven's sake.'

'Maybe it's a shotgun wedding?'

'No . . . she'd have told us.'

'Well, we've still got the hardest part to come.'

'Yeah? What's that then?'

'How are we going to break it to Louis?'

'You think he's going to take it badly?'

'He always said that if he weren't gay he'd marry Gray.'

'Maybe that could be our answer.'

'No way, they'd end up fighting over who wore the dress!'

'No, no; no, no, no, no, no; no, no, no; no . . .'

'Well I know you said he'd take it badly . . .' I grimace at Tanya, 'but if I'd have known *how* badly I'd have put off telling him, until like . . . never.'

Tanya raises her eyebrows at me, and puts a reassuring hand on the slumped shoulders of Louis, who's currently sobbing into Tate's kitchen table. 'Don't worry, darling, we're as against this as you are. Ollie and I have had a long talk and we have a plan.'

'You do?' Louis stops banging his forehead despondently against the kitchen table and looks up hopefully.

'A *cunneeng* plan,' I say in a stupid French accent to try to make him giggle. It doesn't work, so I just end up vaguely embarrassed instead.

I shush Tanya who's giggling, not at my bad impression of Inspector Clouseau, but at Louis. This is really rather an inappropriate moment to giggle at Louis, because he's so genuinely upset. If I can ignore the fact that he's now got a squashed stray pea from Sunday lunch stuck right in the middle of his forehead, like a large mint-green Bindi, then so can Tanya.

'We're going to convince her she's mad for accepting Stuffy Stu's proposal by tempting her with an endless supply of beautiful, interesting, single, solvent, successful, succulent men,' I tell him, deftly removing the pea, by pretending to push his hair out of his eyes.

'And where do you propose we find this endless supply of perfection?' Louis asks, his big blue eyes damp and distrustful. 'Because unless you know a lot of people that I don't . . . which you don't . . . Or do you happen to know of a new wonder store where you can shop till you drop for a drop-dead gorgeous poppet? Toy Boys R Us perhaps? Big Girl Heaven maybe?'

'Oh, that's just a technicality.' Tanya waves her hands airily. 'It can't be that difficult to find Gray someone more appealing than Stuart with a U.'

'A bad-tempered balding cannibalistic Pygmy with a one-inch willy would be more attractive than Stuart with a U,' spits Louis jealously.

'Well, I think that's a bit extreme, but how on earth did a man like him manage to get our Gray out of her knickers?'

'Oh well that one's easy,' Louis looks up at us mournfully. 'He probably bored the pants off her.'

Maybe Tanya has a point. My sister Ella says that the best way to get over one man is to find yourself another one.

I'm still working on this theory.

Not that I have any particular men to get over. I've had a couple of relationships that were vaguely serious, but nothing more: I don't have time for men anyway. Tate's has been my life for the past two years.

I'm not saying I'm a total nun. I do look. But I tend not to touch. I'm far too wary.

Men promise you the earth, and you end up with dirt. They say that women are the romantics. I think maybe that it's impossible for our romantic ideals to ever be fulfilled by a man, because from what I can gather they don't want the same as us women from a relationship. A male friend of mine insists that men never really fall in love, not the way that women do. Sure they have infatuations, sometimes obsessions, but as for love the way women perceive it? Well he's adamant that that's a no-go area for the male of the species, and of those men who get married the majority do it for very different reasons than love, ranging from stupidity to convenience.

I have of course researched this theory further. Of those men who responded to my questioning without bursting out laughing or backing off scared, so far there's a sixty/forty split; sixty percent agreeing with this rather scary theory, and forty percent claiming it's completely untrue. I'm hoping that the sixty percent who agree, do so simply because they've never actually had the dubious pleasure of falling in love themselves.

I even asked Claude what he thought, but his response was to burst into a sadly tuneless version of 'Love is a many splendoured thing', while suggestively waving a large Bologna

61

sausage. I gave up at this point, but it's just another nail in the coffin of my petrified love life.

Our first attempt to drag Gray out of LaLa land and back into reality takes place at Tanya's rather exclusive health club down in Docklands. It's the sort of place I wouldn't normally dare bare my bod in, where beautiful girls wear full make-up to do a complete workout in a leotard made from dental floss and two Dairylea Triangle wrappers. Empty ones, of course; cheese would be far too fattening. I wonder if I could get away with wearing an ankle-length sweatshirt. At five foot four and nine stone, I'm certainly not fat, but standing next to an eight stone, five-eight stick insect certainly makes me feel it.

We're currently standing in the waiting room.

Waiting.

Tanya has booked us a session with her personal trainer, the aptly named Mr Brawn. Mr Brawn is already ten minutes late. Gray is re-tying her Nikes for the fifth time, fiddling with her sports socks, and looking at her watch, no doubt wishing she was curled up on the sofa with Stuffy Stu watching a gardening programme, preferring the sweet Alan Titchmarsh and the swinging Charlie Dimmock to anything this club has to offer so far.

'Where the hell is he?' I hiss at Tanya. 'Any minute now Gray's going to make her excuses and leave.'

'He'll be here in a minute,' she reassures me. 'Probably just buffing up his biceps.'

'Do you think he'll like her?' I whisper.

'He doesn't have to, he's a professional flirt. Besides we're not fixing for her to date the guy, we just want her to see what else the world has to offer.'

'She's already seen what else the world has to offer.'

'And she settled for Stuart?'

'Maybe underneath the corduroys, he has the body of an athlete.'

'Well, he should give it back as it's losing muscle tone!' Tanya quips. 'Ooh, hang on a mo, he's here.'

I follow Tanya's gaze to see the personification of 'Hunk' walking over toward us. He's about five ten tall, and three feet wide, and never before have I seen such a perfectly honed,

62

golden, toned body. Not some horrible muscular monster, but beautifully proportioned, and breathtakingly handsome in the fashion of a young, golden-haired Greek Adonis. He leaves a trail of open-mouthed women gazing after him, as he strides through the gym area to where we are waiting.

'Girls, this is Eric,' Tanya announces proudly.

Three heads bend sideways in unison, as Eric smiles broadly, and bends down to pick up some weights.

'Would you look at the arse on that . . .' breathes Tanya quietly, as though she hasn't looked a hundred times before.

'Nice arse,' agrees Gray. There's a one-minute silence in honour of the perfect backside, before Gray adds, 'But the name just doesn't do it, I'm afraid.'

'What do you mean?' Tanya stops looking at Eric, and looks at Grace in surprise.

'It doesn't pass the shriek test,' I explain. 'You have to imagine yelling their name at the height of passion, and "oh Eric, do it to me, Eric", doesn't exactly have the right ring to it.'

'I suppose I've never really looked at it like that.' Tanya gazes sideways at Eric's incredibly toned gluteus maximus again, finger on lips as she contemplates. 'You could give him a nickname,' she offers eventually. 'I normally call them all the same thing anyway, either babe or stud seems to do the trick.' Tanya shrugs as we look at her in horror. 'They seem to like it, you call a man stud and he seems to think you think he is one. Besides, it saves yelling out the wrong name when you're getting down and dirty under the duvet.'

'Stuart isn't exactly a height-of-passion moniker either,' I say cautiously to Grace.

'Ooh, I don't know.' She suddenly becomes animated for the first time this morning. 'I think it's a lovely name. Strong and manly. You know, like something out of *Braveheart.*'

Tanya and I exchange an incredulous glance. She must be well and truly hooked to think something like that.

Love is blind. A well-known phrase that is definitely proven true in the next hour.

As the demi-god that is Eric Brawn goes through his moves, flexing the majority of the muscles in that amazingly well-honed bod, the entire female population of the gym is straining to look. Even I'm watching him with hard-to-disguise lust.

63

As for Grace, well to my absolute amazement, she's totally unaffected. I've sat in a bar with Grace and Tanya for three hours whilst they watched and discussed the individual merits, or de-merits as the case may have been, of the arse of every guy that walked past our table. Eric's arse, despite being the tastiest bit of cheek I've certainly seen in a very long time, doesn't even rate a second look from Grace.

In fact, normally the first to drag us off to the pub after every outing, she doesn't even join us for an after-gym glass of wine in the restaurant next door, just rushes off to hit the M1 at the first possible opportunity, and break the world land-speed record to Derby for the rest of the weekend.

'Well, that didn't work very well, did it?' I state morosely to Tanya, as she fills my glass with cold Frascati. 'So what now?'

'We haven't changed our minds about Stuart not being right for her, so we just have to keep on trying, don't we?'

'What do we do next then?'

'Don't worry.' Tanya raises her glass to me. 'I've got quite a few things in mind.'

The re-education of Grace is a far harder thing to achieve than we first thought. After giving her invites for countless nights out, which would be the perfect opportunity for her to meet a far more suitable man, the majority of which she refuses, we decide we have to be a bit more ingenious.

Our first plan is to sabotage her car, so that Tanya's gorgeous roving mechanic can come round and fiddle with her spark plugs. Tanya's mechanic is a total honey. Add grease-stained overalls, and the macho expert handling of a large spanner and we should be well away. Grace's fantasy man.

In our dreams.

Reality bites. She makes him a cup of tea, offers him biscuits, then leaves him to get on with things whilst she settles down on the phone to Stuart for an hour.

Next attempt. We put a spanner in the works of her plumbing, then call for Tanya's own personal plumber to come and give her pipe work a thorough going-over. Take a man that Tanya gives twelve out of ten for technique, strip him to the waist in ripped jeans, and get him sweating in a hot bathroom. On her usual form, Grace would have made her move within ten minutes, fifteen if she was being subtle. She makes *him* a cup of tea, doesn't bother to offer him a biscuit, then leaves him to get on with things whilst she settles down on the phone to Stuart for the rest of the evening.

Getting more desperate, we send Tanya out to scour the local bars to find the ones with the cutest customers and the best-looking bar staff, so that when we can eventually tempt Grace out for a drink, she's surrounded by sexy men at all times. We even start to send her pre-paid pizzas when we discover that the delivery guy at her local pizza parlour is the spitting image of Ewan McGregor. This is followed by me faking a cold and sending Grace firstly to the chemist for flu remedy because if you squint your eyes the dispenser looks a bit like George Clooney in glasses, then off to one of my fish suppliers, who's very dishy and a big fat flirt.

Louis even blags her onto the set of a Brit flick he's got a minor bit part in so that she can drool over the latest Jude Law in-waiting, but reports back in disbelief that she got more of a thrill from the lunch-time on-set catering than she did from the latest hot-film hunks.

What has happened to Grace the party animal, Grace the man hunter, Grace the insatiable? It's as if she's suddenly started wearing man blinkers. No longer is her head turned by the sight of a pert bottom in tight denim, a wicked smile, or teasing eyes creased with laughter.

Driven by desperation, Tanya has – not so much a brain wave – as a brain storm. 'I know,' she announces during one of our Saving-Grace sessions. 'I'm going to buy her a man.'

'Well, they're hardly something you can buy in Harvey Nics: the men's department sells clothes, babe, not actual males.'

Ignoring me, Tanya grabs the Yellow Pages, and flicks through to the 'E's'. Finding the page she wants, she turns the book around so I can see.

'Escorts!' I splutter.

'Exactly.'

'You can't do that.'

'And give me one good reason why not.'

'I can give you more than one! Grace'll go ballistic.'

'She might not, she might enjoy it. We can just get someone to take her out, wine and dine her, entertain her with scintillating conversation, make her realise what a real man's like.'

'What – arrogant, ignorant, and egotistical?'

'Come on, babe, it's got to be worth a try?'

I shake my head. 'I know we're desperate but . . .'

Tanya's shoulders slump, but she puts the Yellow Pages down nonetheless. 'I suppose you're right. But what now?'

'Know any newsagents with delivery boys that look like Jean Claude Van Damme?' I smile weakly at her.

'What? The Muscles from Brussels cycling round Islington on a Chopper? You'd be lucky. My delivery boy must be at least . . . oooh, all of . . . twelve.'

'Well, she did go through a phase once of liking younger men . . .'

Claude is off with supposedly a mild case of food poisoning following a weekend in Amsterdam, although the common agreement is that it's far more likely to be a severe case of alcohol poisoning. Nonetheless whatever the cause he can't be allowed anywhere near my kitchen until certified clear. I have therefore been head chef for a week.

I like food. Strike that, I love food. I own a restaurant, so it kind of goes hand in hand, but whilst I really do enjoy cooking, it's more of the intimate-dinner-party-for-friends type of thing, rather than three courses for fifty people.

It should have been my night off tonight. By rights, I should be dressed to the nines and partying with Tanya in a club somewhere.

Reality bites. I'm currently having a wrestling match with a recently boiled lobster. I'm the one that had to boil the lobster, so it wasn't a particularly good start to the evening. I did consider gassing it in the oven as a more humane end, until the bloody thing decided that attack was the best form of defence. It's Louis's job to make sure the first-aid box is always fully stocked. I'm now sporting a blue Snoopy plaster on my left thumb, and a grumpy frown on my face.

When the four of us are in the restaurant we just about get by. Mel does most of the waitressing, with Louis running the bar and some of the smaller tables, Claude does the cooking, and I run around filling in everywhere, be it cooking, from the exotica to garnishing plates, pulling pints, taking orders, or washing up. We've got a couple of student part-timers who come in to cover for days off and holidays, or times when it's just too chaotic to cope, but it's too late to call either of them in tonight. They'll have pulled on their best togs and be hitting the town by now.

Which is where I should be!

Life sucks.

'Gorgeous guy alert!'

It's halfway through the evening. Melanie reverses into the kitchen bum first, balancing plates and glasses, which she quickly dumps in the sink.

'Where's my lippy?' she demands, looking round the kitchen for her handbag. 'I need to redo my face!'

'That good, eh?' I struggle to manage a weak smile.

'Better. I had to take their order twice. I was so busy drooling, I forget what they asked for the first time, and Louis keeps serving them drinks they haven't ordered so he can suss him out.'

Louis trots into the kitchen with a broad grin on his handsome face. 'Get Gray down here now!' he babbles excitedly. 'That's what I call a real man.'

'As opposed to what?' I snap.

'He just oozes sex appeal.'

'Well, he'd better not be oozing on my floor, it took me hours to clean up earlier.'

'Ooh, what's eating her?' Melanie teases.

'Nothing,' Louis giggles. 'That's why she's so grouchy.'

'There are so many things conspiring to piss me off at the moment, a distinct vacuum in the sex department is well down on my list of major worries.'

'Such as?'

'Apart from the fact that I have a chef who never seems to spend any time actually cooking for me, my best friend's just agreed to marry an anorak she's only known for like all of two minutes, and the business I've spent two years building up is about to be taken away from me by a greedy bastard of a property developer . . .'

'I suppose this isn't the right time for Louis and me to launch into our usual rousing chorus of "Always look on the bright side of life".' Mel smiles encouragingly at me.

'You suppose right,' I scowl.

Mel raises her eyebrows at Louis and escapes back into the

restaurant on the pretext of taking more orders. Louis looks at my frowning face. 'He's very attractive,' he wheedles, 'You should come and have a look, it might cheer you up.'

'Can you please stop drooling over the customers and do some work, Louis, we're too short-staffed to mess about tonight.'

'Yes, sir!' Louis mocks me by saluting before slowly goose-stepping out of the kitchen. Dumping my still-stubborn-even-in-death lobster onto the table, I sink down into a chair and grab the coffee Mel made me ten minutes ago, which I haven't had a chance to touch. Surprise, surprise, it's cold and disgusting.

I feel bad. I know I shouldn't snap at Mel and Louis, who both work as hard as I do and somehow manage to remain frustratingly cheerful for most of the time.

Swapping my coffee for a glass of wine à la Keith Floyd, I take a huge swig, and determine to put my happy face on. There's no point worrying about things. Worrying never changes the outcome, it just makes the waiting worse. Isn't it strange that when you're miserable you really let yourself wallow in it. But when you're happy, you're so worried that you're going to end up miserable again, you don't let yourself enjoy it. It should be the other way round. You should glory in being ecstatic and when you're totally pissed off look forward to being over the moon again. However, this world is full of pessimists, and I know I'm one of them. Why be optimistic and end up disappointed, when you can be pessimistic and perhaps be pleasantly surprised? I think I need to change my outlook on life, and actually enjoy happiness when I get it instead of worrying about how fleeting it may or may not be. The only problem with being an optimist is that it's very easy to have one's cheerfulness misconstrued as mild insanity. After all, surely only someone who's slightly barking can find a reason to smile at mishap. If you don't know what I mean, try smiling inanely at everyone you meet for an entire day. You'll find that people start to skirt nervously around you as if you were contagious.

I often wonder if there is anybody out there in this world who has never had anything bad happen to them. Someone who's sailed through life, had a happy stable childhood, always got what they wanted for Christmas, passed every single exam first time, got every job they've ever set their fulfilled heart on, never been crossed in love. I could blow this happy idyll by saying that not everything in their life is perfect, because they are envied and hated by many for such outrageous fortune, but they're probably too cocooned in their little bubble of perfection to give a damn about that. Maybe that's where the key to happiness lies. Pure self-indulgent selfishness, where other people's misfortune doesn't even bring the slightest quiver to your tear ducts.

Maybe I should stop worrying about Grace and let her ruin her life if that's what she wants to do. Unfortunately, I know that's something I could never do, because I care about her too much. It's the same with Tates. The only thing I suppose I can do is resolve not to let everything get to me so much. Think more positively. That's what I'm going to do.

I make a good start by finally cracking the lobster, and have just managed to slip my face into a smile that's far more comfortable than my previous glum frown, when Louis goose-steps back into the kitchen sporting the broken-off end of a small plastic hair comb on his top lip. He *Sieg Heils* me and I start to giggle.

'Ooh, a laugh!' The comb drops off as Louis speaks. 'That's *much* better. I'd say keep it up, but you're wanted in the restaurant, darling, in your position as "patron".'

I stop laughing. 'Why?'

'It's Mr Gorgeous; he's asking to speak to the owner.'

My resolve to be a more positive person slips instantly. 'Great! As if I haven't got enough on my plate. What's the problem now?'

'Don't know, maybe he wants to compliment you on your cooking . . .'

'Can't he write me a letter?'

'Ollie!'

'Okay, okay,' I huff, pushing my sweat-limp hair out of my eyes. 'I'm going.'

Louis eagerly herds me out of the kitchen and points towards one of the alcove tables. 'He's over there – the one in the blue John Smedley jumper.'

I head over to where Louis is pointing. Mr Gorgeous is seated in Snoggers Corner with three friends. Another guy and two girls, both of whom look me up and down from the safety of their designer clothes.

'You wanted me,' I sigh somewhat ungraciously, annoyed. What do they expect me to do, cook in Gucci?

He turns to face me, and I am met by a pair of steady blue-grey eyes. I'm suddenly momentarily peeved that I'm wearing my Rupert Bear chef trousers, a food-stained set of whites, no make-up, and a rather fetching hairnet to keep my unruly brown locks in place.

Mel was right, he's gorgeous. It's not the face, although the face is pretty damned attractive: strong and masculine.

It's the attitude. Those steady blue eyes are challenging, confident, but one would imagine ready to sparkle with laughter at a moment's notice. Not at this moment though, unfortunately. They currently look a little perplexed.

'I asked to speak with the owner Oliver Tate.'

'Olivia. Ollie Tate.' I hold out a hand, realise it's still covered in the juices of a recently deceased crustacean, and wipe it hastily down the front of my trousers. 'Right person, wrong gender.'

'Oh, I don't know,' he replies, taking my hand. 'I think I prefer you as a woman.'

Although this is obviously a compliment, for some reason his tone makes me bristle. I can spot them from a mile away. Another heart stomper. Too attractive for his own good. Successful, intelligent, and exuding a certain sexuality that is bloody irresistible. The problem is that sexuality is irresistible not just to you, but to a whole queue of other women.

He's exuding that sexuality in my direction right now. Well, here's one woman who for the sake of her sanity is going to make damn sure she resists.

'And you are?' I reply tersely.

'I'm Daniel.' He holds out a hand. 'Daniel *Slater*. Although I think you might know me better as "That Bastard".'

'He deliberately came in to humiliate me,' I grumble to Louis.

I'm face down on the bar, exhausted. It's twelve-thirty and we've finally turfed the last customers out, including Dan Slater who, whilst not attempting to speak to me again having simply introduced himself, was one of the last to leave, nursing a coffee and a very large brandy for what seemed like hours.

70

'I think he came in to beat you up,' Louis grins, and pours me a large brandy. 'Good job you *are* a girlie. Although at the moment,' he adds wrinkling his nose at me, 'I think *I* look a lot more feminine than you do.'

'What's that got to do with anything? If he wants a fight he's bloody well got one!' I reply, ignoring Louis's good-natured insult. Although at the moment, I don't think I'd stand much chance of winning: I feel as limp and wrung out as the dishcloth Louis is now using to wipe out the drip trays.

I take a sip of my brandy, feeling the strong liquid course its way down my throat and curl warmingly into my stomach.

'Instead of fighting with him, you'd probably be better off trying to win him over. I always think charm works better than harm.'

'Well, I can be as charming as you want . . .'

'Oh good,' Louis sighs in relief.

'. . . when I hit him over the head with a brick.'

Louis giggles. 'You know I think he just came in to suss you out. He probably realises he's got a fight on his hands with you, and . . .' he slips into a mock Chinese accent, 'it's always a good idea to know your opponent, Grasshopper.'

'Oh yeah, well at least now *I* know the opposition too.'

'Yeah?'

'Yeah.' I look up at Louis and smile evilly. 'If I ever see him crossing a road, I can *speed up*.'

Louis heads for home, and I decide I need a bit of sympathy and understanding. Reaching for the phone, I dial the one place I'm always guaranteed to get it, even when I don't deserve it, no matter what hour of the day.

The phone rings at least twelve times before it's answered with a rather gruff and sleepy, 'Hello'.

'Tanya? Are you still awake?'

'No, I'm fast asleep.' The sarcasm is heavy.

'Did I wake you up? Sorry,' I sniff self-pityingly.

'Come on, babe, when do I ever go to bed to *sleep*?' she mocks herself.

I sniff a touch more loudly this time.

Tanya notices this time. 'Ollie, darling!' she exclaims, the flip note slipping and her voice suddenly full of concern. 'What on earth's the matter?'

I hear the covers rustle as she sits up in bed. 'I can't cope any more!' I wail.

'I'll be right there.'

She's round in twenty minutes flat. By this point I've regained a little composure, thanks mainly to a rather nice bottle of Australian Shiraz, and a huge plate of buttery sandwiches.

I look up at her with heavy eyes from my usual position – kitchen, slumped at table. 'Thanks for coming round, babe, I just needed some sane company.'

'And you called me?' Tanya quips, accepting the large glass of red I'm thrusting in her direction. 'What's up, Ol, what on earth has happened?'

'I had an unexpected visitor tonight.'

'Don't tell me you've seen Grace. I swear that she's been abducted by aliens, I haven't spoken to her for so long.'

'Nope, wasn't Grace.'

'Well, who then?'

'Dan Slater,' I reply, rolling the three syllables and my eyes somewhat dramatically.

'Who?'

So much for my Sarah Bernhardt introduction, she doesn't even remember the name! 'Slater Enterprises . . .?' I prompt her.

'Him! You're kidding . . . he came to see you, here? *The* Dan Slater.'

'*The* Dan Slater. The man himself.'

'But why?'

I shrug. 'Your guess is as good as mine.'

'So, come on, tell all then . . . what was he like, was he hideous, was there a hump?'

'Well, there was, but I'm afraid it turned out to be the sexual connotation after all.'

'You mean you shagged him?' Her perfectly plucked eyebrows shoot up her forehead.

'No, of course I didn't, silly. But I wouldn't say no. He's gorgeous . . . no he's not, he's a bastard.'

'A gorgeous bastard,' Tanya sighs. 'Just my type. How about I shag him, if you're feeling uncomfortable about it. I could always get you some compromising photographs to blackmail him with.'

'Sorry, Louis already offered on that one. You should have seen him tonight, he was running in and out of the kitchen like a wind-up toy, tongue hanging out so far he could have cleaned his shoes with it. And all talk of spitting in Slater's food went well out of the window. He even gave him extra langoustines, and all the best bits from the fresh fruit salad – he was serving it with tongs instead of a spoon. It looked so good it should have been painted, not eaten. All these little star fruit balanced delicately on the top . . .' I say sarcastically.

'I know, how about you shag him? You know, pay him the extra rent in kind.'

'I'd rather die.' I put on my offended martyr face.

'I can think of worse ways to go.' Tanya winks at me. 'You've already admitted you wouldn't kick him out of bed for eating biscuits. Although I can think of far better things to eat in bed . . . no seriously, if you strike up a relationship with him, he might forget the rent increase.'

'You mean I should sell my body!' I reply in outrage.

'It's better than selling up. Besides, you wouldn't be selling your body, just loaning it out.'

'Come on, Tan, I need some serious input here . . . I'll just have to put my prices up.'

'You might lose custom.'

'Cut the wages?'

'Yeah, I can really see you doing that! I know you, you're a big softy, the only person in that restaurant who'd find less in their pay packet at the end of the month would be you . . .'

'Sell my car?'

'You love that car, besides, you don't need a cash injection, that would only last so long . . . whereas a meat injection . . .'

'Tanya, you're terrible!'

'Well, what alternative can you suggest?'

I'm silent.

'So, there's nothing for it, you're going to have to sleep with him.'

'Either that or the next time he comes in to eat, poison him,' I suggest, managing a grin.

'Well if you don't want to sleep with him, and you're going to poison him anyway, can I sleep with him before you kill him off?'

'Tanny, you've never even met the guy!'

73

'I know,' she grins, taking a huge bite out of one of my sandwiches, 'but if you fancy him then he must be pretty bloody amazing.'

'I didn't say I fancy him!'

'Not in so many words, but you don't have to *say* it, darling,' she mumbles through a mouthful of ham, rocket and Leerdamer. 'I can just tell.'

'Just because I said he was gorgeous doesn't mean I actually want the man. I mean I'll happily admit that er . . . Catherine Zeta Jones . . . now she's gorgeous, and I'll admit it to anybody, but it doesn't mean I want to go to bed with her.'

'No, you're far too straight.'

'What am I going to do, Tan? I've worked so hard to get this place where it is, and now this guy just comes along and threatens to ruin the whole thing.'

'Why don't you just sod the slog, find yourself a rich man and be a lady of leisure and pleasure.'

'Yeah, but where's the sense of achievement from that?'

'Are you kidding? The number of women who want that lifestyle and then to actually manage it yourself? It's like winning a gold at the relationship Olympics.'

'Well that's certainly not my style. If the man's successful, then great, but I think the only thing you should expect from a relationship is exactly that . . . a relationship . . . not a cop-out from hard graft, personal ambition, or the necessity of setting up your own pension scheme.'

'That's the problem,' Tanya jokes, 'I only like spending other people's money. I don't get any enjoyment out of spending my own!'

'I know you don't mean that!'

'Maybe not completely, but I'm not as fiercely independent as you are, darling. If a man came along and offered to sweep me off my feet and into a cocoon of charge accounts, and gold cards, I don't think I'd struggle too hard to keep my Office courts planted firmly on the ground.'

Tanya's answer to life may be to find herself a man with unlimited credit, but that doesn't exactly fit with my ideal of complete autonomy in my own life. All of your life you're answerable to someone. When you're a child, it's parents, siblings, teachers; as an adult, it's still parents and siblings. Fortunately the teachers are a dim and distant memory, but if

74

you're not careful they can be replaced by something far worse – bosses. Is that why people who once hated school can look back upon it, ensconced firmly in a nice pair of pink specs, and remember it as their best years . . . because that scary, grey-haired, foul-breathed, evil-brained teacher who used to terrorise you on the hockey pitch is nothing compared to the deadline-breathing monster that dominates your every working moment? This is one of the reasons I decided to work for myself. Unfortunately I have since discovered that there's always someone out there waiting to tell you what to do. In fact my list has increased significantly, and now includes my bank manager, my accountant, my customers, my suppliers, several interfering government busybodies, and a chef who makes Mr Christian seem like a docile, toe-the-line, cap-in-hand kind of man.

And now I have someone else trying to stick their big fat oar in.

Well, he can go take a running jump into a vat full of cold runny cowpats. Yes, he may own the building. Yes, I may have been paying a vastly reduced rent to the last landlord, who loved my backside, my Bordeaux, and my home-made brioche with equal passion – but only ever managed to get his hands on the last two, honestly. Yes, it is quite possible that a rent increase is a reasonable thing to expect, and yes, perhaps I shouldn't have been quite so rude to his representative, but when you're struggling to survive in such a dog-eat-dog world, the last thing anyone should expect a girl to be is totally bloody reasonable.

Besides, the rumours are still rife about development. He could quite easily drive me out and then come in and tear my beloved Tates to pieces, convert it into a posh pad for some spoilt socialite. Maybe Tanya's right and this situation calls for some drastic measures, some dirty fighting. My resolve hardens.

'Your body is your weapon,' Tanya tells me, as though she can read my mind.

'You've twisted that one a bit, I thought it was supposed to be my body is my temple.'

'Okay, my body is my temple,' Tanya repeats. 'So take your shoes off and come on in!'

'I'm sick of people telling me what to do,' I state firmly, ignoring her.

75

'Ooh, I don't know, it can be quite good fun at the appropriate moment.'

'Is *everything* about sex with you?'

Tanya pauses for a moment, head on side. 'Yep,' she finally answers. 'And shopping . . . it's harder to drown in shallow waters,' she adds jokingly, as I give her a withering glance.

Chapter Four

Tanya has been whisked away for a week of luxury by one of her more ardent, and more solvent, admirers: seven days of total pampering at some spa-type resort in the Bahamas. If she wasn't one of my best friends I could actually really hate her. I'd love a week of complete R and R, and brilliant sunshine. Despite the fact that we've just had the longest day and it's now officially summer, the weather is still distinctly miserable.

I feel totally frazzled at the moment. I seem to spend most of my time either working or worried – or both at the same time, which is far worse.

I'm worried about Grace's impending gain of Stuart with a U as a permanent fixture in her life. I'm worried about my impending loss of Tates, which apart from my friends, is the *only* permanent fixture in my life. If I don't come up with some way of meeting the increased rent demand soon, then I'm sorely afraid that it's going to be a sad farewell to two years of hard labour; a labour of love that it would totally break my heart to say goodbye to.

It's drizzling again today, which totally matches my mood, so I pop into the florist's next door to Tates to buy fresh flowers to brighten up the restaurant, and hopefully brighten up my attitude at the same time. I'm just emerging from the shop with my arms full of bright yellow daffodils, when I spot a familiar face coming out of the antique shop next door to the florist's. I take a sharp intake of breath and quick step backwards into the relative safety and anonymity of the shop doorway.

It's Dan Slater.

He's accompanied by two men in sharp suits, and one of the men is putting a large plastic-cased tape measure in the inside pocket of his Hugo Boss jacket. What on earth are they up to?

I sidle up closer to them, positioning myself behind a large rather well-placed bay tree, and pretend to be very interested in a bucket full of gypsophila. I can just about hear them, as long as no cars zoom by. The man with the tape measure is speaking to Dan Slater.

'You're right, it's perfect, I think it'll work really well. You won't have to do too much knocking about either.'

Unfortunately this is all I get to hear before a big truck grumbles loudly past, and I lose my footing from leaning too far to listen in, nearly falling ear first into the clipped greenery of the bay tree. The fact that I'm now face down in a bucket of carnations wouldn't normally be seen as fortunate. However, the very-pink flowers are covering my very-pink face, and I therefore narrowly avoid being spotted by Dan Slater and his entourage as they head straight past me. As soon as the last besuited (and somewhat muscular – hey I'm a girl, I notice) backside has disappeared from my flower-impaired view, I hurtle round the back scattering daffs as I go, and slam my way dramatically into the kitchen.

'You'll never guess who I just saw in the antiques shop!' I breathe asthmatically at Mel, resting my free hand on the table as I try to catch my breath.

'Dan Slater,' Mel says instantly, shoving her order pad in the front pocket of her white tie-waisted apron. 'And two other guys.'

'But how do you know?'

'They've just come into the restaurant.'

'You're kidding, aren't you?' I shriek, dropping the rest of my dripping daffodils onto the terracotta-tiled floor.

'I know, don't tell me,' Mel sighs, putting her pen away as well. 'He is the enemy, and must therefore be removed from the restaurant immediately.'

'No way!' I bend down and gather up my flowers, depositing them in the sink and switching on the cold tap.

'You what?' She blinks at me in surprise.

'Where are they sitting?'

'Well, I haven't seated them yet. Thought I'd better get permission first!' she adds dryly.

'Where are they now then?'

'I left them having a drink at the bar. Why?'

'Put them in the back alcove. Is it empty?'

78

'Yep. The two lovebirds that were in there have just left. Goodness knows how they managed to eat anything, their mouths have been permanently suctioned onto each other for the past hour and a half. It's nice to see someone so happy though.'

'S'pose,' I mumble, totally distracted.

'Yeah, it means I get bigger tips! Those two left me a twenty! I don't know if it was because they were in a generous mood, or because they were so wrapped up in each other they wouldn't have noticed if they'd left me the entire contents of their wallet! Talking about lack of attention,' Mel ribs me, 'are you actually listening to a word I'm saying?'

'Nope,' I reply honestly. 'Sorry, Mel, but I just saw Dan Slater and his minions heading out of the antiques shop with a tape measure.'

'Really?' she replies, intrigued now. 'What do you think they were up to?'

'I'm not sure, but I'm bloody well going to find out. Take them to their table, Mel, and let me know when they're settled in.'

Five minutes later Mel tips me the wink and I sidle surreptitiously round into the bar, the far end of which is perfectly sited for me to resume my eavesdropping without being spotted. I turn the music down slightly, and start to slowly polish a tray of glasses.

The first voice I hear is one I don't recognise. 'I should think you're really pleased you found it, it's absolutely perfect.' This must be the third man who was with them, who didn't speak whilst outside.

'Yeah, I've been looking for something like this for ages.' I definitely recognise this voice. My nemesis. Demon Dan. 'Do you think you can have the work completed in time to meet the deadline?'

'Yeah, no problem.' I recognise this voice as the man with the tape measure. 'A couple of months you said, didn't you?'

'We've got a little bit longer than that. I've decided to wait until after the summer to market the apartments, say September time.'

Mel, who's far too nosy to be able to resist joining me, grabs my arm and we look at each other open-mouthed.

'Apartments!' I mouth, horrified.

Mel shushes me as Dan Slater starts to speak again. 'Anyway enough about work, let's enjoy lunch. The food in here is really good.'

'Well, if it's as tasty as that waitress . . .' The other man laughs appreciatively. 'She's gorgeous. She looks just like Scary Spice.'

The frown Mel was sporting turns into a broad beam at this compliment.

'Yeah, she's lovely, isn't she? Believe it or not, the owner's rather attractive as well.'

Was that really Dan Slater's voice? I raise my eyebrows in surprise at a still-grinning Mel. Dan Slater just paid me a compliment. I'm torn between feeling ludicrously flattered, and wanting to land a left hook on him.

'Really?' Tape-measure Man asks.

'Yeah, these *big* brown eyes, and the cutest arse; but unfortunately you can forget the Spice part, she's just Scary.'

'Oh yeah?' Tape-measure Man again, laughing.

'Yep. Attitude with a capital A for Arsy!'

I'm not torn any more. My only dilemma is what to go and hit him with.

Dan's still speaking. 'She had Edina Mason losing her rag on the end of the telephone the other week, and you know how she prides herself on being cool, calm and collected at all times . . .'

Unable to hold onto my composure any longer, I storm back into the kitchen, closely followed by Melanie, and let out the repressed screech that has been building up inside me.

'Are you okay?' Mel asks in concern, as I scream loudly, then slump down at the kitchen table, head in hands.

I shake my head.

'It might not be what you think.'

I look up at Mel witheringly. 'Well if it didn't sound to you like they're planning to turn these buildings into apartments, what did it sound like?'

'Ooh, I know, it did sound bad, didn't it? But you only caught part of the conversation . . .'

Mel decides that it's probably a good idea not to push this point. 'Shall I still serve them?' she asks uncertainly.

I smile bleakly at her. I'd love her to serve them. To me. On a platter. Cue vision of Daniel Slater, hands tied, big red apple in mouth, me just inserting the heavy metal spit somewhere distinctly painful.

'Yeah, you can still serve them,' I finally answer. 'Just make sure you add a lot of arsenic to their hors d'oeuvres, okay?'

For some reason I expend a lot of effort on their food. Perhaps some subconscious part of me thinks that if they realise how good the restaurant is, then they'd be more reluctant to close it down. Inside, however, I'm stewing hotter than the casserole of boeuf bourguignon I've got in the oven, and when Mel comes back in to tell me they're leaving, I can't hold myself back any longer. I head after Daniel Slater. He's just put on his coat, and is the last one heading through the door.

'Excuse me.' I tap him on the shoulder. Hard.

He turns round in surprise.

'The lunatic owner would like a quick word with you.'

I'm even more infuriated when a small smile quirks about his lips at this. 'So walls do have ears then,' he replies, his obvious amusement shining in his blue–grey eyes.

'You bet they do!' I reply, my anger overcoming any shame I might have about my eavesdropping becoming public knowledge. 'And now I know exactly what you're up to!'

'You do?'

'Yeah! Coming round here with your toadying minions. You think you can have it all your own way, don't you? Well you didn't reckon on me, matey! There's no way I'm going to let you turn Tates into some overpriced pied-à-terre for some prat with an over-inflated ego.'

The slight smile disappears. 'I beg your pardon?'

'You heard me. If you think you're going to shut down my restaurant that easily, then you've got another think coming. I've worked hard to build this into a place that I'm damn proud of, and I'm not going to let some money-orientated blinkered businessman take it away from me!'

There's no amusement shining in those blue–grey eyes now; in fact they've gone pretty cold. 'I suggest that you get your facts straight before making unfounded accusations, Miss Tate.'

This is the formal, totally in control businessman speaking, and yes I do find him somewhat intimidating. Not intimidating enough to stop me from trying to answer back, but before I've even opened my mouth to speak, he turns and walks out of the restaurant, leaving me mouthing silently at nothing but a closed door.

'How rude!' I spit, ignoring the fact that my verbal assault on the man in full view of every customer I have, isn't exactly classified as polite behaviour.

Every customer I have . . . Oh dear . . .

I turn round to see the gaze of *every customer I have* resting squarely on me. My face turns gradually redder as they slowly, one by one, begin to clap, and I scurry scarlet-faced into the kitchen to a hearty round of applause.

I'm woken the next morning by a phone call from Gray. 'What are you up to this weekend?' she demands, after a brief hello.

'Working as usual,' I yawn, emerging from my duvet. 'Why?'

'We'd like you to come over for dinner on Saturday night.'

'We?'

'Stuart and I. We thought it would be nice if you met a few of Stuart's friends.'

'You mean he's got some?'

This barb goes straight over Gray's head. She bursts into peels of laughter. 'Ollie, you're such a card! I've tried phoning Tan, but I can't get her.'

'She's gone away.'

'Oh.' Gray's voice sounds a little flat. 'She didn't tell me.'

'Well, you have been . . .' I search for the right words, '. . . shall we say, a little elusive recently.'

'Preoccupied would probably be a better word,' Gray giggles lustfully, her voice heavy with sexual innuendo. 'I have been neglecting you a bit, haven't I? That's one of the reasons for dinner. Where's she gone?'

'The rich one's taken her away for the week.'

'Which one in particular? I thought they were all rich.'

'Not all.'

'If not well endowed monetarily, then their worth lies in other areas, eh? I know what Tanya values.'

'A big bank balance . . .'

'Or a big dick!' she finishes Tanya's motto for me. 'Well, lucky old me, I seem to have found a man with both.'

'Yeah,' I sigh. 'It's just a shame he's got no personality.'

Gray laughs loudly again. 'Honestly, Ol, you're a scream. It's a shame about Tanya, it means I'm one short.'

'Have you asked Louis?'

'I would but I need a girl.'

'Well, he almost classifies . . . you're not telling me this is one of those boy/girl, boy/girl things, are you? Can't we all just muck in as we normally do?'

'Absolutely not! It's my first dinner party with Stuart. I want to do it properly.'

'He'll be very upset.'

'Louis will understand . . . I'll save him some pudding.'

'Oh, that will make it tons better,' I reply sarcastically.

'Well, if I had somebody in mind for him it would be different, but I'm afraid all of Stuart's friends are very straight.'

'I can imagine,' I reply dryly. The first few words of Gray's last sentence finally filter through into my tired brain. 'Hang on a mo . . . you're not trying to fix me up, are you?'

'Moi?' Gray feigns innocence. 'Would I do such a thing?'

'Yes.'

'Well, I can't exactly fix you up now, can I? I mean, I can't force you to jump on a man just because I seat you next to him at dinner; but as your friend, I can open the door to the sweet shop a little more – you know, let you browse the dessert menu.'

'The only dessert menu I'll be browsing is the one at Tates,' I mutter. 'As I said, Gray, I've got to work.'

'But, Ollie, you're the boss.' Grace's tone becomes wheedling. 'Can't you give yourself one night off, pleeeeease. I really want you to be there, you're my oldest and bestest friend in the whole world, it wouldn't be the same without you, it really wouldn't.'

'That's emotional blackmail, Gray.'

'I know,' she replies cheerfully. 'Is it working?'

'Oh, all right,' I reply very ungraciously. 'I'll be there. Where and when?'

'My place, eight on the dot, don't be late.'

'Bring a bottle?'

'No need.'

83

'Bring a disgustingly fattening pudding?'

'Everything's in hand. Just bring yourself, and don't be late,' she repeats. 'I know what you're like.'

Saturday night, I leave Louis in charge of the restaurant, sulking desperately because Gray's dinner invitation wasn't extended to him, and grab a cab round to Gray's Victorian terrace in Islington.

I'm late. Then again I'm always late so I'm afraid I've rather unfairly come to assume people will expect it, and make allowances.

By the time I get there, everybody's just sitting down to a first course of hot salsa Tiger prawns, a recipe that Gray has stolen from my menu at Tates. My chair is glaringly empty, bang in the middle of the long table, which is currently seating twelve people, all seated boy/girl as threatened. I feel a little better however, when I notice that the seat to my left is also empty.

'I'm not the last one to arrive then,' I chirp brightly at Gray, who'd answered the door with a slightly exasperated look on her face, before kissing me quickly on the cheek, and ushering me into the dining room.

'Sorry, babe, the occupant of that seat actually managed to arrive on time.' The voice, if not the face, carries chastisement for my tardiness. 'I think he's just popped to the loo or something.' She pushes me into the room, like a bossy primary-school teacher herding a reluctant newcomer into class. 'I'd do the intro thing, but I'm afraid my oven is calling me.'

'Maybe I could help?' I ask hopefully, suddenly feeling a little daunted by what appears to be a roomful of strangers.

'No way, it's your night off, honey. You aren't allowed within ten feet of the kitchen.'

'I don't mind, honestly.'

'Stay,' Gray warns me sternly. 'Socialise.'

With that she turns and heads back toward the kitchen, skirt swirling round her knees instead of her ankles, I'm relieved to report, whilst I head into the dining room, squeezing past those already seated, like an apologetic cinema-goer heading for the loos right in the middle of the grand finale. I sit down slightly self-consciously and slide my

84

eyes surreptitiously round the room whilst pretending to un-orchid my napkin. Gray's dinner party for friends seems to be a dinner party for Stuart's friends rather than any of ours.

Upon closer inspection I find that I recognise three familiar faces. Stuart, who smiles hello as I sit down; the girl seated to his left, whose name escapes me, but I think works with Grace; and Cornelia, who, a bit of a wallflower at the best of times, looks more self-conscious than I do. Boy, I wish Tanya and Louis were here now. I have a feeling this isn't going to be a particularly pleasant evening.

The man to my right, who is pouring his neighbour a glass of wine, turns smiling to me. 'Red or white?' he asks, before the genial smile slips and is replaced by a look of incredulous disbelief, which my own face instantly echoes.

My premonition was right.

'You!' we chorus simultaneously, the look of horror on my face instantly emulated by my wine-toting neighbour.

I'm sitting next to Dan Slater.

I'm tempted to pinch myself to see if I'm asleep and having a nightmare. 'What on earth are you doing here?' I hiss a touch too loudly, so that Stuart stops making polite if rather stilted chit-chat with Cornelia and looks over in concern.

'Having dinner,' he replies with a touch of insolence in his voice, and as if to prove his point, puts down the wine without filling my glass and picks up his abandoned fork.

'Well, I can see that,' I spit. 'I just wondered how come you happen to be having dinner at my best friend's house.'

He momentarily stops forking prawns into his mouth, and raises an eyebrow at me. 'You're Grace's best friend?' he tuts loudly. 'I knew that girl was just too good to be true.'

'What do you mean by that?' I bristle.

He puts down his fork and looks straight at me. 'She's so lovely, and so perfect, I was just waiting for the flaw . . . and *here you are.*' He smiles sardonically, then turns to the beautiful but horse-faced blonde on his left, and engages her in conversation, leaving me faced with a broad back and complete indifference. I stare open-mouthed at said broad back, totally amazed by the rudeness of the man. Okay, so after our last conversation – or should that be confrontation – I wasn't expecting a pleasant atmosphere the next time I saw him, but

85

then again I wasn't expecting to find myself sitting next to him at a dinner party either.

I'm just contemplating slipping a salsa-sauce-covered Tiger prawn down the back of his Ben Sherman in a fit of rather childish pique, when someone slides into the vacant seat to my left.

'Ah, I do hope you're the girl of my dreams,' whispers a rather husky voice.

'I beg your pardon.' I turn to find an extremely good-looking man parking his very attractive bum in the empty seat on my other side. He has tousled golden-brown hair, and bright-green eyes, which are currently smiling in a very friendly fashion at me.

'Between you and me, this is more blind date than dinner. The two of them,' he indicates Stuart and Gray, who has just slid back into the room to distribute warm rolls, and lands a soft kiss on the crown of Stuart's head as she passes him. 'They're so bloody blissfully happy being an "engaged couple", they now feel they have to play Cupid to all of their poor, determinedly single friends. I'd begun to think they were trying to pair me up with Cod Face over there,' he nods toward Cornelia, Gray's boss, 'but I do hope it's you instead.'

He holds out a hand. 'I'm Finn, Finnian Connelly,' he beams at me disarmingly, the green eyes twinkling in the candlelight. 'I'm a journalist, so you better watch what you say to me, I'm a terrible gossip.'

'Ollie Tate,' I reply taking his hand, which is warm and firm.

He holds onto my hand for a fraction of a second too long, before letting go and asking me, 'So where do you fit into this scenario then?' He waves a long-fingered hand around the table at the other guests.

'I'm Grace's best friend – we've known each other since we were little.'

He smiles slowly. 'And what do you do, Ollie Tate? Apart from being Grace's best friend?'

'I run a restaurant in Battersea,' I reply casting a glance over my shoulder at Daniel Slater, who still has his back to me. 'A *very good* restaurant!' I add loudly.

'Ah . . . beauty, culinary skills, and free access to her own wine cellar no doubt. I think you could definitely be my ideal woman.'

Grace chooses this moment to appear with a plate of prawns, and dumps them down in front of me somewhat pointedly. Probably still pissed off that I was over half an hour late.

'And what about you? I take it you're a friend of Stuart's. Have you known him long?' I ask Finn when Grace has flounced back to the kitchen with several meaningful glances thrown back over her shoulder at me.

'About five years now, I think. I met him when I was working for a business magazine. Interviewed him actually for an article on up-and-coming young businessmen. He's a nice guy, a touch on the staid side, but always reliable. We have a mutual interest in cars. I like driving them too fast, and he likes tinkering under the bonnets.'

'And I suppose you know *him* as well.' I jerk my head sideways to indicate that other jerk behind me.

'Dan Slater? Yeah, I know him, but not that well. He's an exec director of Stuart's company. I tried to interview him as well, but he held out on me. Probably got too many dodgy deals hidden in his closets to risk letting a journo into his offices.'

'Really?' I reply in interest.

'Pure speculation, darling,' Finn beams beatifically. 'But I always like to think the worst of people, it makes far better copy. To be honest, I don't know that much about the man. Our social circles are a bit like the Olympic emblem.' He makes an image with his hands of two circles crossing. 'And therefore we have a tendency to bump into each other at parties, but that's about as far as it goes.'

'Next time, couldn't you bump a bit harder and shove him out of a window or something?' I mutter.

Finn, who was taking a slug of wine, just manages to stop himself spitting it out as he snorts with laughter. 'He's actually quite a nice guy.'

'I somehow find that a touch hard to believe.'

'He invested quite a bit of money to help Stuart get up and going – you know, like a sleeping partner.'

'Oh, how altruistic of him,' I reply sarcastically. I glare at Dan's broad back, which is still determinedly facing me like a windbreak blocking, not a cool breeze, but any warmth that might ever radiate from the man. I bet he made sure he's getting a bloody good return on his investment.

'Do you have any sleeping partners, Ollie Tate?'

'Nope. I'm the only one in charge,' I reply loudly, more so that Demon Dan will hear me than Finn. 'I like it like that.'

'That's not the kind of sleeping partner I meant.'

I look away from Dan and back at Finn, who winks slowly at me, a flirtatious smile slowly spreading across his face. Before I get the chance to think of a suitably witty answer, Grace is back. Whisking my plate away before I've had the chance to eat any of the prawns, she catches hold of my wrist with her free hand, and attempts to pull me to my feet.

'Ollie darling, would you mind awfully giving me a little hand in the kitchen.'

'But I thought you ordered me not . . .'

'Kitchen, Ollie,' she hisses. 'Now!'

How can I ignore a summons like that? I get up and head after her.

'What's up, babe?' Once in Gray's immaculate kitchen, I look around for the culinary disaster that I'm sure she's dragged me in for, but there's no smoke emanating from the cooker, no soufflé dish upside down on the floor.

Grace suddenly looks a little embarrassed. 'Sorry about that, darling, but I need you to do me a favour.'

'You do? Don't tell me, you want me to whip up a disgustingly indulgent pudding so you can pretend that you made it yourself.'

'Not quite. It's Finn.'

'What about him? Please don't tell me he's gay, Louis gets all the good-looking men.'

Gray bursts out laughing. 'Finn, gay? I don't think so! If he was it *would* be Louis sitting next to him instead of you.'

'Then what's the problem?'

'I want you to stop monopolising him, I'm trying to set him up with Cornelia.'

'Cornelia? Ah. So he was right then.'

'You mean he's sussed?'

'Well, you're hardly Miss Subtle, Gray.'

'Now that he knows, what do you think he thinks of the idea?'

'I'm afraid he doesn't seem to be that enamoured by it.'

'Are you sure?'

'He called her Cod Face.'

'Oh. Well, that doesn't mean he doesn't like her.'

'It doesn't?'

'You're not helping matters. I put you next to the most gorgeous man in the room, so can't you talk to him for a bit?'

'You mean Dan Slater!' I exclaim. 'For one blissful moment I'd almost managed to forget that he was here!'

'You know him?'

'Know him! He's the bastard who's trying to push me out of Tates.'

'Dan? Surely not! He wouldn't do something like that, he's lovely.'

'It's his bloody company that's bought my building. What the hell is he doing here, Gray?'

'He's a friend of Stuart. More of a business acquaintance really, they don't have that much in common except commerce. But I think he's lovely, so I made sure he got on the guest list. I need as many eligible bachelors as I can get my hands on!'

An awful thought hits me. 'He's not the one that you're trying to . . . you know.'

'Fix you up with? Dan? No . . . Dan's got a girlfriend. Well that's not quite true; strictly speaking Dan has several girlfriends. I think he's been seeing Miranda on and off – the girl sitting next to him – although from what I can gather she'd like it to be rather more on than it actually is at the moment. But you can see why, he's rather gorgeous, isn't he?'

'Well that's not the first word that would spring to mind if I was asked to describe him,' I growl.

'Oh, and what is?'

'Arrogant,' I spit.

Gray nods. 'Very. But in a damned attractive way.'

'Opinionated.'

'But incredibly bright.'

'Egotistical.'

'Has every right to be.'

'Ruthless.'

'I know, isn't that so sexy?'

'Jeez, Gray. You're a one-woman fan club.'

'Well, if I hadn't met Stuart first . . .' she winks at me.

Typical. Tanya and I have busted our guts trying to find someone to convince Gray that Stuart's Mr Boringly Wrong instead of Mr Wonderfully Right, and she finally admits to fancying the one person I wouldn't want her to get together with if they were the only two fertile people left on this planet.

Back in my seat, I realise that I didn't ask Gray who it was that she actually *is* trying to fix me up with. Gray has now none-too-subtly manoeuvred Finn temporarily into the seat next to Cornelia, which has suddenly become empty by her sending Stuart out to the kitchen on some false pretext. This means that I now have an empty seat next to me, and a horrible feeling that it won't be empty for very long. Once Gray has stapled a ready-to-bolt Finn into place next to Cod Face, there's no doubt she'll be dragging my own 'prospect' into view. I look round the table, trying to determine which of the men is being prepared for sacrifice at my altar. I know it's not Stuart, Finn, or thankfully, Demon Dan, so that only leaves me three further options. If you could call them options.

The first, seated to Cornelia's left, is definitely not for me. He's about six foot five in his stockinged feet. How can I tell, you ask, if he's sitting down? Well, the said stockinged feet are currently poking out from under the tablecloth on my side of the table, which would be a heck of a stretch for a short guy. Grace knows full well that I prefer a man I don't have to stand on a box for, being just over five foot four myself, especially a man who wears those awful coloured socks with little stitched diamonds running in a neat naff row down the side. The fact that he's quite obviously got some wandering-hands thing going on under the table with his neighbour to the left, a statuesque brunette I don't know, confirms that he's definitely not the one lined up for me. Thank Heavens.

The second selection, to the other side of Demon Dan's horse-faced blonde, I can't really see without having to lean past Demon Dan, and I really don't want to get too close to that particular man at the moment, well at any moment to be honest. I don't know what to be more concerned about, the fact that I've got him seated to my right, or the fact that Grace is hoping I'm going to fall madly in love with the person who'll soon be seated to my left.

I want to go home! I suppose I could feign a sudden illness, and excuse myself. I'm torn between developing an instant deadly infection, or staying and slowly poisoning Dan Slater a little more with each course of the meal. I'm sure Gray has got some rat poison somewhere in her utility room.

The third guy must be at least fifty-something, and is as bald as a buffed golf ball. I'm sure he's very nice, but I'm also pretty sure Grace wouldn't think I'd had such a radical change in taste, brought on by my current man drought, to consider going out with someone that looks like my father.

This means that the second guy must be mine. The horse-faced blonde to Demon Dan's right pops to the loo, and Demon Dan himself leans forward to pass the girl opposite a bread roll, and the third option of the evening is suddenly exposed.

I think I'll sod killing Dan and just kill myself instead. The guy could easily be Stuart's brother. He has the same haircut, except it's not dark, but a sort of off-blond, the same tortoise-shell glasses, and the same tedious, quiet demeanour. He's currently concentrating quite earnestly on his food, spearing prawns with the fork in his right hand, whilst constantly pushing his glasses back up his nose with his left hand, as they keep following his downwards gaze and slipping plate-wards. I watch as he eats the last few prawns on his plate individually, then, breaking a bread roll, proceeds to methodically mop up every last trace of salsa from the cream porcelain. When he's finished, he takes a sip of water – no wine in his glass, I note – and carefully wipes the corners of his mouth on his cream linen napkin.

Help.

Grace has been waiting for him to finish eating, and as Stuart returns from the kitchen, engineers yet another change in the seating plan. She whispers in his ear, looks meaningfully over at me, takes him by the wrist, and practically drags him round the table to where I'm sitting. It doesn't help that he looks as reluctant to meet me as I am to meet him. Grace is the only one smiling at the moment.

'Ollie, I'd like you to meet someone,' she beams happily. 'This is Stuart's best friend, Leo. Leo, this is *my* best friend, Olivia.'

Oh no. Best friend meet best friend. I might have guessed it.

She's trying to find me a Stuart clone. Trying to emulate the romance she's found, on my behalf. I can't be angry with Gray. She loves me and she wants me to be as happy as she thinks she is. I just don't understand how she can think setting me up with another Stuart could be the key to this happiness.

Leo sits down in the seat next to me. He smiles uncertainly.

I smile.

He smiles again.

I smile.

He smiles.

I'm just about to think of some excuse to hit the kitchen again myself, when I hear a slight snicker of contemptuous laughter from the bastard to my right. Git. He's noticed and he's loving every second of my discomfort. I turn back to Leo. He is as far from my type as a sea slug, but this time I'm determined to scintillate and captivate, just to show you-know-who.

I smile broadly at Leo.

He smiles back.

My smile stretches further than I ever thought it could, but I still can't think of anything to say.

His smile grows larger and more obviously forced, but we're both still silent.

Oh no, here we go again. I soon discover that as well as similar physical features, Leo has about the same conversational flair as Stuart. I wonder if the scientists have moved on from cloning sheep and pigs already without actually announcing this fact to the media.

We eventually manage to make an attempt at a polite conversation, but it's a pretty pathetic one. I haven't even had a glass of wine to loosen me up. I try my nun joke. This usually only comes out when I'm drunk, but at the moment I'm desperate.

It doesn't even raise a smile.

It also doesn't help that Finn keeps making me burst into fits of rather undignified giggles. Whenever he thinks no one's looking he glances mournfully over at me, putting his hands to his throat, crossing his eyes and sticking out his tongue, to indicate that he's currently being bored to death by Cornelia, who I can hear banging on to him about the merits of TV as opposed to tabloid advertisements. Finn doesn't even have the grace to blush when Gray, coming back from yet another trek out into the kitchen for the main course (another recipe nicked from my menu), catches him sticking his fingers in his ear and pulling an imaginary trigger.

I don't know how I control my bladder when he then, in the full knowledge that Grace is back in her seat and watching him, surreptitiously puts a hand behind Cornelia's back and makes winding movements, as though he's working a hurdy gurdy. Even Grace can't hold on to the po-face at this point. She collapses face-first into her wine glass, laughing so hard that Stuart begins to smack her on the back in the mistaken belief that she's choking. Finn looks over at me and crosses his eyes again, indicates Leo, and then yawns widely.

I nod. Finally, when I'm just contemplating administering some rat poison to *myself* instead of Dan Slater, to end the evening rather more quickly, Finn attempts a Steve-McQueen-style escape from Cornelia, dropping his bread roll, literally diving under the table after it, and emerging, feigning severe disorientation, back on my side of the table.

'Sorry, mate, think you're in my seat.' He picks up Gray's carefully calligraphied place name and waves it under Leo's nose.

Leo is far too polite and non-confrontational to put up a fight and after a slightly awkward shufty round the table, ends up in Stuart's place next to Cornelia.

'Musical chairs,' grins Finn, sitting back down next to me. 'I was hoping you'd come and rescue me from Bore-nelia, then I saw that you needed rescuing more than I did.'

'Thank you *so* much,' I mutter through pursed lips, like a ventriloquist.

'Take it you weren't getting on that well with the Big L then? His name's not really Leo, you know.'

'It isn't?'

'No, it's Lionel. He changed it so he'd have more success with women.'

'Shame it didn't work then! Sorry, that sounds so bitchy, doesn't it? He does seem like a really nice guy, but . . . well, let's just say I've had more scintillating conversation with a talking parrot.'

'I don't know, he seems to be getting on okay with Cornelia.'

I look over at Cornelia and Leo, and am surprised to find them already deep in conversation. 'Well, that says something about me, doesn't it!' I exclaim.

'Yeah, that you're not a crashing bore like Leo.'

'What's in a name, a rose by any other name is still a rose,' I misquote badly.

'And an arsehole is still an arsehole.' Finn grins. 'Hey!' He spots my empty wine glass and reaching over, picks it up and surveys the clean glass in disgust. 'This isn't on, you still haven't got a drink.'

'I know,' I say pointedly. 'Somebody's been monopolising the bottles.'

This is a little bit of a porkie. I've actually been too much of a wimp to ask Demon Dan to pass me some wine. As a result my glass is empty, and I also need pepper on my potatoes, because the large grinder is beyond the Berlin Wall of his broad back as well. Finn stands up and leans past me, unwittingly trailing the elbow of his blue Yves St Laurent shirt in the gravy of Dan Slater's Beef in Beer, before grabbing the bottle of red sitting between Dan and Horse-face, and pointedly filling my glass.

'Cheers,' he choruses loudly, clinking his glass against mine.

'My saviour!' I reply, taking a grateful slug of my wine, and feeling the fortifying liquid slide a warm and lovely course down my throat and into my stomach.

'I think we might have done them a favour.' Finn indicates Leo and Cornelia. 'They actually look pretty well suited, unlike some people at this table. You know, I'm not being horrible but I really don't know how old Stuart managed to get his hooks into a cracker like her.' Finn sighs as Grace leans in to brush a light kiss on Stuart's slightly flushed cheek.

'Hear, hear.' I toast him, waving my recently filled wine glass. 'My sentiments entirely.'

'You don't seem too keen?'

'Between you and me?'

'I'm the soul of discretion.'

'You're a journalist.'

'All right, I'm a heel instead of a soul, but I won't tell on you, I promise.'

'Well,' I ventured guardedly. 'I'm sure he's a thoroughly nice guy . . .'

'Oh, he is a nice guy,' Finn assures me. 'I can vouch for that at least.'

'But we really don't think he's right for Grace.'

'We?'

'Me, and practically everyone else who knows her. I mean they're just so . . .'

'Incompatible?' he offers.

'Well, no, not really incompatible as such, they seem to get on really well. It's just that they're so different.'

'They do say opposites attract. And if they're compatible . . .'

'They may attract, but do they live happily ever after? And as for being compatible, they may get on at the moment, but Gray's the ultimate party animal, well, she used to be anyway, and Stuart, well, he's just . . .'

'A bore?' Finn offers as I search for a slightly more polite word.

'Well . . . a very nice one. But yes, I think he is. I'm just concerned that after the romantic idyll has worn off, Gray will be left wondering what on earth she's done.'

Finn pours me more wine and looks sympathetic. 'Well you think Stuart's boring because he's a quiet guy, who's more interested in being *at* home, than clubbing *in* Home. Hasn't it occurred to you that perhaps Grace might have changed her mind about how she wants to live her life; after all you're both getting on a bit now. You're hardly youngsters any more. You can't get away with spending all night on the tiles . . .'

I turn to him in outrage, to see that he's got a huge cheeky grin on his face. 'Don't even say that in jest!' I chastise him. 'I think that might actually be partly something to do with the reason they're together.'

'Really?'

'Really. Grace has got to the age where she thinks she *should* be getting married. Stuart is fortunate enough to be "right place, right time".'

'Is that what you think?'

'Maybe . . . oh, I don't know . . .' I decide it's probably not wise to pursue this conversation, after all I may already feel incredibly comfortable in Finn's company, but I don't know the man very well, and he is a friend of Stuart's . . .

I change tack. 'So what about you? I take it you're young,

free and single yourself, seeing as you've been invited to this dinner party in the first place.'

'I am at the moment, but if Grace has anything to do with it, I won't be for very long,' he jokes fearfully.

There's the sound of a knife being tapped against a crystal wineglass, and Stuart stands up.

'Sorry to interrupt,' he apologises, looking a little nervous. 'But I'd like to thank everybody for joining us this evening. I know that you're all incredibly busy people, and we appreciate the fact that you've made the effort to be here tonight.' He pauses to clear his throat and push his glasses back up the bridge of his nose. 'Now,' he continues, turning to Grace. 'As you all know, I recently asked this lovely woman to be my wife, and to the great surprise of an awful lot of people . . .' I swear he's looking at me here . . . 'Including myself . . .' polite laughter, '. . . she actually agreed. Despite popular opinion, I'm not a total fool . . .' I may be paranoid, but I'm sure he's looking at me again, '. . . and therefore, before she has the chance to change her mind . . .' He pauses and smiles at Grace, who smiles back, touching his leg affectionately and encouragingly. '. . . I've persuaded her to make it completely official, and I'd like to take this opportunity, whilst we're blessed with the presence of good friends, to ask you to clear a space in your diaries for the second of September . . .' He pauses again, this time for effect. 'The date of our wedding.'

One end of the table bursts into a small, yet enthusiastic round of applause. Someone whistles. I almost hear the clang as my jaw hits the tabletop. But that's only two months away!

Obviously already primed, Leo now appears from the kitchen bearing a magnum of champagne, which he hands to Stuart before going back for a tray of glasses. Stuart, having removed the foil and wire with a flourish, is now somewhat embarrassingly struggling to pop the cork and ends up handing it to Grace, who, showing some of her usual form – well, usual before she fell in with Stuffy – shoots the cork into the ceiling, and proceeds to spray the entire table Grand-Prix style.

'Hey, save some of that so that we can drink it!' Finn jeers at her, ducking to avoid an arc of foam jetting in his direction, then holding out his glass in an attempt to catch it.

Congratulations chorus around the table. I try to join in but can't find my voice. Two months, I keep repeating to myself, like a broken gramophone record. Two months.

'What do we do now?' I say despondently.

'We could just get pissed,' Finn suggests, overhearing me, and thinking that I'm talking to him.

Maybe I hadn't been talking to him, but at this precise moment in time this sounds like my best option. 'I'll toast that idea,' I agree, clinking my glass against his.

'Glad you approve. The only problem is we seem to have finished the bottle.' Finn up-ends the wine bottle we commandeered earlier over my glass, and a weak dribble falls half-heartedly from its neck. He looks hopefully at the magnum of champagne, but Grace's enthusiastic drenching of her guests means that after a dribble each for the toast, the bottle is practically empty.

'One of the advantages of being the hostess's best friend,' I tell him reassuringly, 'is that I know where she keeps the alcohol.'

Sliding as surreptitiously as possible away from the table, I fetch a couple of bottles of red from Grace's wine rack. I don't feel too guilty helping myself, seeing as I get most of it for her at cost from the wholesaler. Grace comes in to the kitchen to get dessert and, catching me struggling, uncorks the second bottle for me.

'Would have thought you'd be an expert at this by now.' She reaches into the fridge and pulls out a couple of bottles of white. 'Better put a couple more of these out, the champagne lasted about two seconds!' she laughs, then looks at me curiously. 'You didn't seem to knock back much of yours, babe, are you okay?'

I nod slowly. 'Just a bit surprised, that's all.'

Grace smiles at me guiltily. 'Look, I'm sorry I didn't tell you first. I wanted to tell you myself but that would have spoiled the surprise, wouldn't it?'

'I don't know, I think I might have appreciated the advance warning!'

'You are happy for me, aren't you?' she asks, scrutinising my face.

I hesitate for a fraction of a second too long, before forcing a bright smile onto my face, just in time to stop the smile on Grace's face from slipping away completely. 'Of course I am, babe. If you're happy, I'm happy, you know that.' Well, I suppose that's true enough.

'You don't *seem* very happy,' she accuses me.

I take a deep breath. I don't like lying to Grace, and I think that perhaps it's time to voice a few concerns. It's probably not an appropriate moment, considering Stuart has just announced the date of their wedding, but when is it appropriate to tell your best friend that you think the man she's due to marry is a total waste of space? I manage to find a few words that are a little more diplomatic.

'I suppose, it's just that I'm a little bit worried about you. It all seems to be moving pretty fast. I mean, you haven't known each other for very long really, have you, and he's just so different from you . . .'

'Opposites attract,' she chirps happily, taking fresh glasses from an overhead cupboard.

'Okay, but getting married after just a few months of being together? You haven't even had an engagement party? Oh no, I forgot, Stuart doesn't like parties, does he?' I can't help myself adding sarcastically.

'That's not the only reason we haven't had one.' Grace crosses her eyes at me. 'It's not mandatory, you know.'

'S'pose,' I mutter. 'Why have an engagement party when you can cut the crap and go straight to the wedding?'

Grace looks at me keenly. 'You're *not* happy about this, are you?'

'I told you, I'm worried, you just seem to have changed so much since you met him.'

'I haven't changed, babe. Sure, I don't go out as much, but that happens when you're in a steady relationship. I'm still me: you know, mad, stupid sometimes . . . Okay I'm not quite so impetuous, apart from marrying Stuart, of course. You could say it's a typically "me" kind of thing, rushing into the wedding.'

'There's a perverse kind of logic in that one, yeah,' I smile sadly. 'You're not angry with me, are you?'

'Of course not.' Grace puts down the second bottle of white she was opening, and gives me a hug. 'I'm chuffed you're concerned, it shows you still care.'

'You know I do, you donut,' I insult her affectionately.

'Well, don't worry. I'm deliriously happy. Now, be a good

girl and take the wine out. Oh and don't hog it all yourself, I know what you're like.'

I have no choice but to return to the table and drink myself stupid. I place one bottle of red and one bottle of white as far away from Dan Slater as possible, and put the other two bottles between Finn and me, so that the others at our end of the table can reach them, but they're at *our* immediate disposal.

For pudding, Grace, the chocoholic, is serving the same chocolate-fudge cake that I serve in Tates, but has added an extra jug of hot chocolate sauce for those with the same sweet tooth as her. Stuart is currently shovelling a huge piece of cake down his neck with more enthusiasm than I've ever seen him show before for anything else. I would have thought that after his last experience of hot chocolate-fudge cake he'd have steered well clear.

The table is full of sweet-toothed people. The only person who isn't trying to commandeer the hot fudge sauce jug is Dan Slater.

I might have known he wouldn't like sweet stuff. He's far too sour. I finally manage to get my hands on the jug only to end up fighting over it with Finn.

'You got more sauce than I did,' he cries loudly, attacking my plate with his spoon and scooping most of my hot chocolate-fudge sauce onto his own cake.

'No, I bloody didn't,' I howl. 'Give it back now!'

We proceed to have a bit of a spoon fight, me trying to reclaim my captured chocolate sauce and failing bitterly, the only spoonful I manage to get slipping off and landing on the cream linen tablecloth, much to my embarrassment.

Dan Slater isn't laughing at me any more. He still isn't talking to me either. He's spent most of the evening with his back toward me, chatting to a disgustingly simpering Miranda, who's coquettishly tossed her long blonde hair over her shoulder so many times this evening, I'm surprised she hasn't developed whiplash as a result. I am now, however, rewarded with some recognition in the form of a very disapproving look from Dan, at such childish chocolate-sauce behaviour.

This only serves to encourage me to misbehave. I'm very tempted to aim a large spoonful of chocolate cake at him, but decide that this would simply be a waste of good food.

In order to encourage mingling amongst those guests who still haven't paired off with their pre-picked partner for the evening, Grace decides that after pudding, coffee will be served in the drawing room. Having consumed at least a bottle and a half of wine between us, Finn and I are rather drunk by now. Giggling furiously, we refuse coffee, commandeer a bottle of brandy, and slump down in a corner of one of Grace's large red Heal's chesterfields, forming our own two-man clique.

'What on earth have they got on?' Finn wrinkles his nose, as Stuart puts some new CDs onto Gray's sound system. 'I thought this was supposed to be a party, not a party political broadcast!' He yawns widely. 'It's enough to send you to sleep.'

'Maybe it's their way of saying it's time for everyone to go home now!' I joke.

'Hardly.' Finn looks at his watch. 'It's only eleven-thirty.'

'Well, it must be way past Stuart's bedtime time then, mustn't it!'

'He does look a bit sleepy.' Finn assesses Stuart through narrowed eyes, head swaying in an effort to remain upright without full focus. 'Perhaps we should do something to wake him up?'

'Absolutely, what do you suggest?' I slur, taking another swig of my brandy, and grimacing as it burns a course into my stomach.

Finn looks sideways at me and winks heavily. 'I have an idea,' he pronounces. 'Back in a mo.'

Finn slides off the sofa and onto the floor and begins to crawl SAS style across the carpet toward the CD player. I'm nearly wetting myself with laughter, as he weaves through the ankles of those in the room who are slightly more sober and are looking down on him with incredulity, some laughing, some, no need to mention names, looking on in surprised disapproval. Over the gentle sound of Bach, I can just about hear Finn humming the theme to *Mission Impossible*. Once he reaches the CD player, there's a slight pause in music whilst he ejects the concerto, and swaps it for something else. Then he's crawling back to me, huge wicked grin on his handsome cheeky face.

'Mission Accomplished!' he crows, dragging himself back

100

onto the sofa, as Fat Boy Slim blares from the speakers. 'Fancy a boogie?'

I never thought I'd end up doing 'Funk Soul Brother' round Gray's sitting room, especially in front of a group of people who've already been staring at me disapprovingly for the last couple of hours, but here I am tanking it round the edge of a Persian rug, making train movements with my arms, my head bobbing like a nodding dog in the back of a speeding car.

Perhaps I shouldn't have had so much to drink.

The fact that I have had so much to drink is now not only telling on my behaviour, but also straining on my bladder. What goes in, must come out. I'm suddenly desperate for a pee, and telling Finn that I'm just heading off to the little girl's room, break off our two-man shuffle, and stagger upstairs to the bathroom. I sit on the loo and, overcome by a sudden feeling of alcohol-induced weariness, close my eyes, then open them again quickly as the room begins to spin sickeningly fast.

I stay there for at least ten minutes, waiting for the spinning to stop, and for my legs to stop feeling as if they're made of jelly, and start working again. When I eventually recover enough to reclaim my knickers and stagger back downstairs, I find Grace waving people goodbye in the hallway.

I'm highly relieved through my drunken haze to see that the disapproving face she's currently sporting is struggling to stay in place, due to the amusement at my behaviour that is currently fighting her frowning muscles and threatening to make her laugh. 'Bad Ollie,' she tells me, catching my arm as I sway dangerously on the last step.

'Sorry, babe,' I slur, clutching onto her hand.

'I think you need to go home to bed.'

'Can I take Finn with me?' I smile lasciviously. 'I think I like him.'

'Not tonight, babe. Dan's giving you a lift home.'

'What! No, he's bloody not!' I back away from Gray as though she's just threatened to give me a frontal lobotomy, rather than arrange for someone to drive me back to Tates. 'I'll get a taxi. Somebody call me a taxi . . .'

'You're a taxi,' Grace jokes. 'Ollie darling, you're as pickled as a gherkin.'

'So what's new?' I slur, backing into the doorframe of the

101

drawing room, and collapsing gratefully against it. 'I've had a WONderful evening, Gray.'

'I can tell,' Gray says, rolling her eyes and, leaning in, gently wipes chocolate sauce from the left corner of my mouth.

'And I'm not going to spoil it by getting a lift home with jerk-face.'

'I'm not letting you go home on your own.'

'I won't be on my own, I'll be in a taxi. Besides, Finn said he'd take care of me,' I state defiantly.

Grace leans past me and kicks open the door to the sitting room with the toe of her embroidered kitten-heel mule, to reveal Finn, passed out face down on the sofa, left arm hanging over the side, hand palm down in a plate of guacamole dip, which had been passed round with tortillas prior to my arrival.

'Oh yeah?' she laughs softly. 'And who's going to take care of him?'

Dan is saying goodbye to Stuart, shaking hands. Through the now-open door, he catches sight of me swaying in the hallway and, cutting short his goodbyes, comes into the hall, shrugging a cashmere jacket over his Ben Sherman shirt. He warmly thanks Grace for a lovely evening, kissing her on the cheek, but although he's smiling at her, when he looks at me his face is strangely expressionless.

Grace helps me on with my coat, and wraps my unco-ordinated fingers around the handle of my handbag, before kissing me on each cheek, and ushering me out of the front door. I manage to make it down the three steps to the pavement on my own without falling over. Dan Slater's car is a hundred yards down the road. He doesn't actually have to drag me there kicking and screaming, but my sulky face says that I'm as ungrateful for his 'kind' intervention as I would be if he were trying to make me walk the plank. I find I'm too drunk to protest as he feeds me into the passenger seat of his large black BMW, then getting in himself, he leans over and pulls on my seatbelt, brushing close to me as he pulls it across my chest.

Involuntarily, I breathe in the scent of him, as his body brushes against mine. I must admit he smells pretty damn good. Shame he's such a heartless bastard. My dulled and drunken brain reminded of this fact, I manage a pretty good glare at him as he slips the buckle into place. A look that he strangely returns with one of amusement, tinged with slight puzzlement. Fortunately before I get the chance to be insufferably rude to someone who, although he is a total bastard, is actually a kind-enough total bastard to take the pickled gherkin home, I find myself lulled to sleep by the gentle throb of the powerful engine.

When I wake up, the glowing digital lights of the car's dashboard clock tell me that it's one in the morning, over forty minutes after we left Gray's house. The engine's still and as I look around me, amazingly disorientated, I realise that Dan is simply sitting still, watching me. Embarrassed, I avert my eyes out of the window and am highly relieved to see the sign for Tates on the other side of the road. He's brought me home.

Well, what did I expect him to do, murder me on the way home and then take vacant possession of the restaurant?

I've still got a vacant possession sign up on my skull. I think my brain moved out about four glasses of wine ago. It doesn't normally take forty minutes to get back from Gray's house. How long have we been parked here? Maybe he was waiting for me to wake up naturally. Probably thought if he shook me awake, I'd assault him with a loaded handbag or something.

Although my natural propensity for good manners is somewhat smothered by alcohol, and by my abstract feelings for the man sitting next to me, I feel that perhaps some thanks is called for at this moment, for being safely delivered back to my flat. Unfortunately when I open my mouth to slur a brief *merci beaucoup*, the only thing that's forthcoming is a very large belch. I instantly cover my hand with my mouth, not to smother any further belches – fortunately, or unfortunately, you could look at it either way, that was a belch to end all belches, and I don't think I could manage another one for at least two years – my hand's over my mouth to smother the really inappropriate fit of giggles that I've just dissolved into.

I'm still giggling as Dan gets out of the car, and coming round to my side, opens the door for me. I'm still giggling as he guides my shaking, key-clutching hand toward the lock of my front door, and I'm still giggling, though heaven knows why, as he practically carries me up the stairs, kicking open several doors before he finally finds the bedroom. He guides me into a position from where I can safely fall backwards onto my bed, and watches with a slight quirk of a smile on his lips, as I promptly do so.

I blink up at him from my prostrate position.

He looks down at me. He doesn't speak, and he doesn't make a move to leave either.

Unfortunately I feel the need to fill the silence. Even more unfortunately I'm in no fit state to say anything remotely sensible. 'Aren't you going to tuck me in? You know, read me a bedtime story?' is the first thing that slips out of my mouth.

I know I should be horrified at myself, I mean I think I hear a small shriek coming from the compos mentis part of me that is hidden underneath the three pints of red wine and copious amounts of brandy that are currently coursing through my veins, but frankly, I'm at that stage of pissed where I realise what I'm doing, but am too paralytic to worry about it. 'No?' I ask, as he still remains silent. 'What about kissing me goodnight then?'

Oops.

Even though my alcohol level was high enough for me to say this last, it isn't quite high enough to cover any regrets for saying something so downright embarrassing. However, just as my face is turning the same shade of dark pepper-red as my duvet, Dan Slater's deadpan face actually breaks into the slightest of smiles, and I watch in complete amazement as he walks over to the bed, leans down toward me, and very slowly, brushes the softest most delicious kiss across my lips.

I wake the next morning to find there's a bucket by the bed, a large glass of water on the bedside table, and an invisible man with a hammer drill attacking my skull.

I never get hangovers. Well, very rarely anyway. Boy, I must have been SO pissed last night to feel this bad now. My five seconds of ignorant, post-awakening bliss is over, and my memory wakes up and I suddenly feel ten times worse when I remember exactly how my evening ended. Ooooh dear.

I cringe and slide beneath the duvet as though this will hide the embarrassment I feel crashing over me like a tidal wave.

I asked Dan Slater to tuck me in.

How could I have done! Things were bad enough between the two of us before I completely lost any remnants of dignity!

I suddenly have another horrible thought. I don't actually remember getting undressed. I look about and heave a sigh of great relief to see my clothes strewn haphazardly about the room. Only I could be that messy. As long as I didn't do a wild strip in front of him. Eeeek! Abandoned my clothes in a drunken fever of bump and grind.

It's then that I remember the worse part. 'Oh my God!' I shriek, sitting bolt upright. I asked him to kiss me goodnight.

And he did!

And then I passed out.

My face goes as red as my duvet again. Daniel Slater kissed me. Why on earth did he actually kiss me? Sure I asked him to, but he knew I was totally loaded. Turmoil and confusion add to the hangover, until it slowly dawns on me that the most probable reason for Daniel Slater to actually kiss me, would be because he knew that I'd wake up this morning and die of embarrassment!

Dan Slater wins again!

I can hear noises from the restaurant below. I look over at my alarm clock and almost die of shock to see that it's gone two in the afternoon. I was supposed to be hard at work over four hours ago. I'm surprised they haven't been on the phone or hammering at the door to get me down there. I hear the sound of a flung saucepan hitting the wall, and a muffled expletive and realise that it must be one of the rare occasions when Claude has actually turned up for work.

Good old Mel. She's obviously taken charge with her usual efficiency, and guessing the state of me, left me to sleep it off.

I phone down.

Mel answers. Despite the fact that Claude can be pretty scary when in temperamental-chef mode, she sounds pretty cheery. 'Ah!' she exclaims. 'Ollie! You've finally rejoined the land of the awake and sober then, have you?'

'I think I'm awake, but I'm not sure if I'm sober yet.'

'Have a good time last night, or can't you remember?'

'Don't ask,' I sigh heavily, thinking of my fatal last words of the evening. 'How's everything down there?'

'Louis is still sulking because he didn't get asked out to play with you last night, and Claude's his usual happy self,' she adds, her voice heavy with sarcasm. 'Although he hasn't succumbed to the brandy bottle just yet.'

'You sound amazingly calm considering.'

'When I see the other two in such a whopping great stonk, it makes me realise just how lovely and uncomplicated my own life is. Therefore I feel totally justified in floating round looking incredibly smug, which has a double result: it not only makes me feel good, but it irritates the crap out of them as well.'

'So you don't need me just yet then?' I ask hopefully.

'Ooh, I think I'm feeling so magnanimous that we might just manage without you until tomorrow . . .' she laughs.

'Mel, you're an angel. Remind me to give you a pay rise when I can afford one.'

I'm just sinking into my pillows for another ten minutes when the phone rings. 'Hello, you old pisshead,' booms a friendly voice down the line. It's Grace.

I groan inwardly. 'I know! I'm so sorry, Grace. Was I a complete arse?'

'Total and utter one, I'm afraid, but you were highly amusing so I'll forgive you, darling. Besides,' she adds happily, 'you get brownie points because, guess what . . .'

'Can't guess, brain hurts.'

'Leo's taking Cornelia out for a drink tonight.'

'He is? See, I did you a favour.' I start to laugh, but it makes my head hurt more. 'Does that mean I'm not in your bad books if I see Finn again?'

'Are you really sure you want to, babe, he's a bit of a reprobate according to Stuart.'

A Franciscan monk would be a reprobate compared with Stuart.

'I might. He's got to call first though, hasn't he?'

'He's got to recover from his coma first,' Gray exclaims. 'You should have seen the state of him, Ollie. We ended up covering him with a blanket and leaving him on the sofa all night. I think he finally woke up just before lunch, and was still too pissed to drive home. We poured him into a cab about one o'clock.'

'In that case I'll be lucky if he remembers me,' I sigh.

'You'd probably be luckier if he didn't!' Grace jokes. 'What about Dan?'

'What about him?' I reply, suddenly sullen due to extreme embarrassment.

'Get you home safely, did he?'

'Yes thanks.' I decide it's safer to gloss over the subject of Dan Slater. In fact I think at the moment it's best if I pretend to myself that he doesn't exist. 'Do you remember if I gave Finn my phone number?' I ask, trying to change the subject.

'Well if *you* don't remember how on earth do you expect me to,' she laughs lightly.

'I think I did.'

'Well, he's probably lost it.'

'Why's that then?'

'He lost everything else: most of his brain cells, the breakfast I tried to feed him when he finally woke up . . .'

'I know what you mean!' I groan. 'I'm feeling a little delicate myself this morning.'

'You only have yourself to blame. Stuart thinks you're totally mad, you know.'

'Does he?' I don't know if that's an insult or a compliment, coming from him.

'Yep. Raving.'

'Just tell him I've lost my marbles. Oh and Gray, if Finn *has* lost my number, then give it to him for me, okay?'

'That's not exactly subtle, is it, darling?'

'Just give him my number, Gray.'

'You wouldn't rather play hard to get?'

'I've been single for over two years, Grace, how much harder to get do you actually want me to be?'

Attempting to relegate all thoughts of Dan Slater to the 'Access Denied' part of my brain, where I keep the most embarrassing life events, my bank card pin number, and the whereabouts of my spare set of car keys, I turn my mind to Finn.

I like Finn. I haven't liked a man for some time. It's not that I'm totally averse to the idea of having a relationship. The fact that I've spent the past two years building up my business means that I haven't exactly had much time for anything other than work. Not that I think I'm missing out on that much: relationships are far too scary a commodity. They breed a new type of insecurity that I don't know how to handle. You suddenly find yourself with the one thing in life that you dread losing: it's a terrible responsibility. It's not as if you can tape a man inside your knickers so that you don't mislay

107

them, much as the man would probably enjoy this. I prefer friends, they're far less demanding and far more considerate. Most of the time, anyway.

Besides, it's a well-known fact that men only want you until they've got you. The old thrill of the chase. It goes back to the cavemen really. Once they've coshed you over the head a few times, you become far less attractive, and it's time for them to go out again and find a woman with fewer dents in her face. Well, I had decided that I was just going to keep on running. You'd have to be Linford Christie to catch up with me, but even if you were and you did, I probably wouldn't fancy you anyway. I'm fussier than a health and safety inspector in Mrs Miggin's Pie Shop.

It's silly the things that can put you off someone. Give me a perfectly decent man, and I'll always find you a flaw. I dread to think what I'd be like if I ever had children, a daughter especially. I think I'd be the worst prospective mother-in-law in the world. I'd make the Spanish Inquisition look like gentle questioning. I'd probably do the Sinbad-style impossible-quest test: you want to marry my daughter, then you must find me a purple chinchilla wearing a feather boa that dances on tabletops whilst singing 'If you wanna be my lover'. You can't find one? Tough! Stick your head on this block so I may chop it off.

Finn is the first man in quite some time who's actually occupied my thoughts for longer than a drunken nano-second. My solitary status hasn't really bothered me too much though. Marriage and motherhood. It's something I *think* I want, but it's also something that scares me to death.

I can't ever see Tanya settling down. She'll be a ninety-year-old mock Mae West with blue eyeshadow tattooed permanently in her wrinkles, a pampered pink poodle as a child substitute, and several septuagenarian toy boys.

As for me, I think I'd like to settle down with the right person, but as we all know, Mr Right is one of those urban myths, right up there with Seaman Staines, and Roger the Cabin Boy from Captain Pugwash. Talked about frequently, but never actually existed. In the meantime, I pretend that I really enjoy living on my own – which I suppose isn't a complete pretence, it does have bonus points, but usually of the 'I can be a complete slob if I want to' variety, which doesn't really do your self-esteem much good.

All I can say is, if Cinderella knew what an extreme effect she'd have on womankind, she'd have thought more than twice before opening her mouth to sing those six immortal words 'one day my prince will come'. He may come, but he'll probably make you sleep in the wet patch, leave before breakfast and never call you again, even though he promised he would. Never mind the handsome man on a gee-gee charging round saving damsels in distress; who made them distressed in the first place, that's what I want to know! Men! That's who.

Dan Slater isn't a shining prince. He's the Black Knight. Rampaging round London in his black BMW, intent on building up his own kingdom, and sod the serfs.

And as for Finn? Could he be my Sir Lancelot? I really don't know, but I think he might make a pretty good court jester, and I've found that a sense of humour can be far more important than a propensity for throwing coats over puddles.

Maybe Gray has got the right idea. Find yourself a Captain Sensible instead of a dashing-but-diabolic knight who's going to ride roughshod over your heart on his snorting foam-mouthed charger. I mean, if you have a man who has no personality and never goes out anywhere unless it's with you, then you never have to worry about what he may or may not be getting up to. I've always ended up being disappointed by men. I think my ideals must be way too high. Like how on earth can I have integrity on my list of requirements?

A man with integrity?

The Tooth Fairy.

Chapter Five

Tanya has returned from her holiday, as brown as a berry and glowing with the healthy gloss of the recently pampered. 'He did what!' she shrieks so loudly that, despite the loud music throbbing throughout the busy bar, the people at the next table look over in alarm.

Tanya has only just recovered her composure after discovering that Grace is actually getting married in just over two months time. Perhaps I should have saved the story of Daniel Slater and the drunken kiss for another time.

'Well, technically I did ask him to,' I reply looking down at the tabletop in embarrassment.

'Yeah, but you were pissed,' Tanya states. 'You know what that means, don't you?'

'Yeah, total humiliation.'

Tanya ignores me. 'It means he must like you.'

'Don't be ridiculous,' I reply, my head snapping up so quickly something in my neck twinges painfully.

'Would you kiss someone you didn't like?' Tanya asks me bluntly.

'I suppose not, no.' I pick up my wine glass and take solace in its comforting contents. 'But this is different.'

'How so?'

'Because, as I said, I was drunk and I asked him to.'

'Yeah, but he could have just walked away.'

'That would have been the sensible option, yeah.'

'Then that proves it. He likes you.'

'I think I'll stick with my theory, it's far more likely.'

'What, that's it all part of some sad mind game?'

'To undermine me, yeah.'

'And why would he want to do that?' she asks mockingly.

'Because he wants to get his hands on Tates.'

111

'He already owns the building, Ollie.'

'Yeah, but he can't redevelop it with me and my business still in place, can he?'

'And you're sure that's what he wants to do with it?'

'Pretty much so, yeah. I told you about when they came into the restaurant, him and his business cronies, didn't I?'

'Sure you did, but what you heard didn't prove anything, they could have been talking about anywhere. In fact he told you you'd got it all wrong.'

'He's hardly going to admit it to me of all people, is he?'

Tanya sighs. 'Okay, so say it's true, how does kissing you further his cause then?'

'I don't know,' I stutter. 'To confuse me. To make me want to leave the country. I don't know,' I repeat hopelessly.

'Are you sure that's all he did then? You know, kiss you. Nothing else happened?'

'Yes!' I howl. 'Of course it was . . . I think . . . oh crikey . . . no!' I take a breath and try to reactivate the rational part of my brain. I don't actually remember getting into bed. I remember getting onto the bed, but the taking off my clothes part . . . and then there was the glass of water and the bucket he fetched from my kitchen. So he didn't leave straight after kissing me for whatever strange reason it was that made him comply with my drunken request.

Tanya cocks her head to one side and smiles slightly at me. 'So . . . what was it actually like then?' she asks.

'Oh, Tanya, no, please don't ask me that!' I wail, my brains still trying to de-fuzz the events of Saturday night.

'Oh come on, Ol. You and Dan Slater snogged. I need details.'

'I was pissed. I passed out two seconds later.'

'That could have been the effect of the kiss!'

'It wasn't that good!'

'Aha, now we're getting somewhere. So it wasn't any good then?'

'I didn't say that! I just said it wasn't the kiss that made me pass out, he didn't have me swirling deliriously into a passion-induced coma.'

'So you're saying it wasn't a bad kiss, but it wasn't the best you've ever had either. You know, a knicker-elastic snapper, instant drawer-dropper.'

'Tanya, considering what's just happened, this isn't the most sensitive line of questioning.'

'Bugger sensitivity,' Tanya grins wickedly, pouring me another glass of wine in the hope that more alcohol might loosen my tongue a little. 'Dan Slater sounds absolutely delicious, I want to know what it was like to actually snog the man.'

'I reserve the right not to answer that question on the grounds it might incriminate me,' I mutter, refusing to look at her.

'It *was* good, wasn't it?' Tanya crows triumphantly, as if she's Hercule Poirot, and she's just outed the murderer.

I nod, still not looking up.

'Yes.' Tanya claps her hands and falling off her stool, starts to dance embarrassingly around the table. 'I knew it,' she crows, coming level with me and clapping her hands on my shoulders. 'I knew it from the start. You've always been far too venomous about him. Dead giveaway.'

'Okay, I admit it!' I say grudgingly, as she peers over my shoulder, forcing me to look straight into her eyes, 'I find him attractive . . . in a repulsive kind of way.'

'What on earth do you mean?'

'I mean that he's an attractive man, but he's not an attractive person. The way he's messing my life up at the moment I don't feel as if I *should* fancy him.'

'Well that sounds about right,' Tanya nods. 'Humans are pretty perverse beings, we always seem to fancy the wrong people, the ones we're not supposed to like.'

'Could that explain Grace and Stuart?' I wonder aloud.

'Nothing could explain Grace and Stuart.' Tanya frowns. 'Nothing that wouldn't figure on the *X-Files* anyway,' she adds a touch too loudly.

I shush Tanya as Grace, who organised this Sunday mid-morning drink, returns from the bar to the table bearing another bottle of wine. Grinning at us, she plonks the bottle of cold Chardonnay down between our glasses and then, putting her wallet back in her massive handbag, digs around a bit and pulls out a diary that's really too large to be portable. It's stuffed full of clippings from magazines, some of which fall out onto the table as she opens it to the right month.

'Okay, I called you here because . . .'

'You've missed us dreadfully, and were desperate to see us,' Tanya cuts in with a hint of sarcasm.

'Well yes, there's that,' Grace laughs lightly. 'But I also need some dates from you.' She heads back into the bag again and pulls out a pen, the ragged end of which immediately goes in her mouth to be chewed even further.

'Are we going out?' Tanya exclaims excitedly.

'Like in the old days,' I add wistfully.

'We're going dress hunting.'

'Shopping! Great.' Tanya's face immediately brightens. 'Anything specific?'

'Well duh, yeah!' Grace raises her eyebrows at Tanya. 'Only a few little things we need like erm . . . a *wedding* dress, and *wedding* shoes, and *wedding* underwear, and erm oh . . .' She pauses and smiles hopefully at us, 'We'll be needing a couple of bridesmaid dresses as well . . .'

'Bridesmaid dresses?' Tanya repeats cautiously.

'Yeah. What kind of thing do you fancy?' Grace picks up one of her clippings and waves a glossy cut-out photograph of a smiling blonde-haired model in a pink-fondant-fancy creation, that I realise from the small bouquet and floral headband is actually a bridesmaid dress and not something from the Dame Edna Everage Catalogue of Crimes Against Fashion.

'You mean I'm . . . er . . . we, Ollie and I . . .'

'Of course! You're my Matron of Dishonour, and Ollie's my Old Maid of Honour.'

'You can forget the Matron part, right now!' Tanya shrieks horrified. 'Dishonour, I can cope with, but I'm not that old, thank you!'

'Don't know what you're worrying about,' I shake my head, 'you just got Matron; that only hints of age. In fact it makes me think of Carry On films, and busty, sexy women. I got "old". There's no beating around the bush with "old".'

'Will you?' Grace looks at us pleadingly.

I look at Tanya, who distorts her lips and eyebrows into a kind of 'Help' expression.

'Of course we will, you silly sod.' I turn to Grace and hug her, tears welling in my eyes. I'm torn between feeling so proud, and so pissed off. I'm honoured to be Gray's Old Maid

114

of Honour, but I just wish it was for a wedding where she was marrying a man who'll actually manage to make her happy for the rest of her life, like he'll bloody well be vowing to.

'Tan?' Grace asks cautiously. 'I know it's not exactly your scene, but if I promise not to put you in anything too hideous.'

'How could I say no?' Tanya replies.

'You can't.' I look sternly at her, but fortunately I was the only one who caught the vocal inflection which made this question definitely not the rhetorical one Grace thought it was.

'I feel such a two-faced cow.' Tanya listlessly polishes a drip tray with a J cloth, before returning it to the pump and starting on the next one.

Tanya, bless her, has dumped the couture, and is currently in jeans and an old sweatshirt helping me clean up at the bar at Tates. Normally Grace would have come back to help out too. It used to be a monthly ritual. I'd close up for the evening, and the four of us would gather together to clean out the pipes and consume the vast quantity of beer that normally gets wasted in the process, usually resulting in one hell of a party.

Today it's just Tan and me. Louis, who also normally joins us, has an acting job. We did ask Gray if she wanted to come, and bring Stuart with her, but apparently Stuffy is taking her to a Steam Rally this weekend, and having re-stacked her diary with cut-out pages from *Bride* magazine, she shot off up the M1 toward Leicestershire straight after our morning confab. Informing her that it's actually a large gathering of traction engines, Grace cruelly quashed Tanya's initial excitement that a Steam Rally was something to do with saunas and running nude into cold lakes. This is a great shame as I think she was just about to grant Stuart some kudos.

'We're doing all we can to sabotage this bloody wedding, and there's me smiling sweetly and agreeing to be a bloody bridesmaid.' Tanya shakes her head. 'I've never been a bridesmaid before.'

'This will be my third time.'

'Three times a bridesmaid, never . . .'

'A bride,' I finish the quotation for her. 'That's not such a bad thing, considering I've never met anybody I wanted to marry.'

'Ah, poor Ollie!' Tanya hugs me. 'I know what'll cheer us up!' she exclaims. 'Let's go clubbing.'

'That's your solution to everything.'

'No seriously, come on, let's organise a proper girlie night out. It'll take your mind off your problems.'

'What, heading to a place full of nubile nineteen-year-olds, in outfits with less material than my underwear, shaking their youthful cellulite-free stuff on the dance floor, is going to make me feel better?'

'Free-flowing alcohol, mind-blowing dance music, and the all-night burger place after,' Tanya tempts me.

'I'll call Louis.'

'That's not the only person I had in mind to invite.'

'Don't tell me, you want to drag your latest conquest along? Won't that cramp your style a bit?'

'Me, take a man *to* a night club? Talk about coals to Newcastle! I actually meant Gray.'

'You're kidding, aren't you?' I reply huffily. 'Grace hasn't been out with us for ages. This morning was the first time I've actually seen her since their dinner party.'

'Exactly, and this could be the next step in our attempt to wean her away from you-know-who. Find her another man and we don't have to wear pink satin . . .' Tanya tempts me.

'She won't come. She's probably arranged an evening of scintillating macramé with Stuffy Stuart. "Oh, I can't possibly come out tonight," ' I mimic Grace sarcastically. ' "Stuart and I have arranged to strip down his Land Rover. Tomorrow? Sorry I'm busy then too, he needs someone to hold the sheep so it doesn't struggle too much . . ." '

'She'll come,' Tanya says knowingly, suppressing a giggle at my cruel impression. 'Tell her you're desperately depressed and only her company will stop you hurling yourself off Tower Bridge before the night is out. You know what a sucker she is for a sad story. I mean you only have to look at Stuart . . .'

After a lot of coaxing, we somehow manage to pin Grace down for our girlie night out on the following Friday evening. It's arranged that we'll all meet up to get ready at Tanya's place. A ritual that I've really missed since Grace became a stay-at-home.

It does cheer me up a bit stuffing myself into one of Tanya's sexiest Moschinos, and my pair of gorgeous Christian Louboutin sandals, which I couldn't resist in the last sale, and therefore resurrected my 'for emergencies only' credit card to buy.

I pirouette in front of the mirror, and actually find myself grinning. I'm so used to living in restaurant gear, which at the moment tends to be my increasingly stained kitchen whites, due to the number of time Claude's been a no-show recently, I'd forgotten what I looked like with a bit of war-paint on, and I'm actually quite pleased with the result. Maybe I could have a little fun myself tonight, take my mind off the impending doom of Gray's wedding and Tates' funeral. I feel a surge of long-lost optimism, and turn to the other two, who are fighting good-naturedly over one of my favourite Karen Millen dresses.

'Come on you 'orrible lot, get your war-paint on, and let's hit the town. I think we're in for a wicked evening! Oh and let Tanya wear the dress, Louis,' I add as Grace comes out of the bathroom. 'I'm afraid it suits her much better.'

'Boy, do I feel old,' I sigh, watching yet another herd of nineteen-year-olds sashay past, giggling, necking Bacardi Breezers, and looking disgustingly young, lithe, and gorgeous.

'*You* feel old! You're five years younger than I am!' exclaims Tanya. 'If you're old, then I'm positively geriatric. You don't have to comment on that last statement!' she warns, as a slight smile quirks about my lips. 'Anyway, the mature woman has a lot more to offer than some young bimbo.'

'I don't think I like that word . . . mature.'

'Such as intelligent conversation,' Tanya ploughs on with her pet theory regardless. 'A more balanced view of life, financial independence, advanced sexual skills.'

'Cellulite, wrinkles, and a biological clock that's turned into a time bomb,' I add cheerfully.

She silences me with a withering glance. 'Whereas all you get with a younger woman,' she continues pointedly, 'is slightly slimmer thighs . . . in some cases,' the withering look is passed to a seventeen-year-old with puppy fat, whose ample

117

figure has been squeezed into a not-so-ample dress, 'and a lot more hassle.'

'Anyway, talking about hassle, where's Gray got to?'

Louis sighs heavily and looks at her sideways. 'Guess,' he replies.

'She hasn't left already, has she?' Tanya exclaims in horror. 'It's only eleven-thirty!'

'Not quite as bad as that, no,' he replies. 'But you remember those public phones we passed in the foyer . . . let's just say one of them is probably a hot line to Leicestershire right now.'

Tanya shakes her head despondently. 'I think I need a drink!'

She returns from the bar clutching a bottle of champagne, with four glasses balanced between the fingers of her other hand.

'Ooh, champagne!' exclaims Gray, who's returned from phoning Stuffy and eyes the bottle greedily. 'My favourite! What are we celebrating? Not that I care. Gimme now!'

'I haven't seen you for three weeks, so isn't it cause enough that we're all together again for once,' Tanya replies sarcastically, tossing the frothing liquid into the glasses and handing the first one to Grace.

'Sorry, darling. You know what it's like, find a new man . . .'

'Dump your friends.' Tanya crosses her eyes at her.

'That's not *quite* what I was going to say.' Gray pulls a face at Tanya, and lifting her glass proposes a toast. 'To good friends,' she says.

'Friends,' we repeat solemnly, touched by this accolade.

'Who still love you even when they're feeling sorely neglected!' she teases Tanya, swooping in for a hug as Tan's lips set into pout mode.

'I would have invited you to my dinner party,' she reassures her. 'It's not my fault you were off for a dirty week and missed all of the fun.'

I smile sympathetically at Louis, who I know for a fact is still smarting over the fact that he didn't even make it onto the guest list. 'Talking of which,' I ask her, trying to change the subject slightly as Louis begins to scowl moodily. 'Did you give Finn my number?'

'Of course. Hasn't he called you?'

'I suppose he may have done whilst I was down in the

restaurant,' I reply, a touch disappointed, and not wanting to say a blunt 'No', and admit to myself and everyone else that he probably hasn't bothered.

Grace raises her eyebrows at me in disbelief. 'He's not your type anyway,' she states kindly, trying to make me feel better.

'How do you know that?'

'Well, he's lovely, but he's not very reliable. You need someone more in control, stronger ... Someone like Dan Slater,' she adds slyly.

'What!' I explode.

'Dan likes you.'

'No, he bloody doesn't,' I reply, giving Tanya a warning look as she opens her mouth to protest. I haven't told Grace about our little saliva-swapping session, and I have absolutely no intention of doing so either, due to the fact that this would probably fuel her little fancying fantasy.

'Why on earth did he give you a lift home from my place then?' Grace is still insistent.

'Because you asked him to,' I say flatly.

'No, I didn't,' she replies, emptying her glass. 'He offered.'

'He did?'

'Yep, *and* he was asking questions about you.'

'I hope you didn't tell him anything!' I grumble, sinking my face into my drink so I don't have to look at her.

'Nothing too personal, no, but I did ask him about the restaurant.'

'Oh, Grace, you didn't?' I ask in alarm. 'You promised me you wouldn't say anything.'

'Well, I can't just sit back and watch you struggle. Don't you want to know what he said?'

'Do you know, I'm not sure that I do, no.'

'I'm going to tell you anyway,' Grace persists. 'He said he only came into the restaurant initially to take a look at the person who could flap the unflappable Edina Mason ...'

'Edina Mason?'

'His secretary ... sorry, his Executive Assistant. Apparently she's disgustingly efficient, but a total battleaxe, and you're the only person who's ever managed to render her totally speechless. And he also said that he had no idea that the property management department had already asked for an increased rental payment.'

119

'I might have guessed he'd deny it all.'

'Perhaps it's the truth. He seems to be a pretty honest person.'

'Yeah, and you've known him for all of six weeks. You're just blinded by a handsome face.'

She swoops in on this one like a circling vulture. 'Ah, so you admit you think he's handsome then?'

'Wouldn't anybody?' I hedge. 'But that's not the point at all. The point is, it's his company that's threatening my livelihood, and that's enough to make him a total git in my book.'

I refill my glass, and take a fortifying swig of one of our favourite tipples. 'Anyway,' I add, desperate to change the subject. 'We're actually here to forget about our problems, not talk about them. I propose another toast.' I pause whilst I try to think of something. The toast isn't down to a desperate urge to pledge to something, it's an excuse to get Grace to chance the subject from Dastardly Dan Slater, and to drink some more. 'To . . . er . . . to . . .'

Tanya rescues me. 'To all the men we've loved before,' she announces, 'and the legions yet to come.'

Louis and Grace echo this toast with differing degrees of enthusiasm, Grace tailing off before she gets to the men-of-the-future reference. The other two notice this as well. Tan immediately reaches for Grace's nearly empty champagne flute, and fills it to the brim for the third time.

'Are you trying to get me drunk?'

'Yes!' we chorus, pouring more champagne into her glass.

We spend the next half an hour feeding Grace alcohol and pointing out attractive men, noticing that Grace gets more appreciative of the opposite sex as she gets increasingly drunker. Not surprisingly, Grace soon heads for the loo.

'What goes in must come out,' she chirps brightly.

'She's pissed,' Tanya hisses happily to me.

'Just a touch,' I reply. 'All these weeks of quaffing mineral water. Plays merry hell with your ability to cope with alcohol.'

Tanya, Louis and I take the opportunity to scout the room for a potential victim. We have fairly varied tastes. Louis seems to go for lithe, bald men with lots of piercings, which I really don't think Grace would appreciate. Tanya is a sucker for a handsome face or an expensive watch. I'm hunting for a Brad Pitt lookalike, not for me – I'm more of a Tom Cruise girl myself – but I know Grace is a bit of a sucker for the gorgeous one, especially since watching him sweat his way through *Fight Club*.

After five minutes, however, I'm fortunate enough to spot someone that all three of us actually agree is pretty damn tasty, and more importantly all three of us agree that Grace will probably think is pretty damn tasty too. 'Now he's nice.' I point him out to the others.

Tanya peers over to the end of the bar.

'Which one?'

'Dark hair, green Ben Sherman.'

'Can't see his face.'

'Greg Wise crossed with Max Beesley.'

'Sounds promising.'

He turns to look our way and Tanya takes a sharp intake of breath. 'You're right,' she exhales, sighing lustfully. 'He *is* nice. So nice in fact I wouldn't mind a go myself.'

'I know, but think of the cause.'

'Couldn't we find her another one, this place is full of men.'

'Sure it's full of men,' Louis tells her, 'but it's not full of men that Grace would like enough to drag her away from Stuffy Stuart. You'll just have to make the sacrifice for Gray's sake.'

'Okay, okay.' Tanya waves her hands in submission. 'Grace can have him.'

'So how do we get them together then?'

'It's going to have to be the oldest cliché in the book.' Tanya gets to her feet.

'What are you going to do?'

'Watch and learn,' she smiles.

She sashays across to the bar, Louis and I trotting close behind her, and homes straight in on the chosen guy, leaning on the bar next to him, and launching straight into the immortal line, 'Excuse me, but my friend fancies you.' She does it in such an obviously kitsch way that fortunately instead of telling us to get lost, the guy bursts out laughing.

'Really?' he grins at Tanya, a few lines of amused incredulity puckering his forehead.

'Really,' Tanya affirms, pointing to Grace who's just coming back from the loos.

It's an opportune moment. Her hair's a little dishevelled from a quick blast with the hand dryer, and she's wearing a touch too much lipstick hastily reapplied in front of the smoke-stained loo mirror. She looks slightly drunk, slightly wanton, and totally gorgeous.

'Wow,' he states appreciatively. 'In that case I'm a very lucky man.' He has the slightest softest touch of Irish brogue to his voice, which would already be an incredibly sexy voice without this added aphrodisiac. Up close he looks more Greg Wise than ever, with unruly black curls, cut-glass cheekbones, and smoke-grey eyes.

It turns out that his name's Declan, and he's out on a stag night with friends. As the best man, Declan is sworn to keep the groom from being tied naked to London Bridge, or posted by rail to Aberdeen, and he is therefore still relatively sober. The rest of his party, however, are currently stampeding round the nightclub totally pissed, taking it in turns to see who can be the last to pass out, and Declan is therefore grateful for some company.

Whilst Tanya stays to chat up Declan on Grace's behalf, Louis and I go to work on Gray.

'I'd almost forgotten what fun it is to go on a girlie night out,' she announces when we sit back down with her, up-ending the champagne bottle into her glass, but only getting about a centimetre more. 'Oh poo, it's all gone!' she pouts.

Perfectly on cue, Tanya returns to the table with the delicious Declan, who is carrying a fresh bottle. 'Grace, this gorgeous man is Declan,' Tanya tells her. 'Declan, this is Grace.'

Smiling, Declan leans over and fills Grace's glass for her.

'Cheers, Declan.' Grace toasts him with her newly filled glass. 'Here's to you.'

'She likes him,' Louis hisses to me.

'What's not to like?' I reply. 'But how can you tell?'

'She didn't tell him to F off,' Louis replies simply. 'That's a first this evening.'

I think Louis is right. I watch Grace move over on the banquette she's perched upon, to make room for Declan to sit down, smiling at him as he squeezes in next to her, sitting far closer than he actually needs to. They sit talking together for over an hour, steadily working their way through the rest of Declan's bottle of champagne. I can't hear what they're saying but they both seem to be laughing an awful lot.

Tanya gives me an ecstatic thumbs up across the table, as, much later, they get up together, and we watch Declan lead Gray onto the dance floor and pull her against his lovely broad chest into a slow smooch. Frustratingly, however, we soon lose them in the crowd of couples that are hitting the dance floor for a quick grope to a slow song, and almost resort to smooching with each other so we can get closer and watch progress. Two girls wrapped around each other on the dance floor warrants far too much male attention, however, so we grab Louis and both sort of dance with him as well as each other, manoeuvring clumsily round the dance floor in a strange smooching threesome until they're back in view.

'Are they kissing?' Louis has his back to them.

Tanya cranes her neck, to look over his shoulder. 'No, I think she's just slumped in a drunken stupor against his chest.'

A herd of drunken city boys stampede across the dance floor, arms locked around each other's shoulders in a kind of rugby scrum. When our view has cleared again Grace and Declan have gone.

We quickly split up, heading in different directions to see if we can spot them anywhere. Tanya and I meet back up at our table ten minutes later. Neither of us has managed to find them, but Louis who trots back a few minutes after us panting heavily, had more luck.

'Did you find her?' Tanya demands.

Louis, still slightly out of breath, nods excitedly. 'She went outside with delicious Declan,' he wheezes, grinning happily.

'Yes!' Tanya and I punch the air in triumph. 'We did it, we finally did it!' She grabs me and we canter round the dance floor like a pair of grinning idiots then, grabbing Louis, head back to the table for a celebratory glass of champagne.

Twenty minutes later, after we've started on another bottle of Moët, Gray staggers back inside, alone, but with Declan's jacket slung about her shoulders.

'What a lovely man,' she slurs happily, collapsing on the stool next to me, and pinching my glass of champagne.

'Really?' we chorus eagerly.

'Yeah, eversonice,' she hiccups softly. 'He lent me his jacket because it was cold outside.'

'And what exactly were you doing outside . . .?' Tanya pants eagerly.

'Well, he was so nice . . .'

'Yes,' we prompt.

'That he let me borrow his mobile to call Stuart. You know, it's been a luvverly evening, but I'm missing him SOOO much.'

'Aaaah!' Tanya lets out a screech, her head falling forward, forehead thumping on the table in despair.

'Is she okay?' Gray slurs, leaning over and patting Tan ineffectually on her shoulder.

'Yeah, she's fine, babe,' I sigh heavily. 'She's just had a bit of a stressful evening.'

'Such a waste . . .' Tanya mutters into the tabletop. 'Such a bloody waste.' She slowly raises her head from the table, and peers up at me, her glittering green eyes suddenly purposeful, and reaching out grabs her glass from the table, knocks back the dregs of her champagne in one go, then stands up and grabs the jacket that Gray has abandoned.

'Where are you going?'

Holding the jacket to her face, and breathing in the scent of warm male and CK One, Tanya turns and smiles lasciviously at me. 'Well, this jacket has a rather luscious owner, and if Gray doesn't want him then . . .'

I'm totally knackered. After our late and rather drunken evening on Friday, Louis and I coped with a private party on our own last night, didn't close until 2:00am, and spent the next hour and a half clearing up. I then had to get up again at 7:00am to prepare for a booked-out Sunday lunchtime. Louis has the day off; I'm not so fortunate. If I'm not careful I'll fall asleep headfirst in a roasting tin. I've already singed my eyebrows twice through taking the gravy pan away from the flames but not actually moving back myself.

I get the major part of lunch over and done with then, leaving Melanie, Claude and one of my student casuals to cope with the last vestiges of the Sunday-lunch-time crowd, I head upstairs and fall backwards onto my bed, too tired even to pull off my pinny, or drag myself into the bathroom to shower off all of the excess roast fat. I've had my eyes closed for approximately thirty seconds however, when there's a knock at my front door. Groaning, I drag myself out of the bedroom.

'You lot can't cope without me for two minutes, can you? I don't care if you've just had the entire Arsenal team arrive by coach, demanding four courses all round, I'm not coming down again,' I announce, pulling open the door.

It takes a moment for me to recognise the face of the man standing on my doorstep. It's a very attractive face, with lively green eyes, and a mouth that's curling at the corners with laughter at the sight of me. And when I say sight, I mean a real 'sight'. He's immaculately casual, in black moleskins, and a chunky cream Nicole Fahri jumper, his winter-sun-bleached, golden-brown hair as groomed and carefully carelessly tousled as David Ginola fresh from the showers and ready for 'camera *and* action'.

I've got butter in my hair, dark purple-red cabbage stains all over my jeans, singed eyebrows which I'm sure are still smoking, and a streak of gravy browning on my forehead.

Perfect timing.

'Hi, Finn,' I murmur, adding to the attractive look by rubbing my hand across my eyes, and trailing the blob of sleep lodged in one corner across the top of my cheekbone.

Maybe I'm lucky and he goes for the disastrous dinner lady look – NOT.

Finn doesn't comment however, but simply leans in and kisses me on the cheek that isn't covered in eye gunk, then pulling back smiles broadly. 'You smell wonderful!' he announces.

'I do?' I reel back slightly in surprise, both at the kiss and the compliment.

'Absolutely. Roast beef and Yorkshire pudding. Delicious. I could eat you.' He peers closer. 'In fact I could eat off you. You must have enough food on you to serve at least another three people.'

'Oh dear.'

'No, it's great, you look like abstract art.'

Okay, so it may be corny, but it's the nicest a man's been to me recently. A little flattery is good for a girl's flagging ego. He's grinning at me. Perfect white even teeth. I'd smile back but I've probably got pork crackling stuck between my two front teeth or something.

'Sorry I didn't call first, but as well as losing most of my brain cells at Grace's dinner party, I also lost your telephone number. That is, if you gave me your telephone number. I'm afraid I really can't remember. I know I could have got it from Grace,' he adds, echoing the thought that had just flashed through my head, 'but I prefer springing surprises on people. Must be the journalist in me. Would you like a journalist in you?'

'I beg your pardon!'

He bursts into peals of laughter. 'You heard. Worth a try. Well, if you don't fancy an afternoon of debauched sex, how about coming out for a drink?'

'I had planned to spend the afternoon in bed . . . alone and asleep!' I stress, as the wicked grin returns to Finn's face.

'Sounded good until the alone and asleep part . . . Come on, Ollie, I need some company. I can't think of anyone I'd rather spend the rest of the day with.'

More flattery. I like it. Besides, I've spent so much time at this place recently, I think it would probably do me good to get out and about. Escape for a couple of hours, think about something other than food for at least ten minutes.

'I thought we could take a drive into the country and have dinner or something,' Finn adds, thinking I need further temptation as I haven't given him an answer yet.

Well it's still food, but if somebody else is cooking it, who cares. 'Sounds great. But . . .' I indicate my mode of dress. 'I really think I could do with changing first.'

'You don't have to, I kind of like the rough-and-ready look.'

'I look rough-and-ready! In that case I'm definitely changing!'

Just for this particular good-natured insult I make Finn wait whilst I not only shower and change, but style my hair, do my make-up, and try on three different outfits.

'Wow, you scrub up quite well, don't you?' he enthuses, when I finally emerge from my bedroom.

I don't know why I spent so long on my hair: Finn drives an old MG Roadster. For once, the sun is out, so the top is down, and by the time we reach the riverside pub in Warwick that he's chosen for dinner I look as if I'm sporting a larger messier beehive than Patsy from *Ab Fab*.

Whilst I attempt to drag a comb through my hair in the ladies, Finn orders us drinks, and finds a table on the terrace overlooking the river.

'Has Grace forgiven us yet?' Finn asks, handing me a large gin and tonic as I sit down opposite him.

'For the drunken behaviour or for not going along with her matchmaking plans?' I ask, accepting gratefully.

'Either.'

'Yes on both counts, fortunately. Did you hear about Leo and Cornelia?'

'No, but I can guess what you're going to say. I told you that they were a good match. I have a nose for things like that.' He taps a finger on the side of his nose as he speaks. 'Talking of which, are you going to tell me why you dislike Dan Slater so much?'

Oh dear. Why did he have to mention that name? Ever since that evening I've been pushing that particular man to the darkest recesses of my mind, in the vain hope that I can forget . . . well, you know what it is that I want to forget.

'Well?' he prompts me.

'Was it that obvious?'

'Yep,' he states bluntly. 'Even without the body language, I think the request to bump him off was a bit of a giveaway.'

There's a pause whilst a waitress brings us some menus, which I peruse with what I hope is an expert eye, prevaricating between a homemade fish pie, and Spanish chicken.

'It's quite simple really,' I say when I've finally plumped for the fish pie, and Finn has asked for medium-rare steak. 'His company has basically just bought my street.'

'Oh I see,' he says slowly.

'And what do property developers normally do?'

'Er . . . develop property, naturally,' he sighs, fully understanding.

'Exactly. I've spent two years working my socks off building up my business, then along comes Slater Enterprises.'

'Maybe they won't want to redevelop?' he suggests.

'And what else will they want to do with the properties?'

'You get income from rentals, don't you . . .?'

'Yeah, tell me about it. The first thing I got from them was notice of a rent increase, shortly followed by an offer to buy out my lease. Hopefully we can just about take in the increase and still scrape by, but I'm so fed up with just scraping by. We'd started to do well, and I was enjoying it!'

I tell Finn about the time that I saw Dan and the two other

127

suits coming out of the antiques shop, including what I can remember of the overheard conversation from their lunch in Tates. For some reason I omit the part where I verbally attacked Dan Slater afterwards.

Finn sits back and listens. Not just pretends to listen, but I mean really listens to me. It's great to be able to talk to someone who isn't somehow involved in the whole scenario. Someone objective, instead of biased. He lets me rant my way through our entire meal, with hardly an interruption. Very therapeutic for me, but hardly a scintillating evening for him.

I stumble to a halt, and apologise, an apology which he ignores, simply closing the fingers of his hands together, before leaning his chin on them, and looking me directly in the eyes. 'Why don't you utilise the assets you already have,' he states simply.

'Such as?'

'Well, apart from an incredible pair of . . . eyes . . .' His charmingly wicked grin stops me from kicking Finn under the table at this point. 'How about the restaurant?'

'Well, that was the obvious one. Don't you think I haven't thought about ways of increasing business? We can't make the place any bigger. We're only closed when it's not cost-effective to open. I've already negotiated with my suppliers to within an inch of their profit margins, and I've put an extra two percent on practically everything on the menu and behind the bar. I've done everything I can.'

'Are you sure about that? People don't only eat at lunch or dinner times, you know.'

'What are you driving at, Finn?'

'Think about it. If I stayed overnight would you give me breakfast, or could we pop out for it?'

'What?'

'Think about the question, Ollie, not the connotations.'

'Okay,' I reply, thoughtfully. 'Well *in*, I suppose, because there's nowhere nearby to take you . . . there's a place we go to near Tan's, but that's miles away.'

It's like a light slowly dawning in my head. It's so simple it's genius. 'Ooh, Finn, I love you!' I shriek, leaping from my chair and throwing my arms about his neck.

'It's a bit early to start talking about love,' he laughs into my hair, 'but you could show your gratitude in other ways.'

'Oh yeah, of course.' I lean in closer, smiling softly up at him; then, just as he thinks I'm going to land a soft kiss on his waiting lips, lean sideways, pull my bag from under his chair, and whip out my wallet. 'I'll pay for dinner . . .'

It's Monday night; Tates, as usual, is closed for the evening, and Tanya and I therefore have the restaurant to ourselves. We're enjoying a rare evening with just the two of us, seated at one of the best tables, with a bottle of my most expensive red, and a special treat in the form of a huge plate of bubble and squeak, and temptingly curling but awfully fat-laden Cumberland sausages.

'I think I've come up with a solution to my financial crisis,' I tell her, cutting into a spitting sausage with great relish.

Tanya's still reeling over the fact that I've actually been out on what she thinks is tantamount to a date for the first time in ages. 'When am I going to get to meet Finn then?'

'Oh . . . let me think . . . probably . . . never?'

'Um, I don't think so, babe. You know the form: new man has to be introduced. It's the rule. Even Stuart with a U had to adhere to the rule. Unfortunately!'

'He's not my new man. We just went for a drink, Tan, that's all.'

'Yeah, but for you that's like Elizabeth the First announcing her engagement! Come on, tell all, what's he like?'

'He's nice.'

'Nice!' she exclaims in horror. 'Nice! Please don't use that word, Ollie, or I might think you're going down the same sorry path as our poor Grace.'

'No! Not that sort of nice!' I hurry to reassure her. 'You'd like Finn, he's a laugh.'

'Oh well, thank heavens for that.'

'Anyway,' I cut in urgently, 'I've got something far more important than that to talk to you about . . .'

'Yeah sorry, babe . . . carry on.'

'Well like I said, I . . . well Finn and I . . . think we've come up with a way of making enough money to cover the rent increase.'

'You're going with my idea of selling your body?' she quips.

'Hardly, I don't think two pounds fifty is going to get me very far, do you?' I joke. 'Nope. I've come up with a much

129

better idea. I'm going to start utilising the assets I already have to a greater advantage,' I tell her, echoing Finn's wise words.

'So you *are* going to sell your body.'

'Tanya, get out of the gutter, I'm talking about the restaurant. I'm going to start opening for breakfasts.'

She pauses for a moment, chewing thoughtfully on a forkful of potato and cabbage. 'Are you sure that'll be cost effective?' she finally asks cautiously.

'I've sat down and gone through a few figures, and I really think it'll work. I don't need to get Claude in. I can do the cooking, which is good considering my labour's pretty much the only thing around here that's for free at the moment, and Louis said he could do with the extra shifts.'

'His novel's not going too well then?'

'Let's just say Armistead Maupin needn't worry just yet.'

'What about the music?'

'More Red Lion than Red Rock.'

'Acting?'

'Well, he's convinced *EastEnders* could do with another gay character, but he hasn't had the casting call just yet.'

'So in the meantime he's going to continue being the most talented waiter in London.'

'Yeah, and he's promised not to sing to every customer that he thinks could possibly be a talent scout for EMI.'

'And no more breaking into Hamlet whilst he's serving. It really puts you off your lunch when he does "Alas poor Yorick" with half a Cantaloupe, especially when he follows it with a stabbing scene with a steak knife and fruits of the forest sauce – all those lumpy red bits . . . ugh!' Tanya shudders.

'You think that's bad? Have you ever seen him doing *Watership Down* with the floor mop and a packet of chocolate raisins?'

'No, please, don't!' Tanya covers her face with a hand.

'Fortunately he restricts that one to the kitchen! Anyway, what do you think?'

'To what?'

'My idea, breakfast.'

She shakes her head. 'Sorry, I'm still struggling with visions of Louis with a mop head rammed between his buttocks! Sounds great, babe,' she says not very convincingly, 'if you're sure you can cope with the workload.'

'I'll have to, won't I? It's either that or close, and there's no way I'm going to let that bastard Dan Slater beat me.'

'I wouldn't mind letting him beat me . . .' Tanya muses with a far-off look in her eyes. 'Nice bit of soggy celery, handcuffs, maybe some leather . . . I'd go for a blindfold too, but I think I'd rather look at what he has to offer . . .'

Unfortunately not everyone is as enthusiastic about my idea as Finn, Louis, and Tanya.

'You're going to do what?' Grace shrieks indignantly.

It's Tuesday afternoon, just after the lunchtime shift, and Grace and I are sitting in the restaurant kitchen flicking through some brochures containing several pages of frills and chills masquerading as bridesmaid outfits.

'Anybody would think I'd just told you I'm going to turn Tates into a lap-dancing club,' I grumble, flicking quickly past a disgusting ice-pink ensemble that would give even the most dedicated seventies' fan a heart attack.

'You may as well do that from the good this is going to do you, Ollie. You've spent ages building up your reputation, and now you want to send it all down the plughole by turning the place into a Greasy Spoon!'

'If it wasn't for your awful friend Dan Dastardly, I wouldn't even have to be contemplating it,' I snap.

'Dan? Dan wouldn't deal with something of this level.'

'Oh, I'm far too lowly for Mr High and Mighty, am I? Well, in that case why does he keep coming into the restaurant to eat then? I call that pretty hands on, don't you? Doesn't pay someone to come in and harass me, just comes and does it himself.'

'Dan eats in here?'

'Don't sound so bloody surprised, after all we do have rather a good reputation,' I mock her. 'Good enough even for somebody as far above me as Daniel bloody Slater.'

'You know I didn't mean it like that, darling.' Gray refuses to rise to this one, merely looks thoughtful for a moment, and then smiles enigmatically.

'What are you grinning about?' I mutter grumpily.

'I've just had the most amusing thought.'

'I'm glad somebody manages to find this situation amusing.'

She raises her eyebrows at me.

131

'Okay, okay, so why do you think Demon Dan has suddenly taken to filling his face in my restaurant, if it's not some part of his fiendish plot to get me out?'

Gray continues to look Mona Lisa'esque.

'Come on!' I chide her. 'Spit it out.'

'Well . . .' she finally admits, looking coyly at me. 'Perhaps he fancies you.'

'Fancies me!' I splutter. 'Yeah, and I'm going to dance naked at your wedding!' I reply sarcastically.

'That's not so implausible,' the Mona Lisa smile slides into a huge grin, 'depending on how much champagne you manage to sink when I'm not watching!'

'Don't start that one again, Gray, I had enough of it the other night. You've got no excuse now you're sober. Daniel Slater fancying me is about as likely as me giving up this place without a fight,' I tell her, glad I never mentioned the 'kiss' episode.

'It makes sense to me: why else would he suddenly start eating here, and he *did* insist on taking you home . . .'

'I told you . . .'

'Oh for heaven's sake, Ollie, stop with the gunpowder, treason and plot, will you?'

'Well, it's more plausible than your latest theory.'

'I can't see how him providing you with extra custom is going to help, if his main aim is to drive you out of here. We've been out with Dan a few times and he really knows how to party.'

'Yeah, I can imagine,' I reply dryly.

'And why not,' Grace replies indulgently. 'He's single, solvent and totally sexy.'

'Blimey, Grace, you're a one-woman Daniel Slater fan club. Heaven knows what you're doing marrying Stuart . . .'

'Making myself a very happy woman,' Grace replies smugly. 'Perhaps I should wave my Cupid's wand in yours and Dan's direction, and we could make it a double wedding.'

Grace ducks as I throw a packet of bacon at her – hard. 'Talk about adding insult to injury,' I mutter, retrieving the rashers from the box of sliced white they fell into. 'Anyway Cupid doesn't have a wand, he has a bow, which is far more lethal. You can aim an *arrow* straight for Dan Dastardly's heart if you want to, as long as it's a *really* sharp one.'

'I'm being serious here, babe. I think it's quite plausible that he eats in here because he likes *you* as well as the food.'

'Great, he can just add me to his list then, can't he? Another number in a not-so-little black book. Right below miserable Miranda the boot-faced bottle blonde . . .'

'The list isn't that long,' Grace counters, ignoring my jibe about Miranda. 'I just don't think he's found the right woman yet.'

'Try telling that to Miranda.'

'Just because *she* thinks she's the right woman, doesn't mean Dan has the same opinion.'

'I can imagine the right woman for Dan Slater would be pretty hard to find.'

'Yeah,' muses Gray, missing the sarcasm completely. 'She'd have to be pretty special.'

'She'd have to be a saint.'

'She'd have to be very attractive. You're very attractive, you know.'

'Ooh, I know,' I mock. 'Lard does wonders for your complexion.'

'She'd have to be bright. Funny. Interesting. Independent. Maybe run her own business . . .'

'Stop hinting, Grace, it's all in your head. Besides, if it's up to Dan Slater, I won't be running my own business for very much longer now, will I?'

'Look, I'm pretty sure that Dan wouldn't actually *personally* have anything to do with this, but if you want, I could ask Stuart to have a word . . .'

'Don't you dare,' I warn her. 'I can fight my own battles, thank you.'

'What, with eight pounds of bacon, and twelve sliced loaves?'

'Don't knock it, this is the key to my future financial stability.'

'You're seriously going to do this, aren't you?'

'Yep,' I reply firmly.

'I must admit I admire your determination, but honestly, Ol, bacon and eggs . . . it's hardly haute cuisine.'

'I'll just have to make it the *new* haute cuisine then, won't I? I'll become renowned throughout London for my smiley faces made of two eggs and a curling bacon rasher. Joking apart, Grace, I don't care if it is junk food, as long as it gives me the chance to carry on trading.'

'Are things really that bad?'

'They will be when my rent goes up,' I admit. 'I need to do something drastic, and this is it.'

Grace takes my hand and squeezes it gently. 'Well, in that case I really hope it works for you.'

'Me too, babe. Me too.'

'Now!' She lets go of my hand, and, smiling broadly, picks up her open bridesmaid dress brochure. 'We had better get on and choose you and Tan a dress or you *will* be dancing naked at my wedding!'

Chapter Six

The kitchen door swings open, and Tanya's immaculately coiffured head pops round. 'Helloooo,' she purrs, smiling broadly. 'I came down to see how you were going on your first day as a "Caff", you know, maybe buy a bowl of muesli to show my support, but judging by the crowd out there you don't need it.'

'I am the Queen of Grease,' I grin, waving a spatula at her. 'I think I might change the name from Tates to Travolta's! Olivia Newton John. Olivia Bacon Bun.'

Tanya heads over and hugs me hard, risking exposing her gorgeous Gucci jacket to a whole host of stain-making substances, like bacon fat and bean juice. 'To be honest, babe, I didn't think there'd be much call for a greasy spoon round here.'

'Are you kidding, I've had entire dance classes from the school round the corner sneaking in for full English! I should just sod the original menu and offer bacon and eggs all day. The good old English fry-up. Who ever thought it could become the new haute cuisine,' I crow, thinking back to my conversation with a less-than-enthusiastic Grace.

'I must admit I did have my doubts,' Tanya grins. 'But I'm glad I was wrong.'

'Don't worry, babe, Grace didn't think it was such a great idea either, it's just she was more vocal about her concerns!'

'Talking about Grace, which I know we weren't really, but we should . . . I mean, I know you've had a lot on your plate recently . . . pardon the pun,' she adds, as I flip fried eggs, sunny side up, onto a plate already loaded with bacon, and mushrooms. 'But this bloody wedding's getting closer by the day, and she still seems set to go through with it.'

'So what are you saying?'

'We need to step up the campaign. Nothing we've tried so far has worked, has it?'

'Perhaps that should tell us something?'

'Yeah, like it's time to do something drastic.'

'Yeah, like leave them alone. I'm rapidly coming to the conclusion that if Grace is happy, then we shouldn't mess with her life.'

'Do you think she's happy?'

'She thinks she is, isn't that what counts?'

'Sure, until two weeks after the wedding, when she realises she's just pledged to spend the rest of her life with a boring moron.'

'Well, when you put it like that . . . Got any suggestions?'

'As Matron of Dishonour, and Chief Old Maid, we're duty bound to arrange her hen night.'

'Tanya! If we don't want her to go through with this wedding, the last thing we should be doing is encouraging her by arranging a bloody hen night!'

'I know, but I think it's a really good excuse to drag her out on a major-league man hunt, not that she'd know it was a man hunt of course.'

'I suppose so,' I shrug. 'What do you suggest?'

'I was hoping you might have some ideas on that one.'

'You're supposed to be the ideas girl.'

Tanya chews on her bottom lip. I can almost hear her brain ticking away as she thinks. 'How about a weekend away?' she finally suggests. 'A girlie weekend where the aim is to pub, club and man hunt till we drop?'

'Good idea. Where to?'

'I don't know . . . what about Blackpool? One of the girls from work had her hen night there and she said it was five blokes to every girl.'

'Yeah, a load of drunken arseholes in kiss-me-quick hats . . . really tantalising.'

'What do you have in mind then?'

'Something a little bit more romantic maybe?'

'Bognor?' Tanya asks sarcastically.

'Rome,' I reply.

'Italy?'

'Well, that's where it was the last time I looked, yeah.'

Tanya suddenly brightens perceptibly. 'Ooh, Italian men.

Italian shoes. Italian handbags. Italian clothes,' she breathes, her excitement mounting with each exclamation.

'I take it you approve then.'

'Approve! I'm going home to pack!'

Half an hour later, another head pops round the door of my kitchen.

'How's it going?' Finn's friendly handsome face beams broadly at me, not seeming to notice that his usually immaculate hair is flopping over his forehead and obscuring the vision of his left eye.

'Absolutely brilliant.' I stop washing mushrooms to give him a slightly soggy embrace. 'You're a wonderful man. In fact you're just in time for a full English, on the house.'

'I'd love to,' Finn grins, removing a piece of loose grey mushroom skin from the shoulder of his pale-blue Ben Sherman shirt, 'but you'll be pleased to know you haven't actually got any free tables out there. Even the pavement ones are taken, and it's not exactly warm today. I know, seeing as you're wonderfully busy at the moment, how about I take you out for a drink one night instead, to celebrate?'

'I've got a better idea. How about I take *you* out for a drink to say thank you. This was your idea after all.'

'Not so much my idea . . . I just planted the seed. You've done all the hard work.'

'Why don't we go the whole hog and do dinner, and then we can congratulate each other.'

Mel rolls her eyes. 'The Finn-and-Ollie self-appreciation club. Great.'

'Sounds great,' he replies, sticking his tongue out at Mel. 'How about tonight?'

'I can't, I'm working.'

'Tomorrow?'

'The same.'

'Thursday?'

'Take a guess.'

'Friday?'

My apologetic smile says it all.

'Are there any nights when you don't work?'

'Yeah sure . . . about twice a month, and Tanya's booked them all out for the next four months. I know, why don't you come here? I think I can get away with a night off if I'm not actually off the premises, if you know what I mean. Then I'll sort of officially be at work if there are any problems.'

'It's hardly getting away from things . . .'

'The food's really good . . .' I tempt him. 'And I can guarantee you'll get the best table in the house. There's even after-hours drinking if the owner's in a good mood . . .'

He pauses for a moment, and then smiles broadly. 'Okay, you're on. As long as you promise you won't end up spending all night in the kitchen, whilst I'm stuck out in the restaurant on my tod.'

'If that happens I promise I'll send Mel and a bottle of Bolly out to keep you company,' I offer.

'It's a deal!'

Mel blushes furiously as Finn winks broadly at her. 'So which night?'

'Is Thursday any good for you? I don't think we've got too many bookings yet.'

'It's a date.'

'Ooh, it's a *date*,' Mel mocks me, after Finn has gone. 'Can you remember what one of those is, Ollie? No, hang on a mo, you had one with him the other week, didn't you, so officially speaking this is a *second* date. My god, Ollie's going on a second date, does this mean . . . no, it can't be . . . you can't actually be having a *relationship* . . .' She pretends to faint into one of the kitchen chairs.

'Put a sock in it,' I tell her good-naturedly. 'We're just mates.'

'That's the oldest line in the book. We're just friends honest, guv . . . as if!'

'It may be a line, but in this case it's true,' I insist.

Despite Mel's disbelief, it is true. Finn is great. Perhaps a bit too perfect for me. Any man who spends longer than I do in the bathroom concerns me. However, he's totally gorgeous to look at, great fun to be with, kind, considerate, intelligent, but as for sexy . . . well, yes, he is. Undeniably so. But is it *my* kind of sexy? I don't know. We get on really really well, but has he got the 'It' that I'm looking for. Unfortunately it's one of those 'Its' where even I don't know what it is until I find it. So how do I know if he has 'It' or not if I don't know what it is I'm looking for? I'm afraid that he probably hasn't got 'It' because I think if he had I wouldn't be wondering whether he had or not, I'd know. Confused? Don't worry. So am I, but there's a strange kind of feminine logic in there somewhere.

It's kind of scary that the feelings most resembling desire that have been stirred up in me recently were caused by something I'm trying to pretend didn't happen.

That kiss.

You may remember the one in question. Yes, I may have been pissed and on the point of passing out, but not before I felt a wave of hot lust flush through my entire body. No, I was NOT going to admit this to Tanya, even if my very life depended on it. That kiss sparked off a whole riot of emotions, but amidst the horror, confusion, repulsion even, there was undeniably a huge spark of attraction. In fact it was more than a spark, it was a great big spitting Catherine Wheel, which still turns somersaults in my stomach whenever I think about it.

Dan Slater is arrogant, rude, insufferable, insolent, a complete and utter Sod with a capital S, but as for sexy . . . somebody wipe me down with a dry cloth, I think I'm drooling. Unfortunately, he makes me feel really insecure about myself. That's not good. If I had a relationship with someone like Dan, I'd spend the rest of my life fighting off the legions of women who throw themselves under his size eights. Anyway, what am I going on about? A relationship with Dan Slater? The only relationship I have with Dan Slater is mutual hate. It would make life so much easier if I didn't fancy the pants off the man.

Oh my goodness, I've finally admitted it to myself. I fancy Dan Slater. Badly.

Ollie Tate, drama junkie, if things were easy I wouldn't want them so much.

Thursday night rolls round faster than the Runaway Train at Disney World. Louis and Mel have insisted that Finn and I have the alcove table by Cupid, lying through their teeth when I protest, that this is the only table free in the restaurant this evening. When I make a show of checking the booking diary, I find that we have an awful lot of Smiths pencilled in at various 'specifically requested' tables, who I can almost certainly guarantee will be no shows.

139

Finn is a bit late, and I take this opportunity to make sure everything is set up in the kitchen, ready for an evening that should be as hassle free as possible.

I can hear Claude and Louis arguing as usual as I head toward the kitchen door, Claude's broad Scots accent echoing loudly enough to be heard above the soft music in the restaurant.

'Move your fat arse out ma way, ya fat fairy. Ai'm tryin' tae add ma Coq to the Vin!'

'We always knew you'd stick it in anything, you old Scotch tart, but that's a bit OTT, even for a total pervert,' Louis counters.

By the time I reach the kitchen ready to break it up, they're fighting Star-Wars style again. Louis as usual is Lukewarm Skywalker with a French stick as his light sabre, whilst Claude, his fat red cheeks wobbling as he parries, is a strange Totally Daft Vader in his chef's blue-check trousers and white button-through tunic, wheezing heavily from a fifty-a-day Benson and Hedges habit, and wielding a massive salami as his meaty weapon. One salami lunge later, and Louis's French stick is in two pieces.

'Ah always said a man with a huge pork sword wins over a man with a lot of bread any day,' Claude quips.

Louis looks forlornly at the small bread roll he's left clutching.

'Use the forcemeat, Lukewarm,' Claude rasps in his best Alec Guinness impression, waving his salami challengingly at Louis.

With a huge demonic grin Louis picks up a bowl of sausage-meat and stuffing and launches the contents straight at Claude's head. Claude swings with his salami like Babe Ruth at the height of the season.

'Quick, duck!' Louis yells, spotting me in the doorway. 'Uncooked Flying Offal heading your way.'

Claude's salami connects with the ball of meat, and the whole thing explodes on contact like the Death Star at the end of *Star Wars – The Movie*.

'Children!' sighs Mel, who's just come through the door, peering over my shoulder at the resulting mess. 'Don't worry, Ollie, I'll play nanny whilst you get to relax and have dinner with a handsome man . . .' She pushes past me, tutting loudly at Claude as she bends down to clear splattered sausage meat off the kitchen floor. 'Can't you ever behave like an adult?' she sighs.

'Ah know, ah've bin a very bad boy, hen, haven't ah? Here, take this . . .' He hands her his industrial-size spatula, and turning, bends and braces against the kitchen table. 'Ah'm ready for ma punishment . . .'

Finn arrives at eight-fifteen, looking and smelling absolutely gorgeous. Hair as carefully dishevelled as usual, green eyes sparkling with pleasure as he greets me with a kiss to each cheek, much to the amusement of the other two, who are hovering in the background, as close by as possible without being totally obtrusive.

Unfortunately, when I take him over to our table I find that Mel and Louis have taken advantage of my time in the kitchen and have really gone to town to make sure that Snoggers Corner is even more conducive to love than usual; in fact so much so, it could now easily be re-christened Bonkers Corner.

I nearly die of embarrassment as I spot the extra candles on the table and window ledge, and the small glass vase of red roses that Louis and Mel have also placed there, even sprinkling pink rose-petal confetti all over the wooden surface of the table, and replacing the usual Tates match book with a packet of three.

Gesturing for Finn to sit down, I quickly remove the trendily tacky red-plastic heart-shaped napkin rings that Louis has also added, and sweep most of the confetti onto the floor, whilst Finn looks on in amusement.

'Honestly, you just can't get the staff these days,' I say dryly, and quite loudly, pretty sure that the two 'staff' in question are earwigging. They almost had a stand-up fight earlier over who was going to serve us this evening, until they made a pact to have a mutual eavesdropping session and update each other on all gossip.

Giving them as little opportunity to come to the table as possible, I've already placed the menus, an open bottle of red, and a bottle of good white in an ice bucket on the table. Along with a corkscrew, and fresh rolls and butter, this cuts out at least four opportunities for either of them to wait on our table.

'You'll have to forgive me if I fall asleep on you,' I apologise

141

to Finn, pouring him a glass of red wine. 'These early mornings are killing me!'

'I won't forgive you at all,' Finn laughs. 'I'll take it as a total insult, and assume that you find me completely boring.'

'Considering you fell asleep on me at Grace's dinner party, I'd say it was only fair.'

'I did wait until you'd left the room,' Finn counters.

Mel, who obviously won the toss on this one, arrives somewhat prematurely to take our orders. We've only been sitting down for about two minutes, but her curiosity is too much for her. 'What can I get you?' she chirps cheerfully, winking heavily and far too noticeably at me.

Finn, who despite my hurry to clear the table has noted *all* of the extra touches, and the over-attentive waiting staff, winks at me too, but Mel doesn't see. 'Well,' he drawls, leaning back in his chair, and picking up the menu. I've seen that look on his face before, just as he was about to slide off the sofa at Grace's party and make his one-man assault on the stereo system. 'I think I'd like the *oysters*, followed by steak, *rare*,' he almost growls this last word. 'No potatoes, thanks, don't want to get *love* handles. Salad but absolutely *no onions*. Then for dessert I think it has to be the *passion* fruit torte, with *passion* fruit coulis.'

Mel's face is a picture.

'Do you think that worked?' he laughs, as soon as I've placed my order and Mel has scuttled back to the kitchen to tell all to a waiting Louis.

'Absolutely, our ears should be burning so hard we could grill your steak on them.'

'Mean, aren't I?'

'No. It serves them right. Besides I think you might have made their evening.'

'There's only one problem.'

'What's that then?'

'I don't like oysters.'

'You're kidding.'

'Afraid not. I hate them! I won't even try to describe what I think it feels like you're swallowing. Ugh.' He shudders at the thought.

'Don't worry, you can share my prawns.'

142

'That'll be food for gossip, pardon the pun. Can I share your chips too? I love chips.'

When the starters arrive, we hide the oysters in the miniature orange tree sitting on the window ledge, and then take great delight in peeling and feeding each other my starter of Tiger prawns as lasciviously as possible, with much suggestive sucking of fingers, and lip licking every time we catch one of them looking our way.

This is one night when I'm pleased the restaurant is fairly quiet. As I guessed, not one of the entire Smith clan apparently booked in for this evening has shown and so far we've had an uninterrupted evening. Well, if you don't count Louis's and Mel's frequent attempts to sidle past nonchalantly in order to check out the action. Not that there's been any action for them to check out. Only the fake stuff put on for their benefit.

They haven't had an excuse to come over since serving us our main course, and Louis is hovering behind us like an anxious bluebottle stuck behind window glass. 'Is everything okay?'

'Fine, thank you.'

'Yeah, absolutely great,' agrees Finn. 'I'm impressed.' Although the implication is that he's impressed with the food, Finn makes sure that it's me he's looking at as he says this to Louis.

It doesn't go unnoticed. Louis winks heavily at me in excitement. I ignore him.

'Can I get you anything?'

'No, thank you,' I reply shortly.

'More wine perhaps?'

'We still have plenty, *as you can see*.' I glare at him, motioning with my eyeballs for him to go away.

Louis grins cheekily, but leaves as bid.

'Honestly!' I turn back to Finn. 'Are your friends quite so nosy? I'm lucky Tanya's date had theatre tickets tonight, otherwise I'd have found her and this evening's man waving at us from the next table.'

'Tanya?'

'Oh, of course, you didn't meet her, did you? She would have come to Grace's dinner party but she was away. I'll have to introduce you, you'll love her. She's quite like you actually.'

143

'What totally gorgeous, but slightly insane.'

'Right on both counts . . . but I think you beat her on the second,' I tease him.

Finn sticks his tongue out at me, before picking up the third-full bottle of Burgundy, and reaching over to refill my almost empty wineglass.

I put my hand over my glass. 'No more for me, thanks. Red wine always makes me sleepy, and I don't need any extra help this evening.'

'And I thought I was being scintillating company,' he jokes again.

As Finn fills his own glass, my eyes wander out of the window. It's been a beautiful day, and this has now turned into quite a balmy evening. It's still almost light, a mid- to dark-blue sky stretching above the London skyline, with just a few wisps of cloud meandering slowly across it. The birds that nest in the thick lilac that clings to the courtyard wall are still singing, fooled into thinking that night hasn't yet fallen by the light filtering from the restaurant windows. There's one noise missing though. It's only then that I realise that the little fountain is switched off, and I can't hear the usual melodious sound of running water. Looking around, I realise that Cupid would find it a little difficult to be taking his usual well-aimed pee, in the get-up that he is currently sporting.

This includes a party hat, a party blower, a condom on the correct part of his anatomy to be wearing this kind of item (that part from which the fountains usually gushes in case anyone needs any further description), and a little handwritten placard stating 'I'm in the mood for Love', thrust into his bow hand. This could only be the handiwork of Louis. He must have sneaked outside without us noticing. Probably sent Mel out to distract us whilst he set to work.

I can't help it, I start to snigger, almost choking on a mouthful of lambs lettuce. Finn follows my gaze, and catches sight of the recently re-equipped statuette.

'I'm going to kill Louis!' I tell him, pulling myself together with great difficulty.

To my relief his face too crumples with amusement. 'No, don't, that's brilliant! A definite improvement. You should leave him like that all the time.'

144

It's great to find someone with a similar sense of humour to mine.

Over the main course, which fortunately Finn actually ordered because he does like steak, we discover that we're both into Douglas Adams novels, Billy Connelly, Victoria Wood but only live, and we both absolutely adore Carry On films. I'm just telling Finn my favourite nun joke, knowing that he'll actually appreciate it sober, when the door to the restaurant is pushed open, and in walks Dan Slater.

I stop mid joke, and gaze open mouthed as an excited and fawning Mel stops trying to eavesdrop on us, and rushes over to show him and his companions to a table.

He's here again.

I don't believe it. Everywhere I turn, he's there. I can't even sleep without him popping into my dreams, usually in some highly disturbing manifestation. I recognise the two men with him. Tape-measure Man, and the other guy who was with them in the antiques shop. They've probably come to measure up! Well, if they dare to whip out a tape measure in here they'll be in for a big shock.

Finn's spotted them too. 'What on earth is he doing here?' he asks.

'My question exactly. You wouldn't believe the number of times he's come in here to eat since they bought out nearly all the buildings in the street.'

'Probably checking up on his investment.' Finn's craning to see who it is that Dan is seated with. 'I don't know him,' he says, surreptitiously gesturing towards Tape-measure Man, 'but that other guy's Rupert Lock. He's an architect.'

'How do you know him?'

'That's one of the things I was going to talk to you about tonight. I've been doing a little bit of digging for you. There are advantages to having a journalist for a friend, you know. Apart from the obvious. You know, charm, wit, devastating good looks . . .'

'And what did you find out?' I interrupt, laughing.

'I checked with the district council and they haven't applied for any planning permission as far as this place is concerned. What they have done however is bought the old warehouse at the end of the road. The one that was a lighting factory.'

'And?'

'And they've put in an application to alter it for domestic use – they want to convert it into six luxury apartments.'

'But nothing on Tates?'

'Not yet, no.'

'But what about all that business next door, when I saw them in the antiques shop?'

'Actually I checked on that too.'

'How?'

'Simple. I went in and asked what they were doing there.'

'And the owner told you?'

'Not at first, of course. But when I explained to him who they were, he was very helpful. He's worried about losing his livelihood too, you know. You're not the only one who's been asked to pay a higher rent.'

'Well?' I demand impatiently. 'What were they doing there?'

'They were buying a fireplace.'

'A fireplace!'

'Yep. Pretty impressive it is too. Apparently it's to go in some hideously expensive penthouse apartment in a Mayfair building that they're doing up at the moment. The guy in the shop gave me the delivery address and it all checks out.'

I suddenly feel myself turning the same shade of blush-pink as the rose-petal confetti which still litters the floor around our table, as I remember how I lambasted Dan Slater so publicly, after catching what was obviously only part of their conversation, and getting totally the wrong end of the stick.

'Oh my goodness.'

'What's the matter, Ollie? I would have thought that was good news so far.'

'Oh it is, of course it is, but . . .' I explain to Finn exactly what happened.

'Well, don't feel too bad,' he reassures me, when the whole sordid story is told, 'just because they haven't applied for planning permission yet, doesn't mean they won't. They actually stand more chance of achieving permission to change the use of this property if it's not still housing a thriving business. So there's every chance they're simply waiting until your existing lease ends, and hoping you can't cope with the rent increase of the new one.'

'You think so?'

'Of course I hope that's not the case, but you can't rule out the possibility, Ollie. You have to be prepared for it.'

'Well I am more so, thanks to you.'

'Breakfasts still going well?'

'As you know, it's only the first week, but if things carry on the way they are, I'll be able to cope with the rent increase, and you never know, we may get a little boost in profit too.' I raise my glass to him. 'Thanks to you,' I repeat, glancing sideways at Dan.

Finn smiles modestly. 'Glad to be of assistance. Anyway it would have come to you sooner or later. I just did the prompting.'

'How about we make this a proper celebration . . .' I look around for Louis or Mel, both of whom are hovering between my table and Dan Slater's table, neither quite knowing where the most interesting scenario lies. Louis is slightly quicker.

'Fetch me a bottle of champagne, Louis. Vintage!'

'Vintage, eh? What's the occasion?'

'Just celebrating the fact that there's a much stronger chance we'll all still have jobs this time next month. No thanks to some people!'

Did I say that loud enough for Dan Slater to hear? I certainly tried, but I don't know if it would have carried across the hum of voices, sounds of eating, cutlery against plates, glasses clinked together in toasts, and soft music. He might have heard me. He's watching me yet again with a disapproving look on his face as I noisily pop the cork, and with a huge happy grin on my face that's more to rile him than anything else, fill our glasses. Probably doesn't like me celebrating, as it may herald bad news for him and his dastardly plans!

Suppressing a very childish urge to stick my tongue out at him, I raise my champagne glass to Finn, and propose a toast. 'To the future!'

'To the future,' Finn echoes, taking a large swig of fizzy stuff.

I slide another surreptitious glance sideways at Dan Dastardly. He's still watching, and boy does he look pissed off.

Good.

I get this lovely warm glow, not from the champagne, but from knowing that it's me upsetting *him* for a change, instead of the other way round. Feeling rather magnanimous, and

147

also slightly tipsy, we send the rest of the champagne out to the kitchen for Louis, Mel and Claude to share our toast, and then share each other's puddings instead, Finn making sure that he gets the lion's share of both, until we're almost duelling with spoons. We then move onto coffee, fighting over the chocolate mints that come with it, despite the fact that, knowing how much I love them, Mel has given us over twice the amount that we'd normally get.

We round the evening off with two large brandies, which we nurse whilst chatting and laughing loudly, until the restaurant is nearly empty, save for ourselves, a young couple in the other alcove, and Dan and his companions.

'I'm completely stuffed,' I announce happily to Finn, leaning back in my chair and nursing my full stomach.

'Yeah, food's not bad here, is it?' he jokes.

'Probably because for once I'm not cooking. You know I nearly died of shock when Claude actually turned up for work tonight . . .'

'Well, I'm glad he did. Mel's as sexy as hell, but it wouldn't have been the same as having dinner with you.'

'Yeah, it's been great.'

'Can I walk you home?' asks Finn, with a slight laugh, knowing full well that home is five steps to the left of the kitchen door.

'Ooh.' I suck in air through my teeth in mock indecision. 'Let me think . . .' I pause for all of one second. 'Okay then.'

We slip away from the table whilst Louis and Mel are both out of view. Dan Slater looks up at me as I walk past and I could swear he almost smiles, then Finn slips his arm through mine, and raises his eyebrows in a silent greeting to Dan. The half-smile slips away, and he returns Finn's greeting with a brief nod, and then promptly turns away again. I normally go home via the kitchen, but in order to avoid the curious stares and the inevitable gossip, we leave like most normal customers, through the front door, and walk the length of the road until we come to the alley where we can cut through to the service road at the back of the street. This way if there's any further questioning, and I'd be happy to bet the entire restaurant that there will be, then I can insist that I was just walking Finn to his car, and any invitations to come in for coffee certainly weren't issued by me.

We're both silent until we get to my door, which Finn promptly leans against with his elbow, looking down at me, with a slightly amused expression on his face. 'Well, it's that time of the evening,' he tells me, as I fumble in my pocket for my front-door key.

'What time?'

'The one where I have to debate whether it's the right thing to kiss you goodnight or not.'

'You're not usually backwards in coming forwards,' I tease him, 'but I was actually going to ask you in for coffee.'

'I know, but I'm never one to miss a good patch of moonlight.'

Smiling, we lean together and kiss: the easiest and most comfortable first kiss I've ever experienced. Too comfortable even . . . I mean, I wasn't expecting fireworks, but . . . I pull away to see the same slightly puzzled expression on Finn's face that's on mine.

'Was it just me?' I ask him.

He shakes his head. 'How about you?'

I shake my head. 'Nothing. Absolutely nothing.'

'Not a flicker,' he agrees. Finn looks disappointed. 'Can we try that again?' he sighs. 'Just to make sure.'

I nod.

We kiss again.

My eyes flicker upwards toward the roof where my drains appear to be sprouting grass. I'm in the middle of a passionate embrace and all I can think about is that the guttering needs clearing? I pull my eyes away from the weeds sprouting in my plumbing, and turn my gaze back to Finn's face in the hope that the sight of his gorgeous Jude Law-esque features might just trigger some emotion.

Still nothing.

My gaze wanders over his shoulder, whilst Finn, obviously trying harder than me – a male pride thing I think – keeps his eyes doggedly shut, and gives me his best lip shot, sliding one hand up the back of my neck, until his fingers are lacing with my hair. He's a good kisser, I'll give him that, and my eyes are just sort of half closing, when they blink wide open. I'm sure I spot a black BMW driving slowly past the end of the alleyway.

No. Can't have been. I'm imagining things. My paranoia about Dan Slater is really getting out of hand. Back to the job in hand. Or rather the man in hand. I think the man in hand has given up though.

'How about that time?' I ask him, pulling away as his mouth finally gives up and stops moving.

He shakes his head again. 'Still nothing!'

'Me neither. It was like kissing my brother. Not that I'd kiss my brother,' I add hurriedly. 'Not on the lips anyway.'

'Don't worry, I know what you mean. I wouldn't kiss my brother either.'

It's not fair, the first man I meet in ages that I really like, and I don't fancy him. That was one hell of a kiss by anybody's standards, but my perverse hormones flatly refused to kick in.

There's only one thing for it. 'Friends?' I ask him.

'Friends,' he replies, taking my outstretched hand and shaking it.

'You can never have too many friends,' we chorus some-what flatly.

'Still want to come in for a coffee?'

Finn's face brightens a little. 'Do I get to watch *Carry on Camping*?' he asks hopefully.

'Damn right you do.'

'And can I freeze-frame the bit where Bab's bra springs off?'

'As many times as you want.'

'Then lead the way.'

Tanya's round first thing the next morning for a full rundown of what she's entitled the 'Hot Date'.

'So how did it go?' she demands, pinching some toast I'd just made for a customer and sitting down at the table with a cup of tea and a pot of lime marmalade.

'It was nice; we had a good time,' I reply guardedly.

'Nice?' she spits. 'Good? Don't start that again.' Ignoring the butter, she dollops a huge knifeful of marmalade onto her granary toast, and spreads it thickly. 'We've had enough of nice with Stuart with a U. So, did you invite him upstairs for coffee then?'

'Yep.'

'Really!'

'Don't get too excited. We stayed up until four watching Carry On films, and then he fell asleep on the sofa.'

'Is that it?'

150

'That's it, I'm afraid.'

'You sound a bit disappointed?'

'I am a bit. He's lovely, and we get on really well but, don't ask me why, there's just no romantic spark. We're really good mates but that's it. In fact he reminds me of you a little bit, apart from the obvious differences.'

'Don't tell me, apart from anatomical, he's not a total tart?'

'You got it.'

'What time did he leave?'

'He hasn't yet.'

'What!' The toast Tanya was steering toward her mouth is dropped back onto the plate.

'He's in the restaurant having breakfast. He was going to eat it in here, but I needed the table space,' I tell her pointedly.

'He's still here and you haven't introduced me!'

'I haven't got the time! Or the inclination,' I add teasingly.

Tanya gathers up her toast, and the marmalade jar. 'Which table? If you won't introduce me, then I'll just have to introduce myself, won't I?'

'I can't believe you have to make an appointment to try on dresses,' I mutter, as Grace ushers us excitedly through the doors of a disgustingly exclusive bridalwear shop.

Tanya's looking pretty fearful. I suppose for her, going into a bridal shop is a bit like an escaped prisoner strolling around a police station open day.

I must admit this isn't my chosen way of spending one of my precious days off either, especially as ten minutes after entering the shop, I'm squeezing myself into three acres of what the large jolly shop assistant optimistically labelled the 'terracotta' taffeta that Grace has apparently chosen.

'This isn't terracotta, it's orange,' Tanya hisses in the huge changing room. 'I look like a blancmange,' she mutters through closed teeth, her red face, as she emerges hot and bothered through the scooped neckline, clashing furiously with the material. 'A big, fat, *orange* wobbly hideous blancmange.'

'We're here as a foil for the bride,' I tell her, trying to remain calm myself as I catch sight of my equally terrifying Uh-Oh-You've-been-Tangoed image in the huge mirror. 'Although I must admit we do look rather as if we're wearing outsize sixties lampshades, we have to remember the main job of the bridesmaids is to make the bride look good.'

'We'd make Lily Savage look good dressed like this.'

'Smile,' I warn her, as we push through the heavy velvet curtain back into the main body of the shop. 'If this is what Grace wants, this is what Grace gets.'

'With any luck she'll be bringing them back to the shop for a refund pretty soon,' Tanya hisses.

'Amen,' I reply.

We step out to face a waiting Grace with two matching fixed grins on our faces.

'Oh, I say!' Grace exclaims. 'You look . . . fabulous! Absolutely perfect! Give us a twirl.'

Tanya and I reluctantly do a shuffled pirouette, only to realise that Grace is sitting behind us sipping a complimentary coffee and trying extremely hard not to burst into paroxysms of raucous laughter.

'You cow!' I scream, as I realise that we've been set up.

'I'm sorry, I just couldn't resist it,' she howls, slopping coffee onto the red velvet upholstered seat she's perched on. 'Your faces! I wish you could see your faces! You honestly thought I was going to make you wear those hideous things, didn't you?' Grace is practically rolling on the floor in amusement. She'd better not roll too close, I might kick her.

'Ha, bloody, ha!' exclaims Tanya, reaching behind her and beginning rather viciously to unhook the eyes of the bodice.

'These definitely aren't the ones?' I ask fearfully, before starting to wriggle out of my nightmare as well.

'Do you honestly think I'd make you wear something like that,' Grace giggles. 'No, the real ones are tons better, and *sooo* unusual. You know, I never knew you could get bridesmaid dresses in brown plaid . . .' She laughs again at our equally horrified faces. 'No, you don't fancy that . . . well how about the Little Bo-Peep look? You'd look so cute in the bonnets, and it would be so easy to accessorise too, there are plenty of sheep in Leicestershire!'

Chapter Seven

'Passport?'

'Check.'

'Suitcase with suitably sexy clothes, no skirts below crotch length allowed?'

'Check.'

'Plane tickets?'

'Check.'

'Great! Now all we need is the victim herself.'

August has arrived, and finally so has the sunshine. The forecast for the weekend is excellent; ironic really, because this is the weekend that unbeknownst to Stuffy Stu with a U, we're spiriting Grace out of the country. It's Friday afternoon, and Louis and I are going through the last minute details, before our nine p.m. flight.

'I've arranged to pick her up from her office at six-thirty. She thinks we're coming back here to change, and then we're going clubbing,' I tell him, stowing Grace's and my tickets safely into my huge leather handbag.

'She thinks we're going clubbing?' he laughs nervously.

'What else was I supposed to tell her? If I'd told her what we're really doing, she might have come up with an excuse not to come. It is kind of tradition to whisk the bride away on a surprise hen night.'

'What are we going to do to get her through the airport then? Drug her like BA out of *The A Team*?'

'I thought we could blindfold her.'

'Oh right, yeah,' Louis replies sarcastically. 'Bing bong, this is the last call for Flight Number 6969 to Rome for all brides-to-be who are hopefully going to be seduced into dumping their boring fiancés . . .'

'Ear plugs?' I suggest weakly.

'I think we'll just have to hope that when we hit the airport, she'll be pleased,' Louis says, as if he doesn't actually believe this could happen.

'Do you think she will?'

'Well, we told her where we were going was a surprise and she seemed quite happy about that.'

'I know, but she probably didn't think we meant out of the country.'

I had been despatched to Grace's house to surreptitiously pack a suitcase for her, picking a night when we knew she was up in Leicestershire with Stuffy. I took the opportunity to fill it with all of her old bum huggers and crotch brushers. I'm sure she hasn't noticed that they're missing. The most risqué thing she's worn recently was an above-the-knee skirt.

I'm outside Grace's office building by five-thirty on the Friday evening. She doesn't actually finish until six, but I'm not taking any chances. As soon as she puts one toe of her Faith courts out of the revolving glass door, I'm manhandling her into my car and whisking her away. From what I can gather, old Stuffy wasn't too happy about her heading out on what has been billed as a night of drunken debauchery in celebration of her forthcoming nuptials. I wouldn't put it past him to make a last-minute attempt to lure her up to his place instead.

Grace comes out of the building at ten past six, and falls wearily into my car. She looks tired, and confesses that all she'd really like to do this evening is head home for a hot bath and an early night.

Great start. The only good bit is that she has her eyes closed for the first fifteen minutes of the journey and by the time she opens them we're well on our way. 'This isn't the way back to Tates,' she ventures, taking in her surroundings.

'I know.'

'Why isn't this the way back to Tates?' Grace asks tiredly.

'Because we're not going back to Tates.' I grin at her kind of inanely.

'Ollie, what's going on?'

I smile briefly at her again, and indicating, take a left turn.

'Ollie!' she demands again, suddenly looking far more awake.

'It's your hen night, babe.'

'Well, I know that, don't I?'

'So we're throwing you a surprise party.'

'Oh right. So if it's a surprise, should you have just told me about it?'

'Trust me, babe, you'll still be surprised.'

'That's what I'm worried about!'

Making our way slowly through the Friday late-afternoon traffic, we finally arrive in Mayfair. I pull into the no-parking zone outside Tanya's flat, where my car and I are regular visitors, and honk my horn. For the first time ever, Tanya is totally organised, and I don't have to wait half an hour for her to appear. She totters out of the front door on the most ridiculously high pair of Manolos, closely followed by Louis, who, despite the warmth of the evening, looks like a gorgeous little teddy bear in a fake-fur coat. We had the foresight to put their luggage in my boot the night before, so as not to give Grace any clues that we're about to leave the country, but the fact that Louis is also sporting an old-fashioned leather flying helmet is a little bit of a giveaway! Fortunately Grace is so used to his eccentric dress code, it doesn't even register.

When we finally hit the M4, and an increasing number of signs for Heathrow, however, Grace works it out. 'We're going away, aren't we?' she asks a touch apprehensively. Nobody answers her. 'We are, aren't we? Where on earth are we going?'

Tanya, Louis and I share a look, and an enigmatic smile.

'Oh come on, you guys, you've got to tell me where we're going!'

'No way.' Louis sticks his tongue out at her.

'It wouldn't be a surprise then, would it?' adds Tanya.

'What about clothes? I haven't got anything with me.'

'All in hand,' I grin, picking up Grace's house keys from the centre console and rattling them at her.

'What about Stuart?'

'He can't come!' Louis replies quickly.

'That's not what I meant and you know it. He thinks I'm just going out for the evening, he's expecting me home about midnight, he'll be waiting in Islington for me.'

'Okay, okay,' I tell her as her voice rises in panic. 'You get one phone call to tell him you won't be back tonight, all right?'

'Can't I at least tell him when I *will* be back? It's only fair, otherwise he'll worry.'

Despite her voiced misgivings, I can see that Gray is actually kind of thrilled, in a petrified sort of fashion. I recognise that old light in her eyes, and even though her voice is getting pretty high-pitched, I'd bet a week's takings that it's mainly through excitement rather than agitation. I hand her my mobile. 'Tell him you'll be back on Sunday . . . VERY late.'

'Sunday!' Grace exclaims.

I wink heavily at her, relieved that she doesn't instantly demand that we stop the car, turn around, and take her home, but simply punches in her own home number. I recognise the tone in Stuart's voice, especially as he's loud enough for not only Grace to hear him, but the rest of us as well.

'He didn't sound too happy,' I say to her when she hands back my phone.

'Just a little concerned, but I told him you'd look after me.'

'Of course we will!' Louis puts a reassuring arm around her shoulders. 'When we're conscious.'

Once in the departure lounge, we manage to blinker Grace enough to get on the plane without her actually knowing exactly where we're going. It's hard, but Tanya and the tantalisingly off-limits Duty Free shopping prove a pretty major distraction.

'So, now are you going to tell me where we're going?' she finally asks again, when we're boarded and in our seats.

We all hesitate.

'Look, I'm on the plane, the doors are shut, and we're taxiing down the runway. What can I do about it anymore?'

'Well . . .' Tanya begins.

'Don't you think that the fact that the plane had AlItalia written in huge letters on the side was just a bit of a giveaway?' I cut in, teasing her.

'Italy!' Grace shrieks. 'We're going to Italy!'

As if on cue the pilot's heavily accented voice cuts across the cabin. 'Good evening, everybody, and welcome to Flight 102 to Rome . . .'

Grace's shriek of excitement drowns out the rest of his announcement. 'Rome, oh my God! I've always wanted to go to Rome! But you knew that, didn't you, babe? Oh, thank you, thank you, thank you!' she shrieks, pressing her call button for the steward. 'Vodka!' she tells him when he hurries down the aisle to find out what the pre-takeoff problem is. 'Lots of vodka to say thank you. Ooh, what are we going to do first; I want to go to the Viale Vaticano, The Pantheon, all of the Gallerias.'

'Are they night clubs?' Tanya asks, smiling at Grace's enthusiasm.

'No, they're culture,' Louis replies dryly.

'Oh dear.'

It's well after midnight when we finally arrive at the Hotel Vincenzi, which Louis instantly, and somewhat hopefully I think, re-christens as the Hotel SinSexy. The air is warm and still, and heavy with the unusual and exotic aroma of a foreign country. The hotel itself is gorgeous: an imposing baroque palace built several hundred years ago, for some minor Italian Popette-type person. Tanya and Louis are a little disappointed to find that I've booked us inter-connecting twin rooms, which according to them is great fun for a midnight dorm fest, but not exactly practical for pulling. Grace and I are in one room, and Louis and Tanya in the next. Grace staggers sleepily into the en-suite bathroom, whilst I begin to unpack her case before she can spot exactly what kind of clothes were packed for her.

'Right,' I whisper to the other two, who have both perfected speed unpacking, and are now lounging on my bed watching me hang up the clothes from my one overnight bag, 'we've got two days to get her drunk . . .'

'And get her laid . . .' cuts in Louis a trifle too loudly, beaming broadly.

'That wasn't quite what I had in mind.'

'It wasn't?' The other two look at me wide eyed and disbelieving.

'Oh, all right, so maybe that idea *had* floated through my imagination for just a micro second. But I thought we were trying to open her eyes . . .'

'And not her legs,' Louis giggles.

'Open her eyes . . .' I insist, '. . . to other er . . . possibilities.'

'You mean other men,' says Tanya.

'Exactly,' Louis agrees.

I silence the other two with a look as Grace emerges from the bathroom and, sitting down at the dressing table, starts to remove her make-up with a pink cottonwool ball and some Nivea.

'What are you doing?' Louis demands.

'Er . . . getting ready for bed?' Her reflection looks at him quizzically. 'Why?'

'You're kidding, aren't you?' he wails, leaping up from his prostrate position. 'The night is still young.'

'Maybe, but I'm not any more, I need my beauty sleep.'

'But I thought we could go out, hit the town. You know, when in Rome . . .'

'I'd imagine most normal Romans are in bed by now, so that's exactly where I'm going,' Grace announces. Stripping quickly, she slides into her single bed next to mine, pulling the covers up to her chin, and eyeing a disappointed Louis defiantly.

His bottom lip is trembling slightly. Louis the hardened clubber is ready for a weekend where sleep is the last thing on the agenda.

Grace is not to be swayed however. 'I need some sleep,' she states, as his bottom lip stops trembling, and begins to wobble as precariously as the Millennium Bridge in a high wind. As if to underline this statement she switches off the lamp on her bedside table. We all look at each other in disbelief. Give us back the old Grace and she would have been the one dragging us out to find an all-night bar.

'Oh and remind me to phone Stuart,' she murmurs, burrowing her head into the pillow. 'I promised I'd call when we got here but I think it's just a touch too late now, don't you?'

'Yeah, it's definitely too late now,' agrees Tanya, surreptitiously reaching for the phone cord which is plugged in next to my bed and pulling it loose. 'You wouldn't want to wake him up, would you?'

Louis wakes us up at six. I really wish I knew where he gets his energy. He's like an over-excited Labrador puppy on only four and a half hours of sleep. Whilst I'm wading to the bathroom with eyes like slits in the top of a piggy bank, he's running between the bedrooms chivvying us all on as if he's on speed.

By eight o'clock we're dressed, we've had breakfast in the beautifully ornate hotel restaurant, served to us by beautifully handsome Italian waiters that I was far too sleepy to appreciate, and we're in a taxi heading out for the first day in Rome. This is one hell of a way to wake up: both of the windows in the back of the car are down, and the driver is pretending he's Fittipaldi at the Italian Grand Prix.

'I really wish Stuart could see this. It is just *so* beautiful!' Grace is hanging out of one of the taxi windows gazing at the gorgeous architecture.

'Yeah . . . it's fantastic,' breathes Louis, who is hanging out of the other window, but certainly isn't looking at stonework. 'Cor, would you look at the arse on that!' He nearly gets whiplash as the mad taxi driver rounds a corner at breakneck speed.

'I'd love to look at both arses and architecture,' I reply dryly, 'but I can't see anything through the hair that's being blown into my face!'

With Grace begging for culture, Louis angling for a major man hunt, and Tanya flexing her Gold Card and muttering about leather every five seconds, we finally manage a compromise and, after a mad morning of sight-seeing and shopping combined, end up in a bar.

The first of many. Julius Caesar's follows. Then Big Mama's in the Trastevere. We finally end up three hours later, and kind of rolling, in Monte Testaccio, a haven of bars, restaurants and people, which Tanya immediately rechristens the Monte Testosterone for obvious reasons.

'So many men, so little time,' she breathes, rushing between bars like a kid in a sweet shop.

'I thought it was the Italian men who were supposed to run round pinching bottoms,' I say watching her.

'Well, you know how much Tanya's into sexual equality,' Grace grins.

Ten o'clock on a Saturday night, and we've somehow found our way into a sleazy bar cum nightclub, that Louis has insisted we enter because they sell Carlsberg, and at this stage in his drunkenness no other drink will do.

Grace is fretting about Stuart. 'I really should phone Stuart.

I tried from the room this morning, but the phone wasn't working for some reason.'

Tanya smiled slyly at me. Thanks to our deliberately hectic schedule, and a route around Rome that has cleverly avoided telephones of any type, Grace still hasn't checked in with Stuffy as she promised she would.

'There's a pay phone out by the loos,' Louis tells her, waving a handful of lira in the hope of attracting the attention of a lethargic barman.

'Louis!' Tanya howls, as Grace totters off to call home. 'What on earth did you tell her that for?'

'Don't panic, Mr Mannering,' Louis grins drunkenly at her. 'I passed it on my way to the loo and the phone's actually broken. She's so drunk it'll take her ten minutes to work out it's not working, and by that point she'll have forgotten she wanted to phone Stuart in the first place.'

Unbelievably Louis is right, and ten minutes later Grace staggers back and slumps down next to me on a bar stool. Making no mention of Stuart whatsoever, she ignores the vast array of bottles on offer, and suddenly decides that the thing she now wants most in the whole world is ice cream. So much for man hunting. I'm surprised that Tanya hasn't actually pulled yet either. She's flirted for Britain, but that's it. This doesn't last for very long though. It's not long before Tanya's tugging at my elbow with tales of her latest conquest.

'Ollie! You are not going to believe this.'

'What?'

'I've found Romeo!'

I have visions of Tanya hanging off a balcony. 'What do you mean?'

'I've found a gorgeous man, and guess what . . . his name's actually Romeo.'

'You're kidding, aren't you?'

'Nope.' She shakes her head, grinning broadly.

'Well, that's an omen if ever there was one,' Louis announces. 'Where's Grace?'

'Asleep face first in her ice cream, I think.'

'Wake her up and wipe her down, she's about to become Juliet for the night.'

'But he's *my* Romeo,' Tanya frowns petulantly. 'I found him.'

'Be charitable, Tan,' Louis wheedles, 'it's for a really good cause.'

'But I've never had a Romeo before . . .' Tanya's bottom lip wobbles, but I can see that she's wavering. 'I probably never will again . . .'

'Never say never,' Louis grins. 'Anyway, what better to tempt Grace away from a dreadful mistake, than a real . . .' here Louis slips into a fake-American accent, '. . . gen-u-ine bonafide Romeo. How could she resist?'

'Oh okay, you can have him,' Tanya sighs. 'But there's only one problem, he can't speak a word of English.'

'There's no language barriers for love,' says Louis optimistically.

'Well, you go and talk to him then, he hasn't understood a word I've said to him for the past ten minutes.' Tanya takes us through the small crowded dance floor, and over to a table in a darkened corner, where a shorter stockier David Ginola is chatting to two dark-haired, doe-eyed friends.

He looks up on catching sight of Tanya and beams excitedly. *'Ciao, bella,'* he calls out to her, getting up and heading over.

'He's not exactly what I expected,' I shout to Louis above the music.

'What do you mean?'

'Well, he's hardly Leonardo DiCaprio.'

'I don't know – I think he's kind of cute.'

'I'm not really into men who think they look good with hair past their collarbone.'

'You don't have to fancy him, Ollie, as long as Grace does.'

'I don't think Grace fancies anything at the moment, unless it's called Stuart. I can't believe how much she's changed since she met him: have you noticed we've been in at least ten different bars and she's hardly looked at any of the talent?'

'That's probably because she's so pissed she can't see straight.'

Tanya's trying to explain to a puzzled Romeo that she wants him to seduce someone for us. As his obvious intention from the outset was to try to seduce *her*, I think he's finding this pretty confusing. 'She's getting married soon, she needs a last fling,' Tanya enunciates as if he's a toddler.

'She needs several last flings,' adds Louis, over Tanya's

161

shoulder, 'in the hope that she'll realise they shouldn't be last, but continuous.'

'*Cosa?*' Not surprisingly, Romeo screws up his heavily handsome face in confusion.

'Let me, I speak a little bit of Italian.' Louis elbows past Tanya, through to the front. '*Buona sera. Come stai?*'

Romeo's puzzled face breaks into a huge smile at the sound of his own beloved language. So far he's been transfixed enough by Tanya's cleavage to put up with these mad English shouting at him, but he's beginning to get a little fed up.

'Ah, *buona sera.*' His relief is evident. '*Parli Italiano?*'

'*Si, si,*' Louis nods sagely. '*La Telefono a sono.*'

'*Prego?*' queries Romeo in confusion.

'I thought you said you spoke Italian,' I laugh.

'That was Italian.'

' "The telephone is ringing" – really relevant, Louis.'

'I was just warning up,' he slurs, waving me away. 'I think I can just about remember enough to teach him an English chat-up line. After that I'm sure it won't matter that he speaks a different language. In fact it'll probably be an added turn-on.'

'You think?'

'Yeah, not that he needs my added turn-ons, have you seen the bulge in his trousers? Either he's hung like Red Rum, or he runs a salami shop and takes his work home with him.'

I leave Tanya and Louis coaching Romeo with his one very important line, to tip a black coffee down Grace's neck in order not to sober her up – we want her drunk – but to wake her up a bit. At the moment she's so knackered, she's just sliding not very gracefully off her barstool towards the fairly dirty floor. Romeo can hardly sweep her off her feet if she's already flat on her back on the bar floor. I stand and watch Grace's eyes blink open again as the loaded caffeine of a double double Espresso I've just forced down her neck hits her stomach, then begins to course through her veins. Waking up enough to realise that she desperately needs the loo, Grace grins lopsidedly at me, and staggers off towards the ladies.

Louis joins me a few minutes later.

'How's he doing?' I ask.

'I'm not sure. I've either just told him that Grace fancies him, or I've asked him to buy me a wardrobe. I'm afraid I tend to get my Italian mixed up with my French sometimes. I've

162

got him just about perfect on his chat-up line though, and when I pointed out exactly whom it was we wanted him to chat up he got all enthusiastic again. The only problem is I think he wanted me to arrange a threesome with him, Grace *and* Tanya. Is she awake yet?'

'Yeah, she just went to the loo to splash some cold water on her face or something.

'Perfect,' Louis grins, 'we'll get Romeo to move in on her way back.'

The three of us wait by the bar in anticipation, as Romeo is despatched to intercept and intercourse – verbally, for the time being. Unfortunately by this point the dance floor is pretty packed with drunken revellers attempting to do the Macarena, and even when I stand on my barstool, I can't spot either Grace or Romeo. Five minutes later, however, Grace can be seen tottering through some hand-jerking, hip-swivelling drunks, alone.

'This horrible little man just pinched my arse and offered to take me back to his place for some "wold socks",' Grace tells us in outrage, falling onto the bar stool next to me.

'What did you do?' I ask keenly.

'Told him to get lost. He may have been Italian, but he certainly understood "eff off".'

We look at each other in disappointment. 'So what happened?'

'He did as he was told,' Grace giggles. 'He effed off.'

'He's gone?' says Tanya, her face falling.

'He went that-a-way!' Grace sings drunkenly, pointing toward the door.

'Oh Romeo, Romeo, wherefore art thou, Romeo?' Tanya slurs mournfully.

'He's just sped off up the road on his Piaggio,' Louis tells her, passing her his bottle of Sol.

'Hardly the romantic exit Shakespeare had in mind,' I snort into my third tequila.

We finally make it back to the hotel at midday, close the shutters, and fall into bed, all passing out at pretty much the same time, apart from lovely Louis, who I can vaguely hear as I fall into a deep dreamless slumber, humming the Macarena in the bathroom.

★ ★ ★

I'm woken from my total blackout by a shrill shriek from the next room, and watch through a blur of sleep dust in my forced-open eyes as Tanya runs through into our room butt naked and panicking.

'Ollie, Grace, Ollie, Grace.' She agitates between our beds, like a large bluebottle trapped in a bay window. 'Wake up, wake up!'

'What? What?'

'We've missed the flight!'

'What!' I sit bolt upright far too quickly, which sends my head spinning again like the girl from *The Exorcist*.

'We've missed the flight?' shrieks Grace, falling out of bed, and scrabbling around underneath it for the clothes she abandoned six hours earlier.

'Well, not technically yet, but it's due to leave in exactly thirty minutes, and I hardly think we're going to be able to pack and make it to the airport by then, do you?'

'Shit! Shit! Shit!' Grace is currently trying to put her left leg through the right sleeve of the wispy little Kookai cardigan she was wearing the night before.

'Does that mean I can go back to sleep?' I ask weakly, lying back down and pulling the covers over my head.

'No, it bloody doesn't!' Grace howls, hopping past me. 'We've got thirty minutes, we're bloody well going to try to get there.'

Grace and I run around like complete lunatics, throwing clothes into bags, sweeping entire shelves of deodorants and shampoos from the bathroom straight into holdalls, and actually manage to pack all of the stuff in the entire two rooms in just under eight minutes, before we realise we're missing one important thing.

'Louis,' Grace shrieks. 'Where the hell's Louis?'

'Knowing him, he sodded off out again!' says Tan, who's been wafting round getting in the way.

'I don't think so. I woke up about two hours ago, and he was here then.'

'You woke up two hours ago?' Grace echoes in disbelief. 'Well, why the hell didn't you wake us up then?'

As Grace darts into the bathroom in the wild hope that perhaps Louis has fallen asleep behind the shower curtain or something, I take the opportunity to quiz Tan. 'Did you do this on purpose?'

'What's that, darling?'

'Well, I haven't mentioned it to Grace, but someone switched off the alarm.'

'They did?'

'Yeah, I set it this morning, so we'd have plenty of time. Did you switch it off?'

'Me?' She puts a hand to her chest. '*Moi*? Do something like that?'

'You did, didn't you?'

She pauses open mouthed for a moment as though horrified that I would even suggest she could do such a thing, then sighs in mock guilt. 'Okay, you caught me out, I admit it, guv. It was me that did it! Are you cross?'

'Cross?' I exclaim, 'Cross! No, I'm bloody furious . . .' Tanya's face falls. 'Bloody furious,' I add, 'that I didn't think to do it myself.' I step forward and give her a big hug. 'Ooh, you clever girl, now all we have to hope is that we can't find Louis and that's it, we're stuck in Rome!'

Unfortunately, there's a yell two minutes later as Grace finally locates Louis on the balcony, still gloriously drunk and totally oblivious to the chaos that had been unleashed inside. He's reclining on a sun lounger, with a bottle of vodka in one hand, and a pair of opera binoculars – heaven knows where he stole those from – glued to his eyeballs, scrutinising the Italian talent as they parade the streets below in their Sunday best, arses defined better than some of the Roman sculptures in designer jeans that must have been spray-painted onto them. For some strange reason he's dressed in a floaty floral sundress that belongs to Grace, a pair of DMs, and some trendy Ray-Bans, and is giggling like a Banshee as he bottom-watches. 'I'm an Italian Leerer,' he snorts, as we lever him up from his sunbed, and manhandle him inside.

None of us is very surprised to find that by the time we get to the airport we're far too late.

'What the hell are we going to do now?' Grace asks in a tremulous voice, rubbing her temples, as her angst adds to her hangover.

'Get the next flight,' Louis slurs cheerfully, totally

165

unperturbed by the fact that he didn't have time to change and is still sporting a pink-and-orange frock, and is getting a mixture of amused, amazed and fearful looks from the other travellers in the terminal, not purely for his mode of dress, but also due to the fact that in his devastatingly drunken state, we decided it was easier to carry the luggage and load Louis onto the airport trolley.

'It's not like getting on a bus, Louis!' Grace snaps in exasperation.

'It isn't?'

'Well I don't think there'll be another one along in ten minutes, no.'

Amazingly Tanya is the most sober of the four of us, so she's despatched to the check-in desk to find out our options. She's back twenty minutes later. 'Do you want the good news or the bad news?'

'Good news, definitely good news,' Grace begs, obviously thinking of Stuffy waiting at home for her.

'Well, there's another flight early tomorrow morning.'

'Hurray!' Grace is the only one that cheers.

'Don't get too excited! Like I said, there's bad news too.'

'Go on then, hit us with it.'

'There are only two available seats.'

'Well, that's no good; we either all go home, or we all stay here,' I tell her.

'One for all,' choruses Louis, high-fiving Grace.

'And all for one,' finishes Grace a trifle reluctantly.

'I know, but the next flight with four free seats isn't until Wednesday.' Tanya winks gleefully at me.

'But that's three days away! So what do we do?'

'Well, they've put us on standby in case people don't turn up for the morning flight, so all we can do is wait.'

'I vote we head back to the hotel and see if they can put us up for a while longer,' I suggest.

'I think we should wait here a while,' Grace counters in concern. 'At least to see if we can get on the morning flight.'

'But why sit here all night when we could take the opportunity to go out and party again?'

'What and miss the next flight too?' Grace asks in agitation.

'Just humour her for now,' Tanya whispers to me. 'I didn't

put us on standby, I just put our names down for the Wednesday flight instead.'

'Clever girl!'

We find ourselves a corner with four seats and a view of the runway. We're just settling ourselves down as comfortably as possible for the long wait, when I notice that one of our party has gone walkabout. 'Where's Grace?' I ask Tanya.

'Probably gone to the loo.'

'You mean she didn't say?'

When she's still not back after twenty minutes, we start worrying. We're just about to send out a search party, when I spot her weaving her way through the departing holiday-makers towards us, waving two bottles of cheap champagne and looking decidedly more cheerful than she did half an hour ago.

'Gray! Where on earth have you been, we were worried.'

Putting down the champagne, Grace, no longer looking at all worried herself, grins broadly at us. 'I've been sorting out our little transport problem,' she announces. Grabbing Louis's hands and pulling him to his feet, she bundles him back onto his luggage trolley. 'Come on, you 'orrible lot, we're going home.' She starts to pick up her bags and her bottles, and piles them on top of a surprised but unprotesting Louis.

'What? But how?'

'We're getting a lift.'

'What on earth?'

'I phoned Stuart.'

'So?'

'And as I said, he's arranged for us to get a lift home.'

'How on earth has he managed to do that?' I ask her, stumbling to my feet.

'He has friends in high places,' she says cryptically. 'Very high places. Like thirty thousand feet . . .'

'Trust Dan Slater to have a bloody personal jet,' I mutter crossly, swatting at a rather-too-persistent fly with a rolled-up copy of *Cosmopolitan*.

'It's not actually Dan's, it belongs to a friend of his who owes him a favour,' Grace replies, offering me a swig from her nearly empty champagne bottle.

'Friend! Favour! Huh! More likely somebody he's fleeced in

167

business,' I growl, knocking back a large mouthful of fizz.

'This is just SO sexy,' breathes Tanya for the twentieth time.

'Flash git,' I repeat, also for about the twentieth time.

Following Grace's surprise announcement, she herded us into a taxi to drive a hot and dusty fifty kilometres to a private airstrip on the outskirts of the city, and we are now slumped in the shade of an olive tree, watching the sun go down, swigging champagne, using our overnight bags as furniture, and getting progressively more drunk as we wait for Demon Dan to zoom in like James Bond on a rescue mission.

Flash git.

The plane finally arrives at two in the morning, just as I'm taking a quick pee behind a bush that is just a touch too spiky to bare your bottom near. The lights on the plane sweep down the runway like searchlights in a prison yard, picking out my bush – no pun intended – and causing me to haul up my G-string in a hurry, in case the pilot thinks there are two moons out tonight.

To Tanya's extreme disappointment, and my extreme relief, Dan isn't actually on the plane. Stuart with a U is though. As soon as the little jet pulls up on the runway, he's tumbling out of the door before they can even unfold the steps, and falling into the open arms of a waiting Grace.

'You would not believe how worried I was!' he exclaims, holding her so tight I hear her take a sharp intake of breath.

Am I imagining it, or is Stuart with a U actually *glaring* at Tanya and me? Well, you couldn't really call it a glare – I don't think he could form his sane, sensible features into anything resembling malice – but he doesn't look particularly happy.

I start to feel a touch guilty, until Grace, hanging off a touchingly protective Stuart's arm, turns to us as we're boarding, winks broadly, and waving the now empty bottle of champagne she's still clutching in her other hand, slurs expansively, 'Hell of a time, girls, hell . . . of . . . a . . . time.'

I spend the entire flight home sulking desperately. It may seem a bit petty of me, but I can't help feeling that this is yet another occasion where bloody Dan Slater has put another one over on me.

Tanya's happy. She's spent the entire flight in the cockpit, chatting up the dishy pilot. Louis is happy. He's spent the entire flight chatting up the very camp air steward. A whole air steward for a small private jet. Flash git! The only damper on their trip is the fact that Stuart and Grace have spent almost the entire flight liplocked, as if the minor vacuum caused by the shutting of the external door sucked their lips together, never to be prised apart again. At least until we land.

The camp air steward stops pouting provocatively at Louis long enough to offer me a drink. I'm desperate for something alcoholic, but I'm even more desperate not to owe Dan Slater more than I have to, which includes turning down any offer of in-flight hospitality. Telling myself that I should have more than enough alcohol in my blood stream to last me until England, I eventually fall into a fitful sleep, only to have the most disturbing dream. Dan Slater, dressed in a Superman outfit, is trying to land a helicopter full of my friends on the roof of Tates, whilst I'm running round stark naked with only a fly swat in hand to protect my modesty, and to protect the restaurant from imminent destruction as the approaching helicopter turns into a meteorite the size of a small country.

Chapter Eight

On Wednesday evening, having spent the rest of Monday and most of Tuesday in bed recovering from our foreign jaunt, I stagger downstairs still nursing a hangover, and major league small posh jet lag to find that my errant chef has let me down again.

'Claude's just phoned in sick,' is the first thing an equally weary, but far more chirpy Louis tells me, as I stagger hollow-eyed through the back door.

Louis looks down at the order pad he scribbled Claude's telephone message on. 'He said he's got . . .' he squints as he tries to read his own writing '. . . distemper. That's it, he's got distemper.'

'Distemper! *Dogs* get distemper, Louis, not humans.'

'Well, he's an old dog, does that count?'

'No, it bloody well doesn't!' I howl crossly.

'Hey, don't shoot the messenger.' Louis holds up his hands in surrender, then raises his eyebrows at Melanie, who mouths PMT at him.

'I do NOT get PMT, okay,' I snap at them both. 'I can be in a shit mood without having to blame it on my hormones!'

'You know what it is, Mel, don't you?' Louis winks at Mel, determined to do some stirring. Mel giggles but wisely says nothing. 'She's got L.O.S.T.'

'What on earth?' Mel asks.

'Lack Of Sex Tension. I tell you she's totally L.O.S.T. at the moment.'

'Very funny,' I growl, grabbing my chef's apron from the back of the kitchen door and tying it morosely round my waist.

I had hoped to spend the entire evening doing the patron thing; you know, hanging out near the bar, gossiping with the

171

regulars, chatting up new customers in the hope they might become regulars, drinking expansively, all the perks that being the boss can afford me on a good night. Now, however, I'm stuck sweating in the kitchen all night.

Happy happy happy.

Several hours later, though, I suddenly find that being stuck out of the way of the customers does have some advantages when Louis skips merrily into the kitchen, a devilish grin on his handsome face and announces, 'Guess who's here again!'

'I don't know,' I reply, in no mood for guessing games.

'Go on, guess.'

'Why don't you just tell me, Louis,' I reply tiredly.

'Oh honestly, Ol, you're no fun at the moment.'

I raise my eyebrows at him.

'Oh all right . . .' he tuts, but even I can't kill the happy mood, 'I'll tell you . . .' He pauses for added drama.

'Louis!' Mel and I shriek at him in unison: Mel through frustrated anticipation, me through sheer frustration.

Louis looks at me, then at Mel, and grins. 'Satan Slater the devilishly delicious developer,' he growls lustfully.

'He's back!' shrieks Melanie joyfully, dropping a cake slice in her excitement. 'I knew he'd come back. That means he likes me.'

'Maybe he just likes the food,' replies Louis jealously.

Maybe he just likes pissing me off. As you can imagine, I'm not as overjoyed about the arrival of our latest customer as the other two are. Dan Slater. Ollie hater. I'm sure he comes in just to taunt me. He's either very brave, or very stupid . . . after all, I could so easily spit on his scallops . . . or do something far worse in his pasta in pesto . . .

'I've put him on table three.' Louis throws Mel a triumphant glance, this being the table furthest from any of the ones that she covers.

'You'll just have to turf him out again, won't you?' I announce tiredly.

'What?' Louis howls.

'It's ten-thirty, Louis.'

'So, we usually take orders until eleven.'

'I've decided that tonight we only take orders until ten-thirty.'

'But, Ollie!' Louis wails like a kid who's just been told he can't stay up and watch *EastEnders*.

'No buts, Louis, I've had enough and I want to shut early, okay.'

Louis's bottom lip starts to protrude sulkily. 'You'll have to tell him he can't eat, 'cause I'm not going to,' he mutters. 'Not after the way he rescued us . . .'

Fine by me. I wipe my hands down the front of my tie-waisted apron, and stride past Louis determinedly. It's bad enough that Dan Slater keeps coming in here, without my disloyal staff listening to their libidos instead of my warnings, and treating him like the prodigal every time he deigns to enter the establishment.

The restaurant's full. A sight I'm always appreciative of. One that doesn't fill me with quite as much glowing warmth is the sight of Dan Slater seated at a table near the huge open fire, which due to the wonderful change in weather is no longer lit but full of fresh flowers as is usual in the summer months. His companion is, somewhat predictably, Miranda. She's looking extremely pleased with herself, a smile of Cheshire-cat proportions plastered across her heavily made-up face. The smile slips down to her kneecaps, however, when she spots me heading over to their table, to be replaced with a look of extremely pissed-off surprise, which is far less attractive, but much more bearable than the smug look.

I weave my way through the tables towards them, my backbone unfortunately getting weaker with every step. It's one thing to want the thrill of kicking him out, it's another to actually go through with it. Besides, I don't know if I can be so rude . . . after all, as much as I hate to feel beholden to him, there's no escaping the fact that he did go to a hell of a lot of trouble to make sure we got back safely from our Italian escapade. I know it was for Stuart and Grace's sake, certainly not for mine, but I did benefit from his altruism . . .

Altruistic. I'd never have thought of that word as a suitable adjective for Dan Slater. Sighing heavily, I stop in my tracks. I can't turf him out, no matter how much I want to. I'm just about to return wearily to the kitchen and despatch Louis with menus and his order pad, when Dan's voice rings out across the restaurant.

'Excuse me, waitress.' It takes me a moment to confirm that he is actually addressing me. 'Ah, waitress.'

I stand and glare at him in disbelief.

'I say, *waitress*.' The voice gets more impatient and he clicks his fingers imperiously at me, a wicked grin sliding over his face. 'Honestly, the service in here tonight is just dreadful,' he says in a rather loud aside to Miranda, who giggles in a slightly embarrassed way.

It takes me another moment to realise that he's pissed. Gloriously and undeniably rolling drunk. For some reason, I find this Dan Slater far less intimidating. I think it's the slippage of the usual calm cool control. I also find this Dan Slater highly offensive. My previous resolve to let him have his cake and eat it, just for this evening, flies out of the window. Summoning as much calm and dignity as I can muster, I walk over to his table with my 'patron' head on.

'I'm sorry, sir, but the kitchen has just closed . . .' I'm not lying. Despite his best efforts, this is still my restaurant, and I can shut the kitchen whenever I want to.

'Well, open it again then.'

'I'm afraid I can't do that, sir.'

'Why not?'

This one throws me. 'Because I don't want to,' somehow seems a little inadequate. Even in his drunken stupor Dan obviously senses my hesitancy, and throwing his menu down on the table, leans back in his chair in a somewhat insolent fashion and demands to know what the day's specials are.

I ignore him. 'I'm afraid the chef isn't here tonight, and we're closing early,' I reply in my officious patron's voice, which I normally reserve for my bank manager when he's pissing me off, or shoddy suppliers.

He ignores me. 'What are tonight's specials?' he repeats.

'We're closed.'

He looks around him, eyes narrowing drunkenly. 'You don't look very closed to me.'

'I'm surprised you can see when your eyes are so bloodshot and blurry . . .' I reply sarcastically.

Miranda, who appeared initially to be enjoying the confrontation, goes bright red as our voices get progressively louder, and grabbing her bag, mutters that she needs to pop to the little girls' room, and hurries off to hide in the ladies.

Ignoring my last comment, Dan begins to look around him. 'Well, if you're going to be a bore and not tell me what the specials are, the least you can do is help me find a bloody menu,' he mutters, without looking at me.

'Tonight's special appears to be *arseholes*,' I reply venomously.

'What was that?' he asks distractedly, still looking round for the menu, despite the fact it's still where he left it on the table.

'Arseholes,' I growl under my breath.

He hears me loud and clear this time. 'I beg your pardon!' he slurs, looking at me challengingly.

Miranda, who was just daring to venture back from the toilets, turns abruptly and goes straight back in.

'Arseholes,' I repeat loudly, refusing to let him stare me out. 'Arseholes on toast, arseholes with beans, chips or fried bread, poached arseholes, fried arseholes, boiled arseholes, lightly sautéed arseholes, or great big fat arseholes that keep coming into my restaurant and . . .'

I feel a firm hand clamp over my mouth as Louis slides up behind me and drags me back into the kitchen, muttering something to Dan and the remaining customers about me not having taken my pills this morning. I struggle free as we fall through the swing door, and turn spitting furiously at him. 'What the hell do you think you're doing?'

Louis returns my furious gaze with one that's steady and highly amused. 'I was going to ask you the same question.'

'Arrogant, arrogant sod!' I howl, practically jumping up and down in frustration. 'How dare he stagger in here at this time of night, drunk as a goldfish in a bowlful of gin, and start demanding service as if he owns the place.'

'I hate to remind you, Ollie darling, but he does own the place.'

'He may own the building, but it's my bloody restaurant. Two different things, Louis, two completely different things!'

'Look, you take a chill pill, and I'll go and take their order.'

'You can order him straight out of here, that's what you can do,' I huff, folding my arms across my chest.

Louis turns to Mel who's hovering in the background, bouncing from foot to foot with glee at the unexpected excitement in what's usually a straightforward evening of hard slog. 'Be a darling, Melly Belly, and get me a bottle of red from the wine cellar, and make it a good one.'

'I told you not to serve him!' I storm.

175

'It's not for him precious, it's for you.' Louis installs me in a chair, and when Mel dashes back from the cellar with a bottle of red, hands me a large glass and orders me to drink.

'Better?' he asks when I've obediently swallowed half a glass.

'No,' I scowl at him.

'There's no point in deliberately trying to antagonise him, Ollie.'

'Why not? That's what he's doing to me.'

'You don't know that, Ol. Besides he really helped us out at the weekend . . .'

'I know, I know, that's the only reason I didn't turf him out straight away.'

'We owe him, Ollie. As much as you hate to admit it . . . I, for one, would like to buy him a large drink . . .'

'Well, I was going to let him have a complimentary bottle . . .'

'You were?'

'Yeah, but I couldn't work out how to get him to bend so I could insert it!'

After a little more persuasion on Louis's part, I finally unbend enough myself to let him go out and take their order.

'What do they want?' I growl ungraciously when he comes back into the kitchen five minutes later.

'Well the right madam will have the crab bruchetta, followed by the lamb tenderloin.'

'And what about "the Bastard",' I snarl.

Louis sticks the end of his Biro between his lips, and curls the free side of his mouth into a half smile. 'The Bastard,' he announces, 'said that he would like pan-seared tuna to start, followed by . . .' here he pauses, looks down at his notebook, then back up at me, his striking blue eyes crinkling with mirth '. . . one arsehole and chips, medium rare.'

Finally at nearly one in the morning, the restaurant is empty, and the kitchen is cleared, ready to start work again in just under five hours. Kicking everybody out, I throw Morcheeba on the restaurant stereo, and grab the remains of the bottle of 1995 Errazuriz that Louis insisted on forcing down my throat earlier, and sit down at the table closest to the fireplace, taking solace in the calming effect of the delicious scent and soft

176

colour of the sweetpeas filling the grate.

Five minutes later, however, I hear the kitchen door being unlocked, and the creak of the swing door as someone comes back into the restaurant. Louis is the only one with a set of keys. Louis also wanted to stay behind and help me finish the wine, but after such a shit evening, I'm on a Greta Garbo kick.

'Fuck off, Louis,' I bite grouchily. 'I told you I want to be alone.'

'Isn't that a bit clichéd?' drawls an amused voice that's vaguely familiar, but certainly doesn't belong to Louis.

I turn my head slowly in cautious disbelief, to see Dan Slater leaning in the doorway, eyes glazed, cocky grin on his far-too-handsome face. I'm out of my chair and on my feet in seconds. 'How the hell did you get in here?' I shout accusingly.

Completely unperturbed, he waves a massive bunch of keys at me, the effort making him sway a little. 'Figured one of these might fit, and as luck would have it . . .' He walks over and takes the seat opposite my hastily vacated one, helps himself to my glass of wine, and downs half of it in one go.

I stare at him in open-mouthed disbelief. 'Look, you may own the building but that doesn't give you the right . . .'

'It gives me the right of access,' he cuts in, pouring more wine into my glass, and pushing it back across the table toward me.

'It gives you the right to *reasonable* access, at an *agreed* time,' I spit, emphasising the two words, 'and letting yourself into *my* restaurant at some ungodly hour of the morning is not what I call being bloody reasonable.'

He leans back in the chair, pushing the two front legs off the ground with his feet, and surveys me calmly. 'You know you're very attractive when you're angry.'

I stop my tirade, and blink at him in surprise. Well that one was a blindsider. A major cliché. But still one I wasn't expecting. I slowly back away from him.

'Look,' he slurs, 'you and I have a few problems to work out, so why don't you grab another glass, sit down, and we'll talk about it.'

'Maybe that would be a good idea if you were sober,' I reply cautiously.

177

'I'm *totally* sober,' he assures me, swaying slightly.

'Yeah, and I'm the Queen Mother.'

'Why don't you take a pew, Your Majesty. Literally,' he adds, looking at the seating. 'Boy, has this place got some weird furniture.'

'I like it,' I reply defensively.

'And believe it or not, Olivia, so do I. Why do you think I eat here so frequently?'

'Because you're a sadistic bastard.'

'I'll ignore that one.'

'I don't want you to ignore it, I want you to leave.'

'You don't mean that. Not when I've come here specifically to try to help you out.' Yeah, help me out of the restaurant so he can get his bloody hands on the property. 'I think we can come to some sort of arrangement,' Dan continues, pushing a hand through his short brown hair, then letting it fall back onto his distractingly firm moleskin-clad thigh, 'I know you might have trouble meeting the new rent. And believe it or not I actually applaud the way that you've been opening for breakfast every morning . . . but you can't go on working the hours you have been.'

'Have you been checking up on me?'

'Yeah,' he replies completely unperturbed. 'As a matter of fact, I have. I like this place. I actually think it's a sound business, a solid investment . . . I'd be prepared to invest in you, Ollie. A partnership maybe?'

'I don't want a partner.'

'But you can't deny you need some help.'

'I'll get by.'

'Do you think so?'

'I'll have to. You've got me over a barrel and you bloody know it.'

Dan's firm mouth quirks into a slightly lop-sided smile. 'Oh, would that I had,' he drawls slowly. 'Over a barrel, over a table . . . hey, how about coming into my office and trying it over the desk, that's always been a fantasy . . .'

I stare at him in open-mouthed disbelief. 'Are you coming on to me?'

'Maybe.'

'How dare you! Talk about adding insult to injury.'

'Most women look upon it as a compliment . . .'

178

'You arrogant bastard!'

He gets up from his seat and comes round to my side of the table. 'You're far too uptight, Ollie Tate,' he slurs, as I instinctively flinch away from him.

'I think you should leave,' I reply angrily.

He doesn't move.

'Well, if you're not going, then I bloody well am.'

As I go to push past him, he catches my wrist and swings me round to face him. 'Going already? Aren't you going to kiss me goodnight then?' he challenges. He's mocking me.

As hard as I'm trying to retain some calm and dignity, I can't stop the flush that colours my face at the memory of the last time I heard those words coming from my own mouth. Before I can think of a suitable response he takes hold of my other wrist, and pulls me into him so tightly that I can feel his heart beating through his shirt against my chest. Unlike mine, which is on double time, his is as regular as a steady controlled drumbeat. Holding me in an iron grip, he bends his head and slowly kisses me straight on the lips, eyes boring into me as he does so.

I try to pull away, my own eyes blazing back furiously at him, but he's far too strong for me. I feel like Scarlett struggling with Rhett. Shit. I shouldn't have thought that, now I feel horny. What a fantasy! Blimey, he's a good kisser. And he's strong as well. His arms have slipped tightly around me, muscles tensed as his grip strengthens against my struggling. It's no good, I've got to kiss him back. It's like having champagne tipped in your mouth, feeling the sweet taste tempting your tastebuds, and the bubbles tickling your tongue, and then trying not to swallow it. Impossible. Ignoring my head, and letting lust wash over me, I stop fighting him and my eyes slowly fall shut as an intense pleasure takes over from the outrage, but when I finally open my eyes again it's to see that his are wide open, and they're . . . laughing. He's laughing at me.

This is another one of his bloody power games! Pleasure legs it into the night and outrage returns with a vengeance. Struggling like a pet rabbit trying to escape the suffocating embrace of an over-affectionate child didn't work very well. Time for short but sharp. The next time that too-delicious tongue comes snaking into my mouth, I go for the kill, and chomp down hard on the edible but evil interloper. Dan lets out a yell, and drops me like a hot brick.

He's not laughing now. In fact he looks furious. Bloody furious. Frighteningly so. Apart from the fact that I'm sure he wouldn't hit a woman, I think he'd hit me. There's only one thing I can do. Kick him on the shins and run like hell.

Five hours later, after hiding out in my bedroom, wide eyed, trembling, and sleepless, expecting a hammering on my front door at any minute which never actually comes, I creep downstairs, and let myself back into the restaurant, almost expecting him to leap out from the shadows and accost me with one of my own meat cleavers.

The place is empty. So is the wine bottle that I hadn't even got halfway through. I pick it up and study it, shaking my head in disbelief.

I'd shot up the stairs to my flat, half expecting him to be seconds behind me ready to take revenge for my counter-assault. Instead of heading after me as imagined, sporting a carefully sharpened steak knife, and a murderous rage, he must have stayed and finished the wine. Sat back down and calmly worked his way down the bottle. There's even a plate on the table, next to the wine glass still stained with my lipstick, sporting a half-eaten slice of toast, and a mug of English Breakfast.

I feel the teacup. It's still fairly warm. He must have sat and waited here nearly all night. What if he's still here some-where? I glance around fearfully, but the room is empty. He's not hiding out in the loos either, waiting to leap out and either kill me or kiss me. When I'm sure that I'm definitely alone, the leftover fear turns to outrage.

I angrily sweep the remains of his vigil from the table and throw them unceremoniously into the kitchen sink. There's more evidence of his presence in the kitchen, a knife on the table covered in melting butter, a used tea bag in the central waste disposal unit of the sink. I head back out to the bar and find an empty brandy glass on the glass sink drainer. Talk about making yourself at home! He already thinks this place is his own. Well he's not going to get me out that easily.

I jump six feet in the air as I hear the back door into the kitchen, which I left wide open when I came in, slam shut, and heavy footsteps marching across the kitchen floor.

'That's it, I quit!' My heart crawls back into my rib cage as Tanya slams through the kitchen door, and going straight behind the bar, helps herself to a chilled bottle of Diet Coke from one of the glass-fronted fridges. 'I just give up!' she repeats, sitting down on a barstool.

'So do I,' I reply miserably, joining her.

'You don't even know what I'm talking about yet.'

'I don't need to, I'm giving up on everything.' I try to tell Tan about my encounter with Desperate Dan, but she's not listening.

'Do you know, I actually persuaded her to come out with me last night, and I took the rare opportunity to introduce her to some of my favourite men, you know my absolute best, the cream of the crop, but all she did all evening was bang on about bloody boring Stuart with a U.'

'You mean Grace?' I sigh.

'Who else,' Tanya replies dryly.

'As it's not working with Gray, perhaps we should try the other side.' I surprise myself by saying this. My encounter with Dan must be bringing out the man-hater in me.

'Stuart?'

'Yep.'

'And what do you suggest?'

'Find *him* someone else. Lure him away with another woman.'

'You're kidding, aren't you? Who on earth do you think we could find to do that?'

'You could seduce him,' I reply wearily.

'Me?' shrieks Tanya, eyes widening with horror at the thought.

'Well, that says it all really,' I sigh bitterly. 'Even *you* wouldn't touch him with a barge pole.'

'I don't think I like what you're implying,' Tanya replies archly.

'Maybe not, but you know what I mean.'

It's Tanya's turn to sigh heavily. 'The problem is, I do . . . although I really didn't think I was *that* indiscriminate,' she adds quickly.

I raise my eyebrows at her.

'I don't just sleep with *anything*.'

I try the eyebrow thing again, my recent encounter with Dan blighting any hope of tact, and she lapses into a semi-hurt silence, chewing her bottom lip in a sudden burst of self-conscious contrition. 'Okay,' she admits, 'so I'm not that fussy, as long as they've got a big dick, a big heart, or a big wallet, but I do draw the line at Stuart.'

'With a U, and an A,' I joke, suddenly feeling guilty.

'Not an E, and a W,' she agrees, smiling again.

'Perhaps Stuart is a secret Lothario,' I announce, more to make her laugh than through actual belief in what I'm saying. 'Beneath that innocent exterior lurks the heart of a serial rat. The mild-mannered manufacturer is really a decadent duplicitous dirtbag.'

'I have a feeling that this is as likely as Tanya declaring that she's actually a virgin,' says a voice from the kitchen doorway behind us. It's Louis, arrived for the breakfast shift, looking as bleary-eyed and tired as I do. 'Talking about Lotharios, did you tell Tan who turned up again last night?' he asks me, rubbing his eyes as he walks into the room and joins us at the bar.

'I was just about to,' I reply. 'But you don't know the half of it, Lou.'

'I don't?' he asks, wide-eyed. 'Blimey, I thought the bit I did know was enough, what on earth else could there be?'

Louis and Tanya sit enthralled as I fill Tanya in on the whole evening, and Louis on the part that he missed, conveniently skipping the fact that for a moment I kissed Dan Slater back as hard as he was kissing me, and emphasising the mad struggle to get away from him instead. I finish my story to sympathetic noises and shoulder-patting from Louis, but when I look at Tanya, she's sort of smiling in a far-off-fantasy fashion.

'You're taken in by him, aren't you?' I cry incredulously. 'You're not supposed to be impressed by his behaviour, you're supposed to be appalled.'

Tanya has the grace to look a little guilty, but nonetheless doesn't deny it. 'It's just so . . . so . . . macho,' she replies dreamily. 'Shame we can't fix him up with Grace – that would kill two birds with one stone.'

'I like the idea of killing him,' I growl, 'but I think I'd rather Grace be with Stuart than that bastard.'

'Really? At least she'd get some excitement with Dan.'

'Unless Stuart is actually a secret Lothario, as you put it,' Louis says hopefully.

'Hardly,' laughs Tanya. 'That's like suggesting you're really heterosexual.'

'But he might be given half the chance. Stuart, not you!' I tell Louis, who's looking a bit put out at this last. 'They say that all men are bastards deep down.'

'So you're suggesting we give Stuart the chance to bring out his bastard side.'

'Exactly. He probably hasn't had much chance to sow his wild oats. To be a two-timing wild wanton warthog, you actually have to have a social life that involves more than a quick trip to your local hostelry for a pint of Yorkshire's finest.'

'So if the opportunity arose . . .'

'Then it's possible he might take it.'

'And how do we give him the opportunity then?'

'Well, that's the slightly tricky part.'

'*Slightly* tricky?'

'Don't you know anybody who'd be game? What about Mel? Could you convince her?'

'Doubt it very much.'

'But it's such a good cause.'

'Look, the only person I know who wouldn't need much persuading to chat up a perfect stranger would be Claude, and he's hardly a suitable candidate now, is he?'

'Well in that case, it's going to have to be one of us,' states Tanya.

'You're kidding, aren't you?' I exclaim in horror.

'It's got to be done, Ollie.'

'It hasn't *got* to be done. There must be some other way to make Gray see reason.'

'We've tried everything that we can think of.'

'Why can't you do it? You're the expert seductress.'

'Because that's not fair, we need to do this democratically. I know,' she grins, 'we'll draw straws for it.'

'I take it you're not including me in this little poll of yours?' Louis grins, going behind the bar and helping himself to an orange juice.

'And why not? You never know, it might take a man to do this job, if you know what I mean,' Tanya laughs, winking at him. She turns back to me. 'Got any straws?'

'Only cheese ones.'

'Good, I'm starving.' Louis's stomach obligingly emits a loud rumble as if to back up this statement.

'I was joking.'

'How about paper?' suggests Tanya.

'Doesn't taste very good.'

'Shut up, Louis,' we chorus.

I fetch Tanya an order pad, and Louis a packet of Smoky Bacon crisps. Tanya painstakingly cuts a piece of paper into three even pieces, and pulling out a Chanel lipstick from her handbag, makes a red cross on one. She then screws them into tight balls, wrestles one of Louis's Mickey Mouse socks from his foot, and chucks them in ready for a home-made ballot.

'Okay, whoever gets the red cross does the seducing.'

'X marks the "on the spot",' I mutter, gingerly reaching into the sock and pulling out the first piece of paper.

Louis follows suit, leaving Tanya with the final piece. We open them together. The other two's smiles of relief are closely followed by my open-mouthed, bulging-eyed expression of horror when I realise that my scrap of paper has a big red lippy cross on it. Why me? I couldn't kiss old rubber lips if somebody offered to pay me a million pounds and completely re-sculpt my body into a far more flattering shape, something resembling Jennifer Lopez perhaps, though a touch lighter on the butt front.

'No way!' I exclaim, screwing the piece of paper into a small ball, and throwing it at the waste bin.

'I'm sorry, babe, but we did agree whoever got the marked paper. No backing out.'

'I know,' I sigh heavily. 'If you or Louis had got it you'd go through with it.'

'Well I would,' says Louis. 'But I still don't think it would have done any good. He's definitely not a man's man, if you know what I mean.'

'So it's down to me,' I sigh, resignedly.

The other two nod, immovable.

Grace has invited us down to Stuart's for the weekend. It's agreed that the dirty deed will be carried out then. Oh well, at least it gives me time to emigrate, and if I can't get an exit visa I could always throw myself under the next passing bus.

Chapter Nine

Tanya turns up at Tates in a taxi, twenty minutes after I've kicked out my last customers from the hectic Friday lunchtime session. I've thrown a few essentials into an overnight bag and I've only just had time to change into some clean jeans. With no make-up and hair still wet from the shower, I'm a little peeved to see my elegant friend step out of the cab looking as if she's modelling for a Vogue fashion shoot. It also looks as if she's bringing the entire shoot wardrobe with her.

'We're going away for the weekend, not for the next year,' I moan, as the taxi driver hauls several pieces of Louis Vuitton out of his cab and onto the back seat of my car. 'I'm supposed to be picking Louis up as well, you know,' I insist as she simply smiles, but apart from this mute greeting, ignores me. 'You remember Louis,' I say sarcastically. 'Five foot nine, dark hair, good looking, normally sits in the back seat?'

'I know,' she finally answers, turning her attention from supervising the safe transfer of her precious luggage to me.

'There won't be any room left for him at this rate,' I inform her archly as the taxi driver, bald head gleaming with sweat from his exertions, heaves yet another case into my poor car. 'Couldn't you put your cases in the boot?'

'Louis can sit in the boot,' Tanya replies with a slight smile, paying the taxi driver and sliding into the front seat. 'He's easier to clean than kid skin.'

Louis is waiting outside his house for us, perched on a wall, jabbering away into his mobile phone, and looking gorgeous in black velvet jeans, matching jacket, and a plain Ted Baker T-shirt, his spiky black hair tinged cobalt blue at the ends to match his eyes.

Spotting my car turning into his road, he ends the call, and

185

jumps off the wall waving excitedly as we approach. As he's stretching up on tiptoes to wave at us, he reveals that for some odd reason, under the flared velvet, he's wearing green wellies.

Louis has almost as many cases as Tanya does. We somehow manage to squeeze these into the boot, squeeze Louis onto the back seat, and set off. It takes us over three hours through the Friday afternoon traffic to reach Leicestershire, and another hour to find Stuart's house. It doesn't help that it's set back about a mile from the main road, with no signpost whatsoever. Unbeknown to us we have driven past it about three times before we find ourselves almost thirty miles away, and end up phoning Gray on Tanya's mobile. She navigates us through the countryside, mainly by public house, which is a fairly good sign that she does have some form of social life outside of London, and hasn't lapsed into middle age and settled mode completely.

Stuart's house is rambling yet elegant, one of those properties that have had a different wing built every century to form an eclectic, yet beautiful mix of architectural styles.

'What a gorgeous house,' breathes Tanya as, approaching the end of the long oak-lined drive, its magnificent façade comes into full view. 'Well, this is a bonus point.'

'Why?' I mutter, still sulking that I got the job of attempting to seduce Stuart with a U this weekend, and not at all happy that we've finally arrived. 'Gray's not the mercenary type.'

'No, but you'd have to be blind not to notice how wonderful this house is. I'd date Quasimodo if he lived in a place like this.'

'You'd date Quasimodo anyway,' I say, agitation making me bitchy.

'Specially if he had a big dick, I know,' Tanya sighs. 'You really must get over this dreadful image you have of me, Ollie darling.'

'It's not an image, it's a reality.'

'Yes, and you should be very proud of me. You don't realise how much hard work it is being a total slapper,' she jokes.

Louis is curled up on the back seat, fast asleep, buried between Tanya's suitcases in his black velvet, like a little snoring mole. He soon wakes up however, when I brake to a stop on the turning circle in front of the house and a vanity case that was perched precariously on the parcel shelf, and contains enough Estée Lauder to sink the Titanic, falls onto his head.

As we stumble out of the car, dragging Louis from the small suitcase avalanche he's buried under, one of the double doors leading into the main entrance of the house swings open and Grace falls out, surrounded by a small army of dogs. They're a real liquorice-allsorts collection of large, small, and downright odd. One, standing out in particular, looks just like a walking wig that's been thrown off by Cher after a vigorous stage performance, and another resembles a small walking Hitler moustache. On the whole they appear to be fairly friendly, apart from a fat wire-haired terrier that decides it's his duty to defend Chez Stuart from these strange new interlopers with so much aggression that it's hard not to think that he actually spookily knows our main reason for being here is to oust his master from our friend's life.

'Where's the Lord of the Manor then?' Tanya, who firmly believes in the saying *Bite the Biter*, growls back at the terrier then, risking her ankles, brushes imperiously past its bared teeth to plant a kiss on both of Gray's cheeks. 'This place is fabulous, Gray darling. Totally amazing,' she adds, appraising the façade in true estate agent – er . . . sorry, *Property Consultant* fashion, pound signs rolling in her eyeballs like a cartoon character.

'Stuart's out in the stables with his pride and joy,' Grace smiles. 'Come on, I'll take you out so you can say hello. Then I can give you the grand tour!'

In the stables, eh? This sounds promising. Maybe we're finally going to get a glimpse of what Gray sees in Stuart. The Mr Darcy syndrome.

As we follow Grace through an impressively huge entrance hall, and down a long dark corridor to the rear of the house, I have new visions of Stuart stripped to the waist, clad only in a pair of jodhpurs and some highly polished knee-high riding boots, manly chest covered in sweat as he lunges a highly strung stallion, straining lead rope twisted tightly in one hand, lunge whip cracking in the other. I don't know where Stuart suddenly got a manly chest from, but the image is very striking. Somebody wipe me down with a damp cloth, I'm steaming up. I always hoped Stuart would have hidden depths, some redeeming quality that would make us realise he is actually Gray's perfect partner. Let's just hope we find them before I'm forced to do my Mata Hari job. I go from hot and bothered, to just bothered at this thought.

There *are* horses out in the yard. Several of them actually, snorting and stamping, and eyeballing us nervously from the safety of a row of loose boxes. Tanya obviously has the same Jane Austen-fuelled visions as I do. She gets quite excited, even bending to pet a rather pretty tortoiseshell cat that has the audacity to wind itself around the leg of her Joseph trousers, until one of the horses sticks its head out of its stable door in friendly fashion, only to dribble green horse drool onto Tanya's leather Gucci jacket, inducing her to turn a similar shade of green and mutter furiously that she 'hates the country'.

We finally find Stuart in a large barn at the end of the row, and my little fantasy bubble is quite severely popped. Stuart is tending, not to some highly bred Arab with flowing mane and flared nostrils, but to a big black and shining traction engine. Bang go my visions.

He emerges from underneath when Grace calls him. He's not even covered in oil and wearing a tight pair of overalls or a ripped pair of Levi's and little else, which would have redeemed the situation somewhat. Instead he's decked out in a pair of old brown cords, a green checked shirt, some sort of waistcoat contraption which is more pocket than anything else and, horror of horrors, a checked flat cap, à la George Formby.

'How do, everybody.' Smiling broadly at us all, he wipes an oily hand down the side of his cords and holds it out. As the other two are still looking at the flat cap in total horror and make no move whatsoever toward him, I decide it's up to me to accept the not-so-pleasant pleasantries. I take his hand. Last time it was sweaty. This time it's sweaty and greasy. Luvverly!

'Wonderful to see you again.' I force a smile and, rummaging in my bag for a tissue, manage to wipe down my hand on the pretext of blowing my nose. 'Fantastic place you've got here.'

'Really. Thank you,' he says as if he's only just noticed this fact himself.

'He's been working on this thing all day,' Grace announces

indulgently, gesturing to the engine as if she's actually proud of this.

'If anybody fancies a ride? You only have to ask, be more than happy . . .'

'I could go for that,' I reply enthusiastically. 'I used to ride when I was younger.'

'I think he meant on the engine,' Louis whispers to me, as Stuart wipes a finger across the nameplate of the Bedford Belle to remove an imaginary speck of dirt.

Great. He doesn't mean an exhilarating charge on horseback across the surrounding fields; he means a slow chug on the big black boring beast he's been tinkering with. Declining politely, we decide that unpacking has got to be more interesting, and head back out the front of the house to my car.

It takes us three trips to get all of the luggage up to our rooms. 'I hope he's got a cleaner,' I say to Grace, as we head up the stairs and down the mile-long corridor which runs between the bedrooms for the third and hopefully last time. 'Can you imagine having to do all of this yourself?'

'I hope he's got a butler,' Tanya exclaims. 'It's at least a mile to the kitchen! Who's going to fetch me a cup of tea in the morning?'

'If he had a butler,' Grace grumbles good-naturedly at her, 'do you think we'd be carrying your luggage?'

'And no,' I add, as Tanya looks over at me hopefully. 'I will not be waking you up tomorrow morning with a bright smile and a cup of Earl Grey.'

My room is straight out of a *Country Living* magazine. I think that I must be in the Georgian part of the house. Two paned sash windows overlook the formal garden just to the back of the house, and beyond that the view of the rest of Stuart's land stretches out before me to the horizon.

It's a beautiful place. Beyond the garden is a large lake where I can see a lone swan leisurely swimming amongst the lily pads and reeds, as if it's just fallen happily into a Monet painting. Behind the lake, there are fields and gently rolling hills stretching to the horizon, where yet more horses are prancing in high spirits, and black and white cattle are calmly grazing.

Inside, the walls are wood panelled, the furniture's old oak,

189

and the linen chintzy but pretty. All I need now is some ivy outside my window for a suitably handsome hero to scale up and I'm made.

It takes me precisely four minutes to unpack. Estimating from the number of cases Tanya brought with her that she'll take just a bit longer than me, I head into the shared bathroom which is situated between our bedrooms, with a weekly magazine that I found in my room. Tanya bursts through the interconnecting door from her room bearing toiletries, just as I'm settling down on the loo for a quick pee before hurling myself into the bath for a read.

'Out!' I shriek, attempting to kick the door to with my toes.

'I've seen you puking in an Italian loo, with sick in your hair. I hardly think catching you on the lav could embarrass you further,' Tanya states matter-of-factly, but she backs out nonetheless.

Twenty minutes later I haul myself out of the bath and wrapping myself in a towel head through into Tanya's room. She's *still* unpacking her cases. First out of what looks like case number three, is a wispy little number from Ghost, then a large white floppy hat with flowers on, a long midnight-blue Audrey Hepburn number with matching velvet gloves, baggy cream slacks, and what looks suspiciously like a cricket jumper. She's been watching too much Evelyn Waugh, her visions of country living fuelled by re-runs of *Brideshead Revisited*.

The next case, however, is full of more typical Tanya attire: Moschino, Miu Miu, Manolo, Vivienne Westwood. Fun, funky, and to die for, but hardly suitable for the green-welly belt. I can just see her now tottering around a field full of cowpats in a delicate pair of Manolo Blahnik sandals and a tightly laced bustier.

I brought two pairs of jeans, three T-shirts, one jumper, and the obligatory little black dress and thread of leather masquerading as a pair of evening shoes, just in case. Just in case of *what* I'm not sure. I have a feeling the high spot of this weekend will be the journey home. Tanya's only concession to relaxed dressing is a pair of Earl jeans that I would have stolen from her by now if only I could squeeze my size twelve arse into their size eight confines, and a Pucci halter-neck top, which on closer inspection appears to be sporting a tomato

190

ketchup stain from a late-night apres-club burger session, although amidst the riot of Mondrian-inspired colour, you'd hardly notice it.

When she's finally unpacked, I have to wait another ten minutes whilst she showers, and another twenty whilst she carefully blowdries her shoulder-length hair, which is currently dyed a rather fetching red-setter kind of colour, into a perfect Jennifer Aniston bob. It then takes Tanya half an hour to decide between the cricket jumper and a rather gorgeous pink-velvet smoking-style jacket that's very Stephen Fry, but clashes violently with her hair. In the end she chooses the smoking jacket and some black trousers, whilst I just pull on a clean jumper, and we head downstairs to find our hosts.

Gray and Stuart are in the drawing room, sitting either side of a roaring open fire. Beethoven's *Für Elise* is playing on an old gramophone in the background. Stuart is reading *Country Life*. I almost expect Gray to be crocheting, or cross-stitching or something, but to my relief she's actually reading last month's *Vogue*. Beethoven rustles to an end, and Bach's *Brandenburg Concerto No 3* bursts out of the sort of speaker you normally see Jack Russells attached to.

'Blimey, it's the *Antiques Roadshow*,' scoffs Tanya, flouncing into the room, her perfect mouth set into a sulky expression. She glances scornfully over at Gray who appears to be wearing her grandmother's clothes again, collar up to her eyeballs, skirt to her feet, where – horror of horrors – she is sporting the sort of sad pin-cord slippers you'd buy a dotty maiden aunt for Christmas.

'And Gray's the prize exhibit.'

Tanya grabs my hand and pulls me back out into the corridor. 'Thank goodness we came down. I knew she was slipping, but this is ridiculous. We've got to do something drastic,' she hisses, her whispered voice sounding dangerously loud in the vast echoing cavern of the hallway. 'If we don't, we could come back in a few years' time, and there they'll be, a few years older, but in exactly the same position, covered in cobwebs, just like Miss Haversham.'

I think Tan's being just a touch melodramatic, but I know what she means. Gray's not even married yet, and already she's acting like the dutiful little wife in a Dickens novel. Next thing we know, she'll be joining the WI, and making jam, instead of hitting the town and making noise.

'Why don't I suggest going out for a drink? There must be a bar or something nearby?'

'That's not the kind of drastic I meant, but it's gotta be better than being stuck in here all night watching Gray play lady of the manor. Perhaps if we chuck a few vodkas down her throat, it'll give her dormant brain cells a bit of a kick-start.'

Back in the drawing room, Louis is doing his version of ballet to Bach. It's an odd sight: a bit like Julian Clary pirouetting onto the set of a BBC costume drama. He pliés across the room and collapses in a Queen Anne chair, rolling his eyeballs at me.

'We're having a bit of a party tomorrow night,' Grace announces as we sit down.

I catch Tanny and Louis surreptitiously rolling eyeballs at each other again. 'Cheese and pineapple on sticks and a fun game of musical antiques,' I hear Louis mouth in Tanya's ear a little too loudly.

'Mum's coming down.'

Tan and Louis perk up a little at this. Gray's mother Tula was an original It girl before that tired phrase was ever coined by some sorry hack. She and Tanya are kindred spirits. She's blonde, brash, bold and a complete and utter man-eater. She scares me to death.

I last saw her at one of our bridesmaid dress fittings; she roared up to the dressmaker's on the back of a Harley Davidson, driven by her third husband Sylvester, who owns a chain of bookies, and dresses like a gangster from the seventies in candy-striped shirts from Jermyn Street. No doubt she and Tanya will spend the evening behaving appallingly, whilst Sylvester tries to chat up anything that breathes, including me, Louis, and probably the cocker spaniel that's snoring on the hearth rug as well when he's had a few bevvies.

I want to go home. The gramophone has rustled to an end. A grandfather clock is ticking away heavily in the corner. I don't know why, but I've always hated the sound of a ticking clock in a quiet room. It's annoying, like the monotonous drip of a tap, but also somehow desperately sad. For some reason it makes me think of loneliness.

It's a frightening picture, Grace stuck in this big old house on her own with Stuart. It's like something out of the twilight zone. If it's desperately dull with all five of us here, just imagine what it would be like when it's just the two of them. Despite the fact that the room's big enough to house a small nightclub, I can almost feel the walls closing in on us. The tick of the clock is getting louder with each moment. We need something to liven up the atmosphere. I glance around the room for a TV or hi-fi system but see nothing except the record player, under which is stacked a dusty heap of old vinyl. I don't think The Prodigy ever did anything you could play at 45rpm.

Tanya and Louis are unnaturally quiet, sitting still and upright, hands in laps, like children in a strict classroom, both looking decidedly unhappy. They perk up a little when, after some heavy hinting on my part, Stuart suggests we go out for a drink, and both disappear upstairs to change. After three-quarters of an hour they're still not ready, so we decide to head off without them, shouting instructions up the echoing stairway that we'll see them in the village pub when they've finally finished changing.

Half an hour later, Louis prances into the local pub in a pair of sparkling blue and silver boot-cut trousers, that I'm sure I saw in the window of Kookai a few weeks ago, and one of my crop-top T-shirts with a big blue flower on the front and the slogan Daisy Head underneath. What nobody here realises is that this is one of his more toned-down outfits. Stuart looks up and nearly chokes on his pint.

Tanya, in a hot pink Moschino dress that would look great in the West End, but in here makes her look as if she's just walked straight out of the sleazier parts of Soho, looks about her at the low-beamed ceiling covered in leather and brass abandoned by the odd careless Shire horse, at the elderly locals stooped over their pints, at the grandmother clock ticking quietly in the corner and crosses her eyes at me in silent despair. Tanya's idea of a kicking nightspot is one that's full of men. Preferably between the ages of twenty and fifty, with gold Amexes, gold watches, bulging portfolios or bulging crotches. She minces across the paisley-patterned carpet on four-inch heels, mouth falling open at the sight of Grace picking up a pint glass.

'Men don't make passes at girls with pint glasses,' chants Tanya, looking in such abject horror at Gray that I almost expect her to reach out and smack Gray's hand as if she's reprimanding a naughty child. I must admit I'm a little shocked to see my refined Miss Perfect attempt to chug a pint of best bitter, and am relieved when the pint is abandoned after half an hour of face pulling, in favour of a large gin and tonic.

Tanya and Louis look about them in horror, mutter something about the Archers, and time warps and, ordering a bottle of vodka, retire to a corner to drink themselves not into oblivion, because that's where they think they've actually just arrived, but out of it.

I attempt to talk to Stuart, having forgotten what hard work this can be. To my surprise however, he's pretty chatty: admittedly he's talking about traction engines, and horses, crop rotation, and textiles, but at least he's making an effort. He must be more comfortable on home territory. More relaxed and ready to open up to us. It's not long before I find myself apologising for the Rome episode. I can still remember his anxious and accusing face on touchdown and am surprised to find myself suddenly feeling a bit guilty.

'Well, we managed to rescue you, so it all came right in the end,' is his magnanimous reply, which he promptly ruins by adding, 'thanks to Dan.'

Thanks to Dan. He had to point that out, didn't he?

When he then starts spouting on about what a good guy Dan is, I decide it's time to join Grace and Louis in their little vodka retreat. I'm lucky, a local in a Barbour collars Stuart for a discussion on boundaries, and I manage to slip off into the happy corner, where Tanya and Louis are drinking like parched dingoes in a desert, and laughing like demons, earning black looks from the more staid pub clientele. The reason for the upward swing in mood is that they're already halfway down the bottle, knocking back glasses full of Russia's finest – and strongest, it's blue label – as if it's mineral water.

'We've decided to get so gloriously pissed that we sleep for the entire day tomorrow,' Tanya announces. 'Then all we've got to get through is the party in the evening, and then Sunday lunch en famille, and then we can go home.'

'Ooh the party,' drawls Louis drunkenly. 'I'm *soooo* excited.'

'Yeah, I can just imagine it now,' Tanya nods. 'Mahler at his most boring in the background, dry sausage rolls, and a warm bottle of Black Tower with seven straws. You know I've just had an awful thought.' She flutters a hand melodramatically to her forehead. 'What on earth am I going to wear?' she drawls sarcastically.

'You could borrow my hot-pink hot pants, darling,' Louis tells her. They roll about together on their bench seat snorting with laughter, the bottle of vodka they've nearly consumed between them obviously taking its toll.

'No,' she snorts, 'there's nothing for it, I'm going to have to pop into town tomorrow and buy something new. A rat catcher perhaps? Or a tweed twin set with green wellies.'

'With a deer stalker,' Louis howls, 'don't forget the deer stalker.'

The following night, Louis, Tanya and I descend the stairs in jeans and a random slash of lippy and little else in the way of make-up – except for Louis of course, who as usual is sporting the obligatory blue mascara – to find the house packed with more designer wear and more people than Paris-fashion week.

Instead of the small family gathering we were expecting, with warm wine and Twiglets at twenty paces, a major-league party is in full swing with at least one hundred people already boozing, and more arriving in a steady flow through the open front doors.

The drawing room has been converted into a disco, where a proper DJ, with speakers the size of an elephant's backside and laser lights that are pulsing in time to the beat, is playing the latest upbeat funk from Limp Bizkit. There's a makeshift bar in another corner of the room, manned by two hired barmen in naff clip-on dickey bows, and across the vast hall, the dining room has been turned into a rather impressive running buffet. Locals in black skirts and neat white blouses are scuttling amongst the guests handing out flutes of champagne. Tanya hits the middle section of the split staircase which leads down from the galleried landing, shrieks loudly and turning, rushes back upstairs to change again, closely followed by Louis and me.

'When did all of those people arrive?' Tanya howls, sprinting down the long corridor towards her bedroom, and flying straight into the bathroom to wash her hair. 'I know I've been flat out for most of the day, but how on earth did I miss that? Honestly, I'm going to murder Gray for not warning us she was having a full-on, full-scale party! The way she was talking last night, I thought it was long-lost aunts and uncles, and a swift game of musical chairs!'

Whilst Tanya hurls herself bodily into the shower, I head back to my room to change. My obligatory little black dress is gratefully pulled from its plastic cover, and left to air on the bed whilst I carefully apply some party make-up. I think I must have worn this dress about a hundred times in the three years that I've owned it. It's an Audrey Hepburn-style number, which thankfully is pretty timeless, and I tend to ignore the fact that my friends have seen me in it at practically every single formal occasion we've been to. A quick brush through my hair and some make-up will do me, but I know from experience that I'll have to wait a while for Tanya.

Ten minutes later, however, a blood-curdling shriek from Tanya's room sends my hand skidding across my face, lipstick slashed across my cheek like a bright red gash. The inter-connecting door is locked. I sprint along the corridor in just my knickers, convinced by the sheer terror in Tanya's voice that she's, at least, being brutally and painfully murdered by a mad axe-wielding intruder, a bright-pink blush the only thing covering my modesty as I encounter Grace's stepfather number two, Sylvester, emerging from the family bathroom in a striped Turnbull and Asser bathrobe.

I burst panting into Tanya's room, to find her cowering in a corner by the bed, wrapped in a large white towel, staring open-mouthed and wide-eyed at what look suspiciously like a pair of shoes.

'What on earth's the matter?' I gasp breathlessly.

She gibbers and points.

'What? What is it?'

'I just got out of the shower, and I found . . .' She pauses, and points again, mouth forming a horrified grimace.

'Found what, Tanya?' I reply in exasperation.

'That!' she replies, the pointing getting animated.

I head over in the direction of her stabbing finger, expecting to find at least a dead and decomposing body, only to freeze in my tracks as my nose is assaulted by a really vile stench. That

196

could be the decomposing part, but fortunately I can't see a body. Yet.

I glance fearfully round at Tanya. 'What on earth has happened?' I demand.

Tanya sniffs heavily with upset, and then coughs, as in doing so she inhales a touch too much of the stench permeating the room. 'One of his dogs has crapped in my new Jimmy Choos!' she wails in horror.

No dead body. But in Tanya's eyes a serious crime has been committed. That's it. Whatever chance Stuart stood with Tan he's just lost. A horse dribbling on her Gucci leather jacket was bad enough. I mean at least that wiped off with a bit of non-green spit and some loo roll . . . but this! Total sacrilege. A big heap of something stinking on a delicate pair of very expensive designer footwear.

'Oh dear,' is all I manage to say in reply. Very succinct, Ollie, very helpful.

'I know who did it!' Tanya shrills, like Miss Marple at a murderous house party.

'*Who* did it?' I ask her, shaking my head to clear visions of a vengeful Stuart squatting over her shoes with his trousers round his ankles.

'It was that bloody dog . . . terrier . . . scrappy-haired ugly . . . thingy!' She spits the insults. 'It gave me a dirty look when I growled at it earlier.'

'It's a dog, Tan. Dogs shit. They don't think, they just shit.' I hardly think a dog would seek revenge, or notice insults, but Tanya's too upset to reason with. I turn my attention to repairing the damage instead of explaining it. 'Well, I think we'd better find you something else to wear.'

'I want to wear this dress. Those shoes go with this dress,' Tanya continues, her bottom lip trembling petulantly. Apart from the fact that the shoes obviously added a pretty hefty lump to her outstanding credit-card debt, Tanya's immediate horror is born from the fact that she now has to re-think her outfit.

My suggestion that we could rinse the shoes out – you know, flush them down the lav a few times, then hit them with the power shower – is greeted with a look of sheer scorn, and the offending pair are finally disposed of, with much pulling of faces, in an empty Sainsbury's bag, using a pair of antique silver salad tongs that I had nipped down and stolen from the buffet laid out on the long table in the dining room.

Getting rid of the stinking shoes was the easy part; trying to persuade Tanya to choose something else to wear takes me twenty minutes and a whole dumper-truck full of well-aimed flattery. She's finally ready, poured into something diaphanous and revealing from Whistles that's just as gorgeous, if not more so, as the previously chosen outfit, but she's still sulking.

Louis, who's missed all of the excitement, dances into the room to see if we're fit to accompany him downstairs. He's resplendent in a very fitted crushed-velvet burgundy jacket that looks as if it's just been thrown off by Laurence Llewellyn Bowen, and a pair of bum-hugging, emperor-purple, boot-cut moleskins. His outfit is complemented by a bare tanned chest, Tanya's pink snake-skin boots, and more make-up than me. 'How do I look?' he asks, twirling on his heels.

'Gorgeous,' announces Tanya kissing him lightly on the cheek.

'Too gorgeous,' I add, thinking of Gray's reaction now that she's become more conservative than Maggie Thatcher.

'Don't you dare ask me to change, Ollie,' Louis pouts. 'I am what I am and if Stuffy Stuart doesn't like it then he can go stick his head up one of his tractor exhausts.'

Once downstairs, Tanya hunts out Gray to severely admonish her. She's in the drawing room, with her mother Tula, who always reminds me of a mixture of Honor Blackman and Patsy from *Ab Fab*. She's sixty, bleached blonde and wrinkled, but still attractive in an OTT kind of way. Tonight she's wearing a bright-orange, fringed-suede minidress, pointy Avengers boots, earrings that could tune you into the Mir Space Station, and more make-up than Louis. She looks as if her dress sense got stuck in a sixties' time warp.

'I didn't realise it was fancy dress,' Louis mutters, raising his eyebrows at her.

'I think she looks *fabulous*!' breathes Tanya, forgetting the recent shoe incident in the excitement that she's going to get to party the night away with someone who's been one of her role models since they first met.

Tula is also berating Grace about springing a surprise party on everybody. 'Trust you, darling. You're the only person I

198

know who would throw an engagement party three weeks before the actual wedding.'

'Well, we weren't going to have one. Then we thought, what the hell, you only get the chance once in a lifetime, and if we don't do it now, we'll be too late.'

'It's their *engagement* party?' I hiss to Louis in surprise.

'You could have told us,' Tula continues moaning at Grace, one of her favourite pastimes. 'We'd have bought you a present.'

'Yeah. A pooper scooper,' Tanya adds savagely, suddenly noticing that the dog in the dock for the murder of her shoes is skulking by the unlit fireplace. 'Or even better a humane mutt killer. Although it wouldn't worry me if it wasn't too humane. You know, I'm *sure* it was that bloody terrier, it keeps looking at me with this stupid smug expression on its face.'

'Dogs can't look smug,' I reassure her.

'Trust me,' she hisses. 'This one does.'

'Where's my future son-in-law?' Tula is now demanding in a loud gin-sodden voice.

'Probably hiding from her,' I whisper to Louis.

'Probably hiding from everybody,' Louis agrees. 'He doesn't like parties, remember. I bet he's out in the barn with the Boring Belle polishing his brass.'

We're both wrong however. We all look over in amazement as, two minutes later, Tula exclaims in delight as she spots Stuart pushing his way through the crowds of people towards us, progress slow as he stops to say hello to newcomers to the party. 'Ah, here he is! Here's the groom!'

The surprise we're all registering however is not because Stuart's actually shown up – I mean this is his house after all, and therefore he can hardly renege on his duties as host – it's down to the fact that Stuart looks good.

Not just good, but *really* good. He's wearing a brand-new, dark-grey Armani suit, and a beautifully tailored shirt, with no tie, just the little collar unbuttoned in an extremely attractive casual way. He's obviously been into town for a haircut, and the radically close-cut George Clooney look is amazingly flattering.

'Ah, here's my man,' Grace coos affectionately. 'Doesn't he look lovely?'

'He looks very well groomed!' Tula laughs at her own joke.

199

For once we manage to agree with Grace about Stuart without actually lying through clenched teeth.

'Gorgeous suit,' breathes Louis, immediately trotting over to quiz Stuart about shop and cost.

'When did he get his hair cut?' I ask Grace.

'Whilst you were sleeping off your hangovers. I really don't know how you lot could have spent nearly all day in bed on such a beautiful day.'

'You mean you managed to drag him away from the Bedford Belle?' Louis teases her.

'I didn't have to drag him anywhere,' Grace replies. 'He went all on his own. He even bought the suit without telling me! I think he's trying to impress someone; if he hadn't promised to marry me in three weeks' time I'd start to worry!'

'Really?'

'No, I'm only joking,' she laughs lightly. 'I just think he's trying to hold his own amongst you fashion victims.'

'He is? He doesn't strike me as the kind of guy who'd give a damn.'

'Well, there's a lot more to Stuart than meets the eye.'

I suddenly feel really bad. We've really been treating Stuart like he's too dense to notice our less-than-warm approach toward him, the sarcastic comments, the whispered asides. I feel a flood of guilt wash through me, and decide it's best to change the subject. 'Is Finn coming to this surprise party then?'

Grace shakes her head, and puts a warm consolatory hand on my shoulder. 'Sorry, babe. Afraid not. He's working on some big story at the moment, couldn't get away.'

'Oh, what a shame.'

'I understand you two have been spending quite a bit of time together recently,' Grace teases me.

Tanya gives me a strange look. 'But you insisted that you were just friends,' she asks me almost accusingly.

'We are. Sorry, babe, I know how disappointed you are about that, having tried your hardest to make it otherwise . . .' I turn to Grace. 'Tan's been plugging Finn to me like Chris Evans with a favourite record. I think she was more disappointed than me that Finn and I didn't get together. She thought I might finally end my period of sexual purdah and join her in wanton abandon.' I turn back to Tan grinning. 'I

200

know you were probably looking forward to some major league stirring, babe, but we're just mates, honestly.'

'Oh yeah?' Grace asks in disbelief.

'Absolutely. Unfortunately. He's really cute, isn't he? Have you ever taken a good look at his backside?'

'Well no, I can't say that I ever have,' Grace admits with a laugh.

I lick my lips lasciviously. 'Very tasty,' I tell her. 'Like a ripe peach you just want to sink your teeth in.'

'So what's the problem?' Tanya asks me. 'If you think he's tasty why not take a bite?'

'I think I prefer my fruit a touch more sour,' I tell her cryptically.

Tanya's face relaxes into a fairly understanding smile, and she turns away to talk to Tula, who, having spotted the arrival of a partner-in-crime, is tapping a bony bejewelled finger on Tanya's shoulder in order to gain her attention. I do feel quite sorry for Tanya, I think she really wanted Finn and me to get together. Having introduced herself to him that morning in the restaurant, she wouldn't stop banging on about him, plugging how lovely he is in a not-particularly-subtle fashion.

I know Tanya worries that I've been on my own for so long, but it's a fact of life that you don't automatically fancy everyone you meet, no matter how funny, good-looking, or nice they are.

I must admit I was kind of disappointed too when Finn and I decided that nothing was happening between us on the sexual front, but now I'm really glad we didn't click romantically, because I've found a really good friend, and we all know that friendships last long after passion has fizzled away. I know many of the longest-standing relationships started off as friendships, but Finn and I are never going to move on from mildly flirtatious. That extra something, that key chemical reaction that turns a friendship into a romance, just isn't there.

I wish he were here tonight though. I could have done with an ally. Especially when, through the crowd of boozing people, I spot Dan Slater standing over by the fireplace, as usual surrounded by attractive and adoring women hanging off his inflated ego.

Despite the obvious adulation, he looks bored, eyes scouting the room as though he's looking out for someone.

'What the hell is *he* doing here?' I mutter to myself. I haven't seen or heard from him since our little contretemps in the restaurant, and I was really hoping to keep it that way. Tula has tottered off on her spiked heels toward the bar, leaving little pockmarks in the wooden flooring where the Chinese rugs have been rolled up and stored for the party.

Tanya turns back in time to hear me grumbling. 'Who? Who's here?' she asks, the obvious angst on my face fuelling her curiosity.

'That bastard over there.' I point him out to her, and she beams broadly at me.

'You mean you know him?' she drools. 'Tula and I were just drawing lots.'

'What for? To see who gets to drown him in the lake?'

'Well, I could stop him breathing with my thighs if you so desire,' she winks at me. 'He's gorgeous!'

'A gorgeous bastard,' I sigh heavily.

Tanya quickly pulls her gaze away from Dan and back to me. 'A Gorgeous Bastard or *The* Gorgeous Bastard,' she asks.

'The,' I tell her.

'That's him?'

'Yep. The one and only. That, my darling slapper, is Demon Dan, Satan Slater, nemesis and all-round nightmare.'

'You're joking!'

'I kid you not.'

'Wow. No wonder you don't know whether to kill him or get kinky with him.'

'Oh don't worry, I'm not so confused any more, not after that night he let himself into Tates. I think the only option I have left is the murder one. That's if I get the chance to stick the knife in before he does.'

'He'll probably be fine, Ol.'

'You think! The last time I saw him, I bit him, kicked him, then legged it.'

'Oh well, perhaps he won't then.' Tanya shrugs helplessly, and heads after Tula towards the makeshift bar in the corner of the room.

I follow, muttering morosely. 'Cheers, Tan.'

'For what?' she asks cheerfully.

'For your understanding and helpful attitude,' I reply sarcastically.

Tanya pulls a fish face at me. 'Just ignore him, Ollie. You don't have to socialise with him, do you? Pretend he's not even here,' she advises me, hovering indecisively over one of Grace's homemade punches. They're normally a lethal concoction of all of the bottles she can find that are nearing their sell-by date. Tanya takes the safe option and asks the camp-looking barman for a glass of dry white wine.

'And don't have too many of those either,' she warns me as I help myself to a glass of the obnoxious-looking punch and, knocking it back rather too quickly, head straight for a refill.

'Why not?' I wail, trying to recapture the glass she's just confiscated from me.

'Because you've got a job to do tonight. An important job.'

'I have?'

'Stuart,' she says succinctly.

I pretend to look blank.

'The seduction of . . .' she adds very quietly, giving me a meaningful look.

'Tonight?' I can feel my already weak knees begin to tremble, and it's not through the ingestion of a glass of ninety-nine per cent proof alcohol either.

'Tonight,' she replies firmly.

'Oh please, Tan, no, anything but that!'

'We decided we were going to go through with it, babe. This weekend.'

'I know, but I'm not sure that I can.' Oh what a night!

Tan puts a reassuring hand on my arm. 'You'll be fine, babe. Just think of Grace.'

'What? Imagine I'm snogging my best mate instead of her fiancé.'

'That's not what I meant and you know it.'

As soon as Tanya's headed off to join Tula again for a mutual man hunt and major bitching session, I hover back towards the bar and help myself to a couple more glasses of punch. It may be obnoxious but it's got one hell of a kick, and that's really what I need at the moment. I quickly knock back another glass, then helping myself to a recently opened wine bottle, I slope off into a darkened corner in which half of the furniture has been pushed so that people can dance, slump down on a sofa, and decide that I could bring new meaning to the phrase 'bottling out', and get so totally and riotously drunk I won't be able to stand or speak, let alone seduce.

I haven't shaken Tanya for long enough though. I'm just sinking my nose into my second glass of wine, when from the corner of my eye I can see her sidling back up towards me. I turn to face the opposite direction. If I ignore her she might go away. Wrong. There's a vicious tapping on my shoulder. She looks accusingly at the glass and wine bottle I'm clutching onto as fiercely as a bargain hunter in the Harvey Nicks sale.

'What are you doing?' she hisses.

'Juggling,' I reply sourly.

'You promised me you wouldn't drink, Ollie!'

'I did?' I reply, feigning innocence.

'Yep.' Her lips purse into a thin line.

'Well I *had* to drink,' I attempt to excuse myself. 'Firstly it's a party, and that's what you're supposed to do at parties, isn't it? It would look pretty suspicious if I didn't drink at all. And secondly, *he's* here.'

'Who?'

'Nasty Dan, the dastardly developer.'

'I know, but I thought we decided that you were going to ignore him.'

'He beat me to it.'

'You what?'

'Well, you can't ignore someone who's already ignoring *you*, because they wouldn't notice that you're ignoring *them*, because *they* were ignoring *you* first.'

'I think I follow that.' Tanya looks pained. 'Just. Don't worry about Dan; if the worst comes to the worst, I'll seduce him for you.'

'Couldn't you offer to seduce Stuart for me instead?' I plead.

'Is that really why you're trying to get drunk, because you can't face chatting up Stuart?'

'Well, it is their engagement party.'

'We had a plan. We should stick to it.'

'But it's their *engagement* party . . .' I repeat.

'Trust you to develop a conscience all of a sudden,' she sighs in exasperation. 'It's not really a proper engagement party, Ollie. Nobody has an engagement party *after* their hen night.'

'Grace does.'

'Okay, so it is an unorthodox engagement party, and so yes, it makes us totally crass, but it also makes our mission far more urgent! Don't you see that?'

'Maybe we should just let sleeping dogs lie. Stuart's not that bad really, when you get to know him a bit better.'

'You're not telling me that you actually *like* him, are you?'

'Well, like is such an insipid word,' I hedge.

'You *do*, don't you!' she squeaks accusingly.

'Let's just say I don't *dislike* him as much as I thought I did. He's been really quite nice this weekend.'

'Nice is such an insipid word,' Tanya mocks me. 'Tell me, do you think he's right for Gray?'

'Well, nooooooo, I suppose I still wouldn't say that.'

'Do you want her to spend the rest of her life smelling of Labrador, scraping mud off his Land Rover, knitting thermal socks, and coming second place to a stupid steam engine?'

'No, of course not.'

'Then we've got to do this for her sake.'

'I suppose so,' I mutter, gazing miserably into the depths of my almost-empty glass.

'You don't want to do it, do you, that's what this is all about. You're chicken, aren't you?'

'Kentucky could coat me and fry me,' I admit.

Tanya looks at me for a moment, then gives a huge sigh, rolling her eyes to the ornate ceiling. 'Well, it's a shame you're not a pullet then, isn't it?' she quips half-heartedly. 'I'll just have to do it myself, won't I?'

I heave a huge sigh too, of relief. 'Oh will you . . .?'

'Yes,' she snaps, 'but you're still coming with me.'

'You mean you want to offer him a threesome!' I squeak fearfully.

Tanya rolls her eyes. 'No, stupid, but I want witnesses in case it turns nasty. Where's Louis?'

'Trying to chat up Velcro man.'

'Who?'

'The barman. He really fancies Louis. He's got Velcro instead of buttons on his shirt, and he keeps ripping it open to show Louis his chest in an attempt to impress him.'

'Quick release clothing, eh?' murmurs Tan, momentarily distracted. 'I like it.' She shakes her head. 'Anyway, enough messing about. It's time for some serious intervention. I'm going to lure Stuart into the stables on the pretext of actually being interested in those great smelly-breathed beasts out there, and then offer him a knee trembler over the stable door.'

'What if he says yes?'

'Well, that's where you leap out from behind a hay bale, and do your accusatory bit.'

'And what if he says no?'

Tanya looks at me as though I've just suggested that the Pope's an alcoholic. 'Since when . . .' says Tanya, hand on hips, outraged that I could even question her undefeated title of Queen of the Come-On.

'There's always a first time,' I mutter weakly. 'Maybe we should just leave well alone. They do seem really happy together.'

Tanya looks over to where Grace and Stuart are standing, holding hands. Grace is holding court in a group of family and friends, the life and soul of the party, Stuart is hanging back behind her, like a shy five-year-old hiding behind Mummy's skirts.

'It's not happiness,' Tanya says flatly. 'It's just temporary insanity.' She turns back to me and smiles encouragingly. 'I'm going to get Louis, then speak to Stuart. We'll see you in the courtyard in ten minutes, okay? And no wimping out.'

Ignoring Tanya's warnings about keeping a clear head, I knock back another glass of wine for Dutch courage. Despite the fact that I appear to have wriggled out of the leading role, this evening is still something I think I'd rather experience through a nice alcoholic haze. Holding out for as long as I think I possibly can, I finally and very reluctantly turn and begin to make my way out of the drawing room. I head for the corridor that I think leads past the kitchen and into the rear courtyard where Stuart keeps his horses and his pride and joy, the dreaded Bedford Belle.

Two footsteps down it, however, an unexpected hand on my shoulder makes my skeleton jump straight out of my skin, and cling shaking to the ceiling by its trembling bony fingers.

'I'm sorry, I didn't mean to startle you.'

I'd almost convinced myself this evening couldn't get any worse. I was wrong. Dan has obviously followed me out of the drawing room. Why he'd want to do this is totally beyond me, unless he's decided to accost me somewhere dark and quiet and kick me somewhere painful. After our last meeting, he probably wants to get me in a shady corner to wreak revenge for his dented shin and swollen tongue.

'I've been looking for you,' he continues, as I simply stare fearfully at him, waiting for him to launch an attack like a rabid dog.

'You have?' I squeak nervously. It's too dark in the corridor for me to see his face very clearly, so it's hard to judge exactly what feeling is behind this sentence.

'Yeah.' He hesitates for a moment, then moves closer toward me so I can actually see him a little better. Am I imagining it, or does he actually look as nervous as I do? I still take a step backwards out of kick range, just in case. What happens next though catches me more off-guard than a right hook ever could.

'Look,' he says, dragging his eyes up off the floor and looking at me earnestly. 'I'm really sorry about the other night.'

He's apologising? If I wasn't already feeling faint from alcohol and not-very-delicious anticipation of the events still to come in the stables, I think I'd pass out from shock anyway. Admittedly he started it, but I was the one who actually committed ABH.

'I was totally out of order,' he continues, actually looking as if he means this. 'I had no right to do what I did. I'm sorry.'

I stare at him open-mouthed. 'You are?'

'Yeah. Very. I shouldn't have let myself in, it was wrong. And as for the rest of it . . .' He tails off, looking embarrassed, but sounding completely sincere. I'm totally thrown by this. I simply stand and stare dimly at him, not really knowing what to say.

'Look, Ollie, I know we've had our differences, but it would make life so much easier if we could manage to be civil to each other.'

Ah. Okay. Now I understand. This is the olive branch, soon to be followed by the wooden club. 'You mean it's hard to negotiate terms for Tates with someone you end up fighting with whenever you meet them,' I say coldly.

It's like a heavy metal shutter has just come down over his

face. He sighs heavily, eyes sliding away, no longer looking keenly at me, but dully at the floor, features heavy with what looks like disappointment. 'Why does this *always* have to be about the restaurant?' he mutters angrily.

'Because that's what this *is* about . . . isn't it?'

He shakes his head. 'What will it take to get through to you?' He looks up at me again, his blue eyes guarded. 'I like you, Ollie,' he says quietly.

'You do?' I ask in surprise. He certainly doesn't act like he does.

'Yes!' he almost screams in frustration. 'You're rude, arrogant, pig-headed, insufferable sometimes, and totally bloody frustrating, but I can't get you out of my head. I don't know what you've done to me, Ollie Tate. I can't even think straight anymore.'

He reaches out tentatively, and when I don't step away, or attack his oncoming hand with my teeth, runs gentle fingers down the side of my face and across my lips. I'm as mesmerised as a mongoose by a swaying snake, seducing before it strikes. His fingers are inducing the same Catherine Wheel of sparking emotions in my stomach as that bloody kiss did. I can feel myself melting like butter on a hot corncob.

Fight it, Ollie, a small voice says in my spinning head. He's only after one thing, and unfortunately it's *not* sex. He's just using his too-bloody-irresistible charms to get his hands on your restaurant, not your hot cross buns. Treacherous sod, he's more devious than I thought. Mentally telling myself to snap out of it, I just about manage to pull myself away from that wonderful touch, and square up to him. 'Oh I get it,' I say slowly. 'Seduce me, soften me up, get me eating out of your hand, and then maybe I'll do anything for you. Anything you want, like even signing over my right to Tates.'

For a moment he looks searingly angry, but then it's like a cloud passing over his face, a cloud of major-league disappointment. He shakes his head slowly, eyes narrowing as he looks at me, then turning abruptly on his heels, he walks away without a word.

I stand dumbly and numbly in the same spot for a few moments watching his back as he strides down the corridor and disappears from view. Then like Cinderella I hear a clock striking somewhere in the echoing hallway, and it pulls me back to reality. Shit. Tanya!

Speeding down the corridor in the other direction, I bump into a body heading hurriedly the opposite way. The familiar scent of Chanel No 19 reassuringly fills my nostrils. 'Tanya, thank goodness it's you,' I begin. 'You'll never guess what just . . .'

'Ollie, where the hell have you been!' she cuts in agitatedly. 'I'm supposed to be meeting Stuart in the stables in about . . .' she looks at her watch and gasps in concern, '. . . thirty seconds! I told him I wanted to get a good look at his bloody traction engine.' She laughs distractedly. 'He jumped at the chance to get out, after all you know how much he hates parties!'

'Tan, I REALLY don't know if this is such a good idea . . .'

'To be honest, babe, I'm a bit nervous myself, but a girl's got to do what a girl's got to do!' She grabs my wrist and starts to tow me down the corridor past the kitchen where the hired caterer is busy filling a row of mini quiche pastry shells with a mushroom and egg mixture, and out through the back door into the cobbled stable yard, looking at her watch once again as she hurries along. 'Louis should be in place already. I told him to get behind a hay bale or something.'

'What should I do?'

'Just stay outside in case I need you, okay. You can peer in through the top window if you stand on a hay bale, I'll shout if . . . aaaaaah!' There's a loud shriek as Tanya, hurrying way too fast on slippery cobbles in three-inch killer heels, loses her footing and, still grasping hold of my wrist, crumples in a heap on the hard, damp floor.

There's deathly silence for a moment, when all I can hear is the noise of the party going on indoors, then the sound of a pained groan from the hunched body of my friend on the floor. 'Tan! Are you okay?' I hiss in concern.

There's a huge sniff from Tan's downturned face.

'Can you get up?'

'I broke my heel,' she says, her voice choked.

'Another pair of Manolos bites the dust!' I joke weakly. 'Don't worry, babe, we can swap shoes,' I say hopefully, as Tanya makes no move to get up from the floor. 'I know mine aren't exactly designer but . . .'

'I would, babe,' her voice is tremulous, 'but that's not the only thing I think I've broken.' Tanya finally looks up at me. Her face is drawn with pain, and I can see tears stinging in the corner of her eyes.

Bending down quickly in concern, I gently feel Tanya's ankle. 'It doesn't feel as if you've broken any bones, you've probably just twisted it. Come on, you old fogey, we'd better get you back inside.'

'We haven't got time!'

'What on earth do you mean?'

'Stuart will be waiting.'

'Well, he'll just have to carry on waiting, won't he? This is more important.'

Tanya shakes her head. 'No, Ollie, *this* is more important.' She tries to stand up, but fails. 'It's no good, Ollie, *you're* going to have to do it.'

'Can't we take a rain check?' I suggest feebly.

'They're getting married in three weeks, we haven't got any more time left; it's now or never.'

'How about we settle for never, and just make sure we're there for her during the divorce proceedings?'

Tanya doesn't even need to speak, one look says it all.

'Okay.' I give in under the frown. 'Okay. I'll do it. But goodness knows how. What on earth do I say to him?'

'Just get him talking about how he fixed up that heap of crap he's got in there, and then tell him what a clever boy he is, he'll lap it up. All men love flattery.'

'But I don't . . .'

'Just go, he'll be waiting.'

I hesitate. 'Are you going to be okay . . .'

'Fine. Go, Ollie. Now. Before you miss him.'

I head reluctantly over to the large Dutch barn. The door is open and a light is on inside. I take a deep breath, look back at Tanya, who impatiently motions me to go in, and then step inside.

Stuart is already there. He's taken off his smart jacket, which is hung over the end of a rake that's propped against the wall, and with shirt sleeves rolled to his elbows, is lovingly polishing the brass section of the chimney of the Bedford Belle, with a clean yellow duster. He looks far happier in here than he did inside the house.

210

'Er . . . Hi.' I say it so quietly the first time, my voice paralysed by nervous fear, that Stuart doesn't hear me. I cough to clear my throat, and catching this noise, he turns around. 'Hi,' I try again. 'Tanya said you were out here. Not enjoying the party very much?' I'm so nervous my voice sounds like Larry the Lamb on helium.

Stuart shrugs apologetically. 'Not really my kind of scene, you know, crowds of people, small talk. Not my forte, as you've probably observed,' he says in a self-deprecating manner. 'I'm kind of lacking in the social-skills department.'

Oh bless him. I falter for a moment, both impressed and touched by such modest honesty, but Tanya's words are still fresh in my ears as well. I take a deep breath and slide in to seductress mode with all the ease of an old unoiled bicycle trying to go from first to second gear. 'Well, it looks like your skills lie in other directions.' I motion to the engine, then, perhaps a touch too Mae West, I sashay over to him, swinging my hips in fifties' seductive-starlet mode. 'This really is a lovely piece of craftsmanship.'

I've never been good at drama, apart of course from the high drama in my own life. Even I think I sound insincere, but when I flick my eyes nervously over at Stuart again, he's smiling proudly. This gives me the courage to continue my theme. 'It must have taken you ages to get it looking so good.'

'I've been working on it a little every day for the past three years,' he replies, gazing adoringly at the engine.

'Wow, now that's what I call dedication.' Oh my goodness, I'm simpering. The *shame*. 'Every day for three years!' I echo, as if I'm impressed. Blimey. The man's obsessed! My best friend is marrying a man who looks at a traction engine with more lust and affection than he does at her. Tan's right, we can't let her do this. No matter how much my instincts are telling me otherwise, I've got to go through with this. For Grace's sake.

I move in closer and run my hand in what I hope is a seductive fashion over a painted black fender, before bringing it to rest on Stuart's arm. 'You're a clever man, Stuart. Grace is a really lucky girl,' I murmur in my best come-to-bed voice.

He catches the new note in my voice, feels my hand on his elbow, and turns to me with a puzzled expression on his face.

'A *really* lucky girl,' I repeat, moving my hand rather shakily up to his shoulder, not realising until it's too late that I've left

211

a trail of black dust on his shirtsleeve from where I rubbed my hand across the black fender of the Belle.

Our faces are now only inches apart. It's no good, I've got to close my eyes. Not through some misguided spark of passion, but simply because I can't bear to see what I'm doing! I lean in towards Stuart, puckering up as if I'm about to take some disgusting medicine instead of presenting my face for a passionate kiss. I open one eye. Stuart is standing surprised and hideously transfixed in front of me, eyes as wide and frightened as Bambi in the face of the forest fire. He looks as though he wants to be kissed as much as I want to do the kissing. Oh hell. It's now or never.

I grab a fistful of shirt, and pull him towards me, planting a hard smacker on his shocked and rigid lips. It's like pressing my lips against a cold wooden surface.

'What the hell do you think you're doing?'

I drop Stuart like a chastised dog being ordered to loose a stolen ham bone, as an angry voice booms across the vast barn, echoing into the high ceiling. I just want to curl up in a corner and die. Of all the people that could catch me doing this it had to be him, didn't it! Where on earth is Louis, he's supposed to be my lookout!

Dan Slater strides into the barn, eyes blazing with anger. Looking around in panic, I catch a glimpse of Louis lurking terrified, eyes agog, behind a hay bale, as Dan grabs me just above the elbow, and drags me out of the stable, leaving Stuart to bolt off in the other direction, like a nervy greyhound released from the traps.

'I don't believe you,' Dan's muttering, his voice whilst low pitched as venomously angry as a trapped wasp. 'You selfish little bitch. You just couldn't bear to see her happy, could you? She's your best friend, for heaven's sake! How could you?'

'It's not what you think.'

'I know what I saw and what I heard!' His fingers are digging into my arm quite painfully in a vice-like grip, as he literally carries me across the courtyard and back into the house.

'I suggest that you get your facts straight before making unfounded accusations, Mr Slater,' I snap at him in a faint echo of the words he threw in my face that day in the restaurant.

212

He stops and swings me round to face him, catching hold of my other wrist so that he has both of my arms trapped in his strong grip. We're back at the spot in the corridor where we were twenty minutes ago, but there's absolutely no trace of the warmth that was in his eyes then. In fact they are now cold, hard, and kind of frightening.

'I don't know what your game is, Ollie Tate, but I don't like it.'

'And what the hell has anything I do got to do with you?'

'When you're trying to screw up my friends then it has a hell of a lot to do with me. Or should that be trying to *screw* my friends?'

'I wouldn't sleep with Stuart if you paid me,' I mutter.

'Then what the hell was going on in there?'

I stare at him truculently, embarrassment and anguish at being caught doing something so outrageously awful as trying to snog my best friend's fiancé, especially by Dan Slater, making me appear as sullen as a schoolgirl on permanent detention.

'And where do you think you're going!' he snaps as, refusing to answer, I wrench away from his grasp, and head down the corridor towards the stairs, intent on escape.

'I'm going to my room to pack if you must know,' I spit, trying to hide the tears, which are welling rather embarrassingly in my eyes.

'And totally ruin Grace's party? No, you're bloody not! You're going to get back in that room with a fucking smile on your face, and act like nothing has happened.'

'I can't do that!' I wail.

'Then tell me what the hell's going on.'

'I can't do that either.' I sink down on the bottom step of the wide stairs, and let my red face fall into my cold hands.

'You can't stay there, Ollie,' Dan says minutes later, when I still haven't moved or uttered a word. People are giving me curious looks as they head from the living room to the buffet in the dining room, probably assuming that I'm the worse the wear for drink. Oh how I wish I were!

'I need a drink,' I announce, suddenly standing up and brushing past him. As I head towards the living room and the temporary bar, I feel Dan's arm slide through mine, and with an iron grip, he guides me back to the darkened corner where

213

I was perched half an hour ago on one of the sofas. Would that I could wind back the clock. I'd have just stayed here and saved an awful lot of hassle. He pushes me down onto a sofa and then, accosting a wandering waitress, takes two champagne glasses, and puts both glasses in my hands. 'You stay here,' he commands me.

I want to tell him to stick his orders up his backside, but I haven't got the nerve or the energy, and for some strange reason I do as I'm told, and stay put, morosely drinking from alternate hands.

He comes back into the room twenty minutes later accompanied by a pale-faced Stuart, who, completely ignoring me, goes to join Grace and her mother who are dancing to 'Come on Eileen' on the make-shift dance floor at the end of the room.

Dan comes back over into my corner and sitting down next to me, takes one of the half-empty glasses from my hand, and drains it. 'You're lucky,' he says, putting the empty glass on the floor next to his feet. 'I've managed to persuade Stuart that you're drunk, depressed and desperate, and that the best thing he can do is put whatever it was that happened out in the barn down to a moment of madness on your part, and forget about it.'

'Ooh I'm *soooo* lucky. Drunk, depressed, and desperate, thank you so much!' I reply, dully. 'I think I'd rather have told him the truth!'

'Which is?'

'Which is nothing to do with you,' I reply, looking around hopefully for more kind ladies dispensing alcohol. Dan's right in a way, I am depressed, and now I'm desperate to get drunk.

'Still following that theme, are we?' he replies sarcastically. 'I have the right to remain silent, on the grounds that I might incriminate myself . . .' He reaches out a hand towards me and I instinctively flinch away, assuming he's either going to try to slap the truth out of me, or slap some sense into me, or both. He does neither, simply runs a surprisingly gentle hand down across my cheek until his fingertips are resting against my temple and, shaking his head, says more to himself than me, 'What's going on in there, Ollie? I really wish I knew . . .'

A sudden unexplainable urge to confess all is fortunately interrupted by the appearance of Tula. It's the first time in my life that I've actually been pleased to see her, despite the fact that, as usual, I am in the wrong in her eyes, this time for my apparent wanton monopolisation of Dan. 'Come now, Olivia,' she purrs, swaying in front of our sofa on her Post-Office-Tower heels. 'You can't keep the best-looking man in the room to yourself *all* evening.'

'I'm afraid it's *I* that am monopolising Ollie and not the other way round,' Dan cuts in, smiling in a charming but slightly frosty fashion at Tula, who either has a problem with her false eyelashes slipping, or is winking quite heavily at him. 'We have a few . . . er, business items that we need to discuss . . .'

'Well, in that case I *definitely* have to get you on the dance floor, this is a party after all. I really think business should be saved for the boardroom.'

'Unless it's funny business, and then you're much better off in the bedroom, eh, Tula?' I cut in acidly, knocking back yet more champagne.

Tula stops winking at Dan, and turns to glare at me instead. I glance at Dan, expecting him to be joining her on the glare-at-Ollie front after my ill-timed attempt at sarcastic wit, but to my surprise, he's struggling not to laugh.

'It's only the very unimaginative who limit sex to the bedroom, Ollie darling,' Tula states icily.

She turns abruptly away from me and, leaning over Dan, wraps her hand around his wrist, her whole demeanour softening as she leans toward him. 'Come and dance with me, darling,' she breathes, gin fumes floating around us like exhaled cigarette smoke.

The Lambada begins to throb from the surround-sound speakers, and Tula starts to shimmy in front of Dan like a lap dancer moving in for the thrill, her bony hips cracking loudly as she performs a series of pelvic thrusts that would threaten rupture for an abdomen less toned on a woman her age. It's the first time I've ever seen Dan Slater look scared.

He begins to proffer an apology on the grounds that he's not a big dancer, but Tula's having none of it. 'Oh but I insist!' she trills, tightening her orange-painted talons around Dan's wrist, and practically hauling him to his feet. 'It's tradition for the usher to dance with the mother of the bride.'

I've never heard of this one before, but who am I to argue

215

the point. I mean, as much as I dislike Tula, I'd rather Dan was being carted round the dance floor by her than playing Torquemada to my heretic prisoner. And it certainly doesn't look as if Tanya or Louis will be galloping in to save me either. She and Louis have now managed a pretty major disappearing act themselves. Where the hell are they? I'm hoping that any minute now they'll come back in the room and rescue me from Dan, but no such luck.

As she leads her prisoner onto the dance floor, I don't know whether to laugh or be annoyed as I hear Tula say in a rather loud whisper, 'I thought I'd better come and rescue you from Olivia, she's a nice enough girl but far too dull for someone like you.'

I wish Dan did think I was dull. It would be better than the view he seems to have of me at the moment. Mentally deranged hussy would probably be a pretty apt summary of his opinion of me. I don't think I better ask him to kiss me goodnight this evening! I think the only kiss Dan would willingly give me at the moment would be a Glasgow one.

Taking the opportunity to sneak away from the party, I head upstairs and fall thankfully into my room. Closing the door firmly behind me, I lean back against the solid wood for a moment, whilst my poor heart attempts to reduce a few beats per second, and then turn around and push the heavy metal bolt home to lock myself in. I know Dan is currently trapped between Tula's skinny thighs as she tries to Lambada her way into his underpants, but I wouldn't put it past him to come looking for me if he manages to make a break for it and escape.

In fact I wouldn't be surprised if he positions himself outside my room for the night, standing sentry, making sure I'm not going to try to slip along the corridor in the buff and attempt to seduce Stuart with the lure of my naked body. Ugh! I don't know what would be worse: Dan thinking that I actually fancy Stuart, or him knowing the truth.

This one will have to remain theoretical. Even if I tried to explain what was actually going on out there, I don't think Dan would listen to me now. The only thing I fervently hope is that he managed to convince Stuart that I was suffering from a never-to-be-repeated lapse in sanity. The more I think about it, the more I'm convinced that this is actually the truth anyway. I must have been mad to think such a stupid scheme would work. And even if it had done, and Stuart had been unable to resist me puckering up to him like a sour sink plunger, it may have made Grace think twice about marrying him, but what repercussions would there have been on a friendship that means more to me than most things in my life? What repercussions might there still be?

Two minutes later my poor nerves, which are already as strung out as a wrung dishcloth, take another battering as the en-suite bathroom door swings open, and Louis's pale face slides cautiously through, making me jump six feet off the duvet.

'Are you alone?' he whispers nervously.

I nod, heart pounding.

'Are you okay?'

I shake my head.

'I am *so* sorry we just abandoned you!' He shoots through the door, and comes and sits next to me on the bed, enveloping me in a big hug.

'Where have you been?' I mumble miserably into the warm and familiar comfort of his velvet-clad shoulder.

'Casualty.'

'What?' I look up in alarm. 'What's happened?'

'Well, after Dan frog-marched you out of the barn, I tried to follow, only to find Tan crumpled in a heap in a dark corner, nursing an ankle that looked like black pudding.'

'Oh no, I'd forgotten all about that. Is she okay?'

'Nothing major. Just a bad sprain. She'll be up in a minute, she just got mobbed by sympathy wishers on our way back in. It's amazing how much attention a pair of crutches can get a girl. I've already got first dibs on borrowing them when she's better.' He laughs half-heartedly.

'Did you tell her what happened?'

'Yep.' He nods. 'It filled the one and a half hours we had to wait in casualty. Well, wasn't that a total disaster . . .'

I let my head fall wearily back onto Louis' shoulder. 'You can say that again,' I mumble.

'Well, wasn't that a total disaster?' repeats a tired mocking voice.

I look up and see Tanya hopping slowly through the bathroom door on her crutches. 'I'm so sorry, babe!' she pouts,

217

heading awkwardly over, before tumbling down onto the bed on the other side of me, bandaged ankle stuck out in front of her like a poker. 'I feel as if it's all my fault! I saw Dan coming, but I just wasn't quick enough to warn you.'

'What do we do now?' Louis asks.

'I think the best thing we can do is leave, as quickly and as quietly as possible.'

'What, now?'

'No, that would look a bit odd, wouldn't it? Besides, I can't drive, what with the vodka from last night, and then tonight's alcohol added on.'

'What the hell was Daniel Slater doing out there anyway?' asks Louis in a fit of pique.

'I think he was following me,' I reply slowly.

'Why would he do that?'

'He wanted to talk.'

'About the restaurant?'

Was it about the restaurant? I thought so at first, but now I'm not so sure. I shrug helplessly. 'Do you know something? I don't know, I really don't know.'

In the total mess that has been this evening, I'd almost managed to forget that Dan said he liked me. Well, I bet he doesn't any more.

We're a motley crew leaving the next morning, all of us pale and drawn, although unfortunately for us, not from the hangovers that are dogging most of those who actually had a pretty good time last night.

Tanya, limping and leaning heavily on her crutches and a po-faced Louis for support, makes herself feel a little better by momentarily managing to connect the heavy rubber end of one of her crutches with the scrawny arse of her sadistically snarling doggie tormentor.

I've volunteered to carry most of our luggage in the hope that I can slide out unnoticed, hidden behind it, a walking wall of Louis Vuitton. If I could, I'd cover myself from head to foot in LV logos and pretend to be a suitcase. Instead of simply a *mental* case.

Unfortunately, there's a leaving committee waiting to say goodbye. Grace is still on a party high, grinning happily at everyone, kissing her goodbyes once, then so pleased that the party, in her view, was such a major success, and so sad that everybody's leaving already, running round to kiss everybody again. Stuart hovers uncertainly in the background, shaking Louis's hand, smiling distractedly at Tanya and avoiding me fearfully as if I had a vicious strain of contagious leprosy.

Hurling Tanya's expensive luggage unceremoniously into the boot, I get gratefully into my car, and have the engine started before the other two have even set foot inside, almost spraining Tanya's other ankle by pulling off before she's actually managed to lower herself completely into the front seat. With Grace calling out to ask for the twentieth time whether we're absolutely positive we can't stay for Sunday lunch, I fire up my engine, wave distractedly, and hurtle down Stuart's long drive, scattering pheasants, and freaking out Louis as I narrowly miss flattening a confused rabbit, which zigzags dangerously in front of the car before hurling itself desperately into a grass-filled gully at the side of the road.

We're all silent until we hit the M1, when the joint sigh of relief is heavy enough to mist up the windows.

'That's it, from now on we stay well out of it,' I state emphatically. 'I am never, repeat NEVER, going through something like that again. Let's just hope that Stuart keeps his trap shut or Grace'll be sacking us as bridesmaids.'

'She'll be sacking us full stop,' Louis grumbles from the back.

'You mean we're just going to sit back and let her go through with it?' Tanya asks in concern.

'Exactly,' I reply. 'We're going to go to that bloody wedding, put on the dresses, put on the smiles, and make like we're happy for her. After all it is supposed to be the happiest day of her life . . .'

'Yeah,' Louis adds sullenly, 'and the most miserable of ours!'

'Blimey,' I say, looking round, all three of us as glum as a lottery winner who's just thrown his ticket out with the trash. 'We're a right bridal shower, aren't we?'

After dropping the other two off, I finally arrive home at about midday. Sunday lunch is in full swing in Tates, but I'm not needed in the restaurant having arranged cover for the whole weekend. I wasn't exactly expecting to be back this early. I'm just debating whether to go down and help out anyway, rather than being alone with my thoughts, which is quite frankly not advisable at the moment, when my private telephone line rings.

'Hey, babe, I hear you had a bit of a disastrous weekend.' It's Finn. For some reason the sound of his cheerful friendly voice brings the tears stinging to the corners of my eyes.

'How on earth do you know about that?' I ask, raking the back of my hand across my eyes to brush them away.

'Come on, Ollie, you know better than to ask a journalist that question. I knew you couldn't stay out of trouble without me there to look out for you.'

'Oh don't,' I reply. 'It was awful, Finn, really awful.'

'Fancy some company?'

'Oh yes, please,' I sigh gratefully.

'Put Sid James on, I'll be round in half an hour.'

Finn arrives bearing wine, a box of Jaffa cakes, and a big hug, which is what I needed most of the three, although desperately grateful for all. He uncorks the wine, hands me a large glass, and settles down on the sofa, whilst I tell him the whole sad sordid story with much melodramatic sighing, gesturing, and a certain degree of embarrassment, especially when it comes to telling him about the bit where I puckered up and plunged in.

I finally winge my way to the end, only to look up expecting automatic sympathy and see that he's actually laughing instead. 'It's not funny!' I admonish him. 'I used to be able to talk to Grace about anything. Now I'm keeping a secret from her. A big, fat, horrible secret that would probably blow apart our friendship if she ever found out the truth. Maybe I should just tell her everything, and lay myself at her mercy . . .' I sigh melodramatically.

'You only want to tell her because it would make you feel better,' he says rationally. 'It might help you cope with the guilt, but trust me, it's not always the best thing to be completely honest. I think there's less harm done by just trying to forget about what happened. Believe me, you'll look back on this in a few years' time and laugh.'

'You think so?'

'I know so.'

'Maybe you're right, but that's easier said than done, Finn.

220

Even if I could just forget about it, there are other people who I'm certain won't be forgetting what happened quite so easily.'

'Like who?'

'Well, there's Dan for one, and Stuart, and what if either of them said something to Grace?'

'From what you said, Dan seems to be attempting a clean-up operation. You know, damage limitation. He won't say anything.'

'Maybe not, but he's probably drawing up my eviction order as we speak,' I say morosely, refilling both our wineglasses. 'I know it sounds a really crass thing to say considering, but one of the worst things is the fact that Dan probably thinks I actually find Stuart with a U attractive. I mean, he caught me trying to molest the guy, what else is he going to think?'

Finn watches me silently for a moment. 'You like him, don't you?'

'Be serious!'

'I am.' He studies me closely, an infuriatingly knowing smile on his face. 'It's not the way you react. It's the way you *over*react.'

I pause for a moment, then decide that out-and-out denial is just a waste of time. 'Okay,' I admit, 'so I find him attractive. But it's such a contradiction to how I feel about him. You know, I don't think I've ever seen anything nice about him. For someone I don't know that well, he's always managing to stick his bloody oar into my life!' I stop when I realise that Finn's stopped smiling and is once more laughing at me.

'There you go again. Pure passion.'

'Well, he's messing with something I'm passionate about.'

'And why do you think he's messing?'

'Because he's a hard-bitten businessman, who doesn't let human kind, of which, incidentally, he's not a fully paid-up member, get in the way of a fast buck.'

'But you still fancy him.'

'Yes,' I sigh. 'I still fancy him.'

Finn reaches a long arm around my shoulders and hugs me hard. 'Life can be a bitch sometimes, can't it,' he murmurs.

I rest my head wearily on his shoulder, taking strength from his warmth and non-judgemental understanding. 'You smell good,' I tell him, breathing in the clean citrus smell of his aftershave. 'Sometimes I really wish I fancied you instead.'

221

'I know, sad isn't it? It's not the end of the world though. We could still go for some gratuitous sex?'

Pulling away, I grab one of the sofa cushions and wallop him with it.

'Ooh, play fighting. This is tantamount to foreplay, you know. I'm just kidding!' He holds his hands up, as I throw him a mock-disgusted glance. 'As a matter of fact, I couldn't fool around with you, even if I wanted to.'

'Oh yeah.' I stop my next cushion attack in mid-flight. 'Is there something you want to tell me? Or maybe *someone* you want to tell me about?'

'Not just yet,' he replies grinning coyly. 'It's far too early days, but let's just say, you should hold the front page . . .'

Chapter Ten

The following Monday night – well Tuesday morning if we're being literal – Tanya is staying over at mine after what was supposed to be a wild night out to cheer us all up, but turned out pretty flat in the end, none of us really being in the mood to party. Even Louis was happy to go home just after midnight, with none of the usual pleading to join him at a club somewhere to rave his Lycra legs off until dawn.

Tanya and I are just toasting an entire granary loaf in the minuscule flat kitchen, having been hit by a bad attack of the midnight munchies, when the doorbell starts to ring repeatedly.

'Who on earth could that be at this time?' I exclaim, dropping a slice of toast butter-side down onto the table, as the sudden noise makes me jump.

'Louis?' suggests Tanya.

'He's got a key. He'd just let himself straight in.'

The doorbell rings again, longer this time. Tanya peers out of the kitchen window. 'I can't see who it is. You'd better answer it.'

I'm tempted to pick up the knife that we used to cut the bread, just in case I happen to have an escaped axe-wielding convict on my doorstep but, telling myself that I'm being majorly paranoid, I clatter down the stairs with just a piece of toast in my hand. A slice of dripping granary is hardly a defensive weapon, but I suppose I could always go for assault and buttery. Whoever it is on my doorstep appears to have permanently glued their finger to the buzzer, which is now on constant ring. 'Okay, okay, hold your horses,' I yell, pulling the door open.

Grace must have been leaning on the door as well as the bell. As soon as I yank it open she falls through into the

223

hallway, and lands in a heap at my feet. 'Oh shit!' she exclaims, rubbing her knee, which she bumped on the bottom step.

'Grace?' I say in surprise.

She looks up at me; her eyes are red from crying, but they're also blazing with outrage. Surprise makes way for major concern.

'Gray, what on earth's the matter?'

Shaking her head, she gathers herself up off the floor, and pushes past me, heading up the stairs to the living room. I drop my toast on the doorstep and, hastily pulling the front door shut, run after her in panic. 'Grace, what is it?' I demand again, puffing after her. 'Tell me.'

She turns to face me, eyes hollow and sad, yet blazing with indignation. 'I've left Stuart!' she shouts angrily.

'You're joking!'

Tanya, who's just coming out of the kitchen, mouths, 'Yes' and does an expansive thumbs up and a little dance of joy behind Gray's back, which is fortunately cut short by her still dodgy ankle giving way again.

I, however, can see my best friend's face. I don't *like* what I can see.

I guide her to the sofa. 'What on earth happened, babe?'

'You're not going to believe this,' she says bleakly, sinking into the seat. 'You're really *not* going to believe this.'

'Tell me,' I reply urgently.

She looks up at me, eyes hollow. 'Stuart he . . . well, he . . . oh!' She sighs and shakes her head quite violently as though doing so will dispel whatever it is that is upsetting her so badly. 'Oh, Ollie, I can't believe it . . .' She pauses again and looks up at me, face pained and frowning. 'Stuart . . . he actually suggested that you were coming on to him at our engagement party!'

I feel the blood drain from my face.

'Tanya maybe,' Grace continues, throwing a very half-hearted smile in her direction. 'I mean we all know she's a bigger flirt than Mata Hari, it's practically a pre-requisite that she chat up every man she meets regardless of circumstance, but to actually suggest that *you* were trying to chat him up. The arrogance of the man!' She slumps backwards against the sofa cushions and looks back up at me again through slitty blood-shot eyes. 'And the worst thing was the way he told me. All fake concern for my welfare! Said he didn't want to tell me, but thought it was best that I knew what had happened in case I heard it from somewhere else and got even more upset!'

'Oh shit. You don't believe him, do you?' I ask fearfully.

'Believe him! I *know* you don't fancy Stuart,' she states adamantly. Then in a weaker voice adds, 'You don't fancy Stuart . . . do you?'

'Of course I don't,' I reply, highly relieved that I don't have to lie to her on this front.

'Of course you don't,' she repeats. 'I don't know why I even asked. I can't believe he'd tell me such dreadful lies, Ollie. It's like I never knew him at all.'

I sit down next to her and, unable to speak, start to pat her somewhat ineffectually on her shoulder.

'And then he even said that he thought that you've been trying to split us up since we first got together!' Grace turns and sobs into my shoulder.

I look over at Tanya, who has gone as white as me.

'I don't know how I could have been so blind!' Grace wails. 'It's not you that's been trying to split Stuart and me up. It's him that's been trying to get me away from you. He's just trying to push a wedge between me and my friends so that he can have me all to himself. It's sick! He can't bear me to be with anybody but him. Twenty-four seven. Well he's gone and blown it, hasn't he?'

She goes quiet for a moment, and I can feel the tears sliding down her face and onto my bare shoulder. When she speaks again, the anger has gone from her voice, but she sounds interminably weary. 'Can I stay here with you? I don't want to go home. I don't want to be on my own, and I don't want to talk to him either. He doesn't know your number. For heaven's sake, he doesn't even know my best friend's phone number! What does that say about us?'

Abruptly, Grace pulls away and stands up again, taking a few deep breaths as though attending an ante-natal class. 'Maybe this is all for the best. We're two very different people.'

She's talking to herself, not Tanya and me, and is now pacing up and down the room, looking at the carpet. 'I thought we complemented each other, but maybe I was wrong. Well, there's no maybe about it.' She stops walking and her voice falls to a harsh whisper, 'How could I have been *so* wrong about someone?'

Glancing in mortification over at Tanya, I take Grace, who has simply stopped in mid-pace like a toy whose batteries have run down, by the shoulders and steer her into my bedroom, where she needs no prompting to fall fully dressed, face down into the pillow, where she remains totally still, not asleep but completely and utterly shattered.

'I'll make you a coffee,' I tell her, pulling my duvet cover over her inert form. As usual the heat is sauna-like in the bedroom, but she feels cold to the touch.

Tanya's waiting in the kitchen. Ever able in a crisis, she already has a bottle of wine uncorked, has topped up the pot of coffee we started earlier to go with our toast, which is now bubbling away like a mini geyser, and has emptied a packet of disgustingly thick chocolate biscuits onto a plate. 'Is she okay?' Her face and voice are both full of concern, despite the fact that her mouth is also full of biscuit.

I shake my head, and sitting down at the table begin to play with the empty biscuit packet. 'What have we done?'

'Exactly what we set out to do,' Tanya replies, trying to be matter of fact. 'It may seem dire now, but it's for the best. You know it is.'

'We've finally got what we wanted,' I say, ripping the flimsy plastic apart as though it's the wrapper's fault that my best friend is so devastated, 'so why doesn't it feel as good as we thought it would?'

'Because she's hurting, and it's awful to see her in pain.'

'Yeah,' I look up at Tanya bleakly. 'Especially when it's us that have caused it.'

Grace stays at the flat for two days, barely speaking, spurning meals, but then eating everything in sight as soon as she's on her own. I've never gone through so many packets of biscuits and bags of mini Mars Dark in such a short space of time. Calling in to work sick, she spends her time sitting by the telephone, pretending that she's not there on purpose, but jumping six feet every time it rings. She then visibly sinks with disappointment when she remembers that Stuart doesn't have my number, unless he's been so desperate to contact her that he's jumped through hoops of fire to actually get his hands on it. Not that she wants or expects him to have done this, of course, because as she now declares quite vehemently, she hates him as passionately as she once thought she loved him.

I'm waiting as well. Waiting for the relief to kick in that we've finally saved Grace. Waiting for the feeling that what we did was the right thing to come washing over me in a flood of self-righteousness. Unfortunately the only thing that I'm drowning in at the moment is guilt. Be careful what you wish for, because one day you might get it.

By the end of the second day she can't stand it any more and goes home, to pretend that she's not sitting by a telephone for which Stuart actually knows the number.

I drive her back to Islington with mixed feelings. I really don't want her to be on her own when she's obviously so unhappy. The problem is, knowing it's mainly me that's brought on such unhappiness makes it very hard for me to be with her at the moment. I can't look her in the face. And although I truly do sympathise with all my heart when she cries on my shoulder at two in the morning, I feel such a total hypocrite in doing so.

I can't think of what to say to her half the time, especially when she goes through their final conversation for the umpteenth time, repeating everything Stuart said about the incident in the Dutch barn, and repeating again how she can't believe that he would lie to her like that. She keeps pointing out that I spent most of the evening glued to Dan Slater and wouldn't have had a chance to go anywhere near Stuart, and therefore soon comes to the conclusion that he is stupid as well as dishonest.

I'm so scared that I've not only ruined her relationship with Stuart, but I've ruined our relationship too. I've lied to my best friend. I'm still lying to her by omission, by my failure to counter any allegations against Stuart with the truth.

I drop her off at her house with much prolonged hugging, and instructions to come straight back if she's feeling too bad, or to call me at any time of day or night if she needs me. Both of us say goodbye with an incredibly heavy heart.

The following day, I'm relaxing in the kitchen with a vast

sandwich and a trashy tabloid, after a long breakfast session, followed by a busy lunchtime. Mel, who was over an hour late for the lunchtime session, due to her own major drinking session the previous night, is now guiltily making up her lost time, despite my protestations that she really doesn't need to, by cleaning the stove. She's currently on her hands and knees, head in the oven. Not the best thing with a hangover, but she insists that if she starts to feel really bad, she can always turn on the gas.

I'm just contemplating getting us both something a bit stronger than the mug of coffee I'm drinking, hair of the dog for Mel, and hell, any excuse for me at the moment, when I hear the front door of Tates being pushed open. I was so distracted today, I must have forgotten to lock it. Sighing at the prospect of having to kick out what is probably a hungry, irritable, food-seeking, non-English-speaking tourist, who seemed to make up most of my clientele this lunchtime, I put down my paper reluctantly and get to my feet.

'I'm sorry, we're closed now,' I begin tiredly, heading back through the kitchen door into the restaurant. 'I'm afraid we only serve until three on a . . .' I stop dead in my tracks.

Dan Slater is standing in the middle of the room. For some reason I'm not that surprised to see him, but this doesn't stop my heart from joining the half-eaten pastrami and tomato on rye in my stomach.

'Hi,' he says quietly.

Mel staggers into the room from the kitchen, pulling off her apron, which, due to the fact that her waist is so slender, is tied around her twice and therefore rather well knotted. 'I've just finished cleaning the oven so can I go home now, you old slave driver?' she jokes. 'I neeeeed sleep . . . oh.' She stops dead in her tracks as, finally looking up from attempting to unravel her apron strings, she catches sight of the new arrival.

Dan and I finally drag our equally cautious gaze away from each other and look over at Mel. We all stand there silently for a moment, eyeing each other like gunfighters waiting for the clock to strike noon, eyeballs bouncing from one to the other, each waiting for somebody to react.

Finally after what seems like five minutes, but must only have been about five seconds, I turn to Mel. 'Yeah, it's okay, you go home, Mel, we're through here.'

'Are you sure?' she hesitates looking warily at Dan. 'I can stay if you need me.'

'Honestly, it's okay, we're all done here, you go home.'

'Well, if you're sure . . .' she says slowly, making no attempt to move.

I nod, looking far more confident than I actually feel.

'You know where I am if you need me.' She leaves reluctantly. I've never seen her take so long to gather up her belongings at the end of a hard shift; she's normally dialling for a taxi as she serves the last coffee, and sprinting for the door the moment the last customer has drained the dregs.

Dan watches her leave, then looks back at me, as I stand warily some distance away from him. We have the awkward-pause thing all over again, where I decide that I'm far too world weary to worry about why he's here, and then he finally speaks. 'I'm not here to fight. In fact I was hoping for a temporary cease-fire.'

I shrug. 'Glad to hear it. I'm too tired to fight. Do you want a drink?'

He looks at me in surprise, then slowly nods his acceptance. I head over to the bar. 'What's your poison?'

A smile quirks at one side of his mouth. 'I think I should be wary how I answer that question, considering the person who's asking it.'

'Don't tell me, anything so long as it isn't rat or arsenic?'

'A beer would be good.'

I open him a cold bottle of Bud, and offer him a glass which he declines, then make myself a large gin and tonic. He's followed me over to the bar and is now seated on one of the stools. My instincts are to stay put with a three-foot width of mahogany and several pointed beer pumps standing like sentries between us, but I somehow find myself going round to join him on the other side, sliding onto the next bar stool, which is fortunately near by but not thigh-touchingly close.

I sip my drink slowly. I desperately need a good strong slug of alcohol, but I think it's wiser to keep all of my senses as alert as possible at the moment. Whenever I'm in the same room as Daniel Slater I feel like a rabbit trapped in a fox's lair. It's almost as though I can smell the predatory aura that the man gives off.

Dan's leaning with his back against the edge of the bar,

staring into the unlit grate of the fireplace. He drinks nearly half of his bottle before he actually says anything to me. 'I've just been to see Grace.'

'Oh,' I reply slowly, watching his mouth as he raises the bottle to his lips again. He looks sideways at me, and I look away. 'Is she okay?'

He shakes his head slowly. 'She's in a bad state. She really trusts you, Ollie.'

'I know.'

'Which means she no longer trusts Stuart.' He turns to look at me, his normally direct blue eyes clouded with concern. 'Which isn't exactly fair, considering the fact that we both know who's telling the truth.'

Here comes the guilt again. 'It wasn't what you think,' I blurt.

'I know that,' he replies quietly.

'You do?' I ask in surprise.

'I had lunch with a mutual acquaintance yesterday.'

'Oh yeah,' I reply, trying to regain my composure and act nonchalant.

'Yes, Finnian Connelly. He told me what you were really doing that night.'

'He did?' I ask in surprise. I don't know whether to be pissed off or pleased that the loveable, but not dreadfully discreet Finn has told all. In a way I'm glad Dan knows the truth, that I'm not some awful fucked-up bitch who'd try to steal my best friend's man. I just hope that he doesn't think the real reason I tried to snog Stuffy is worse though. I don't know why but I want Dan to have a good opinion of me . . . well, I do know why. It's a weird feeling, liking someone that you've spent so much emotional energy loathing.

Dan is nodding in response to my last question. 'Yeah. He told me everything, Ollie, as far as he knew it. You'll probably be pleased to know that he took quite a bit of persuading to rat on you though. He's very loyal.'

'He's a good friend.'

'Yeah, that's what he said.' He slides a hard-to-read glance sideways at me. 'You're just good friends.'

I have a feeling we've temporarily moved onto a slightly different subject than Stuart and Grace, another underlying issue that we've both been trying to ignore – well that *I've*

230

been trying to ignore. I certainly haven't forgotten our conversation in the corridor of Stuart's vast house, and I'm strangely relieved that he seems to be acknowledging the fact that he now knows that Finn and I aren't an item.

My perceived subject change is only fleeting however. Dan finishes his drink and puts the bottle down on the bar behind him. 'Maybe Stuart's not your ideal man, but this isn't about what you want, is it, Ollie?'

'I want the best for Grace,' I reply cautiously.

'And who are you to judge what's best for her? No, maybe Stuart's not as dashing or as intellectual or as interesting or as funny or as sociable as you think he should be, but have you ever seen her as happy or contented with someone before?'

I hang my head. I don't need to answer this one. We both know that he's right.

'You can lie to yourself, Olivia, but if you really care about Grace as you say you do, then for heaven's sake stop lying to her.'

I sigh heavily, not able to look at him. 'I can't tell her what we did,' I mumble to the floor. 'She might hate me for it. And I know I deserve that . . .' I add before he can, '. . . but it would hurt her even more than she's been hurt already, she's my best friend.' I hang my head in my hands, overcome by what a mess we've made of things, still unable to look Dan directly in the face.

'Stuart's a good man, Ollie.'

'I know that,' I reply quietly. I jump slightly as I feel the unexpected touch of his hands on mine as he gently pulls my hands away from my face and still holding onto them, smiles softly at me. I don't think he's ever smiled at me before.

'Look, I know you thought you were doing the right thing, however misguided . . .' His voice is tinged with kindness. This is worse than being told off by him. I can't take kindness. Not from Dan, and especially not when I don't deserve it.

I can't help myself as the fat, hot, salty tears that were balancing on the edge of my lower eyelids begin to tumble down my cheeks. 'What am I going to do?'

Letting go of my left hand, he reaches out and gently wipes away my tears with the ball of his thumb. 'You'll sort it out.'

'But how?'

He smiles again, but this time it has a touch of irony to it.

231

'Well, you've been pretty resourceful so far. I'm sure you'll think of a way.'

'What about Stuart?'

'Well,' he sighs heavily, finally letting go of my other hand. 'I've spoken to him. I explained what I could without hurting his feelings too much. Like I said, he's a good man, but that doesn't mean he's completely inhuman. He told Grace the truth and she chose to believe you instead of him. He loves Grace to bits, but he has his pride, Ollie. And it's been hurt pretty badly . . .'

Great! I now have visions of Stuart in the same me-induced misery pit as Grace. I'd managed to push most thoughts of him to a completely unused part of my brain. The fact that he could be just as unhappy as Grace had somehow managed to slide past me. I suddenly realise that we'd cruelly and conveniently dehumanised Stuart into something with no feelings, never once considering that what we were doing would hurt him badly too. I didn't think I could feel any guiltier than I already did. I was wrong!

Dan finishes his drink and, standing up, puts the empty bottle on the bar, smiling sympathetically at my miserable face. 'Don't worry too much, Ollie. Believe it or not, I'm a very firm believer in fate. If Stuart and Grace are meant to be together, then they will be regardless of interference from you, me or anybody else for that matter. But whatever happens now, I'm sure that *you'll* try and do the right thing.'

He reaches out as though to take my hand to shake it, but then obviously changes his mind, and as we both hesitate, my hand hovering in midair as well, we end up simply and briefly touching fingertips instead. He turns and makes for the door, and as his fingers closes around the handle, I call out to him. 'Hey.'

He pauses and turns back to look at me.

It takes me a moment to form the words, whilst he looks at me quizzically.

'I'm sorry,' I finally manage.

One side of Dan's mouth quirks into a smile. 'It isn't me you should be apologising to.' He pauses for a moment, and the smile slowly extends to the other side of his face. 'Although it *was* pretty shabby of you to abandon me to my fate with Tula the Terrible the other night. Do you know she got the DJ to play the Lambada *four times in a row.*' He grimaces, and jokingly rubs his lower inner thigh as though in pain. 'The bruises are slowly disappearing, but as for the mental scarring . . .' He shakes his head.

Despite my recent wallow in the murky puddle of self-pity, I find that I too am smiling. 'Thank you,' I tell him slowly.

He shrugs. 'Don't mention it.'

'No I mean it.'

'I know,' he replies quietly, and smiling again, pulls the door to behind him.

Moving over to the window, I watch as Dan walks down the road toward his car. I was wrong: Dan Slater is a nice man. If I was wrong about that, then maybe I'm wrong about a lot of other things too.

The same evening Grace comes back to stay again. Stuart's hurt pride has obviously meant that the telephone at Grace's house has been resolute in its silence, and she therefore feels it's the lesser of two agonies to stay at my place. It's all very well him not phoning her on a phone that he doesn't know the number for, but she really can't handle him not phoning on a number that's stored as speed dial number one on his home and mobile phones, and is the first on his list of BT friends and family. Although she has compromised and brought her mobile with her.

The initial outrage has subsided and she now sits slumped in miserable silence in front of the TV all day. I've never seen her so unhappy.

I spend the weekend working, my concentration not on the restaurant, but on several foolish plans for righting the very big wrong that we've committed. Come Monday evening, a week to the day after Grace arrived in floods of tears on my doorstep, I leave her glued to my sofa watching *National Velvet*, comforted by a box of Kleenex, a bottle of Frascati, and the presence of her mobile phone, and slope off downstairs to the restaurant with the excuse that I need to do some stocktaking. As soon as I hit the kitchen, I'm on the phone to Tanya and Louis, calling them in for an emergency meeting.

Louis, who was on his way to see us both anyway, arrives first, looking worried. 'Is she okay?' he asks, his face a picture of concerned guilt. 'I brought her some books and some mags,

233

and a huge box of chocs to try to cheer her up.'

I shake my head. 'I've never seen her so miserable. Splitting with Arty upset her, but this is another league entirely.' I pour Louis a cup of tea from the pot I have ready on the table.

'It's only me!' Tanya's head appears around the door. 'What's the panic, babe?' she asks coming into the room. 'I was right in the middle of something important.'

'So I can see,' I reply, as her trendy Burberry trenchcoat slips as she sits down, to reveal that all she's wearing underneath is a set of Agent Provocateur underwear and a warm glow.

'The last time we did this we were plotting Stuart's removal,' she laughs, as I hand her a glass of wine as well, but there's no humour in the laughter.

'It's a very different agenda for today's meeting, guys.' I pause, and look from one to the other, desperately willing them to be with me on this one. 'It's Grace and Stuart,' I announce slowly, as they wait intrigued. 'I want to get them back together.'

'You want to do what?' Tanya shrieks.

'I hate to admit it,' I raise my hands defensively at an open-mouthed Tanya, 'but I really think there's only one thing that's going to make Grace happy again.'

Louis sighs and shakes his head. 'I agree,' he says. 'I really hate to admit it too, but that's what I've been thinking.'

'But we've just rescued her from a marriage that would have made her *so* miserable!' Tan objects.

'I'm sorry, Tan,' I state firmly, my conviction that I'm finally doing the right thing making me determined not to waiver, 'but Stuart made her happy. It's *us* that have made her miserable.'

Tanya looks at me defiantly for a moment, and then her face crumples. 'You're right . . .' she sniffs. 'Completely right. I feel like a total heel!' She wails the 'heel' loudly, dropping her head melodramatically onto my collarbone, and sniffing into my T-shirt. 'It's all such a mess!'

'Well, we made the mess, now we're going to have to sort it out.'

'How?'

'By telling her the truth?'

'We can't do that!' Tanya quickly pulls away from my

234

shoulder and stares goggle-eyed at me in horror at such a suggestion.

'She'd understand. We only did it because we love her.'

'We can't just tell her everything outright,' Tanya says. 'I honestly don't think that would be the right thing to do, trust me. It's got to be subtle.'

'How subtle can I make it? I've got to admit that I did actually make a pass at her fiancé,' I mutter sulkily.

'Yeah, but you wouldn't have followed through, would you? We were just hoping that he'd accept the offer to shag in the stables . . .'

'And then we'd know that he's a *real* arsehole and we wouldn't have felt so bad about trying to break them up for no good reason . . .' Louis states morosely. 'Because that's basically what we were doing. Trying to break them up for no good reason.'

'For our own selfish reasons,' I add.

'We could say that we love her so much we were testing him. You know, to make sure that he'd be faithful. And that he passed with flying colours,' Tanya suggests.

'Do you think she'd fall for it?'

'Well, it's got to be better than the ugly truth that her friends are complete rats who thought they'd try and wreck her love life for her,' mutters Louis, getting up from his chair and raiding the fridge as he usually does in a crisis. Leaning against the work surface, with the fridge door still open for instant emergency access, he begins to munch miserably on a handful of grapes he found in the salad tray.

'Don't beat yourself up too much, babe. We *thought* we were doing the right thing,' I tell him reassuringly, 'and now it's time for us to actually *do* the right thing.'

'Yeah, I think we're all agreed on that,' Tanya sighs. 'But what on earth are we actually going to do?'

'I'm not sure, but as someone said to me earlier today,' I tell her, the image of Dan flashing through my brain once again, 'we'll think of something.'

We decide to keep the first plan of action as simple as possible, and I am despatched upstairs to try to persuade Grace to call Stuart, which would at least be a positive step in the right direction.

235

It's far harder than I thought it would be though. She's still totally torn between desperately wanting to speak to him, and never wanting to speak to him again for telling what she feels were outrageous lies about the people who mean the most to her in the world. We don't deserve such dogged loyalty.

'Call him. I know you want to,' I say for the sixth time in fifteen minutes.

'No, I don't,' she replies, her face set in a sulky miserable expression.

'You can't blame Stuart too much . . .' I venture hesitantly.

'I can't blame him! You know what he said about you. He said you'd been trying to split us up since we first got together.'

I take a deep breath. 'Well, we might have given him that impression,' I confess to her. 'You know how protective we are.'

'Really?' For a moment Grace looks hopeful, and then her face falls back into the miserable expression it's been wearing all week, and she shrugs in fake nonchalance. 'Well, even if you did, he hasn't even bothered to contact me. If he cared he'd have called me. And he hasn't so he obviously doesn't,' she states with a depressing kind of logic.

'You're the one that left him. He's probably sitting by the phone right now, hoping and praying that it's going to ring, that you're going to call him.'

Gray blinks up at me through tear-filled eyes. 'Do you think so?'

I nod vigorously, and she ponders this fact for a moment, before shaking her head again. 'I'm not phoning him!' she insists stubbornly. 'He still lied to me about you. That bit was unforgivable, Ollie.'

I know I should tell her the truth and salvage Stuart's honour in her eyes, but I just can't bring myself to do this. I'm a horrible person. Maybe I could go with Dan's drunk and desperate story, but I can't bring myself to do that either. I'm a wimp. I give up.

Leaving Grace with her wine, I head back downstairs to where the other two are waiting for me in the restaurant kitchen. Tanya is still seated at the kitchen table, clutching a large cup of strong black coffee. Her nerves must really be on edge, as she's also smoking a very rare cigarette. Louis as usual has his head stuck in the huge fridge seeking out comfort food.

'Any joy?' Tanya looks up quickly as I head back into the room.

I shake my head despondently.

'I don't believe this,' she smiles weakly. 'We struggled so hard to split them up, and now we're going to have to fight to get them back together again.'

Louis emerges from the fridge, a fork in his right hand, on which is speared a large piece of chocolate-fudge cake. 'I think I've had an idea,' he announces. 'Chocolate feeds the brain cells,' he adds, as I raise my eyebrows at his stolen bounty.

'Come on then, spit it out. The idea, not the cake,' I tell him as he looks despondently at his piece of nicked pudding.

Louis makes us wait whilst he swallows his forkful before I change my mind and confiscate it. 'Well, she fell for him before when he rescued her,' he says, sucking the sticky fudge from the prongs and savouring the last sweet sensation.

'So what are you saying?'

'We need to re-create that moment. Turn Stuart from heel back into hero.'

'So what do you propose this time?' Tanya says sarcastically. 'Kidnap Gray and send Stuart a ransom note? Tie her to a train track and hope he makes it on time?'

'Um, not bad,' I joke half-heartedly, 'but a touch risky. Trains never run to schedules these days.'

'She had a car accident last time, didn't she?' Still hungry, Louis sticks his head back in the fridge to see what else he can purloin.

'I don't think arranging for her to end up engine-down in a ditch again is a very good idea, do you?'

'I'm not suggesting we cut her brakes or anything!' Louis protests.

'Then what are you saying?'

Louis emerges from the fridge again, a cold sausage left over from breakfast balanced between his nose and his top lip as a makeshift moustache. 'Now listen very carefully,' he grins, making his sausage wobble precariously. 'I shall say zeese only wernce!'

It's seven o'clock the following evening. The sun for once is

237

shining, the birds are still singing in celebration of this rare occasion, and Tanya, Louis and I are skulking in a country lane somewhere near Woburn Abbey. Fortunately Louis has left the balaclavas behind this time, but we're still on an undercover mission. Figuring Woburn was about midway between Islington and the outer reaches of Leicester, and timing being pretty crucial, we've found ourselves what appears to be the only isolated and still-working phone box in the vicinity that takes money instead of phonecards, something none of us happen to carry. I know we have mobile phones, but the phone box itself has a crucial part to play in the said devious mission, as it's the only landmark for about six miles on this particular stretch of road, which is deserted apart from the odd timid deer lurking in the woodland.

With me and Tanya crammed together into the bright-red box and Louis hanging off the heaving door, I do the dialling first. Grace is obviously still sitting next to the phone, as it's answered almost before it rings out.

'Hello,' she says breathlessly.

'Grace, it's me.' I hear a soft exhale of breath which registers disappointment that I'm not a particular steam-engine-loving male, and then she sounds pleased to hear from me, despite the fact that she's obviously still as miserable as a dog who's been denied its daily walk.

'Hi, babe. What's up? Where are you? Mel said you'd gone out for the afternoon, but you didn't tell me you were going anywhere, and I've been calling your mobile for ever.'

'We need help!' Louis wails dramatically in the background.

'Great acting, Lou,' Tanya mutters, 'but a bit OTT for a car breakdown.'

'We've broken down, Grace,' I tell her, crossing my fingers behind my back as I lie to her yet again. 'Can you come and get us?'

'Oh shit. Of course, straight away.' I hear the rattle as Grace grabs her car keys from their usual spot next to the telephone. 'Where are you?'

'Bedfordshire.'

'Bedfordshire!' she repeats loudly. 'What on earth are you doing in Bedfordshire?'

'Er . . . we've been shopping.'

'You went shopping . . . in Bedfordshire . . . without

238

me?' her voice breaks a little at the exclusion.

'Well, we wanted to get you a surprise to cheer you up,' I improvise quickly, 'so we could hardly take you with us.'

'Yeah, and it's going to be some surprise!' Louis chuckles in the background, before being shushed by Tanya.

'Can you come, babe? We're really stuck.'

'Of course I'll come. Don't worry. I'm on my way. Just tell me exactly where you are.'

'You can't miss us. We're on the A4012 just outside Woburn, next to an old red phone box.'

One down, one to go.

'She's on her way,' I tell the other two, squeezing out of the way and passing the phone on to Louis, who's volunteered to stage the next move in our game for obvious reasons: I think if I tried to phone Stuart, he'd probably put the phone down on me.

The phone seems to ring forever. What if he's not there? Oh crikey, I hadn't even thought of that.

When we're just about to give up, someone finally picks up. 'Hello?' It's a male voice. He too sounds breathless, as if he's been running.

'Stuart?' Louis asks, then nods excitedly at us. It's obviously him. 'It's Louis. Yeah, fine thanks. How are you? Yeah, I know. Well, that's who I'm calling about. She needs you, Stuart. She's had another accident . . . no, no, we think she's okay, but she's all on her own, and we can't get to her to pick her up. I didn't know who else to call.'

There's a long pause and then Louis beams broadly and does a thumbs-up with his free hand. 'Ooh, you're a total saint. Where? Yeah, you can't miss her, she's on the A4012 just outside Woburn, next to an old red phone box.'

Almost exactly two hours later, Grace's car pulls up next to the phone box. We watch her from behind the safety of the hedgerow where we're lying, hidden somewhat uncomfortably in the camouflage of some scrub at the edge of a spinney. Louis immediately stops grumbling about blisters, having had to park his car in a secluded clearing over a mile down the road and then walk back up to us, and, letting go of his left foot, falls down next to me like a paratrooper spotting the enemy and diving for cover.

Grace sits in her car for a moment obviously completely perplexed as to why we're not where we said we would be, then gets out and looks around in puzzlement. A minute later, she gets back in her car and looks at her map again.

'Come on, Stuart!' I mutter through clenched teeth, hoping against hope that our very rough calculations on time, distance and weight of traffic for both of them were right. 'Knowing our luck he's got stuck in traffic.'

'Or his Land Rover's broken down.'

Louis looks at his watch. 'Where the hell is he?' he hisses. 'Now she knows we're not here, she won't hang around for very long on her own.'

'She probably thinks she's got the wrong place,' I hiss in concern.

Grace gets back in her car and, putting the key back in the ignition, picks up the handset of her car phone, and punches in a number. Fortunately my mobile's set to vibrate for a while before it rings, and I catch it before it starts making any noise. That'd be really great. Grace calls me, and the bush over the road starts belting out 'I'm in the Mood for Love', which Louis downloaded from the internet onto my mobile in a fit of sarcastic teasing over my non-existent love life.

My instinct is to divert the call to voicemail, but Tanya motions for me to pick it up. I ignore Tanya and follow my instincts, pressing the clear button to cut the call.

'What did you do that for?' Tanya whispers.

'I didn't know what to say to her, I'd have blown it.'

Grace starts the car again.

'Quick, she's going. Call her. Call her on her mobile.'

'And say what?'

'I don't know, tell her we'd gone to see if we could find food or something, tell her Louis was starving, and we're heading back and to wait where she is.'

'What about Louis's car?' I ask Tanya. 'Won't she want to know where it is?'

'And what if she suggests that she drives and get us from wherever we are, as it would be quicker?' adds Louis.

'Tell her we've hiked across the fields because we saw a light and she can't reach us by car.' Tanya shrugs. 'I don't know, wing it, but stop her from going!'

I hastily tap in Grace's number. To our extreme relief, as

soon as her phone starts to ring, and she recognises my number, she switches off her engine and pulls on her hand-brake before answering hurriedly.

'Ollie darling, where the hell are you? I thought I'd arrived at where you told me, but I don't think I can be in the right place, because you're not here!'

'Are you outside a red phone box on the A4012?'

'Yes.'

'And is there a . . . er . . .' I look around wildly trying to improvise, '. . . a big tree . . . yeah, a tree just beside it with one branch right next to the third pane of the phone box door that looks like it's doing a V-sign at you.' Tanya rolls her eyes.

Grace pauses for a moment. I watch her look around, then smile in relief as she spots it. 'Yeah,' she replies. 'There is, I can see it. Trust you to notice something like that!'

'Then you're in the right place. We'll be back there in about fifteen minutes, don't move a muscle.'

'But where are you, Ollie, and where's Louis's car?'

'What was that? Sorry, the line's breaking up . . .'

'I said, where's Louis's car?'

'Shkkkkkkk,' I hiss through closed teeth. 'Sorry, babe, can't hear a thing, darling, dreadful signal, see you in a mo . . . and for heaven's sake . . . shhkkkkk . . . stay where you are!'

I punch the disconnect button and roll my eyes at the other two. My heart's beating so hard I can feel it knocking against my rib cage like a rent collector who just knows that his rent-owing tenants are actually in the house and hiding under the kitchen table.

We watch with baited breath as Grace punches out a number on her car phone again. She's obviously trying to call me back, and I hastily switch off my mobile, but to our intense relief she doesn't start to drive off again. Unable to contact me, Grace gets out of the car and walks the length of the road to where it bends into obscurity, and back again, looking out for us, before getting back into her car and picking up a news-paper from the passenger seat.

Another nail-biting fifteen minutes pass agonisingly slowly. Grace skims her paper, looking at her watch almost as much as we do. She's just got out of her car again to look worriedly back and forth down the road, when we finally see car headlights sweeping down from the North.

241

Thank goodness. There's a collective sigh of relief, until we notice that it's not actually Stuart's Land Rover heading down the road toward us. There's a moment of panic as a sleek black Porsche pulls up behind Grace's car, and we think she's going to be rescued by the wrong man, then Stuart practically falls out of the driver's seat, and stumbles toward her.

'He's got a new car!' hisses Louis in amazement.

'And he's wearing jeans!' adds Tanya.

'And a Red or Dead T-Shirt!' I add incredulously.

'Good sign . . .' Louis whistles quietly through his teeth. 'HUGE effort, I mean HUGE.'

Stuart is calling anxiously to Grace. 'Grace, Grace, are you okay?'

As he moves forward, away from the car, he falls into the beam of the headlights, which he left on, and Grace is now able to see the identity of the new arrival. For a moment her face lights up like a beacon, then, as if somebody's pressed a panic button, the shutters come down, and her face goes cold and unwelcoming. 'What on earth are you doing here?' she asks stiffly.

'I got a call from Louis. He said that you were in trouble. That you'd had another accident.' Stuart's voice tails off and he frowns as he takes in Grace's very clean, sleek and obviously undamaged car.

Grace loses some of the frostiness, and looks at him in puzzlement. 'But Ollie and Tanya called *me* and said that *they'd* broken down.'

They both pause and look at each other, realisation slowly dawning. 'I think we've been set up,' Stuart says, slowly raising his eyebrows.

Grace nods, biting her bottom lip. They both look at each other in silence, then I see a slight smile lifting Grace's tired features. 'And you came all this way to make sure I was okay?'

Stuart nods.

'Well, I'm afraid I don't need rescuing after all,' Grace finally says, trying to be light-hearted, but the break in her voice betraying the pain she feels.

'That's a shame.' Stuart tries to laugh lightly too, but ends up turning it into an embarrassed and emotional cough instead, before adding wistfully, 'Rescuing you has to be one of the high points of my life.'

Grace can't help herself from smiling slightly at this, giving Stuart the encouragement he needs to ask her, 'What happened to us, Grace?'

The smile slips, and her face immediately loses the warmth again. 'Well, I think it was something to do with what you said about Ollie,' she replies shortly, and turning steps back towards her car.

Stuart hurries forward and catches her arm before she can open the car door. 'I didn't lie to you, Grace, you *must* know that,' he says desperately. 'I don't know what was going on with Olivia, but I do think it was all some big stupid misunderstanding.' His voice drops to a soft whisper. 'You must know I wouldn't lie to you, Grace, ever. I've always been truthful with you . . . you're too important to me . . .'

'Then what happened?' Grace demands, turning back to face him.

'Do you know, I'm not quite sure. But what I am sure about is that I love you. More than ever, and not being with you is tearing me apart. I swear on my life, Grace, I've *never* knowingly lied to you, or tried to mislead you.' His voice breaks a little and he turns away from Grace so that she can't see the tears gathering in his eyes. I can see them though, and it's all I can do to stop myself from flying out of my hiding place to convince Grace that Stuart is telling her the truth. 'Please don't let a stupid misunderstanding ruin the best thing that's ever happened to me,' he whispers, unable to face her, and unable to hide the emotion in his voice. 'We were so happy together.'

Grace pauses for the longest moment, and then she speaks, her voice an almost-inaudible whisper. 'We still could be.'

'What did you say . . .' Stuart asks, turning, not daring to believe what he thought he just heard.

'We still could be . . . happy together . . . if that's what you want.'

'If that's what I want . . .' he replies incredulously. 'Oh Grace, I'm so sorry.'

'I'm sorry too.'

'Pur-lease! Somebody pass me the barf bag,' Tanya pipes up from her clump of long grass.

'Shhhhhh!' hisses Louis. 'This is better than *Coronation Street*.'

'I've missed you so much,' Grace whispers, stepping towards him.

'I've been totally miserable without you,' he replies, taking a tentative step forward as well.

Tanya sticks two fingers down her throat and makes a retching noise.

Stuart reaches out and gently, hesitantly, touches Gray's face, then when she doesn't pull away, he becomes bolder. Pulling her into his arms, he looks lovingly down at her, and finally moves in to kiss her, a lingering, passionate kiss, that yes, is maybe a little too sloppy and lacking in technique for our liking, but brings a huge sweet smile to Gray's face for the first time in two weeks.

'I love you,' Grace whispers, her lips still touching Stuart's.

'I love you too,' he replies, closing his eyes and resting his forehead against hers. 'And there's something really important I need to ask you.'

He reluctantly pulls away from her, then still holding onto one of her hands, sinks down on one knee in front of her, Grace smiling down incredulously, the tears beginning to stream unchecked down her pale face as she realises what it is that he's about to do.

'Grace . . .' Stuart begins hesitantly, then taking a deep breath, he regains control, and looks up at her sincerely. 'Grace Ellerington, will you marry me?'

We hold our breath for what seems like the longest of moments, and I feel I'm just about to pass out when I finally hear Grace whisper, 'Yes please,' before she pulls Stuart to his feet and back into another embrace, holding onto him as if she never wants to let go.

'Yes!' Louis and I shriek, leaping into the air and high fiving in exhilaration, before falling back into the bushes, shushing each other, as Stuart and Gray turn in surprise at the sudden noise.

As I burrow back into the undergrowth, I turn grinning to Tanya and am amazed to see that she's dabbing her eyes with a handkerchief. 'Are you crying?' I whisper incredulously.

Tanya whips the handkerchief away from her eyes and hastily shoves it back in her jacket pocket. 'Of course not!' she snaps. 'Bark dust.' She coughs unconvincingly, turning crimson and turning away. 'Plays merry hell with my contacts . . .'

★ ★ ★

When Stuart and Grace have finally released each other from what must have been the longest embrace in history and, getting back into their respective cars, have both headed off to our relief towards the London road, already chatting together on their hands-free sets, we emerge from the undergrowth, picking debris from our hair, and brushing twigs, leaves, and bits of earth from our clothing.

Louis, who seemed to enjoy rolling round in scrub, looks like Stig of the Dump; his black hair, which is normally spiked up with blue tips, is still spiky, but now has a fine layering of dark-green bark dust, which doesn't quite go with his eyes so well.

'Well, we did it,' Tanya says a touch morosely, watching Stuart and Grace disappear around a bend.

'We did the right thing,' I tell her, giving her a hug.

'I know.' She sighs, but this time she allows the smile that was threatening her lips to grow to its full stretch.

'Group hug time!' shrieks Louis excitedly, joining in and smothering us both in more dirt. Extricating ourselves from the muddy hug, we start to walk the mile and a half back down the road to the clearing where Louis left his dirt-encrusted Mini. We're cold, tired, and filthy, but there's a mutual feeling of elation, marred only slightly for me by the fact that I'm desperately in need of a pee, but loathe to clamber into the undergrowth again.

It takes over half an hour at a weary shamble to make it back to Louis's Mini, by which point we're more than grateful to clamber into a car that was the epitome of discomfort on the journey out but is now as welcoming as a big squishy duvet on a cold night.

'I vote we find the nearest pub,' suggests Louis, inserting his keys into the ignition.

'Seconded,' Tanya says firmly from a reclined position on the back seat. 'I really need a large drink.'

'I hope the nearest pub isn't any more than five minutes away,' I squirm, crossing my legs with great difficulty in the confines of the front passenger seat. 'I really need a long pee.'

'Civilisation, here we come,' Louis grins, turning the ignition. 'I'm sure we passed a pub a few miles down the road. I think we should get a bottle of champers to celebrate

245

and I hope they're still serving food, I'm starvi . . .' Louis's voice trails off, as he realises that although he's turning the key, the car isn't actually firing up, simply spluttering like someone who's swallowed a mouthful of food the wrong way. Looking fearfully at me, Louis turns the key again and the engine fires into life. He looks round at Tanya and smiles in relief, puts the car into gear, and pulls away. We've travelled approximately ten yards, however, when the engine splutters again, coughing like a flu victim, and dies a grim and grisly death, accompanied by the sound of some pretty drastic grinding of metal from the engine compartment.

'Oh shit.'

'What's happened?' Tanya, who'd just sunk back into the seat and closed her eyes, sits bolt upright in concern.

'Well,' Louis replies, shaking his head in disbelief at the irony, 'it looks as if we might have broken down!'

There's a strange sort of strangulated, sobbing noise from the back seat, and I turn around expecting to find a tired Tanya in floods of tears. She's crying, but to my amazement, it's tears of laughter.

We finally make it back to Tates just after midnight, all three of us crashing out in my huge bed, as tired as dogs.

I drag myself up when the alarm sounds at six, and trying not to wake the other two, who slept straight through it, shower, dress and head downstairs to start preparing for the breakfast session. Fifteen minutes later, a sleepy, slitty-eyed Tanya and Louis join me, and silently begin to help. I could kiss them both, but I don't have the time or the energy.

Sod's law, it's one of the busiest mornings I've ever had. I normally get a clear hour at least between the end of the breakfast crowd and the beginning of the lunchtime trade, but today we work through solidly until well past four o'clock.

With their help, we make it through, until the restaurant is finally empty, all three of us on autopilot, barely speaking. We don't have the energy for anything but the task in hand. The poor student that I have on shift today, convinced that he's done something drastically wrong and has been sent to Coventry as nobody is speaking to him, is then totally con-fused when I give him a hug and a twenty-pound bonus for putting up with us all day before he goes home.

We're also still living on our nerves somewhat because, as yet, we haven't heard a word from Grace. We haven't dared to contact her since the culmination of Mission Impractical and her reunion with Stuart, figuring that if she wants to talk to us, or should that be if she's *still* talking to us, then she'll be in touch.

As my student casual rushes off to spend his twenty-pound bonus in a pub with friends, we all gather round the bar with three earthenware bowls of hastily reheated lasagne and a bottle of Shiraz, to toast what was hopefully our success. Two forkfuls into our food, however, there's a loud and persistent knocking at the front door of the restaurant.

'Ignore it,' Tanya suggests, taking a big slug of wine.

'I've got to,' I reply. 'Even if I wanted to answer it, I haven't got enough strength left to pull back the main bolt.'

'We're closed!' Louis yells as the knocking continues, adding a 'Bugger Off' under his breath.

The knocking on the door stops, but two seconds later there's a face at the window. It's Grace.

There's a stampede to let her in, Louis making it to the door first and wrenching it open hurriedly. We sort of collide into the back of him, reshuffle, and then step back to let Grace get into the room, standing round like awkward teenagers at a party, eyeing each other nervously, but not quite knowing what to say first. I'm trying to read Grace's expression, but her face is amazingly impassive, leaving us no clues as to whether she's going to hug us or hit us.

She finally speaks. 'I know I probably should have contacted you sooner,' she says, 'but I'm delighted to announce that I have just spent the entire day in bed with my fiancé.' She looks round at us, scrutinising our faces, trying to read our reaction to the news she's just imparted with such obvious delight. 'My fiancé,' she continues, waving her left hand, which is once more sporting the engagement ring Stuart gave her. 'The man that I will be marrying Saturday week.'

'The wedding's definitely back on?'

Grace nods, a broad grin spreading ecstatically across her pretty face.

'Yes!' Louis punches the air, Tanya and I fling open our arms in excitement, and we all pile in, for the group hug of a lifetime. Grace, squashed in the centre, looks around at us, her smile still on full-beam, but now full of delighted incredulity, relieved to see that our congratulatory smiles are, this time, totally genuine.

'Thank you,' she whispers, hugging each of us in turn, 'for last night. You're all totally insane, but I love you to bits.'

Oh dear, I know we've sorted things out now, but I get a sudden rush of guilt again at the thought of having lied to someone I love dearly too. I have to confess.

I glance at Louis and Tanya and raise my eyebrows. They know what I'm thinking, I can see it in their faces too. Tanya grimaces, but nods, as does Louis. I take a deep breath. Here goes.

'Grace,' I say slowly, pulling away, 'we've got something we should tell you.'

But before I can speak further, Grace shakes her head. 'Don't.' She puts a finger over my lips. 'I don't want to know.'

'But,' I mouth against her finger.

'No.' She shakes her head again, pulls her finger away, and looks round at us all. 'Things have gone a little mad recently,' she says, laughing dryly. 'I'm not really sure what's been going on, but what I do know is that Stuart loves me with all of his heart, and that being apart from him was *sooo* hard it proved to me that I don't want to be without him. Ever. So, you see, in a way, what's happened has been a good thing. A test . . .' She sighs, and then begins to smile again, looking coyly at us from under her eyelashes. 'And as for you lot . . . well, I know by now that whatever you do, you do because you really care about me. Okay?'

I nod, biting my bottom lip in an attempt to stop myself from bursting into tears.

'Because you love me,' she continues, 'as much as I love you bunch of idiots.'

Louis hasn't got the same kind of control, he's currently blubbing heavily into the shoulder of Tanya's little designer cardi.

'Stop snivelling, you gits.' Grace wipes her own eyes which are suspiciously damp. 'Let's just forget about the past few weeks, okay, and look to the future.'

Louis stops weeping like a fifties' movie starlet, and nods. I quickly fetch another glass from behind the bar and pour Grace some wine.

'The future!' we echo her, raising our glasses in a toast.

Grace drinks deeply, then puts her glass down on the table amidst the almost untouched remnants of our late lunch. 'Right, you 'orrible lot,' she commands sergeant-major style. 'Now we've finally got everything sorted out, there's only one more thing to do. Finish your drinks and get moving, we've got a wedding to reorganise and only a week to do it!

Chapter Eleven

Fortunately Grace has been unable to bring herself to cancel anything, so all we have to do to reorganise the wedding of the year, is reassure her closest relatives that they still have to get their hats out of mothball-ridden boxes and hitch a ride up to Leicestershire, where in defiance of tradition, Grace and Stuart are marrying in Stuart's local church.

When it gets to Friday, the day before Grace's wedding, all I have left to do is struggle through a morning of work, before picking up my dress, which has had to be altered due to all of the weight I've lost through the last few weeks of worry, and then pick up Tanya, Louis and Finn respectively, who are all hitching a ride to Leicestershire with me.

On the Friday morning, however, I make it down slightly late for work to find not only Louis, but Tanya and Finn in the kitchen as well, bags packed and ready to go whenever I am. Louis has made a start on breakfast: bacon is sizzling away under the grill, a heap of freshly washed plump white mushrooms are sitting on a chopping board waiting to be sliced, and croissants are warming through in the oven, filling the room with a heavenly aroma of fresh baking. He is now refilling the industrial toaster with half a loaf of thick white bread. Finn and Tanya are ostensibly helping, by spreading Anchor thickly on each warm slice already made, but they appear to be eating more than they're buttering for the customers. I look at the clock on the wall, it's only seven-thirty. This is the first time I think I've ever seen Tanya up and dressed before ten on a day she doesn't have to go to work.

Louis offers me a mug of tea and, as it's still fairly quiet in the restaurant, I sit down at the table with the other two to drink it. 'It's always lovely to see you,' I tell them both, sinking my nose into my steaming mug. 'But what on earth are you doing here at this time of morning?'

'Couldn't sleep,' mumbles Tanya, not quite meeting my eye. 'Probably pre-wedding nerves or something.'

'I thought they were reserved for the bride,' I tease her. 'What about you?' I turn to Finn. 'Surely you haven't got pre-wedding jitters as well?'

Finn shakes his head. 'Far from it,' he mumbles through a mouthful of toast and Marmite. 'I've actually got some good news for you, and I couldn't wait to let you know, so I thought I'd kill two birds with one stone and come straight round, instead of meeting up with you later.'

'So what's the news?' I help myself to a piece of toast from his plate.

'It's about Slater Enterprises.'

'Oh please no. Not today.' Dropping my toast, I get up from the table and back away, hands held in the air as if to fend off any thoughts of Slater Enterprises from entering my mind. 'I just want to forget about them until after the wedding, please.'

'Well, that'll be difficult seeing as Dan Slater is one of the ushers.' Finn looks sideways at me, to see how this particular piece of news is being digested.

As far as I'm concerned this is as difficult to swallow as a piece of uncooked bacon rind. 'Grace never told me that!' I cry in consternation.

'Well, she wouldn't, would she, in case you came up with some fantastic excuse to wriggle out of your bridesmaid's frock and not go. I think she's still harbouring secret hopes that you two will give her an opportunity to be an old maid of honour herself.'

Tanya digs Finn good-naturedly in the ribs with her elbow. 'Stop teasing her, you rat!' She turns to me. 'Grace thinks nothing of the sort, babe. Well, nothing quite so drastic anyway, she's just still convinced that you two would make a pretty good couple if you'd only stop fighting and admit your true feelings.'

'Which at the moment are slightly less on the loathing side than they used to be. But you know the old adage, never mix business with pleasure? Well, I've decided that I'd be very wise to stick to it at the moment.'

'I might have agreed with you a couple of days ago . . .' Finn replies, a slight smirk on his face, '. . . but then I got a very interesting delivery yesterday – from Dan Slater.'

'Yeah, I understand you two have been getting a bit matey recently.' I raise my eyebrows at him. 'Lunch last week, letters this? What is it?' I tease. 'A late Valentine?'

'You'd be surprised how close you are . . .' Finn replies cryptically, the smirk getting bigger by the minute. 'Only it's not for me.'

'What are you on about?' I ask in concern.

Finn laughs at my confused face. 'Don't look so worried, babe, it's good news, honestly.' He takes another bite of toast, and chews agonisingly slowly before adding, 'Slater Enterprises *are* developing the area, they've bought practically every building they can get their hands on.'

'Don't I know it,' I sigh, plonking my empty mug down on the table with a dramatic thud. 'And you call that good news?'

Finn nods enthusiastically. 'They're taking it upmarket, Ollie. Don't you see, it's going to be good for your business. Instead of a load of run-down empty buildings, you're going to have some nice new expensive smart apartments around you, containing nice new expensive smart customers for Tates.'

'That's if Tates is still here,' I reply pessimistically.

'Well, that's why I'm here . . .' Finn picks up a long white envelope that was sitting next to his toast plate. 'Dan asked me to give this to you.' He hands it to me.

'What is it?' I ask, shifting it from hand to hand as though it's a letter bomb or something.

'It's your new lease for Tates.'

I should have expected it, my old lease runs out at the end of the month.

'Open it,' Finn urges.

All eyes are on me as I reluctantly rip open the envelope and take out the contents. I put the bulk of the document on the table and scan through the cover letter. 'It says here that they've sent me a revised lease which incorporates certain changes, and supersedes any previous agreements. Can they do that, can they just change it and expect me to sign it? Changes? What kind of changes? What have they done now? Don't tell me they've decided to increase the rent even further!'

253

Tanya, who's picked up the rental agreement, and is currently speed-reading, shakes her head. 'Hardly. I think you'd better look at this.' Tanya holds the paperwork out towards me.

Taking it reluctantly, I read the paragraph she was pointing at. 'Ten-year lease at a fixed monthly rent . . . It's the same amount as I was paying before Slater Enterprises bought the building. What on earth! This can't be right . . .'

'It is right, Ollie. It's all there,' Tanya assures me, smiling slowly, 'in black and white.'

'But why? I don't understand,' I repeat. 'Their last letter distinctly said that the rent would be substantially increased.'

'You thought Dan was faking an interest in you, to get to Tates,' Finn states bluntly. 'I suppose this is the only way he could think of to prove you wrong.'

'You mean Dan's done this?'

Finn nods slowly.

'But . . . I can't accept it.'

'Don't be ridiculous, of course you can! Besides it's too late. It's all done. The contract's drawn up.'

'I'll just have to give it back to him then, won't I?'

'It's not like Marks and Spencers, Ollie,' Tanya exclaims. 'You can't just take it to customer services and ask for a refund!'

'I haven't signed it, Tanya. It's not valid unless I sign it.'

'Well, you'd be a fool not to.'

'I'm not a charity case, Tan!'

'I'm sure that's not how he views you either,' Finn says calmly. 'In fact I think we both know that he thinks a great deal more of you than that.'

I look down at the table. It's been hard to admit to myself in my own head, let alone out loud to my friends, how I feel about Dan Slater. I'm also nowhere near as sure as Finn seems to be that Dan actually has feelings for me. Well, I know he has feelings, but I really thought they were more of the hate variety.

'He just wants you to have a chance, Ollie. And I think he wants the pair of you to have a chance too. And if you can be honest with yourself for a change, you'd admit that that's what you want as well.'

'I can't see that this is the best way. Not with this bloody contract hanging over my head. I'd owe him for the next ten years. And don't you dare suggest that I could pay him in kind!' I round on Tanya, who's grinning so lasciviously it's easy to see what's running through *her* mind at the moment. 'No.' I get to my feet determinedly. 'I've made up my mind, I'm not signing.'

'You mean you're choosing to pay a higher rent?' Tanya asks in disbelief, the smile falling rapidly from her face.

'No, I'm *choosing,*' I echo her, 'to stand on my own two feet.' I stride purposefully out of the kitchen.

'What are you doing?' Louis calls anxiously after me, obviously expecting a repeat of the previous occasion when I had a special delivery from Slater Enterprises.

'I'm going to call them,' I reply.

'That's what I was afraid of,' I hear him mutter as the door swings to behind me.

However, when I get through to Slater Enterprises a polite receptionist tells me that Mr Slater is away on business and isn't expected back in the office until the following week. She does however put me through to a surprisingly obsequious Edina Mason, who, considering our previous encounter, is thoroughly charming to me.

When I push back into the kitchen, Tanya and Finn are shuffling quickly back to their chairs, and Louis is looking red-faced as he rubs his tea towel against a dish that I know he'd already dried earlier. They'd obviously been lined up behind the door trying to listen in.

It's also obvious that they didn't hear anything however, as Louis bursts out almost immediately with, 'What did they say?'

'He's away at the moment,' I reply slowly. 'They're not sure when he'll be back. But they confirmed that the rental amount quoted is correct. How could he have done this to me!'

'You make it sound worse than when you thought he was trying to screw you. Funny, it turns out he really was, just in the biblical rather than business sense.'

'Tan! Your sense of comic timing's dreadful.'

'Okay, back to the serious stuff; what else did they say?'

'Said something about how they're trying to upgrade the area, and mine's the kind of business they want to attract, so

255

this is a gesture to encourage me to stay here.'

'See, that's fair enough. You're doing him a favour by staying put.'

'Well, I suppose it does sound better if you put it like that,' I agree reluctantly, '. . . but I'm still not signing.'

'Why not, Ollie?'

'Well, it works both ways, doesn't it?'

'What on earth do you mean?'

'I don't want him to think that I feel obligated to him.'

Tanya rolls her eyeballs. 'Bloody hell. You two were made for each other . . .'

'You think so?'

'Yeah, you're both ridiculously proud, and infuriatingly stubborn!'

Mel, who's going to be in charge for the whole weekend whilst we're away, has arrived early, and is out in the restaurant taking orders. My two student casuals, one who was helping out at breakfast, and the other who has just turned up, also early, for the lunchtime session, are both scheduled to work all weekend as well. Even Claude, who, surprise, surprise, hasn't made it in quite yet, has signed in blood that he'll be in and on time for every single lunch and dinner shift. I therefore summon the courage to leave Tates entirely in their hands and we head off to Leicestershire early.

We load up the car with cases and presents, bridesmaid dresses wrapped carefully in their protective carriers direct from the dressmaker. I just manage to save the Spode tea set that we bought them from being sat on by Louis, as Tanya and Finn squeeze into the back seat together, leaving him to park his pert bum in the front next to me.

It's Friday, so the traffic is heavy, despite the fact that we've got an earlier start than expected. I'm quite grateful for any delay, as I get more anxious the closer we get. I can feel my stomach knotting like a wrung dishcloth. I haven't officially seen Stuart since the night I cornered him in the Dutch barn, and puckered up to him like a salted slug. We may have managed to get Stuart and Grace back together, but I still don't know what kind of reception to expect from someone we've treated so ill, me visibly more so than the others.

Storm clouds are gathering on the horizon ahead of us, and

the sky is getting greyer the further north we travel. Superstitiously, I take this as an omen, my mood getting greyer in line with the skies.

Tanya and Finn are laughing, joking and teasing in the back seat. Louis is turned half round in the front, seat-belt straining, to join in, his attempts at lightening my obviously low mood finally abandoned after half an hour of his best wisecracks have been met with almost complete silence, interspersed with the odd patch of nervous laughter.

Tanya, finally noticing my mood, leans forward to whisper in my ear that I shouldn't worry. 'Grace has forgiven us. She already said that in not so many words. Even though . . .' she holds up her hand to silence me, before I can say it. 'Even though,' she continues, 'she doesn't really know the full story. Like she said: it's history. Besides, you two have been friends forever, if anybody should be worrying right now it's me and Louis. The longer the friendship the more likely you are to be forgiven.'

I disagree with this. The longer the friendship, the more heinous the crime committed.

I needn't have worried about Grace however. The moment we pull up outside Stuart's sprawling house, Grace bounds out to greet us, fighting her way through the usual pack of dogs, as beaming and delighted to see us as the big chocolate Labrador that's currently thrusting its nose in very friendly fashion up the hem of Tanya's rather short skirt. She throws her arms around my neck and spins me round in a hug that almost has my feet lifting from the ground, then after greeting Tanya, Finn and Louis in a similar fashion, she returns to me and guides me into the house with her arm slipped through mine.

The house is full of people. Those of Grace's family who have already arrived are currently being herded round the house by Tula, who, making herself completely at home, is giving a guided tour, proudly pointing out the house's many attributes, as though it's been in *her* family for generations.

A drawing room to the rear of the house has been turned into a temporary wedding headquarters. Filled with an odd assortment of tables and chairs collected from throughout the house, it is now home to a vast assortment of wedding paraphernalia, from a long trestle table stacked with gifts, to

257

flower arrangements for the reception and church. A fleet of champagne bottles are sitting in an old tin bath full of ice in one dark corner. A small table next to the bath bears three huge boxes, with 'Ellerington' scrawled on the side in black marker. These apparently contain the different layers of the cake, which Grace announces excitedly is made up of one layer fruit, one sponge, and one chocolate, at which point Louis the cake-fiend and thief grins excitedly.

Leaving Louis trying to persuade Grace that he should taste the cakes in order to make sure that they're all right, I wander over to the far side of the room. Through the open French doors I can see several men in overalls erecting a huge marquee on the bowling-green smooth lawn, pausing occasionally to look up at the threatening sky and mutter ominously. Foldaway chairs are stacked in neat rows on the lawn alongside the rapidly growing marquee, and another two men are wheeling a stack of precariously balanced round tables along the patio on a hand cart, swearing profusely as the top table wobbles dangerously before sliding with a resounding crack onto the hard stone floor. Still swearing, they abandon the cart and make to pick it up, then notice me watching them from the window, stop swearing and start muttering apologies instead, the elder of the two even doffing his flat cap.

Smiling, I turn back to face the room and find Tanya grinning somewhat awkwardly at Stuart who is just walking into the room in search of his wife-to-be. He is looking squarely at Grace and has a broad beam on his face, which slips the moment he sets eyes on Tanya and me. He hesitates for a second, obviously not knowing quite what to do, then gives us a cursory nod before turning around and walking straight out again.

'I've got to talk to him.'

'I think it might be better if you just leave it,' Tanya disagrees. 'At least he acknowledged us. When we left the last time we were here, we might as well have been lepers, the distance he maintained.'

'I know, but I've got to speak to him, Tanya. I can't just leave it with him thinking badly of me. Grace is like a sister to me. It means he's practically going to be my brother-in-law.'

I hurry after him. 'Stuart, hang on a minute.'

He stops and turns around, and I suddenly lose the pre-rehearsed, I'm-really-really-sorry speech that I've been running through in my head for the past week or so. I stand and look at him stupidly for a moment, mouth opening then closing as my brain refuses to connect. In the end I come out with a pretty lame, 'Look, I'm sorry.'

He doesn't answer.

'For everything.'

He pauses for a moment, removing his glasses and rubbing at the corner of his right eye with a long finger, then at an imaginary smudge on the lens of his glasses with the hem of his shirt, whilst I look awkwardly at the floor.

'Look,' I venture falteringly. 'I needed to say it, and I really do mean it, so I'll just go now . . .'

I turn to leave but he calls me back. 'Ollie, it's okay.'

I turn back, attempting a hopeful and conciliatory smile.

Stuart takes a deep breath, which he releases as a long sigh. 'I think the best thing we can all do is forget about it.'

I nod my agreement.

'Although I must admit I was pretty pissed off to begin with . . . but then Dan explained everything. You were trying to look out for your friend. Although your tactics were pretty suspect, I suppose it was on the whole a kind of admirable thing to do. Especially as I realise how hard kissing me must have been for you.'

I force myself to look up at him, and am amazed to see a slightly amused smile on his face as he says this. I manage a smile myself. 'We were idiots,' I tell him.

'Well, I'm glad you said that because it means I don't have to,' he replies, but he's still smiling.

'I'm sorry,' I repeat again.

'I know you are. Besides, not all of your mad schemes are bad ones. Thank you, you know, for the other night.'

'The breakdown?'

'Yeah. Now that plan was a touch of pure genius!' Stuart's smile breaks into a broad friendly grin, which literally transforms his face. No, it doesn't suddenly turn him into a younger Mel Gibson, and no, I still don't find him attractive myself, but I can actually see now a little more why Grace does.

'I'd hug you, but I don't think it's a particularly good idea,' I tell him, holding out my hand instead.

'Don't want anyone to get the wrong end of the stick,' he jokes, taking my hand and shaking it slowly.

'Well . . .' I say, letting go, noting mentally that his hands are still sweaty, but not minding quite so much this time. 'Think I'd better head off and get an early night. Big day tomorrow. My best friend's getting married . . .'

'Do you know something?' He pulls a mock amazed face. 'So am I, isn't that a coincidence?'

We smile kind of stupidly at each other for a moment; a new, well, I think *understanding* is the best way to phrase it, between us.

'Suppose I'd better go and relearn my speech. You know me, nerves, and speaking in public,' he rolls his eyes to the ceiling, and taps his forehead, 'add them together, equals complete brain freeze.'

'Yep, I've got a lot to do as well, you know bridesmaidly duties . . . promised I'd help the bride wax her moustache . . .' I tease. 'Got to look her best for the photos . . .'

I turn and walk back to where Tanya is hovering nervously in the entrance of the bridal HQ room, trying not to look as if she's watching us. But before I reach her Stuart calls me back.

'Oh and, Ollie.'

'Yeah?' I turn back towards him.

'Will you do me a favour?'

'Sure,' I say in surprise. 'What is it?'

'Give Dan a break.'

'Which bone?' I joke feebly.

'He's a good guy, Ollie.'

'People keep telling me that.'

Stuart laughs lightly. 'Well maybe,' he replies as his face breaks into another smile, 'that's because it's true.'

The rain against the window is hard enough to wake me from a fairly fitful sleep. Getting out of bed, pulling the counterpane around my naked shoulders, I shuffle over to the closest window and look out into the night. The threatened storm has arrived.

The white marquee is billowing in the wind like a large tethered ghost, attempting a last-minute escape before the finality of tomorrow's festivities. Pools of rainwater are collecting in the sagging folds of the roof, before waterfalling down the sides when the canvas swells with each gust of wind. A spectacular flash of lightning suddenly cracks across the sky like the snaking strike of a neon bullwhip, illuminating a figure in the garden below. A man is leaning against the huge spreading oak tree, taking in the same magnificent view that I am, whilst sheltering from the rain. He has a brandy glass in one hand, and the other is tucked deep into his trouser pocket. Shoulders hunched, hair plastered to his head by the downpour, he is seemingly as mesmerised by the storm as I am.

After a few moments, he turns to go back inside and another bolt of lightning shoots across the sky, illuminating everything in front of me so brightly it's as if someone has turned on a powerful light. As the man looks up at the sky, I see his face. It's Dan Slater.

In the fragment of the second more that the sky is lit with such brilliance, he turns back towards the house and our eyes meet, before he's plunged back into the darkness of the shadow thrown across the patio by the great stone walls of the house. The next second however, as Dan takes another step forward, the security lights blink on, and I can see him still looking up towards my window. He smiles slowly up at me, and then we both jump and look away as the French doors that lead into the rear sitting room designated as headquarters of bridal operations are wrenched open by the wind, slamming with a loud crashing sound into the wall on either side. They obviously hadn't been shut properly earlier in the day.

There are a heap of flower arrangements, meant for the tables in the marquee, stored just inside on one of the tables. The strong wind catches the nearest one, and lifting it like a feather floating on a breeze bowls it out of the window. Like a bridesmaid leaping for the bridal bouquet, Dan swiftly stretches out a hand and catches it as it tumbles past him. He smiles up at me, indicates the flowers and then the marquee with a sweep of the same arm, raises his glass in acknowledgement to me as if to say well done, and then steps inside.

I wake up the next morning to the sound of church bells: the bell ringers are practising in preparation for midday. Pulling back my curtains, I'm relieved to see that the marquee is actually still there, having half expected it to set sail the night before like some great white galleon.

Also, thankfully, the rain that fell in the night is no longer, and has simply acted to wash away the grey skies, and a perfect summer day is unfolding, if a little soggily, as the morning progresses.

Downstairs in the huge kitchen, Tanya, still in her dressing gown, with her hair set in big pink rollers, is hitting the wedding-breakfast Grand Mimosas with a vengeance. Her pre-wedding nerves have now taken hold to such a great extent, she confides in a whisper, that she's spent three hours from just after dawn with her head down the toilet, vomiting up practically everything she's eaten in the past month or so.

Grace, on the other hand, the one person who's supposed to be nervous, is calmer than a sloth on Prozac.

A cheery-looking woman with pink cheeks and soft brown curls, wrapped in a huge apron that is far too big for her, is presiding over three huge frying pans on the vast range. She's currently frying eggs, I'd say about eight to one pan, and smiles at me as I enter the room, blearily rubbing the sleep from my eyes. I smile back briefly, and go and sit at the long wooden table next to Grace.

Tula, already resplendent in an acidic-orange suit that glows more neon than the amber on a traffic light, and a hat that looks as if it's just entered the atmosphere still burning and excited NASA and several *X-Files* fans before landing squarely on her head, is also sinking her nose in a champagne glass. Turning her nose up at the addition of orange juice, she is downing straight Grand Marnier and champagne.

Tanya's particular form of malaise must be catching. I'm fine until the cheery egg-flipper whomps full plates of breakfast down on the table in front of Grace and then me. I thought it was supposed to be the bride that was sick with nerves, I moan to myself, as I watch Grace eagerly tuck into a huge plateful of eggs and bacon, my own stomach growling like a rabid dog, but churning far too much to be fed.

I smile my thanks at what I assume is a hired help, until, turning with a smile, Grace catches the woman's hand to stop her heading straight back to the Aga and announces, 'Ollie, this is Stuart's mother.'

262

'Oh my goodness,' I reply, leaping from my seat and holding out my hand in greeting. 'I'm so sorry, I had no idea.'

'Don't worry about it, love,' she says in a heavily Leicestershire-accented voice. 'Madam Butterfly over there,' she indicates Tula who has just slumped in a basket chair in the corner, and is looking morosely into the depths of her now-empty champagne flute, calling loudly for someone to bring her a large G and T, 'has already told me off for not turning down her sheets last night!' And with that she bursts into a quivering chortle of laughter.

Back in my room, the breakfast I forced down now gone the same way as Tanya's lunch yesterday, I stand solemnly – well, as solemn as I can be in just my underwear – in front of my bridesmaid dress, which is hanging in its protective cover on the front of the wardrobe. After the orange-blob scare came Grace's real choice, a flattering empire-line dress made of the softest lemon silk, delicately embroidered with gold thread, which is so beautiful even Tanya wasn't too loathe to wear it.

It feels like a momentous occasion to take the dress from the hanger and carefully slip it on. Grace's hairdresser Pansy, an exuberant, straight-talking brunette with boobs like pillows that are wonderful to rest between whilst she primps and preens, has been dragged down from London for the day, and my hair is now piled on top of my head with tiny lemon silk roses threaded through it, a style which I was concerned would be a bit Knickerbocker Glory, but is actually so delightfully flattering that I keep sneaking amazed and pleased glances in the mirror at my reflection.

'*You're so vain!*' sings Tanya, stepping carefully into the room, her hem lifted like a Jane Austen heroine treading over a muddy puddle. 'How the hell are we supposed to walk in these things?'

'With great difficulty,' I tell her. 'And I'm not being vain! I'm just amazed that I actually look okay in this get-up.'

'You look more than okay.'

'Are you sure?' I reply, looking over my shoulder at my arse in the huge mirror.

'Don't even ask if your bum looks big in it,' Tanya pre-empts me. 'Believe it or not, you look absolutely gorgeous.'

'I do?'

'Yeah, absolutely.'

'Well, try not to look too gorgeous, you don't want to upstage the bride,' laughs a nervous voice.

Tan and I turn to see a vision in shimmering cream silk glide, albeit somewhat hesitantly, into the room. 'Is somebody going to help me on with my veil then?' Grace asks, as we stand and simply stare at her in open-mouthed silence.

Do you ever have moments in your life that you know you'll remember for ever? This is one of mine. For a moment it's not Grace Ellerington, the successful, attractive twenty-nine-year-old I know and love standing in front of me, but the shy, nervous, hesitant, eleven-year-old I first met, eighteen years ago, with whom I've formed one of the most incredible and wonderful bonds of friendship a person could ever be lucky enough to find. I feel the tears welling as if a dam has just burst at the backs of my eyes.

'Well, how do I look?' she finally prompts us, her face getting more worried by the minute. 'No, don't tell me, I can see it in your faces. You hate it, don't you? I look dreadful, don't I? I knew I should have gone for something else . . .'

Unable to speak, I turn to Tanya and am amazed to see her normally bright eyes also clouded with tears. 'You look . . .' she hesitates. 'You look . . .' she repeats again, but is unable to continue. Turning away, sniffing heavily, she looks around frantically for a tissue, but spotting nothing except a long plastic bag full of pink cotton wool, Tanya picks up one of my abandoned socks, and blows her nose loudly into the red and yellow wool.

'Well, I hope you're not crying because I look a fright.' Grace's smile quivers as she too, rocked by our emotions, feels a single hot tear fall from her eye and roll slowly down her cheek.

'You look fabulous.' Tanya finally finds her voice, albeit a slightly huskier one than normal.

'All brides look fabulous,' Grace laughs, quickly wiping her face. 'But thank you for not sounding *too* surprised.' Suddenly Grace's face falls and momentarily she looks panicked. 'Oh my goodness,' she cries, turning imploringly to me. 'I can't believe I actually forgot.'

'Forgot what?' I rally in concern.

'Something old, something new,' Grace replies. 'I completely forgot.'

'Don't worry, darling, it's only silly superstition.'

'It's not just superstition,' Grace replies in panic. 'It's tradition!'

'Something old – well, you've got that,' Tanya exclaims reassuringly. 'Me. The oldest bridesmaid in town.'

'Something new? Something borrowed?' Grace gabbles.

'Shoes,' I tell her. 'Quickly, swap shoes. These are new, and you can borrow them. Simple. We're the same size, and they're practically the same style, not that anyone can see them under our dresses anyway!' Grace and I hurriedly swap.

'Just one more thing.'

'I think I can help you out there!' choruses a gin-sodden voice. Tula appears in the doorway. I think she must have found her gin and tonic, as she seems to be clutching the frame for support.

'What's this?' Grace asks as Tula, risking life and limb, lets go of the door frame, sashays precariously across the room like a slender tango man, and hands her a magazine.

'Something blue,' Tula winks heavily. 'I found it in Sylvester's briefcase. You can use it to spice up the wedding night afterwards.' Tula kisses Grace leaving two big orange lip marks on each perfectly made-up cheek. 'Just popped in to tell you that I'll see you at the church, darling. Must get there before your Aunty Alba. Have you seen what she's wearing? Her hat's so huge she'll obscure the view of any poor soul sitting behind her!' Tula hurries out of the room, the brim of her own hat only narrowly missing the door frame, as Grace looks in amazement at the copy of *Fiesta* her mother's just handed her.

Tanya moves in hastily to repair Grace's mussed-up make-up, and then hands her the bouquet, a glorious affair of creamy trumpet lilies.

'Ready?' we ask her.

Grace takes a deep breath and nods. 'Ready.'

'Glad to hear it,' purrs a voice from the doorway. 'Because your escort has arrived!' It's Louis, leaning against the door frame, doing a Sean Connery impression. He's decided to shun the morning suit which is being favoured by the rest of the men in the wedding party, and is looking dreadfully handsome in kilt and cummerbund, and for the first time since I've

265

known him, he isn't sporting a scrap of make-up, or hair dye, or even glittery jewellery, although upon closer inspection the kilt does turn out to be Westwood, and a woman's.

He steps daintily across the room, and bowing low before a laughing Grace, straightens and offers her his arm, whispering in her ear as she steps forward to take it, 'You look beautiful, angel, absolutely breathtaking.'

The house is strangely empty as Louis leads us downstairs, practically everyone else having already left for the church. We wait ten minutes in the entrance hall, before having to send Louis back upstairs to coax Grace's sick-with-nerves father out of the bathroom, where he's spent the past two hours avoiding his ex-wife, with a bottle of Jack Daniels, the *Racing Post*, and his mobile phone on the hotline to his bookmakers.

Now late, we load Grace and her father rather unceremoniously into the trap being drawn by the horse that once trailed green drool over Tanya's Gucci jacket. Tanya and I sensibly steer clear of an animal that can emit something foul from either end of its body, and opt to travel behind with Louis in an old Bentley that Stuart unearthed from yet another barn full of engines at the back of the house.

Grace is still clutching my hand, despite the fact that she's now several feet above me. I give her a gentle squeeze and, practically wrenching my hand out of her vice-like grip, trot back to join the others in the Bentley, which, whilst gleaming on the outside, still has a few odd wisps of straw on the floor, and a surprised-looking chicken perched in the open glove compartment. Louis shoos the chicken out of the car, and all three of us get in the back, watching and waving as Grace's trap pulls away and heads for the village. We sit and wait for someone to come out and drive us away. It's only after another five minutes that we realise we're all alone.

Louis looks at his watch. 'We're late,' he chimes excitedly, like the White Rabbit in *Alice in Wonderland*. 'Who's supposed to be driving this thing?'

'I thought we had a chauffeur?' Tanya says, after we've sat in expectant silence for far too long.

'I think Sylvester said he'd do it,' I reply slowly.

The other two look at me in horror. 'But he left with Tula about thirty minutes ago.'

'Then what the hell are we waiting for!' I exclaim. 'Let's go.'

Tanya turns to me, and smiles hopefully. 'Don't look at me!' I shriek. 'I can't drive this thing!'

'Let me,' Louis insists.

'Are you sure?'

'Once you're driven a thirty-year-old Mini you can drive anything!' Louis clambers over the low leather back of the front seat, and slipping into the driver's place, turns and grins broadly at us. 'Hold onto your headdresses!' he teases, but when he tries to turn her over, she refuses to start.

'Oh God,' I moan. 'We're going to miss the wedding!'

'Try again!' Tanya shrieks agitatedly at Louis.

There's a faint click as Louis turns the key in the ignition, but no other activity in the engine department whatsoever.

'We're going to have to walk!'

'But it's two miles away, we'll never make it in time.'

'Taxi?'

'You're joking, aren't you, we'd never get one now.'

'It's downhill nearly all the way,' suggests Louis, 'if we can just get her rolling . . .'

I shake my head. 'We're not thinking straight,' I tell them quickly. 'Stuart's an engine fanatic, he must have something somewhere that works.'

We rush in a straggling line round to the back of the house, looking quickly in all the barns and stables. My suggestion that we could hop on a couple of horses is quickly vetoed, and we're just beginning to get hot, bothered and very despondent, when Louis gives a shout from one of the corner looseboxes. 'You two, over here, I've found something.'

I don't like the way that he says 'something', but seeing as my barn is sadly empty, I head over in the direction of Louis's voice. As my eyes adjust to the gloom I see with a sinking stomach exactly what it is that Louis has found: an old World War Two motorbike, complete with side car.

Tanya skids through the door behind me, pulling straw from her hair. 'Oh my God!' she cries, throwing her hands over her mouth to suppress the laughter. 'You can't be serious!'

'We haven't got time to be choosy,' says Louis, but he still hangs back.

I decide it's time to act. 'Get out of the way!' I push past a

267

reluctant Louis, and tucking my skirt safely in my Janet Reger knickers, straddle the cracked leather seat.

'Ollie! What on earth are you doing?' Tan shrieks.

'I had a fifty c.c. when I was sixteen,' I tell her, kicking out the starter pedal, ready to fire up. 'Sold it when I got overtaken by a milk float; let's just hope this thing's a bit quicker. Now hop on, baby!' I crack down the starter pedal, and the engine fires into life. 'We've got a wedding to catch.'

We arrive at the church half an hour late, Louis wedged in the sidecar, his spiky hair swept back by the wind, his forehead and Ray-Bans plastered with flies. Tanya is perched behind me, clinging tightly round my middle. After the initial fit of screaming as I found full throttle and roared off in the direction of the church, she learnt that it was far wiser to keep her mouth shut and her head down, and is therefore looking by far the tidiest of the three of us. I clamber off the bike, smoothing down my skirts, and picking a large bluebottle from between my teeth with a heavy shudder.

Grace has been anxiously looking out for us. 'Where on earth have you been?' she cries. 'I was just about to send someone back to look for you!'

'Car trouble!' I pant.

'I thought you weren't going to come!' she wails, practically throwing herself around my neck.

'And miss my best friend's wedding?' I tell her affectionately. 'Never!'

The vicar, who had come outside to find out what was delaying the bride, spots Tanya struggling to pull her long skirt from her knickers, and hurries over to help her. The photographer, who's been snapping away at arriving guests like the paparazzi on the trail of Posh and Becks, gives a great booming laugh and captures the moment on film for all eternity, and the front of the local paper.

'What a way to get famous,' Tanya sighs, suppressing her laughter. 'I can just see the tabloids getting hold of that one.'

'Yeah, I can see the headline,' Louis giggles, 'Vicar in Bridesmaid's Knickers Shocker!'

Tula, hanging off the arm of Sylvester, who's dressed like George Melley on his way to a jazz festival, posing like a Tiller girl, looks thoroughly peeved that we've just stolen her limelight, and drags Sylvester into the church to take up residence in the front pew.

We step inside the church just as the choir are coming to the end of 'Oh, for the wings of a dove'. The next minute they've started on a somewhat ambitious rendition of *Pie Jesu*.

'Groom's on the right. Bride's on the left,' says a familiar voice, and Finn appears grinning from the main aisle, top hat perched rakishly on his handsome head.

'I think we're supposed to go up the middle,' I reply, smiling somewhat shakily at him. Through the open doors, I can see that the church is totally packed, each pew stuffed with far more people than they should normally accommodate. If this wasn't enough to make me tremble with nerves, the sight of Dan Slater ushering another latecomer into place, wildly handsome and self assured in his dark-grey morning suit, practically finishes me off.

The Vicar, back in place now, signals to the organist to change the music. Everybody turns and looks expectantly towards the doors as the organist strikes up the Wedding March.

'Here comes the bride, nowhere left to hide!' trills Grace nervously. 'I think my 'lastic's snapped, cause my g-string's on the slide!'

As we all burst out laughing Dan too, turns to face us. For a moment our eyes lock, challenging as ever, and then he smiles. A slow, steady, reassuring smile that fills me with warmth and a new determination. I take a deep breath. 'Well, this is it.' I squeeze Tanya's hand. 'It's finally happening.'

'Maybe we could do a number on the just cause and impediment bit.' She smiles stiffly, without turning to look at me.

'Only if we want to bring new meaning to the word matricide . . . her mother would kill us! Besides, do you really want to?'

Tanya shakes her head. 'Not any more. No.'

'Okay, girls,' Finn prompts us, leaning over to carefully pick a small black beetle out of Tanya's hair. 'Best foot forward, and keep in time, okay.'

As we pass him, I see Finn wink heavily at Tanya and her smile back slowly and very sweetly. Tanya? Sweet? There's something very amiss here.

269

I look from one to the other, both gorgeous, groomed and gregarious; they're either long lost brother and sister or . . .

It suddenly all falls into place. I thought it was weird that Finn knew about the Stuart seduction disaster so quickly. Then there were the veiled hints about a new romance, and yesterday when they both turned up in the kitchen together at an hour of the morning when they'd normally still be in bed. That was pretty suspect. Add to that Tanya's total failure to pull whilst in Rome, when normally she'd be packing something six foot and sexy in her suitcase to take home as a souvenir. She barely put up a fight to keep Romeo for herself which, thinking back, was most unlike her. And perhaps all of that raving from Tanya about how wonderful Finn was, wasn't for my benefit at all. Straight from the heart. Finn and Tanya.

'You and Finn?' I whisper to her.

The beatific bridesmaid's smile remains in place, but I can see the corners of her mouth twitching.

'You're a dark horse,' I tell her. 'It's not like you to keep something like that so quiet. If you were worried that I wouldn't approve, then you were right. No matter how much I love you, Tanya Mathers, I have to say that Finn is far too nice to be humped and dumped by the likes of you, you old tart.'

'I've been faithful to him for over six weeks,' she murmurs without looking at me, the smile never slipping from her face.

I suddenly lose step in the wedding march, staring open mouthed at Tanya's elegant back. Louis is walking behind me. His sporran prods me in the small of my back and I hurry to catch up with Tanya, falling in beside her. 'Six weeks?' I hiss in disbelief, as Grace reaches Stuart's side, and we fall into place behind her.

'Uhuh,' Tanya replies without moving her lips.

'Must be Luh uh uh Love,' hums Louis.

'You knew?' I round on him.

'The Lou'ster knows *everything*.' He smiles smugly.

We're silenced by a look from the vicar, and the service begins. To my amazement and relief, Tanya, Louis and I don't find it too difficult to 'forever hold our peace'. And when Stuart says his vows, he's smiling down so tenderly at Grace, as though he and she are the only people in the church, and the crowds of wellwishers in wide hats simply aren't there. The look in his eyes! If someone ever looked at me like that I know I'd probably be happy for the rest of my life.

Having made a death pact between us that we wouldn't cry, the two bridesmaids and the honorary pageboy begin to wail in unison. Fortunately the honorary pageboy has half a box of man-size stuffed in his sporran.

'You know,' I sniffle through my tissue to Tanya. 'I've suddenly worked it all out. You know what it is, don't you?'

'What?'

'Stuart's nice. And we're not used to nice.'

'A nice man is something of an oxymoron.'

'We can't all have disastrous relationships with heartless bastards.'

'And we don't all thrive on misery and heartache.'

'They're going to settle down in roses-round-the-door bliss with two point four children and be happy ever after.'

'Which is what we all swear we want.'

'But won't get with the heartless bastards.'

'Does this mean we have to find "nice" men to be happy,' Tanya asks fearfully, thinking back over her years of fun and fantastic wild sex with all the wantonly wicked heartless bastards she's had the pleasure to meet.

'Perhaps we can find ourselves a *nice* heartless bastard.'

'Isn't that a bit of a contradiction too?'

'You know, I don't think it is.' I smile at her, and we both look over to where Finn and Dan are standing solemnly side by side.

An hour later, Grace and Stuart step beaming out into the sunshine, Mr and Mrs Masterson, ready to be ferried to the reception on the gleaming back of the Bedford Belle.

It's gone midnight. The meal, speeches, the toasts, the cutting of the cake, the hurling of the bouquet – at which point I would like to point out that I ducked, as Grace none-too-subtly aimed it straight at my head – are all done, and the five-piece jazz band who've played valiantly through the last five hours, are starting to sway tiredly.

I watch Stuart lead Grace out onto the springy hardboard dance floor of the huge white marquee, with a warm feeling

271

in my stomach that hasn't come from the fourth glass of brandy I'm currently clutching. Tanya and Finn are next out onto the dance floor, sliding smoothly into a slow waltz, Tanya's chestnut head falling softly against Finn's shoulder. Despite my misgivings I have to admit they make a beautiful couple.

Leo and Cornelia are up next, Cornelia holding her left hand out rather stiffly, so that everyone they spin expertly past like the lead contestants in *Come Dancing*, can see the blue sapphire engagement ring she's wearing so proudly. Louis is leaning back in his chair on the other side of our round table chatting to the same waiter who was trying to attract his attention all evening at Grace and Stuart's belated engagement party.

Was that really only three weeks ago? It seems like a lifetime. I think the events that happened in between that day and this have taken at least two years off my life, but as I watch Stuart whisper something in Grace's ear, then lean down to place a gentle kiss on her radiant, smiling, upturned face, I realise with a huge sense of relief that everything is now as it should be.

Well *nearly* everything.

'We did it,' says a voice, echoing my thoughts.

I look up, recognising the voice instantly, and suddenly and rather oddly feel shy. As I put down my nearly empty brandy glass, and struggle for something to say, Dan Slater offers me a glass of champagne.

'I think another toast would be pretty appropriate, considering that without your intervention we wouldn't be where we are today.'

'Is that a jibe?' I ask, cautiously accepting the champagne flute.

'No, it's a big congratulations. I don't know quite what you did, Ollie, but it worked.' He raises his glass. 'To the future.'

'To the future,' I echo, toasting as he had Grace and Stuart, but when I turn back to face him, he's looking squarely at me. His usually hostile handsome face is to my amazement full of warmth, but I notice sadly, still wary. I can't really blame him, I suppose. Not after our history to date. He's probably waiting for me to snap and fling the champagne back in his face. He's been watching me cautiously all day, but hasn't come near me

272

until now, like a sheepdog circling an errant lamb to make sure it doesn't go astray. And I noticed with some embarrassment in the church that when the vicar got to the 'just cause and impediment' bit, his eyes immediately shot over to me. It's also been hard not to notice the fact that his every move has been pretty effectively policed too, Miranda, not so much a sheepdog as a devoted puppy, constantly hugging his heels.

'How is . . . everything?' he asks awkwardly.

'Good,' I reply.

'Business?'

'Busy . . . got my new lease.'

He nods slowly.

'And I sent it back . . .' I add, looking into my champagne glass rather than at his face.

'Right.'

'Unsigned.'

'You did what!' he exclaims in surprise.

I look up at him carefully. 'I don't expect any favours, Dan.' This is the first time I've said his name to his face, and I find that I like the way it tastes in my mouth. 'You made your point, and now I've made mine. We're quits.'

'Quits?' he asks uncertainly, his face clouding a little.

'Equal?' I offer, meaningfully.

He smiles slowly, a smile that spreads over his strong handsome face, and into his beautiful blue-grey eyes, making them crease endearingly at the corners. 'That's a better word.'

Tanya and Finn are heading back towards us from the dance floor holding hands. The small band playing away on a raised platform behind the head table had upped tempo from a gentle waltz to a rather vigorous Samba, which they both, knackered and slightly drunk, have struggled to get through, and they are laughing and breathless.

Dan follows my gaze to the dance floor. 'Would you like to dance? It's the last waltz,' he adds, as the band leader announces the end of the evening.

Taken by surprise at this offer, I hesitate for too long. Homing in like a heat-seeking missile in bright-pink lipstick, Miranda totters over to our table, and does a double take as she spots Dan still standing awkwardly next to me.

'Daniel Slater!' she shrieks. 'There you are, you gorgeous man, I've been looking for you everywhere! Come and

273

dance!' She grabs his arm, and pulls him in the direction of the dance floor.

'Well, actually . . .' He hesitates, looking back at me, but I simply smile half-heartedly and shrug, watching as the persistent Miranda drags her prize into the midst of the other dancing couples.

'How could you just let him go like that?' Tanya chastises me, sliding back into the seat on my right.

'She asked him to dance,' I reply, my voice not sounding quite as nonchalant as I intended.

'He asked *you* first.' Tanya raises her eyebrows at me.

'He was probably just being polite.'

Tanya rolls her eyeballs at Finn, sighing heavily in exasperation. 'Jeez, Ollie, what's the poor guy got to do to convince you he actually *really* likes you?'

'You honestly think so?' I turn to her imploringly. 'Because I really need to know . . . I don't want to make a complete idiot of myself . . . not that I haven't already, but I can't make it any worse . . .'

'Of course he does, you moron!' Louis, who has staggered back to the table with a bottle of champagne in one hand, and the barman's telephone number in his breast pocket, almost yells at me in frustration. 'You're the only person who doesn't seem to realise it. Do you need it written in blood or something?'

'Okay!' I hold my hands up in defence. 'Maybe you're right, maybe he does like me, but that's no use when he's already involved with someone else . . .' They follow my gaze to where Miranda is dragging Dan around the dance floor, beaming up at him with a slightly manic look, like Kathy Bates in *Misery*.

'Trust me.' Finn takes my hand and squeezes it gently. 'There is no Dan and Miranda . . . although not through lack of effort on her part, I must admit. You know that night she turned up at the restaurant as we were leaving? Well, he wasn't expecting her, she just followed him there, and decided to gatecrash. That's not the first time either. He's actually worried she's a bit of a bunny boiler . . .' he grins. 'Face it, Ol, he likes you.'

'Well, if he likes me then why does it feel as if he's been avoiding me. This is the first time he's spoken to me all day . . .'

'Hasn't it occurred to you that he might have been waiting for you to speak to him? You can't just sit back and wait for him to make another move, because he might not. He's done *all* the running so far, and look where it's got him. Absolutely nowhere!'

'Yeah, but he's been so subtle you'd have needed subtitles to get the full picture.'

'I'd hardly call some of the moves he made subtle,' Finn laughs humourlessly, 'but it was obviously done in a language you failed to understand.'

'Or were too stubborn to understand,' Tanya adds meaningfully.

'I think the next move is down to you, babe,' Finn tells me.

'You do want to make a move, don't you?' Tan asks softly.

I nod slowly.

'Then what on earth are you waiting for?'

'Courage,' I reply morosely, taking another swig from my champagne, then finishing my brandy quickly as though this will suddenly fill me with purpose.

'Blimey, Ollie, what's wrong with you?' Tanya wails. 'I know you. When you find something you think is right for you, you'll usually fight tooth and nail to make it happen.'

I watch as the final song ends, and everybody enthusiastically applauds the band, who bow briefly before trooping off en masse to revive their flagging spirits at the bar. Miranda, still grasping Dan firmly by the wrist, leads him off the dance floor and back towards her table, pulling him into the seat next to her. Two minutes later, however, he's making his excuses, and heading towards Grace and Stuart to say goodnight. He shakes Stuart's hand warmly, and kisses Grace on the cheek. They chat for a moment, and then he turns and heads towards the exit. Just before he steps outside, he pauses and looks back. Our eyes meet briefly, and for a moment I think he's going to speak, but he simply smiles kind of wistfully, and steps outside.

Tanya and Finn follow my gaze. 'He's leaving already?' Tanya asks in disappointment.

'He's leaving first thing tomorrow morning,' Finn tells us, holding up a salutary hand. 'We were chatting earlier. He's got business in New York. Doesn't know when he'll be back . . .' He looks pointedly at me.

I look from Finn's face, to Tanya's, to Louis, and then across to Grace, who looks at Dan's retreating back, and then pleadingly at me. Taking a deep breath, I push back my chair, and stand up.

'What are you going to do?' breathes Tanya.

'Something I should have done a long time ago.' I take Tanya's champagne flute from her hand, and knock back the rest of her drink in one go. Then lifting my skirts I hurry out of the marquee, and tread delicately across the damp grass towards the house.

Ten seconds later, I hear soft footsteps falling in the grass behind me, and a hand catches hold of my wrist. It's Grace. 'He's in the green room,' she whispers, 'three doors down from you.'

'It's that easy to guess where I'm going?'

'Absolutely!' She leans in and hugs me, hard. 'And if that's not where you were heading, then you bloody well should be!'

'Am I doing the right thing?' I ask her tentatively.

She nods vigorously. 'Absolutely, the only pity is it's taken you so long! Think of all the time you've wasted! Talking of which,' she announces beaming broadly, '*I* am going to go and fetch my *husband* and take him to bed!' She pauses, looks down at the wedding band on her left hand, and smiles incredulously. 'Oh my God, I'm married . . . can you believe I'm actually married!'

We both gaze in awe at her ring finger, before bursting into peals of laughter as the unmistakable voice of Louis, who appears to have hijacked the empty stage, aptly belts out the first melodious verse of 'Rescue Me' over the PA system.

We hug again then, letting me go, Grace gives me a little push towards the house. 'Go on then, I can't wait here all night, I've got a marriage to consummate.'

I shake my head, laughing softly.

'Go on!' Grace urges, as Stuart appears in the brightly lit entrance of the huge marquee. 'What are you waiting for?' She gives me another gentle push towards the house.

I look back when I reach the doorway, to see Grace and Stuart, hand in hand and giggling like maniacs, running full pelt towards the hay loft at the end of the stable block.

Heading through into the kitchen, I go to the key cupboard

by the back door, and take out the huge bunch of house keys that's hanging there. Kind, pedantic, practical Stuart has thoughtfully labelled all of the keys. Not so great if they were burgled, but, hey, it makes life a hell of a lot easier for me, which is great, considering that what I'm about to do is probably one of the most difficult things I've ever done in my life.

I slip upstairs, sighing indulgently as I head past a couple necking on the left-hand turn of the main stairs, oblivious to anything except each other and some heavily spontaneous passion. I start hesitantly down the corridor, past my own room, count three doors on the left to what is hopefully the green bedroom and, hand shaking like a wobbly jelly, insert what I hope is the right key in the lock. To my relief I hear the slight click as the lock yields, and gingerly turning the handle I open the door, and step quietly into the room.

Dan is standing at the bedroom window, looking out over the garden where the party is still in full swing. It's now gone two o'clock in the morning, and the hosts have abandoned their guests to get down and dirty in a heap of straw. He's fresh from the shower, a towel slung about his hips, his hair glistening damply in the moonlight and the light from the garden lanterns swinging gently in the warm breeze, which is filtering softly through the window.

He turns at the sound of the door closing quietly behind me, and is so stunned to see me standing there that he almost loses his towel in surprise. 'What on earth!' he exclaims, grabbing the slipping towel, and hurriedly hauling it securely back into place.

Taking a deep breath, I wave my bunch of keys at him. 'I figured one of these might fit, and as luck would have it . . .'

He loses the surprised expression and smiles slowly if somewhat faintly at me, in recognition of the irony. Encouraged by the smile, I leave the support of the door frame and walk somewhat unsteadily over towards him. Considering the fact that he's the one who's practically naked, and I'm fully clothed, he looks a damn sight calmer than I feel.

I decide to brazen it out, and start swinging my hips like Tanya in a roomful of men, before deciding that it really doesn't suit me, and shuffling quickly to a halt in front of him.

As he gazes gently and questioningly at me I suddenly find

that my brain's still partying at the reception without me.

'What are you doing here, Ollie?' he asks, as I stand stupidly before him, all of my hastily pre-rehearsed witty one-liners flying in formation out of the window like a flock of migrating birds.

'Do you know, I'm not quite sure . . .' I stutter after a moment.

He raises an eyebrow at me, but remains silent, and this time I know he's not going to help me out, it's down to me.

'Can we start again?' I ask hesitantly. 'I mean, I really think we should start again.'

'Okay,' he smiles tersely. 'You go out and come in again, but knock first this time.'

'Well, that's not quite what I meant.' I flush in embarrassment.

'Oh you mean a new beginning?' he asks in a slightly mocking tone.

'I suppose so. Forget the past . . .' I stop and look at the floor, suddenly wishing that I hadn't come. I should have listened to my doubts and stayed put at the party. Of course he doesn't like me, he thinks I'm an idiot.

'I don't know if I want to forget the past,' Dan says quietly.

'Of course,' I reply, biting my bottom lip. 'I just wanted to . . . well, what I mean is, I'm sorry, for causing so many problems and . . . well, I think I'd better go now . . .'

'I don't want to forget the past . . .' Dan repeats, catching hold of my wrist as I turn to leave, and pulling me back round to face him, 'because there are certain parts that I'd kind of like to remember . . .' The firm grip on my wrist relaxes; I can feel his thumb resting gently against my over-active pulse point.

I pull my eyes away from the floor, and look up hopefully at his face. There's no sarcastic smile, no sardonic look, no recriminations, in fact he's smiling at me with a look of almost, well, *tender* affection. Slowly, he reaches upwards, and places his fingertips against my lips, running them down over my chin, and across my neck until his hand is softly cupping my throat.

'You are so beautiful,' he whispers, 'and brave, and loyal, and a complete and utter . . . *idiot* sometimes.' He almost shouts the 'idiot', shaking his head in disbelief, and catching his bottom lip between his teeth. 'You're infuriating, Ollie Tate, maddeningly so. There are times when I could willingly have throttled you.' I feel his fingertips squeeze my throat oh so softly as he speaks, and note with pleasurable concern that the fireworks in my stomach have just started a display to rival that of the Millennium.

'You were like a fox caught in a trap, trying to savage the hand of the poor sod that was attempting to get you out . . .' He trails off, but although his voice was raised slightly, there's no anger in it, only exasperated amusement.

'Would it make you feel any better if I promise not to bite?' I reply, bending my head, and very gently and briefly taking the tip of his middle finger between my teeth. I feel Dan shiver, as I turn the touch into the lightest kiss before looking back up at him.

'Are you quite sure this is what you want, Ollie?' he asks hesitantly. 'With our track record, we could just end up hating each other . . .'

'Well, we're probably still going to fight,' I joke weakly, gasping as his fingers trail away, down my neck and across the sensitive flesh below, brushing against my breasts, as his arm slides around me.

'And then spend a lot of time making up,' he answers. He wraps his other arm around my waist, and pulls me carefully towards him.

'I'm sorry,' I breathe, letting my own arms slide under his and around his waist.

'For what?'

'That it's taken me so long to realise . . .'

'There is one way you can make it up to me . . .' he whispers gently, his mouth so close to mine I can feel the warmth of his sweet breath playing across my lips as he speaks. 'Ask me . . .'

'Ask you what?' I reply, feigning ignorance.

'*Ask* me, Ollie . . .' he hisses, his hands sliding playfully from my waist and over the curve of my arse. 'Please. Because this time I'll know that you mean it . . .'

'Lose the towel, and I might consider it,' I tease, becoming bolder, then reel backwards slightly in surprise as without a word he smiles wickedly, lets go of me, and then drops his towel to the floor.

I stare at him open-mouthed for a moment, as his own eyes steadily return my gaze, completely unabashed, and then this huge, stupidly happy smile slides slowly onto my face. 'Well, when you put it like that . . . how on earth could I possibly refuse.'

I practically collapse back onto the bed behind me, knees a little weak at this point, and, crooking my finger at him, slowly beckon him over to sit beside me.

'Well,' I ask him, my eyes gazing brazenly into his with the same challenging look he's giving me. 'Aren't you going to kiss me goodnight then . . .?'